"I can tell when you're lying, Garrett. Your eyes grow dark, and the right corner of your mouth tightens."

Would his mouth be hard or soft, passionate or gentle against hers when they kissed?

"I don't want you," he said as he moved closer to her lips.

"You're bluffing."

"You're too trusting." He lowered his mouth to her ear. "But I don't have the strength to pull away."

She smiled. "Now you're telling the truth."

With a groan he fastened his lips to hers. She didn't hesitate. She clung to him and let his mouth drive away the memories of the past week. For this wonderful moment all she could think about was his touch.

He lifted his head. "Be very sure, because I won't let you go all night long."

CHRISTMAS JUSTICE

BY
ROBIN PERINI

Published in Great Britain 2014
by Mills & Boon, an imprint of Harlequin (UK) Limited,
Eton House, 18-24 Paradise Road, Richmond, Surrey, TW9 1SR

© 2014 Robin L. Perini

ISBN: 978-0-263-91380-4

46-1214

Harlequin (UK) Limited's policy is to use papers that are natural, renewable and recyclable products and made from wood grown in sustainable forests. The logging and manufacturing processes conform to the legal environmental regulations of the country of origin.

Printed and bound in Spain
by CPI, Barcelona

Award-winning author **Robin Perini**'s love of heart-stopping suspense and poignant romance, coupled with her adoration of high-tech weaponry and covert ops, encouraged her secret inner commando to take on the challenge of writing romantic suspense novels. Her mission's motto: "When danger and romance collide, no heart is safe."

Devoted to giving her readers fast-paced, high-stakes adventures with a love story sure to melt their hearts, Robin won a prestigious Romance Writers of America Golden Heart Award in 2011. By day she works for an advanced technology corporation, and in her spare time you might find her giving one of her many nationally acclaimed writing workshops or training in competitive small-bore-rifle silhouette shooting. Robin loves to interact with readers. You can catch her on her website, www.robinperini.com, and on several major social-networking sites, or write to her at PO Box 50472, Albuquerque, NM 87181-0472, USA.

With love to my aunts, Gayle, Earlene, Sissy (Lynn) and
Barbara. I'm blessed to know you are always there.
No matter what.

Prologue

Today was no ordinary day.

Normally Laurel McCallister would have adored spending an evening with her niece Molly, playing princesses, throwing jacks and just being a kid again, but tonight was anything but typical. Laurel let the wind-driven ice bite into her cheeks. She stood just inside the warm entry of her sister's Virginia home, staring out into the weather to see the family off to the local Christmas pageant. Her fist clutched the charm bracelet Ivy had forced into Laurel's hand.

A gift from their missing father.

He'd been incommunicado for over two months. Then suddenly the silver jewelry had arrived in Ivy's mailbox earlier that day. No note, only her father's shaky handwriting on the address label, and postmarked Washington, D.C. Laurel squeezed the chain, quelling the shiver of foreboding that hadn't left her since Ivy had shown her the package. Her sister had told her they needed to talk about it. Tonight. The news couldn't be good, but it would have to wait.

Bracing against the cold, she met her sister's solemn gaze, then picked up her five-year-old niece. Laurel snuggled Molly closer. At the end of a bout of strep throat, the girl had insisted on waving goodbye to her mother. Ivy returned the farewell wave from across the driveway, apprehension evident in her eyes. And not typical mom-concern-for-her-youngest-daughter's-health worry.

Laurel scanned the rural setting surrounding Ivy's house. With the nearest neighbors out of shouting distance, it should be quiet. And safe. Laurel might only be a CIA analyst, but she'd completed the same training as a field operative. She knew what to look for.

Nothing seemed off, and yet, she couldn't stop the tension knotting every muscle, settling low in her belly. For now, her sister and brother-in-law refused to let the trepidation destroy Christmas for the kids, but Laurel had recognized the strain in her sister's eyes, the worry on her brother-in-law's brow. Too many bad vibes filtered beneath the surface of every look her sister had given her.

Laurel touched the silky blond hair of her youngest niece.

Molly stared after her mother, father, brother and sister, her baby blues filled with tears. "It's not fair. I want to go to the pageant. I'm supposed to be an angel."

The forlorn voice hung on Laurel's heart. She placed her hand on the little girl's hot forehead. "Sorry, Molly Magoo. Not with that fever."

Ivy bundled Molly's older brother and sister into the backseat of the car. Laurel sent her sister a confident nod, even though her stomach still twisted. She recognized the same lie in her sister's eyes. They were so alike.

One of the kids—it must have been Michaela—tossed a stuffed giraffe through the open car door. Ivy shook her head and walked a few paces away to pick up the wayward animal.

Laurel started to close the door. "Don't worry, Molly. They'll be back s—"

A loud explosion rocketed the night, and a blast of hot air buffeted Laurel. She staggered back. The driver's side of the SUV erupted into flames. Fire and smoke engulfed the car in a hellish conflagration. Angry black plumes erupted into the sky.

God, no! Laurel's knees trembled; she shook her head. This couldn't be happening. Horror squeezed her throat. She wrenched Molly toward her, turning the little girl away from the sight, but Laurel couldn't protect Molly. Her niece had seen too much. Molly's earsplitting screams ripped the air.

No sounds came from the car. Not a shout, not a yell.

Laurel had to do *something*.

"Stay here!" She scrambled through the door, racing across the frozen yard. She glanced back; Molly had fallen to the floor in tears. Laurel squeezed her eyes shut against the heart-wrenching cries, then snagged her phone from her pocket and dialed 9-1-1. "Help! There's been an explosion."

Blazing heat seared Laurel's skin. It wasn't a typical car fire. It burned too hot, too fast. Laurel choked back the truth. This wasn't just any bomb. This was a professional hit. A hit like she'd read about in dossiers as part of her job with the CIA.

Unable to look away, she stared in horror at the interior of the car. In a few minutes, nothing would be left. Just ash. They wouldn't even be able to tell how many people had been in the car.

The phone slipped from her fingers.

Ivy's family was gone. No one could have survived. Frantically, Laurel searched for her sister. Her heart shattered when she saw the smoking body lying several feet away from the car. She ran to Ivy and knelt next to her sister's body, the right side blackened and burned beyond recognition, the left blistered and smoldering.

"Laur—" the raspy voice croaked.

"Don't talk, Ivy." Laurel couldn't stop her tears. She could hear her niece's wails from inside the house, but Ivy. God. Her clothes had melted into her skin.

Ivy shifted, then cried out in agony. "Stupid," she rasped. "Not c-c-careful enough. Can't…trust…"

"Shh…" Laurel had no idea how to help. She reached out a hand, but there wasn't a spot on Ivy not burned. She was afraid to touch her sister. Where was the ambulance?

Ivy coughed and Laurel bent down. "Don't give up. Help is coming."

"Too late. F-find Garrett Galloway. Sheriff. Tell him… he was right." Ivy blinked her one good eye and glanced at the fire-consumed vehicle. A lone tear pooled. "Please. Save. Molly." The single tear cut through the soot, and then her eyes widened. "Gun!"

Laurel's training took over. She plastered herself flat to the ground. A shot hit the tree behind her. With a quick roll, she cursed. Her weapon was locked up in the gun safe inside the house. A loud thwack hit the ground inches from her ear. The assault had come from the hedges.

"Traitor!" Ivy's raspy voice shouted a weak curse.

Another shot rang out.

The bullet struck true, hitting Ivy right in the temple.

Horrified, Laurel scampered a few feet, using the fire as a shield between her and the gunman. She panted, ignoring the pain ripping through her heart. She would grieve later. She had one job: protect Molly.

Sirens roared through the night sky. A curse rang out followed by at least two sets of footsteps, the sound diminishing.

Thank God they'd run. Laurel had one chance. She flung open the door and grabbed a sobbing Molly in her arms. She hugged her tight, then kicked the door closed.

Through the break in the curtains, she watched. A squad car tore into the driveway. No way. That cop had gotten here way too fast. Laurel pressed Molly against her, then locked the dead bolt.

She sagged against the wall. "Oh, Ivy."

"Aunt Laurel?" Molly's small voice choked through her sobs. "I want Mommy and Daddy."

"Me, too, pumpkin."

Laurel squeezed her niece tighter. She had two choices: trust the cop outside or follow her sister's advice.

After the past two months... She slipped the bracelet from her father into her pocket, then snagged a photo from the wall. Her sister and family, all smiles. She had no choice. The high-tech bomb, the cop's quick arrival. It smelled of setup.

Laurel raced through the house and grabbed Molly's antibiotics and the weapon from the gun safe, half expecting the cop to bang on the door. When he didn't, Laurel knew she was right. She peeked through the curtains. Her sister's body was gone. And so was the police car.

The flames sparked higher and Laurel nearly doubled over in pain.

The sound of a fire engine penetrated the house. No time left. She snagged the envelope her father had sent and stuffed it into a canvas bag along with a blanket and Molly's favorite stuffed lion.

She bundled Molly into her coat, lifted her niece into her arms and ran out the back door. Laurel's feet slapped on the pavement. She sprinted down an alley. Shouts rained down on her. Smoke and fire painted the night sky in a vision of horror. One she would never forget.

She paused, catching her breath, the cold seeping through her jacket.

"Aunt Laurel? Stop. Mommy won't know where to find us." Molly's fingers dug into Laurel's neck.

Oh, God. Poor Molly. Laurel hugged her niece closer. How could she explain to a five-year-old about bad people who killed families?

Laurel leaned against the concrete wall, her lungs burning with effort. She wished *she* didn't understand. She wished she could be like Molly. But this wasn't a child's cartoon where everyone survived even the most horrendous attacks. Reality meant no one had a second chance.

Laurel had to get away from the men who had shot at her, who had killed her sister and her family.

But Laurel didn't know what to believe. Except her sister's final words.

Which left her with one option. One man to trust.

Garrett Galloway.

Now all she had to do was find him.

Chapter One

Normally Trouble, Texas, wasn't much trouble, and that was the way Sheriff Garrett Galloway liked it. No problems to speak of, save the town drunk, a few rambunctious kids and a mayor who drove too nice a car with no obvious supplemental income.

Garrett adjusted his Stetson and shoved his hands into the pockets of his bomber jacket to ward off the December chill. He'd hidden out in Trouble too long. When he'd arrived a year ago, body broken and soul bleeding, he'd trusted that the tiny West Texas town would be the perfect place to get lost and stay lost for a few months. After all, the world thought he was dead. And Garrett needed it to stay that way.

Just until he could identify who had destroyed everyone he loved and make them pay. He'd *never* imagined he'd stay this long.

But the latest status call he'd counted on hadn't occurred. Not to mention his last conversation with his mentor and ex-partner, James McCallister, had been much too…optimistic. That, combined with a missed contact, usually meant the operation had gone to hell.

Garrett's right shoulder blade hiked, settling under the feel of his holster. He never left home without his

weapon or his badge. He liked to know he had a gun
within reach. Always. The townsfolk liked to know their
sheriff walked the streets.

He eyed the garland- and tinsel-laden but otherwise
empty Main Street and stepped onto the pavement, his
boots silent, no sound echoing, no warning to anyone
that he might be making his nightly nine o'clock rounds.

James McCallister's disappearance had thrown Garrett. His mentor had spent the past few months using
every connection he'd made over his nearly thirty-year
career, trying to ferret out the traitor.

Big risks, but after a year of nothing, a few intel tid-
bits had fallen their way: some compromised top secret
documents identifying overseas operatives and operations, some missing state-of-the-art weapons. The door
had cracked open, but not enough to step through.

Garrett didn't like the radio silence. Either James was
breaking open the case or he was dead. Neither option
boded well. If it was the first, Garrett contacting him
would blow the whole mission; if the second, Garrett was
on his own and would have to come back from the dead.

Or he could end up in federal prison, where his life
wouldn't be worth a spare .22 bullet.

With his no-win options circling his mind, Garrett
strode past another block. After a few more houses, he
spied an unfamiliar dark car slowly making its way down
the street.

No one drove that slowly. Not in Texas. Not unless they
were up to no good. And no one visited Trouble without good reason. It wasn't a town folks passed through
by chance.

His instincts firing warning signals, Garrett turned
the corner and disappeared behind a hedge.

The car slowed, then drove past. Interesting.

Could be a relative from out of town, but Garrett didn't like changes. Or the unexpected. He headed across a dead-end street, his entire body poised and tense, watching for the car. He reached the edge of town and peered through the deserted night.

Nearby, he heard a small crack, as if a piece of wood snapped.

No one should be out this way, not at this time of night. Could be a coyote—human, not the animal variety. Garrett hadn't made friends with either one during the past year.

He slid his Beretta 92 from his shoulder holster and gripped the butt of the gun. Making a show of a cowboy searching the stars, he gazed up at the black expanse of the night sky and pushed his Stetson back.

Out of the corner of his eye, he caught sight of a cloaked figure ducking behind a fence: average height, slight, but the movements careful, strategic, trained. Someone he might have faced in his previous life. Definitely. Not your average coyote or even criminal up to no good. James Mc-Callister was the only person who knew Garrett was in Trouble, and James was AWOL.

The night went still.

Garrett kicked the dirt and dusted off his hat.

His muscles twitchy, he kept his gun at the ready, not wanting to use it. This could be unrelated to his past, but he needed information, not a dead body on the outskirts of his town. What happened in Trouble stayed in Trouble, unless the body count started climbing. Then he wouldn't be able to keep the state or the feds out.

He didn't need the attention.

He could feel someone watching him, studying him.

He veered off his route, heading slightly toward the hidden figure. His plan? Saunter past the guy hiding in the shadows and then take him out.

He hit his mark and, with a quick turn on his heel, shifted, launching himself into a tackle. A few quick moves and Garrett pushed the guy to the ground, slid the SIG P229 out of reach and forced his forearm against the vulnerable section of throat.

"What do you want?" he growled, shoving aside his pinned assailant's hood.

The grunts coming from his victim weren't what he'd expected. With years of experience subduing the worst human element, he wrestled free his flashlight and clicked it on.

Blue eyes full of fear peered up at him. A woman. He pressed harder. A woman could kill just as dead. Could play the victim, all the while coldheartedly planning his demise. He wasn't about to let go.

The light hit her face. He blinked back his surprise. He knew those eyes. Knew that nose.

Oh, hell.

"Laurel McCallister," he said. His gut sank. Only one thing would bring her to Trouble.

His past had found him. And that meant one thing. James McCallister was six feet under, and the men who wanted Garrett dead wouldn't be far behind.

THE PAVEMENT DUG into Laurel's back, but she didn't move, not with two hundred pounds holding her down. He'd taken her SIG too easily, and the man lying on top of her knew how to kill. The pressure against her throat proved it.

Worse than that, the sheriff—badge and all—knew her name. So much for using surprise as an advantage.

She lay still and silent, her body jarred from his attack. She could feel every inch of skin and muscle that had struck the ground. She'd be bruised later.

Laurel had thought watching him for a while would be a good idea. Maybe not so much. Ivy might have told her to trust Garrett Galloway, Sheriff of Trouble, Texas, but Laurel had to be cautious.

The car door opened and the thud of tiny feet pounded to them. "Let her go!" Molly pummeled Garrett's back, her raised voice screeching through the night in that high-pitched kid squeal that raked across Laurel's nerves.

He winced and turned to the girl.

Now!

Laurel kicked out, her foot coming in contact with his shin. He grunted, but didn't budge. She squirmed underneath the heavy body and pushed at his shoulders.

"Molly, get back!"

The little girl hesitated, sending a shiver of fear through Laurel. Why couldn't her niece have stayed asleep in the car, buckled into her car seat? Ever since that horrific night four days ago, she couldn't handle Laurel being out of sight, knew instinctively when she wasn't near.

Suddenly, Garrett rolled off her body, slipped her gun into his hand and rose to his feet with cougarlike grace. "Don't worry. I'm not going to hurt either of you." He tucked her weapon into his pants and stared her down.

She sucked in a wary breath before her five-year-old niece dived into her arms. "Are you okay, Aunt Laurel?"

She wound her arms around her niece and stared up at Garrett, body tense. "You're my hero, Molly." She forced her voice to remain calm. At least the little girl hadn't lost the fire in her belly. It was the first spark Laurel had seen from her since the explosion.

Molly clutched at Laurel but glared at Garrett.

He struggled to keep a straight face and a kindness laced his eyes as he looked at Molly.

For the first time in days, the muscles at the base of Laurel's neck relaxed. Maybe she'd made the right decision after all.

Not that she'd had a choice. There'd been nothing on the national news about her family. No mention of gunfire or Ivy being killed by a bullet to the head. There had been a small piece about an SUV burning, but they'd blamed a downed power line. That was the second Laurel had known she was truly on her own.

Until now.

She hated counting on anyone but herself. She and her sister had been schooled in that lesson after their mother had died. With their father gone, Ivy and Laurel had been pretty much in charge of each other.

But Laurel was out of her league. She knew it. She didn't have to like it.

She held Molly closer and studied Garrett Galloway. Something about him invited trust, but could she trust her instincts? Would this man whose expression displayed an intent to kill one moment and compassion the next help her? She prayed her sister had been right, that he was one of the good guys.

Garrett tilted back his Stetson. "I could have…" He glanced at Molly, his meaning clear.

Laurel got it. She and Molly would be dead…if he'd wanted them dead.

"...already finished the job," he said harshly. "I'm not going to."

"How did you know my name?"

He raised a brow and slipped his Beretta into the shoulder holster and returned her weapon. "I know your father. Your picture is on his desk at...work."

His expression spoke volumes. She got it. Garrett had worked with her father in an OGA. While the CIA had a name and a reputation, her father's Other Government Agency had none. Classified funding, classified missions, classified results. And the same agency where Ivy had worked. Alarm bells rang in Laurel's head. Her sister had sent Laurel to a man working with the same people who might be behind the bomb blast. And yet, who better to help?

Garrett held out his hand to her. "You look like you've been on the road awhile," he said. "How about something to eat? Then we can talk."

Laurel hesitated, but what was she supposed to do? She'd come to this small West Texas town for one reason, and one reason only. To find Garrett Galloway.

She didn't know what she'd expected. He could have stepped off the set of a hit television show in his khaki shirt, badge, dark brown hat and leather jacket. Piercing brown eyes that saw right through her.

If she'd imagined wanting to ride off into the sunset with someone, it would be Garrett Galloway. But now that she'd found him, what *was* she going to do with him?

He didn't pull back his hand. He waited. He knew. With a sigh, she placed her hand in his. He pulled her to her feet. Molly scrambled up and hid behind Laurel, peering up at Garrett.

He cocked his head at the little girl. Laurel sucked in

a slow breath. Molly's face held that fearful expression that hadn't left her since they'd run from Virginia, as if any second she might cry. But then her eyes widened. She stared at Garrett, so tall and strong in his dark pants and cowboy boots, a star on his chest.

He was a protector. Laurel could tell and so, evidently, could Molly.

Garrett met her gaze and she recognized the understanding on his face. "Come with me," he said quietly.

"I have my car—"

He shook his head. "Grab your things and leave it. If anyone followed, I don't want them to know who you came to see."

"I was careful. I spent an entire extra day to get here due to all the detours."

"If you'd recognized you had a tail, you'd already be dead." His flat words spoke the truth of the danger they were in. He walked over to the vehicle and pulled out the large tote she used as a suitcase, slinging it on his shoulder opposite his gun hand. All their belongings were in the bag. "Until I'm certain, we act like you have one."

Laurel stiffened. In normal circumstances she could take care of herself and Molly. As if sensing her vulnerability, Garrett stepped closer.

"*You* came to *me*," Garrett said. "You may have blown my cover. You need to listen."

He was on assignment. She should have known.

She prided herself on her self-reliance, her ability to handle most any situation, but his expression had gone intense and wary, and that worried her. Ivy had been a skilled operative. She had always been careful, and she was dead. Laurel had to face reality. She'd jumped into the deep end of the pool her first day on the run and Garrett Galloway was the lifeguard.

She swallowed away the distaste of having to rely on him, nodded and lifted Molly into her arms. "How far?"

"Across town," he said, his gaze scanning the perimeter yet again.

"A few blocks, then?" Laurel said with an arch of her brow.

Garrett cocked his head and one side of his mouth tilted in a small smile. His eyes lightened when he didn't frown.

"Let's go."

One block under their feet had Laurel's entire body pulsing with nerves. She'd never seen anyone with the deadly focus that Garrett possessed. He walked silently, even in boots, and seemed aware of each shadow and movement.

Suddenly he stopped. He shoved her and Molly back against the fence, pulling his gun out. Then she heard it. The purr of an engine. It grew louder, then softer. He relaxed and tilted his head, looking from Laurel to Molly. "Let's move."

Molly gazed up at him, her eyes wide. She looked ready to cry. He tilted the Stetson on his head. "You ready for something to eat, sugar?" He gifted her with a confident smile.

Just his strong presence soothed Molly. For Laurel, his nearness had the opposite effect. She wanted to pull away, because the draw she felt—the odd urge to let herself move into his arms—well, that was something she hadn't felt before. She'd never allowed herself to be this vulnerable. Not ever.

He could snap her neck or take her life, but he might

also do worse. This man could take over and she might lose herself.

A dog's howl broke through the night, followed by more barking. As Garrett led them through the town in silence, Molly clung to Laurel. Her eyes grew heavy and her body lax. The poor thing was exhausted, just like her aunt.

Garrett matched his steps with hers. "Whatever brought you here, it was bad, wasn't it?" He bent toward Laurel, his breath near her ear, the words soft.

She couldn't stop the burning well of tears behind her eyes. She had no reserves left. She wanted nothing more than to lean closer and have him put his arm around her. She couldn't. She recognized her weakness. Her emotions hovered just beneath the surface, and she'd be damned if she'd let them show.

In self-preservation, she tilted her head forward, expecting her long hair to curtain her face, to hide her feelings, but nothing happened. She ran a hand through the chopped locks. Gone was her unique titian hair, and in its place, she'd dyed it a nondescript brown that stopped at her chin. She had to blend in.

"I understand," he said, his voice gruff. "Better than you know."

Before Laurel could ponder his statement, he picked up the pace. "My house is ten minutes away. Across Main and around a corner two blocks."

With each step they took, the blinking lights and garlands, then the tinsel, came into full effect. He paused and shifted them behind a tree, studying the street.

Molly peered around him, her small mouth forming a stunned O. "Aunt Laurel, lookie. It's Christmas here." The little girl swallowed and bowed her head until it rested on Laurel's shoulder. "Our Christmas is far away."

Laurel patted her niece's back. "Christmas will follow us, Molly Magoo. It might be different this year, but it will still happen."

Molly looked at her, then at the decorations lining the town, her gaze hopeful. "Will Mommy and Daddy come back by then?"

"We'll talk about it later," Laurel whispered. She didn't know what to say. Even though Molly had seen the explosion, she still hadn't processed the reality that her mother, father, brother and sister were never coming back.

She gritted her teeth. As a grown woman, she didn't know how long it would take her to accept her family's death. That she was alone in the world. Except for Molly.

"We need to move fast." Garrett held out his arm. Main Street through Trouble wasn't much. Two lanes, a single stoplight. "Go." They were halfway to the other side when an engine roared to life. Tires squealed; the vehicle thundered directly at them.

Garrett pushed them behind a cinder-block wall, dumped the tote, then rolled to the ground, leaving himself vulnerable.

A spray of gunfire ratcheted above Laurel's head as she hit the ground. Molly cried out. Laurel covered the little girl's trembling body and pulled her weapon. She lifted her head, scooting forward. To get a clean shot, she'd have to leave Molly. Bullets thwacked; concrete chips rained down. Laurel tucked Molly closer, gripping the butt of her gun.

A series of shots roared from behind the wall.

Skidding tires took off.

At the sound, Laurel eased forward, weapon raised. She half expected the worst, but Garrett lay on the ground, still alive, his gun aimed at the retreating SUV. He squeezed off two more rounds, then let out a low curse.

She couldn't catch her breath. They'd found her.

"What's going on out there?" An old man's voice called out, and the unmistakable sound of a pump-action shotgun seared through the dark.

"I'm handling it, Mr. McCreary," Garrett called out. "It's Sheriff Galloway. Get back inside."

A door slammed.

Garrett held his weapon at the ready for several more seconds, then picked up his phone. "Shots fired just off Oak and First, Keller," he said to his deputy. "Activate the emergency system and order everyone to stay inside. I'll get back to you when it's clear."

He shoved the phone in his pocket and ran to Laurel. "Everybody safe?"

Molly sobbed in Laurel's arms. She clutched the girl tighter. Laurel didn't know how much more her niece could take.

"Come on." Tension lining his face, he scooped up Molly. His boots thudded on the ground; Laurel carried their belongings and her footsteps pounded closely behind. He led them down an alley to the rear of a row of houses. Then, when he reached the back of one house, he pulled a set of keys from his pocket. "We've got to get out of sight. Plus, I have supplies to gather. Then we need a safe place to hole up."

"I'm sorry," she said quietly. "I brought this to you."

He gave a curt nod. "Who knew you were coming to Texas?"

"No—no one."

"Who told you about me? Your father?" Garrett said.

"My...my sister."

"Ivy?" Garrett's brow furrowed. "She worked for the agency, but we never tackled an op together."

Laurel bit her lip. "My sister said your name with her dying breath. She said to tell you that you were right."

THE SUV THUNDERED down the highway and out of Trouble. Mike Strickland slammed his foot on the accelerator and veered onto an old dirt road leading into the hellish West Texas desert. When he finally brought the vehicle to a halt, he slammed it into Park and pounded the steering wheel with his fist. "Son of a bitch. Who was that guy?"

"The law," his partner, Don Krauss, said, his tone dry. "You see the badge?"

Krauss could pass for everyman. He was great to have on the job because he excelled at blending into the background. His medium brown hair, medium eyes, medium height and nothing-special face got lost in a crowd.

Strickland had a tougher time. A scar from his marine stint and his short hair pegged him as ex-military. He could live with that. He tended to work the less subtle jobs anyway. But Krauss came in handy for gathering intel.

"No sheriff has reflexes like that," Strickland said. "She should be dead. They both should be."

"The girl avoided us for four days, and she's just an analyst, even if she does work for the CIA. She's smart. Switched vehicles twice and never turned on her cell phone." Krauss tapped the high-tech portable triangulation unit.

All this equipment and a girl in a beat-up Chevy had driven over halfway across the country and avoided them. "She got lucky." Strickland frowned.

Krauss let out a snort. "No, we got lucky when she used her ATM for cash. The only stupid move she made, but she cleaned out her account. We won't be lucky again. And now she's got help." He hitched his foot on the dash. "If Ivy talked—"

"I know, I know." Strickland scratched his palm in a nervous movement. In four days the skin had peeled, leaving it red, angry and telling. Not much made him nervous, but his boss... He forced his hand still and gripped the steering wheel, clenching and unclenching his fists against the vinyl. "We can fix this. Forensics will be sifting through what's left of that car for weeks. I made sure it burned hot, and I've got friends in the local coroner's office. If they stall long enough for us to provide two more burned bodies, no one will ever know. Everyone will believe the woman and girl died that night along with the rest of her family."

"You blew her head off," Krauss said. "Cops had to notice."

"It hasn't been on the news, has it?" Strickland said with a small smile.

Krauss shook his head. "I figured they were holding back details as part of the investigation."

"Hell, no. First guy there threw her into the fire. Everyone else is keeping mum. They think it's *national security*."

"Lots of loose ends, Strickland."

"I got enough on my contacts' extracurricular activities. They won't be talking anytime soon. They know the rules." Strickland slid a glance at his partner. "You read the paper? Remember last year, that dead medical investigator? I had no choice. He was a loose end. Like the boss says, loose ends make for bad business."

Krauss tugged a toothpick from his pocket. "Guess the boss was right in choosing you for this one, because we have two very big loose ends." He turned in the seat, his normally sardonic expression solemn. "You ever wonder how we ended up working for that psycho? 'Cause I'm starting to regret every job we do."

"For the greater good—" Strickland started, his entire back tensing. He cricked his neck to the side.

"Yeah, I might have believed that once," Krauss said.

"Don't." Strickland cut him off. "Don't say something I'll have to report."

"Says the man who's hiding his screwup."

"I don't plan to be on the receiving end of a lesson," Strickland said. "You talk and we're dead. Hell, we're dead if we don't fix this."

"I know," Krauss said, his voice flat. "I got a family to protect. Let's get it done fast, clean up and get the hell out of this town. I already hate Trouble, Texas."

"No witnesses. Agreed?" Strickland turned the motor on.

"The sheriff, too? Could cause some publicity."

"This close to the border, this isolated, there's lots of ways to die."

Chapter Two

"*I was right*. Great, just great," Garrett said under his breath, cradling a sobbing Molly in his arms.

He rocked her slightly. She tucked her head against his shoulder and gripped his neck, her little fingers digging into his hair. He held her tighter while his narrowed gaze scrutinized the alley behind his house. A chill bit through the night, and Molly shivered in his arms. He needed to get them both inside and warm, but not in the place he'd never called home.

Another thirty seconds passed. No movement. The shooter probably didn't have an accomplice, but he couldn't assume anything. Assumptions got people dead.

A quick in and out. That was all he needed.

He led Laurel into the backyard of the house James McCallister had purchased on Garrett's behalf and closed the gate. He wouldn't be returning anytime soon. His time in Trouble had ended the moment he'd tackled Laurel to the ground.

But he needed his go-bag and a few supplies. On his own, it wouldn't have mattered. He shifted Molly's weight in his arms. These two needed more shelter than to camp out in the West Texas desert in December.

Molly clung to him tightly. He rubbed her back and

his heart shifted in his chest. God, so familiar. The memories of his daughter, Ella, flooded back. Along with the pain. He couldn't let the past overcome him. Not with these two needing him. He led them to the wood stack.

"Give me a minute," he whispered. "Stay out of sight, and I'll be right back."

He tried to pass Molly to Laurel, but the little girl whimpered and gripped him even tighter.

"It's okay, sugar. Your aunt Laurel will take good care of you."

With one last pat, he handed Molly to Laurel, his arms feeling strangely empty without the girl's weight. Laurel settled her niece in her arms, her expression pained. He understood. "She's just afraid," he said.

"I know, and I haven't protected her." Laurel hunkered down behind the woodpile. She pulled out her pistol. "I won't fail again."

Laurel McCallister had grit, that was for sure. He liked that about her. "I'll be back soon."

He sped across the backyard, slipped the key into the lock and did a quick sweep of the house, eyeing any telling details. He couldn't leave a trace behind. Nothing to lead any unwelcome visitors to his small cattle ranch in the Guadalupes or to his stashed money and vehicle.

Garrett pressed a familiar number on his phone.

"Sheriff? What happened? Practically the whole town is calling me." Deputy Keller's voice shook a bit.

"Old man McCreary's not putting a posse together, right?" Garrett had a few old-timers in this town who thought they lived in the 1800s. This part of Texas could still be wild, but not *that* wild.

"I talked his poker buddies out of encouraging him,"

Keller said. "It's weird ordering my old high school principal around."

Garrett pocketed a notebook and a receipt or two, then headed straight for his bedroom. "Look, Keller, I'll be incommunicado tracking this guy. I don't want to shoot anyone by mistake. Keep them indoors."

"You need me, Sheriff?"

"Man the phones and keep your eyes out for strangers, Deputy. Don't go after them, Keller. Just call me."

"Yes, sir."

Garrett ended the call. If the men following Laurel and Molly had a mission, his town was safe. Assassins tended to have singular focus. He probably wasn't the target, except as an opportunity. Still, Ivy had known his name. She'd said he was right. He couldn't be certain how much of his identity had been compromised.

If anyone had associated Derek Bradley with Garrett Galloway before today, he'd already be dead. He *might* still have surprise on his side, but he couldn't count on it. And if he'd been right…well, that was all fine. It didn't make him feel any better. There was a traitor in the agency, and he didn't know who. Ivy's message hadn't identified the perp.

Garrett grabbed his go-bag from the closet, then opened a drawer in his thrift-store dresser. He eased out an old, faded photo from beneath the drawer liner.

"It'll be over soon." He glanced at the images he'd stared at for a good two hours after his shift earlier. Hell, it was almost Christmas.

Tomboy that she'd been, his daughter, Ella, would have been after him about a new football or a basketball hoop, while Lisa would've rolled her eyes and wondered when her daughter might want the princess dress—or any dress, for that matter. His throat tightened. He'd never know what kind of woman Ella would have become. Her life had ended before it had begun.

Garrett missed them so much. Every single day. He'd survived the injuries from the explosion for one reason—to make whoever had murdered his family pay. He wouldn't stop until he'd achieved his goal. He'd promised them. He'd promised himself.

He ground his teeth and stuffed the photo into the pocket of his bag. The perps should already be dead. He and James had failed for eighteen months and now... what the hell had happened? Now James's daughter Ivy had paid the ultimate price. And Laurel was on the run. James was... Who knew where his mentor was?

The squeak of the screen door ricocheted through the house. He'd been inside only a few minutes. He slipped his gun from his shoulder holster and rounded into the hall, weapon ready.

Laurel stilled, Molly in her arms. "She has to go to the bathroom," she said with a grimace.

"Hurry," Garrett muttered, pointing toward his bedroom. "We can't stay. I wore my uniform and badge tonight. If they saw it, they'll find this place all too easily."

Laurel scurried into his room and Garrett headed to the kitchen. By the time they returned, he'd stuffed a few groceries into a sack. "Let's go."

Gripping his weapon, he led them outside. The door's creak intruded on the night, clashing with the winter quiet. Pale light bathed the yard in shadows. A gust of December wind bit against Garrett's cheeks. A tree limb shuddered.

He scanned the hiding places, but saw no movement, save the wind.

Still, he couldn't guarantee their safety.

"Where are we going?" Laurel asked, her voice low.

Garrett glanced at her, then Molly. "I have an untraceable vehicle lined up. We'll hole up for the night. You need rest. Then after I do a bit of digging, we'll see."

Laurel had brought his past to Trouble. No closing it away again. If his innocent visitors weren't in so much danger, Garrett would have welcomed the excuse to wait it out. His trigger finger itched to face the men responsible for killing his wife and daughter. Except a bullet was too good for them. They needed to die slowly and painfully.

Garrett might have failed to protect his family once, but he wouldn't allow their killer to escape again. He didn't particularly care whether he left the confrontation alive, as long as the traitor ended up in a pine box.

He just prayed he could get these two to safety before the final battle went down.

LAUREL STOOD ALONE just behind a hedge at the end of the alley, out of sight, squeezing the butt of her weapon in one hand, balancing Molly against her with the other. Garrett had risked crossing those streets to retrieve his vehicle, putting himself in the crosshairs in case the shooters came back.

Every choice he'd made focused on protecting them, not himself. She shivered, but it wasn't the winter chill. She'd made a choice eighteen hundred miles ago to come here. Garrett's immediate response to their arrival had frozen her soul. Now instinct screamed at her to run, to disappear, to try to forget the past and somehow start over.

Maybe she should. He knew what they were up against.

He was worried. Maybe vanishing would be easier. She didn't see Garrett Galloway as a man who would give up easily. But sometimes accepting the reality and moving on was the only way to survive.

A dark SUV pulled into the alley, lights off. Garrett stepped out. "Laurel?" he whispered, searching the hedges with his gaze.

She almost stayed hidden, frozen for a moment. She had some cash. People lived off the grid all the time. So could she.

She could feel his penetrating gaze, compelling her to trust him. What was it about him…?

With a deep, determined breath, she stepped out from behind the hedge. Beads of sap still stuck to her pants from hiding in the firewood pile. The scent of pine flashed her back to memories of camping and fishing and running wild without a care in the world. Her heart broke for Molly. Could Laurel help her niece find that joy after everything that had happened?

Laurel was so far out of her element. She'd taken a leap of faith coming to Trouble and to Garrett, trusting her sister's final words. Her sister had known she was dying; she wouldn't have steered Laurel into danger. Laurel could only pray she had understood Ivy correctly.

She carried Molly to the vehicle. Garrett didn't say anything, but his dark and knowing eyes made Laurel tremble. Did he know she'd almost taken off?

"You decided not to run," he said, opening the door. "I pegged it at a fifty-fifty chance."

He could see right through her. She didn't like it. "I almost did," she admitted. "But I can't let them get away with what they've done." She pushed back a lock of Molly's hair and lifted her gaze to meet his. "Our lives have been turned upside down. Can you help us?"

She didn't usually lay her vulnerabilities out so easily, but this was life and death. She needed his help. They both knew it.

He gave her a sharp nod. "I'll do what I can."

She placed Molly in the backseat and buckled her up. Laurel climbed in beside her. She tucked the little girl against her side. "Where to?"

"I contacted a friend. We need food for a few days. He runs the local motel and does some cooking on the side." Garrett paused. "I don't know how long we'll be on the road. His sister is about your size. I noticed that Molly has a change of clothes, but not you."

Laurel could feel the heat climb up her face at the idea he'd studied her body to determine her size. But he was right. They'd left so quickly, she hadn't had time to do more than purchase a few pairs of underwear at a convenience store. How many men would even think about that?

Garrett didn't turn on the SUV's lights. He drove the backstreets, then pulled up to the side of the Copper Mine Motel behind a huge pine tree, making certain the dark vehicle was out of sight from the road. A huge, barrel-chested man with a sling on one arm eased out of the side door. His wild hair and lip piercing seemed at odds with his neatly trimmed beard, but clearly he'd been on the lookout for them.

Garrett rolled down the passenger-door window. "Thanks, Hondo."

The man stuck his head inside and scanned Laurel and Molly. The little girl's eyes widened when she stared at his arm. "Who drew on you?" she asked.

Hondo chuckled. "A very expensive old geezer, little lady," he said. He placed a large sack on the seat, then a small tote. "You're right, Sheriff. She's about Lucy's size. These clothes are brand-new. Just jeans and some shirts and a few unmentionables." His cheeks flushed a bit.

Laurel scrambled into her pocket and pulled out some bills. "Thank—"

Hondo held up his hand. "No can do." He looked at the sheriff. "If you want them to stay here—"

"After what happened last time, Hondo, I won't let you risk it. Thanks, though." Garrett handed Hondo his badge. "When folks start asking, give this to the mayor."

"Sheriff—"

Laurel clutched the back of the seat, her fingers digging into the leather. She wanted to stop him from giving up his life, but she'd brought trouble to his town. She'd left him with no choice.

"We all have a past, Hondo. Mine just happened to ride in tonight. Something I have to deal with."

Hondo nodded, and Laurel recognized the communication between the two men. The silent words made her heart sink with trepidation.

"Keep an eye on Deputy Keller. He's young and eager, and he needs guidance." Garrett drummed his fingers on the steering wheel. "Come to think of it, you'd make a good sheriff, Hondo. You've got the skills."

"Nah." Hondo's expression turned grim. "I won't fire a gun anymore, and I couldn't put up with the mayor. He's a—" Hondo glanced at Molly "—letch and a thief."

"And willing to take a payoff. I should know. It's how I became sheriff."

Hondo's eyebrow shot up. "You still did a good job. Best since I've lived here."

Garrett shrugged and shifted the truck into Drive. "Goodbye, Hondo."

A small woman with wild gray hair shuffled out of the motel, a bandage on her head. "Hondo?" her shaky voice whispered. "Cookies."

Hondo's expression changed from fierce to utter tenderness in seconds. "Now, sis, you're not supposed to be out of bed. You're just out of the hospital." He sent Garrett an apologetic grimace.

"But you said you wanted to give them cookies," she said, holding a bag and giving Hondo a bright smile.

Laurel studied the woman. She seemed so innocent for her age, almost childlike.

The older woman's gaze moved to Garrett and she smiled, a wide, naive grin. "Hi, Sheriff. Hondo made chocolate chip today."

"We can't say no to Hondo's famous cookies, Lucy."

Garrett's smile tensed, and his gaze skirted the streets. Did he see something? Laurel peered through the tinted windows. The roads appeared deserted.

Lucy passed the bag to Hondo. An amazing smell permeated the car through the open window.

Molly pressed forward against her seat belt. "Can I have one, Sheriff Garrett?"

Hondo glanced at Laurel, his gaze seeking permission. She nodded and Hondo pulled a cookie from the bag. "Here you go, little lady."

With eager hands, Molly took the treat. She breathed in deeply, then stuffed almost the entire cookie into her mouth.

Lucy giggled. "She's hungry."

Hondo placed a protective arm around his sister. "They've got to leave, Lucy. Let's go in."

She waved. "'Bye." Hondo led her back into the house, treating her as if she were spun of fragile glass.

Garrett rolled up the window, lights still off. He turned down the street. "She was shot in the head a couple months ago. We didn't think she'd make it."

Laurel wiped several globs of chocolate from Molly's mouth. "You've made a place for yourself in this town." She resettled the sleepy girl against her body. "I'm sorry." What else could she say?

"They'll find someone else. Things will continue just as they did before I came to Trouble."

The muscle at the base of his jaw tensed, but Laurel couldn't tell if he really didn't mind leaving or if something about this small town had worked its way under his skin. She didn't know him well enough to ask, so she kept quiet and studied the route he took. Just in case.

He headed west down one of the side streets almost the entire distance of town.

Laurel couldn't stand the silence any longer. "Where are we going?"

Garrett met her gaze in the mirror. "I'm taking the long way to the preacher's house. The church auxiliary keeps it ready, hoping they can convince a minister to come to Trouble. It's been empty for almost a year."

"We're just hiding across town?"

"Sometimes the best place to hide is in plain sight," Garrett said. "Besides, I want to do a little searching online. See what I can discover about your sister."

"There was never a news report on the car bomb," Laurel said quietly. On the way here, she'd searched frantically at any internet café or library she could. She kept expecting some news story on an investigation, but she'd seen nothing except a clipping about a tragic accident. In fact, they'd simply stated the entire family had perished in a vehicle fire.

She hugged Molly closer.

They'd lied.

"That tells us a lot." Garrett stopped in the driveway of a dark house, jumped out and hit a code on a small keypad. The garage door rose.

"Small towns," he said with a smile when he slid back behind the wheel. "I check the house weekly."

"Is it safe?"

"The men who took the shot will assume we're leaving town. I would. And I don't want to be predictable."

He pulled the SUV into the garage. The automatic door whirred down behind them, closing them in. Laurel let out a long breath. She hadn't even realized she'd been holding it.

"We're safe?"

"For the moment," Garrett said, turning in his seat. "We need to talk." His gaze slashed to Molly, leaving the rest of the sentence unsaid. *Alone.*

"I know." Laurel bit her lip. She didn't know much. She'd hoped Garrett would somehow have all the answers, that he could just make this entire situation okay.

It wouldn't be that simple. She clutched Molly closer. Laurel had no idea how they would get out of this situation alive.

THE INKY BLACK of the night sky cloaked Mike Strickland's vehicle. Stars shimmered, but it was the only light save a few streetlights off in the distance. Trouble, Texas, was indeed trouble.

"They couldn't have just vanished." Strickland slammed his fist onto the dash of the pickup he'd commandeered.

He'd switched license plates and idled on the outskirts of town, lights off, in silence. He tapped a number into his cell.

"They come your way?" he barked.

"Nothing," Don Krauss said through the receiver, his voice tense. "There are only two roads into town."

"But a lot of desert surrounding it," Strickland muttered in response to his partner's bad news. "We need satellite eyes."

Krauss let out a low whistle. "You request it, the boss'll wonder why."

Strickland activated his tablet computer. The eerie glow lit the cab. "You see the history on this sheriff? Garrett Galloway?"

"Yeah," Krauss said. "So?"

"It's perfect."

"What do you mean?"

"I mean, his backstory is perfect. He grew up in Texas. Went to school at Texas A&M. Joined the corps there. Got a few speeding tickets. Headed to a small town, ran for sheriff."

"Like a thousand other Texas sheriffs."

"Everybody's got something. No late taxes, no real trouble. It feels wrong," Strickland said quietly.

Silence permeated the phone. "What are you thinking?"

"You saw his moves. He didn't learn those in college. Maybe Laurel McCallister didn't get here by chance. Who comes this close to nowhere on a whim?" Strickland glanced around. "And we're at the frickin' end of the earth."

"Still doesn't help to explain if the boss asks about using the satellite."

"I'll say it's a hunch."

Strickland could almost see his partner's indecision. "You gotta learn to take risks, Krauss. If we don't get rid of those two, we're dead. But if my hunch is right, and Garrett Galloway isn't just some hick sheriff, we might be able to feed the boss something new."

"And save our skin. I like it."

"Keep digging on Galloway. Even the best slip up sometimes."

"I'm on it. What do we do until then?"

"I'm contacting headquarters. I want to see a sweep of this part of Texas from the time we arrived until now. This place is dead at night. I want to know who's been moving around and which way they went."

"This could go to hell real fast, Mike."

Strickland scratched his palm. "We just need one break, Krauss. One opening, and our targets won't live long enough to disappear again."

A DIM LIGHT illuminated the preacher's garage. A plethora of boxes provided too many invisible corners and a variety of spooky shadows along the walls. Laurel shivered, but slid out of the car anyway. She bundled Molly into her arms before following Garrett into the preacher's house. He carted in the supplies while she scanned the kitchen, studying each corner, each potential hiding place, each possible weapon. One thing she'd learned in her job: details mattered.

Laurel stepped into the living room. A front door and a sliding glass back door. Not exactly secure. And, of course, doilies everywhere.

The muscles in her shoulders bunched and she cocked her hip. Molly grew heavier and heavier with each movement. She walked back into the kitchen. The decor erupted with grapes and ivy.

So very different from Garrett's house. She'd seen enough of the place to know it hadn't been a home to him, just a way station.

With a sigh, she sat down at the table, shuffling Molly in her lap. She and Garrett needed to talk, but not with Miss Big Ears listening to every word. Molly let out a small yawn. The girl had to be exhausted, but she wouldn't be easy to put down. Even then, the nightmares came all too easily. "Do you have any milk?"

"Warm?" he asked, searching through a couple of cabinets. He pulled out a small saucepan before Laurel could answer.

She nodded. Molly sat up and rubbed her eyes, a stubborn pout on her lip. "I don't want milk. This isn't home. I want my mommy and daddy. I want Matthew and Michaela."

Laurel froze. Molly hadn't mentioned her brother's and sister's names since they'd left Arlington. She blinked quickly and cleared her throat. "I want them, too, honey. But we have to hide. Like a game."

"I don't like this game. You're mean."

The girl's lower lip stuck out even farther and her countenance went from stubborn to mutinous. She crossed her arms, and all Laurel could see in her niece's face was an enraged Ivy. Some might think she could wait Molly out, but her niece could be as tenacious as…well, as Laurel herself.

"It's late, Molly." Her tone dropped, words firm and short. She didn't want to have another drawn-out adventure getting the little girl to bed. Before the car bombing, it had taken some cajoling, at least two stories and two tiny glasses of water before she could get the child to close her eyes. Now…Molly didn't fall asleep until her poor body simply rebelled. "It's time for bed."

"Then why aren't you having hot milk, too?" Molly scrunched her face and crossed her arms.

Garrett turned around. "We're *all* having warm milk, and I made you a *very* special recipe," he said, adding a dash of sugar and a little vanilla and nutmeg to the cups he held.

He set a plastic cup in front of Molly and a glass mug in front of Laurel, then brought over a plate of vanilla wafers. The aroma mingled in the air around them, and Laurel sighed inside. It smelled like home and family. She swallowed briefly, her eyes burning at the corners.

Garrett took a seat, the oak chair creaking under his weight. His large hands rounded the cup. He raised it to his lips, sipped and stared at Molly. She glared back, but when he licked his lips, dunked a vanilla wafer into his cup and bit down, she leaned forward and took a small sip from her cup.

Molly's eyes widened a bit and she tasted more. "Wow. That's yummy. But I want chocolate chip."

"Glad you think so." He slid one of Hondo's cookies toward the little girl and she gifted Garrett with an impish smile.

He winked at Molly, who downed another gulp. Laurel couldn't resist, even though she detested the drink. She chanced a taste. The nutmeg and vanilla hit her tongue with soothing flavors. "Mmm. How'd you come up with this recipe?"

"My wife invented it, actually. Put our daughter to sleep." A shadow crossed his face, then vanished just as quickly. "They're gone now."

"My mommy and daddy and brother and sister are gone, too," Molly said with a small yawn. "I hope they come back soon."

Laurel bit her lip to keep the sob from rising in her throat. "Is there someplace I can settle her down?"

Molly's body sagged against Laurel. A few more minutes and the little girl wouldn't be able to fight sleep any longer.

"Pick a room," Garrett said. "I'll check the perimeter and secure the house."

He strode toward the door.

"Garrett," she said, her voice barely above a whisper. "Thank you. For everything."

"Don't thank me yet, Laurel. Thank me when this is over. Until then, I may just be the worst person you could have come to for help."

GARRETT STOOD SILENTLY in the kitchen doorway as Laurel padded into the living room.

"She asleep?"

Laurel whirled around. Then her head bowed as if it were too heavy for her shoulders. He could see the fatigue in her eyes, the utter exhaustion in every step.

"She was bushed. It's been a rough few days. She just downed the last of her medicine, so hopefully the strep throat is gone."

He tilted his head toward the sofa. "You look ready to collapse. Have a seat. My deputy's been busy tonight calming the town. He received a report of an SUV speeding out of town early tonight. I told him to keep out of sight but watch for it. If they're smart, they'll dump the vehicle."

"But they won't give up," Laurel said.

"I doubt it."

Laurel lowered herself to one end of the sofa, twisting her hands on her lap. "You work for the agency? With my father?"

Garrett sat in the chair opposite her. "In a way." No need to volunteer that he was off the roll. If the agency didn't think he was dead, he'd probably be awaiting execution for treason.

Just one of many reasons he shouldn't allow himself to get too close to Laurel.

But even as he faced her, he felt the pull, the draw. And not because she was gorgeous, which she was, even with that horrible haircut and dye job. Beauty could make him take notice just like any man, but that didn't turn him on half as much as how she'd fallen on top of Molly to protect her.

She was a fighter—a very good thing. She'd have to be for them to get out of this mess alive.

Which put her off-limits. That and the fact that she was James's daughter.

"Your father trained me," Garrett said, trying not to let himself get lost in his attraction for her. "He saved my life, actually."

Laurel tucked her legs beneath her. "I thought it had to be something like that. I used to watch Dad train in the basement when I was a kid. I recognized that move when you dived to the ground." She rubbed her arms as if to ward off a chill. "Ivy worked every night to perfect it. In spite of Dad."

"I heard about the destruction to his office. I don't think James wanted her to join up."

"He was furious, but Ivy has...*had*," she corrected herself, "a mind of her own." Her voice caught and her hands gripped her pants, clawing at the material. "Dad raised us to be independent. She wanted more than anything to follow in Dad's footsteps. She wanted to make the world safe."

Laurel's knuckles whitened and she averted her gaze from his. Every movement screamed at him not to push. Garrett could tell she was barely holding it together, and if she'd given him the slightest indication he would have crossed the room and pulled her into his arms and held her. Instead, he leaned forward, his elbows on his knees, studying her closely. He hated to ask more but he needed information. He had to know. She might not even be aware of the information she possessed. "Where's James, Laurel?"

Her breath shuddered and she cleared her throat. "I don't know. He stopped calling or emailing two months ago. Then out of nowhere a package arrived this week. He sent a charm bracelet to Ivy."

This week. So if James had really sent the package, he'd been alive a week ago. Garrett's shoulders tensed. "Did you bring it?"

Laurel pulled a silver bracelet from her pocket. She touched the small charms and the emotions welled in her eyes. Reluctantly she handed it to him. "Ivy shoved it into my hand as she was leaving that night..." Her voice broke. "She said it was important."

He studied the silver charms. Nothing extraordinary. A wave of disappointment settled over him. Surely there was *something* here. He studied each silver figure, looking for a clue, a message from James. A horse, a dog. A seashell. Several more. Nothing that Garrett understood, but he'd bet Laurel had a story to tell about each one.

The question was, did any of those stories have a hidden message? He handed her back the treasure.

"Tell me about the figures."

She walked through a series of memories. A trip to the ocean with the family right before her mother passed away. Their first dog and his predilection for bounding after fish in freezing mountain streams just to shake off and soak everyone. A horse ride that ended in a chase through a meadow. Her voice shook more with each memory, but the hurt didn't provide anything new. Garrett couldn't see a connection.

He let out a long, slow breath. He had to ask. "How did Ivy die?"

Laurel stared down at the floor. He knew exactly how she felt. Sometimes even looking at another human being could let loose the tears. After Lisa and Ella, he hadn't allowed himself to give in to his emotions. He'd shoved the agony away, buried it in that corner of his mind where it wouldn't bring him to his knees. Garrett had focused on revenge instead. He'd had to in order to survive.

But since Laurel had landed underneath him on the streets of Trouble, the pain he'd hidden had begun scraping at him, digging itself out.

She didn't look up. She simply twisted the denim fabric in her fists. "The explosion burned Ivy almost beyond recognition. She lived. She gave me your name. Then they shot her in the head."

Her voice strangely dispassionate, she went through every detail. When she told him about the single cop's arrival, Garrett closed his eyes. At least one law-enforcement officer on the take. Probably more.

Asking for help was out of the question. And with

James AWOL, they were on their own. She knew it. So did Garrett.

Laurel lifted her lashes and silent tears fell down her cheeks. She wouldn't be facing this alone. In a heartbeat, Garrett knelt at her feet. He pulled her into his arms and just hugged her close.

She clung to him with a desperation he understood. Her fingers dug into his arms. The tiny tremors racing through her tore at his heart. Laurel's heart was broken, and she had a little girl who needed her to be strong.

Laurel needed him, but his body shook as the memories assaulted him. How many nights had he dreamed of his wife and daughter calling out to him, begging for him to save them? But Laurel's pleas were real, in every look, in every touch as she clung to him.

The similarities between Ivy's death and his wife's and daughter's couldn't be denied. He'd find the culprits this time. They wouldn't get an opportunity to hurt anyone else.

Garrett stroked Laurel's back slowly, but she didn't let him go. Her grip tightened.

His pocket vibrated. With one arm still holding Laurel close, he tilted his phone's screen so he could see it. He blinked once at the number. The country code was too familiar. Afghanistan.

"Hello?" He made his greeting cautious, unidentifiable. This was Sheriff Garrett Galloway's phone and number. No one from Afghanistan should know it. That was a life he'd hidden away.

"Garrett?" A weak voice whispered into his ear. A voice he knew.

"James?"

Laurel froze in his arms.

"Garrett, listen to me. The operation has been compromised. Go to Virginia. Get my daughters to safety. They're in danger."

"James, Laurel is with me. What's going on? Where have you been?"

"Oh, God," James cursed. "Ivy knows too much. You have to get her out of there."

Garrett nearly cracked. He didn't want to tell his old friend the worst news a man could receive. Garrett knew the pain of losing a child. Your heart never recovered.

Laurel snagged the phone away from Garrett. "Daddy?" she shouted.

"Laurel, baby. Don't believe what anyone tells you," James said, his voice hoarse. "Promise."

Shouts in Arabic reverberated through the phone. "Find him!"

"Laurel," James panted. "Remember. Ivy's favorite toy."

A spray of gunfire exploded through the speaker.

The phone went silent.

Chapter Three

The phone slipped from Laurel's hand. Her father couldn't be gone. "Daddy?" Her knees gave way and she slid to the floor. She looked up to Garrett. "Get my father back, please."

Garrett scooped up the phone and pocketed it. "I'm sorry. I can't."

He slid his arms beneath her and lifted her. Laurel grasped at him. Her mind had gone numb. She couldn't feel a thing.

With silent steps he carried her to the sofa and sat down on the smooth leather, anchoring her beside him. "Laurel." He used a finger to force her to meet his gaze. "Stay with me, honey."

Her body shuddered, and she couldn't stop the trembling. This couldn't be happening. She wanted to bury herself in Garrett's arms and just forget everything. Pretend the past few days hadn't happened. But she couldn't.

Molly. Molly needed her.

She fisted the material of her jeans, fighting to calm the quake that threatened to overtake her. She had to know. Slowly she lifted her gaze to meet his. "My father? H-he's dead, isn't he?"

Laurel hated the words coming out of her mouth. The

last bit of childish hope, that her father would rescue her and Molly, disintegrated into a million tiny pieces.

Garrett's face resembled a stone statue. He gave nothing away from his expression. He didn't have to say anything.

A burning crept behind her eyes and she pressed the heels of her hands against them, trying to curtain the emotions. "God."

James McCallister had always been invincible. But after the past few months, when she and Ivy had been braced for the worst, for a few brief moments tonight Laurel had gotten her father back.

Now she'd lost him again. Maybe for good this time.

"So many bullets flying," she said, her voice hushed. "How could he possibly survive?"

He hugged her close. "James is smart. And resourceful. If anyone can survive out there, your father can. Right now, I'm more worried about you."

Garrett pulled a small leather case from his pocket and unzipped it before grabbing a small screwdriver. He pulled his cell from his pocket and opened the phone. Quickly, he popped the battery and a small chip from the device and tossed it onto the coffee table before tucking his kit back in his jacket.

"You removed the GPS." The truth hit her with the force of a fist to the chest. "If they're tracing his calls, they know our location. That's what I do for the CIA. Track locations from cell towers and satellites."

"Then you know we can't stay here." Garrett stood.

Laurel swiped at the few tears that had escaped. "How long do we have?" She wasn't stupid. She made her living analyzing data. A price came with being connected at all times. Cell phones, computers, tablets, internet—everyone left a trail. She rose from the couch, her body slightly chilled once she left the warmth of his. She shouldn't get used to it. She knew better. "I'll get Molly."

At her turn, Garrett touched her arm, stopping her. "I'll see you through this."

Laurel paused. "I've driven clear across the country, and a phone call from Afghanistan is bringing whoever killed my family down on top of us...and you. How can it ever be all right? How can I ever keep Molly safe?"

The question repeated over and over in her mind. She knew better than most people how easy it was to track virtually anyone down. Biting her lip, she hurried into the bedroom and wrapped the blankets around Molly. There was no telling where they'd end up.

Molly squirmed a bit. "Aunt Laurel?" she whispered.

"Go back to sleep, Molly Magoo."

"I had a bad, bad dream," she said.

"I've got you," Laurel whispered. "I won't let you go." She hugged Molly tight, humming a few bars of "Hush, Little Baby." Thankfully, Molly snuggled closer, yawned and settled back to sleep.

Laurel exited the bedroom, hurrying to the garage door. It squeaked and she paused, praying Molly wouldn't wake up.

Her niece didn't budge. The dim garage light shone down. Garrett shoved a few last boxes into the back of his SUV and opened the back door, a tender expression when he looked at the sleeping girl in Laurel's arms pushing aside the intensity of just a moment ago. "You better do it. Better if she sleeps."

Laurel gently settled Molly onto the backseat, snapping the seat belt around her.

Garrett closed the door, his movements almost too quiet to hear. "Watch her. I'm going to wipe the house down."

Laurel gave him a quick nod and he disappeared into the house. When he returned, he stuffed a microfiber cloth into his jacket pocket, hit the garage-door opener and slid into the SUV beside her. "Fingerprints would make it too easy for them," he said. "You're on file with the FBI because of your clearance, and so am I."

With a quick turn of the key in the truck, the engine purred to life. He quickly doused the automatic lights and pulled out slowly.

After pressing the outside code, the garage door slid down. The house appeared vacant again.

Laurel looked through the windshield, right, then left, then behind. Tension shivered between them.

Garrett maneuvered onto the deserted street, still without headlights. Trouble had gone to sleep. He didn't plan on anyone waking up as they left town.

He didn't need lights to see anyway. The church auxiliary had gone and wrapped every lamppost and streetlight with garland and twinkle lights, ribbon and tinsel. With each gust of wind the decorations clattered against metal, leaving his neck tense and his hair standing on end.

He gripped the steering wheel, his knuckles whitening. God, he hated Christmas. Hated the memories it evoked. But at least the bulbs lit their way through Trouble.

"Where are we going?" Laurel asked, still alert and searching the surrounding landscape for anything out of the ordinary.

"The middle of nowhere," Garrett said. "Even though some consider Trouble just this side of nowhere."

The vehicle left the city limits, only a black expanse in front of them. This part of West Texas could seem like the end of the world at night, the only light the moon and stars above.

"They'll keep looking for us," Laurel said. "They want us dead."

"No question." Garrett watched the rearview mirror, but no lights pierced the black Texas night. So far, so good.

Laurel shifted in her seat beside him, peering out the front windshield. "It's so—"

"Dark?" Garrett finished.

She glanced over at him, her face barely visible from the light of the dashboard dials. "I've never seen the sky so black."

"When I first moved here from the East Coast, I couldn't get over how bright the stars shone or how dark the countryside could be."

"You didn't grow up around here?"

Garrett quirked a smile. "I was an army brat. I'm from everywhere, but we were never stationed in Texas."

Laurel's eyebrow quirked up. "I'd have taken you for a Texas cowboy."

"I was for a while."

But not anymore.

Garrett focused on the white lines of the road reflecting in the moonlight. No lights for miles around. The tension in his back eased a bit. They were alone.

"It's spooky," Laurel said, her voice barely a whisper. "No sign of civilization."

"You lived on the East Coast all your life?" he asked.

"Dad's job has always been headquartered in D.C. He'd leave town…" Her voice choked. "Someone has to know where he was," she said.

Garrett had been mulling that over. James had been his sole contact since Garrett's attack. He had no backup. No one he could trust.

"What about Fiona?" Laurel's voice broke through the night.

"You know about her?"

"I'm not supposed to. Dad tried to keep his personal life separate, but a few years ago, we caught them at a restaurant. They looked really happy. I'm surprised he hasn't married her. From what we figured out, he's dated her for at least five years."

"More like six," Garrett said. "Though I'm surprised he took her out into public. They work together. That was a huge risk." He drummed his fingers on the steering wheel. "Fiona might be the only person we can trust. She could get at his travel records."

"She could get him backup." Laurel flipped open a cell phone. "He needs help."

"What are you doing?"

"It's prepaid," she said. "I'm not stupid."

Garrett snatched the phone from her. "Not from here. I have equipment we can use to call her. It's more secure. For both of us. We don't want to place her in danger either."

"Dad needs help now."

"James either made it out of that situation alive and is hiding, or there's nothing we can do to help him."

A small gasp escaped from her. Garrett cursed himself, lowering his voice. "Look, I don't mean to be callous, but your dad wanted you safe. That meant more to him than his life or he wouldn't have called. We have to be careful, Laurel. We're alone in this right now, and we have to choose our allies carefully. One slipup…" He let the words go unsaid.

One mistake and they'd finish the job on him and Laurel and Molly would vanish without a trace.

"I understand," she said finally, her voice thick with emotion. "I don't have to like it." She twisted in her seat. "So, this place we're going… How'd you get a secure system?"

"Your dad set it up while I was…incapacitated."

Almost dead.

A small dirt road loomed at the right. Garrett passed it by, drove another ten miles, then pulled off onto a county road heading toward a mine.

"Are we getting close?"

"As close as things get in West Texas," Garrett said. He turned off the lights and the motor. The residual heat would keep them warm for a while.

"We're stopping? We're not that far from town."

Garrett leaned back in his seat and turned his head. "We're waiting. If your tail followed, they should show up soon enough."

Thirty minutes later, the air in the vehicle had chilled. Molly whined in the backseat, wrapping the blanket tighter around her. Garrett cast one last look down the desolate road, then turned the key, and the engine purred to life. He pulled onto the highway, heading back in the direction they'd come.

"You're cautious," Laurel said.

"I'm alive when I shouldn't be." Words more true than he could ever articulate.

"*Who* are you? Really." She shifted and moonlight

illuminated her suspicious expression. "Why did Ivy send me to you?"

The tires vibrated over the blacktop. Garrett refused to let the question distract him. The men following her were good, and he couldn't risk them being seen. Besides, he couldn't tell her. He knew James wouldn't have mentioned his new identity, and if Garrett revealed his previous name, she'd recognize it. As a traitor and a spy.

James had given testimony about Garrett's many infractions. The world had believed the agency's statements. Congress and the covert community trusted James McCallister. Without fail. He might not be a man the public would ever recognize, but in the intelligence community, James McCallister was a legend. The man's lies had saved Garrett's life. And made it so he could never go back. Not unless he wanted a target on his back.

Laurel would have every right to run once she learned the truth, but he couldn't allow that. James's call had done more than warn them. James had risked Garrett's life—and his own—to save the McCallister family. Garrett wouldn't let him down. He owed James too much. He owed the men who had killed his wife and daughter, Laurel's sister and her family—and maybe James— justice. Not courtroom justice, though. The kind that couldn't be bought or bargained for.

"Let's call me a friend and leave it at that," Garrett finally said. "A friend who will try to keep you safe."

"A friend," Laurel mused. "Why doesn't your comment engender me with faith?"

Garrett gripped the steering wheel tight.

"You came to me, Laurel."

"And if I had a choice, I wouldn't be putting our lives in the hands of someone I don't know if I can trust to keep us alive. I like to have all the facts, all the data. You don't add up, Sheriff Garrett Galloway. And that makes me nervous."

What could he say? Her words thrust a sword into his heart. He hadn't been good enough to protect his family. He hadn't seen the true risks when he'd followed up on a small leak at the agency. That one thread had led to their deaths.

Within minutes, the small dirt road appeared. He veered the SUV onto it, the narrow lanes barely visible. The farther they drove in, the bumpier it got. And the more the tension in his chest eased.

Soon they'd started a climb into the Guadalupe Mountains. Leafless branches scraped the sides of the vehicle. Before too long an outcropping of rock blocked their way.

Relieved that the county hadn't seen fit to clear the debris off the glorified cow path, Garrett backed the vehicle into a small clearing. Branches closed over the windshield, barricading them in.

With a sigh he shoved the gear into Park.

"Waiting again?" Laurel asked. "I can't imagine anyone would follow us here."

"The rest of the way to the cattle ranch is on foot. I didn't want the place to be too easy to find."

"I'm known for my sense of direction and I studied the terrain, but even I'm not sure I could find my way here."

"That was the point of buying it," Garrett said. He pressed a button on his watch and the face lit up. "Several hours until daylight. To dangerous to go by foot. One wrong move and we step into nothing and down a two-hundred-foot drop." He reached behind his seat and pulled out a blanket and pillow, thrusting them at her. "Get some rest. When the sun comes up, we'll hike the rest of the way."

"We'll start the search for my father tomorrow?" she pressed, taking the pillow and holding it close to her chest. "I can help. I have my own contacts."

He nodded, but he had his doubts. Laurel might be a gifted analyst, but the moment they ran a few searches, whoever was behind this would start backtracking. Garrett might not know the names of the traitors, but he knew a few dollar amounts. It was in the billions. Too much money was involved for them not to be tracking. Loyalty shouldn't be for sale, but it was.

Which was why Ivy was dead.

Damn it. Garrett should have come out of hiding sooner. He shouldn't have listened to James. He'd wanted to believe his old mentor was close. He'd wanted to believe justice was in their grasp.

"Try to sleep," he said. "Light will come soon."

Laurel snuggled down under the blanket. Garrett shifted his seat back a bit. He'd slept in far worse places.

His hand reached for his weapon. He had to find a way to end this thing. Not only for his family, but before Laurel and Molly paid the price their family had.

The question was how.

James had obviously slipped up.

Garrett couldn't afford to.

A small sigh of sleep escaped from the woman beside him. He tilted his head toward Laurel.

Her blue eyes blinked at him.

"Are we going to get out of this alive?" she whispered. "Truth."

"I don't know."

THE CHRISTMAS LIGHTS decorating every damn corner in Trouble, Texas, twinkled with irritating randomness. Strickland's eye twitched. He leaned forward toward the steering wheel as far as he could and still maneuver the vehicle.

He passed by the sheriff's house for the fifteenth time. Still dark, still deserted.

Headlights illuminated a house ahead.

Strickland whipped the steering wheel and turned down a side street to avoid the deputy crawling all over town. He plowed through a mailbox. With a curse he righted the car.

"Face it," Krauss said, propping his leather work shoe against the dash. "We lost them."

"We can't," Strickland muttered. "She has to die. Her and the kid."

He made his way to Main and pressed the gas pedal. Trouble was a dead end. The SUV shot ahead. The deserted streets of the small town slipped past. They headed into the eerie pitch blackness of the desert without headlights to light the way.

"We have to tell the boss that the McCallister woman is alive, Mike. There's no way we can keep it a secret."

"We still have another day or two," Strickland argued, a bead of sweat forming on his brow. Just the thought made his chest hurt. His pulse picked up speed. He knew what the boss would do. What had been done to others.

"Too risky. If we come clean—"

"We're dead."

Strickland's phone rang.

He yanked the steering wheel and nearly drove off the road. Cursing, he straightened the vehicle.

The glowing screen on the phone turned into a beacon in the night.

Krauss shoved it at Strickland. "It's the boss."

"How—?" He pressed the call button. "Strickland." He forced his voice to sound confident, arrogant.

"The car made the papers," his boss said. "The coroner believes the family died. Well done."

"Thank you." A shiver tickled the back of his neck, as if a black-widow spider had crawled up the base of his skull.

"I have another job for you. It's important."

A string of curses flooded through Strickland's brain. Another job. He had to finish this one first. He couldn't leave it undone. "Of course."

"Two years ago. Another car bomb. Another family. You were in charge."

Strickland remembered it well. No mistakes that time. He'd earned the boss's trust on that job.

"Our target is alive."

Strickland slammed the brakes. The car skidded to a halt. "What?"

"You told me he was dead."

"He wasn't breathing. No way he could have survived those burns." Strickland pulled at his hair. God, a mistake. No. He jumped out of the SUV and paced the pavement. His hand shook as he gripped the phone. Mistakes weren't tolerated. Ever.

"Well, he did. I'm taking care of that loose end. I want you to finish the job. Make certain this time."

Strickland turned on his heel and glared at the twinkling lights of Trouble. He was so screwed. "I'll find him. You can count on me."

"We'll see."

His heart thudded against his chest; his stomach rolled. Bile burned his throat.

"I'll search for him. He can't hide."

"He's not living under his real name."

Krauss rounded the vehicle. Maybe they could split up. It was the only way either man would make it off this assignment alive.

"How do I find him?"

"Your target is Sheriff Garrett Galloway. Trouble, Texas. Kill him this time, Strickland. Be very sure he's dead."

Strickland met Krauss's wide-eyed gaze. He'd heard the words. His partner shook his head in disbelief.

"Oh, and, Strickland? This is your last chance. One more less-than-adequate performance and you'll pray your life will end well before I allow it."

A SLIVER OF SUN peeked over the horizon, the light pricking Laurel awake. She blinked. The muted blue of the winter sky through the windshield brightened with each passing moment. Her cheek pressed against the leather seat. Awareness of the past week washed over her, drowning her in grief.

Ivy, her family. Her father.

Molly.

She jerked her head to one side, then the other, her gaze finally resting on Molly's sweet face.

"She's hasn't stirred," Garrett whispered, his voice low and husky.

Laurel longed to reach out and cuddle her niece, to touch her, to be certain. Molly's pink cheeks were just visible at the edge of the blanket; a small frown tugged at her mouth.

"No nightmares?" Laurel asked, shifting in her seat, combing her hair back from her face with her fingers.

"A few whimpers in the middle of the night. She's obviously exhausted."

"She can't wrap her mind around what happened." Laurel avoided Garrett's sympathetic gaze. She pretended to study the rugged bark of the piñon branches rapping gently against the window. "I can't understand most of the time."

He said nothing, and for that she was thankful. What could he say?

She sent him a sidelong glance. She'd avoided thinking about him as a man, but now, in the close proximity, she couldn't deny her heart stuttered a bit when she looked at him. He was handsome, but that wasn't what drew her. The hard line of his jaw, the determination in his eyes. And his gentleness with Molly. He was the kind of man she could fall for.

Smart, driven and deadly, but with a kind soul. And a heart.

She wanted to reach out and touch him. Just once. She blinked, staring at him. His gaze had narrowed, an awareness in his eyes.

He felt it, too.

The next moment, she wondered if she'd imagined the spark between them. He blinked; the heat doused.

Garrett pulled her SIG from below the seat. "You have extra ammo?"

"Of course," she said. "In my duffel. Dad trained me to go everywhere prepared."

"Not to mention the agency."

"They weren't as tough as my father."

A small grin tugged at the edge of Garrett's mouth.

"So true. I'm going to check out the ranch house. If I'm not back in one hour, I want you to leave." He handed her the keys and a slip of paper. "Contact Daniel Adams. He's the only other person I know who can get you the kind of help you need."

She pocketed the number and clutched the butt of the SIG.

"I'll be back," he said, opening the door.

"Be careful."

He tipped the brim of his Stetson before closing the door softly.

His catlike moves revealed more training than Laurel had. He disappeared around a pile of rocks. She caught a glimpse of his hat for a moment, but within minutes he'd vanished.

She clutched the keys in her hand. She had a full tank of gas, Molly in the backseat. She could run, just disappear.

Forget the past?

The fiery inferno of her sister's car burned the backs of her eyelids. Where was the justice in disappearing?

Her sister never would have let it go. Laurel dug into her pocket and pulled out the prepaid cell. No signal. If anything did happen, how would she find help? Her father wouldn't appreciate it if she put Fiona at risk.

Who could Laurel ask?

There was a reason she'd traveled all the way across the country. She had no choice but to trust Garrett. Him and his secrets.

Her father had called Ivy the judge and jury and Laurel a lie detector. Perhaps it was true. If she had enough information, Laurel could usually figure out the truth. It was what made her good at her job.

As long as the information was solid.

And with Garrett, she had nothing.

Laurel wrapped her arms around her knees, the gun heavy in her hand, comforting in its power. The chill of the winter air outside seeped into the car. She tugged the blanket closer and glanced at the clock. Thirty minutes. And he wasn't back.

A gust hit the tree, scraping the side of the truck. She tensed, gripping the butt of her SIG even tighter.

Forty-five minutes.

Laurel eyed the keys she'd placed on the dash. Fifteen minutes left.

A loud yawn sounded from the backseat. "Where are we?" Molly sat up. "Cars aren't for sleeping." She looked outside, and her eyes widened. "We're in the woods."

Laurel twisted in her seat and faced her niece with a forced smile on her face. "Like the three bears."

Molly gave her aunt a skeptical, you-can't-be-serious expression.

"Look!" Molly squealed, pointing out the window.

Laurel brought the gun to the ready and aimed at the window.

Garrett paused in his tracks and raised his hands with an arched brow.

Molly giggled. "Sheriff Garrett is a good guy. You can't shoot him."

Laurel dropped the weapon and stuffed it into her jacket.

With a forced smile on his face, he opened the back door. "And how is Sleeping Beauty this morning?"

"Hungry," Molly said, rubbing her eyes.

"I think we can take care of that. But first we're going

for a little walk." Garrett met Laurel's gaze and gave her a slight nod. "All clear."

She slipped out of the seat and headed to the back of the truck.

"Don't carry too much," Garrett said. "The terrain is rocky. I'll come back for the rest later." He turned to Molly. "Want to wear my hat?" he asked, holding it out to the small child.

Molly gazed up at him, her blue eyes huge. She nodded and Garrett tipped the hat on her head. It fell over Molly's eyes and she giggled. "It's too big."

"Are you saying I have a big head, young lady?" Garrett asked with a smile, his eyes twinkling.

Molly's grin widened and for the first time in days she lost that haunted look in her eyes. "Bigger than mine," she said. "You're funny. I like you, Sheriff Garrett."

"I like you, too, sugar."

The endearment made Molly smile again, but a swallow caught in Laurel's throat, because the normalcy wouldn't last. It couldn't.

Garrett led them through the jagged mountains, so unlike the woods in Virginia. Craggy rocks, the evergreen of piñon trees, lower to the ground, searching for water. Dry and harsh. Laurel stumbled and fell against a rock, scraping her hand.

Garrett was right beside her in an instant, helping her to her feet, his arm firm around her waist. His touch lingered for a moment, as did the concern in his brown eyes. "You okay? It's not much farther."

Molly stood, holding her lion against her chest. The little scamp hopped from one rock to the next.

"Fine," Laurel said, but her belly had started to ache. It always did when the nerves were uncontrollable. Every moment buried the truth further. They were truly out in the middle of nowhere. Without communication, without anyone but Garrett. How long could it last? How long would they be here?

How could they help her father from here? Much less themselves?

The questions whirled through her mind until a small stone-and-wood structure jutted from an incline.

The ranch house, with a porch surrounding it, wasn't large. Off to the side a small corral appeared more abandoned than anything. She couldn't see any sign of livestock.

"Here we are," he said, climbing up the steps and opening the door. He opened a panel and entered a code. Laurel raised an eyebrow.

"Sensors around the perimeter."

She nodded just as Molly raced in. The little girl's vibrating energy circled the room. She ran from the couch to a nightstand, finally bending down to poke at the fireplace screen. Rocks climbed ceiling to floor, the structure dominating the small living room.

Garrett set a bag in the simple kitchen on one wall.

"Put your things in here." He pushed into a small room with a double bed, chest of drawers and nightstand. No photos, no pictures on the wall. Plain, simple and utilitarian.

"The bathroom is through there," he added. "Just a shower and toilet."

"Is this your bed?" Laurel set down her duffel. "It's fine, but where will you sleep?"

Garrett hesitated. He glanced down at Molly. "Which side of the bed do you want, sugar?"

Molly grinned. "*I'm* gonna sleep in that big bed?" She

ran over and bounced on the side. "When my brother and sister get here, all three of us can fit."

Laurel averted her gaze from Molly, landing on Garrett. A glimmer of sympathy laced his expression.

"I'm going to show your aunt Laurel something. Okay?"

Molly nodded, hugged her lion and started a conversation with the beast.

Laurel took one last look at Molly and followed Garrett into the great room. "I don't know how to explain it to her."

He rubbed the stubble on his chin. "It won't be easy, but she has you. Molly will be okay, eventually. There's going to be a fall when she recognizes that her family is gone. Believe me, I know."

Laurel stilled and took in Garrett's features. Strain lined his eyes and a darkness had settled over his face. She reached out her hand and touched his arm. "I can see that."

He looked down at her hand touching him. "I'll show you my setup here. You may need it."

A step away had her clutching at air. He'd fled her touch. She didn't know why she'd reached out to him, but something in his expression called to her, made her want to comfort him, even as her own heart was breaking.

He unlocked the door leading into the second room in the cabin. She gasped. High-tech equipment she recognized from her job at the CIA lined two walls. Monitoring equipment—a secure phone and a very top secret computer system. A world map hung on one wall. Several pegs dotted some of the more sensitive countries. Below the map, a cot with a pillow and a rumpled blanket seemed to speak volumes.

The bedroom he'd given to her and Molly wasn't where he slept. When he visited this ranch house, he slept here.

"And I was worried I didn't have cell service," she said. "You could contact anyone anywhere in the world from here."

"Hand me your phone," Garrett said.

"It's powered off." She handed it to him.

"Good. They shouldn't be able to trace it to you since it's prepaid, but we can't afford to take chances. It still pings a cell tower." He removed the battery and GPS chip. "Pop in the battery if you have to use it," he said, tossing the GPS in the trash.

"You could track my father with this equipment," Laurel said, moving into the room.

"Maybe." Garrett sat down in one of the chairs and nodded his head at Laurel to take the other seat. "You have to understand, I promised James I'd stay out of the investigation. I have. For his sake."

"But—"

Garrett raised his hand to interrupt her argument. "I get it. Things have changed. We're taking a huge risk, though. I could make his situation worse. You have to understand that, Laurel."

How much worse could it get?

Laurel couldn't sit still. She paced back and forth. Her father could already be dead. But if he wasn't, what if this decision caused him to lose his life? Her mind whirled with confusion. The analytical part of her brain didn't like the missing data.

She lifted her gaze to him before taking her seat again. "If your father were missing, what would you do?"

"If my father were still alive, I'd do whatever it took to find him."

"And live with the consequences?"

"In this situation, yes. The alternative is worse," Garrett said. "Your father has made a lot of enemies over the years, but more than that, if we don't discover who is behind your sister's murder, you and Molly will never be safe. Those men will never stop coming after you."

"Oh, a big kitty! Come here, kitty, kitty." Molly's voice rang out from outside the cabin.

Laurel jumped to her feet at the same time as Garrett. "What kind of cats—?"

"Not domestic."

Robin Perini

Chapter Four

Garrett pulled the Beretta from its holster and slammed through the front door of the ranch house. Laurel's footsteps thundered behind him.

"Oh, God," she whispered.

Molly stood about ten feet from the porch, across a clearing. Her hand reached out toward a large cougar, its long, thick tail swinging to and fro.

"Good kitty," Molly sang out, stepping forward.

The cat crouched, hissing.

"Molly," Garrett said, his tone firm with what his daughter had called his *mean voice*.

The little girl froze. "I didn't do anything wrong."

He guessed the *mean voice* still worked, but the memory also returned that horrible helplessness that he never experienced when facing his own death—or even the death of another agent.

Only a child's death could evoke the fear that seeped through his very soul.

Without hesitation, Garrett aimed his weapon at the animal, cursing inside for the animal to stop moving. As it was, it was going to be an impossible shot.

"Molly." Garrett forced his voice to remain calm.

"That's not a kitty cat. I need you to stay very, very still, sugar. Don't move. I'm going to shoot a gun."

"Too loud," Molly whimpered, shaking her head back and forth, clasping her ears with her hands and squatting down.

Damn it. She'd made herself a target. The cat hunched down on its front paws, clearly preparing to pounce. Garrett couldn't wait. What he wouldn't give for his father's old Remington. He could take out the animal with one shot. A rifle was so much more accurate than a handgun at this distance.

The cat growled, opening its mouth in a show of aggression.

Molly squealed and tumbled backward, becoming a perfect target for the predator.

Garrett ran at Molly, shouting. He had to get closer. Startled, the animal shifted its focus, turning away from Molly. Garrett took four shots at the mountain lion. The big cat yowled once and bounded away, disappearing into the cover of the trees. He'd aimed the shots wide on purpose. Injuring the animal could have done more harm than good, especially if he hadn't been able to take it down. A wounded cat could tear out Molly's throat in seconds.

He'd played the odds.

Thankfully, the animal hadn't gone against its nature. Garrett kept his weapon on hold, searching beyond the shrubs and piñons for the cougar. Cats were normally reclusive, avoiding humans, but they were curious as well.

"Get her," he called to Laurel.

Behind him, she scooped Molly into her arms. The little girl sobbed. Laurel hugged her niece close. "It's okay. You're safe."

Garrett backed toward them, scanning the perimeter,

but there was no movement beyond the tree line. He kept the Beretta in his hand and headed to the house.

"I—I want my mommy." Molly hiccuped from Laurel's arms. *"Mommy!"*

"It's gone," he said.

No need to take chances, though. Within seconds, he'd escorted them inside. Once they were safe, he shut and locked the door. The little escape artist had figured out the dead bolt. He'd have to secure the door another way. It had been a long time since he'd childproofed anything.

His knees shook slightly, and he grabbed the doorjamb for support. Garrett could face down at AK-47 or an Uzi without increasing his heart rate by a beat or two.

A milk-faced Laurel sank into the sofa, rocking Molly in her arms. The little girl's cries tugged at his heart. Laurel rubbed her niece's back, and she turned her head to Garrett.

Thank you, she mouthed.

He'd brought them here, though. He'd put Molly in danger. He should have anticipated. He knew better. Whoever said girls didn't get into as much trouble as boys hadn't lived with his Ella. Or Molly.

"I just wanted to play with the kitty," she said through hiccups. "He's the same color as my lion."

Now that they were safe, Garrett's breathing slowed from a quick pant. He crouched next to the sofa. "I know, Molly, but that kind of kitty doesn't play. He's a wild animal. No more going outside alone. Okay?"

"I want your promise, Molly," Laurel said, her voice stern. "You can't go outside without me or Sheriff Garrett."

The little girl squirmed in Laurel's arms. "Okay."

Laurel allowed her niece to slide to the ground, but Garrett didn't trust that look. His daughter had played the game before. He held Molly firmly by the shoulders, looking her squarely in the eyes. "Listen to me, Molly. Outside is dangerous. We're in the woods and you could get lost. We might not find you. I want a real promise."

Her lower lip jutted out.

"Molly."

She let out a huge sigh. "I promise. Cross my heart, stick a nail in my eye, even if I don't want to."

Garrett held on to a chuckle at the little girl's mutilation of the saying. He stuck out his hand. "Deal."

She straightened up and placed her small hand in his. "Deal. Can I have something to eat? I'm hungry."

Kids. Hopefully she'd been scared enough to mind him. Mulling over how he could keep Molly in the cabin, Garrett walked over to the bag of food on the table.

"Play with your stuffed lion, Molly. We'll let you know when breakfast is ready."

"His name is Hairy Houdini. Daddy named him after me 'cause I always disappear." She ran off to the other room, swinging the lion in the air as if he were flying.

Laurel staggered to the kitchen table and slumped in the chair. She held her head in her hands. "Oh, God."

"You okay?" Garrett asked after pulling a skillet from a cabinet and setting it on the stove.

"My niece was almost a midmorning snack for a mountain lion. Not really."

"She's something else."

Laurel looked at the bedroom door. The little girl had an animated discussion going on with her toy. "Like nothing happened. Is that normal?"

"Kids are more resilient than we are," Garrett said before he could stop himself.

"You've had experience." Laurel folded her hands together. Quiet settled in the room, with only Molly's chatter breaking through.

Garrett's teeth gritted together. He wasn't having this conversation. She didn't need to know how he'd failed to protect his own wife and daughter. Not when he needed her to trust him.

So why did silence feel like a lie? "I'll be back in a few minutes," he said. "I need to get the rest of our supplies." He hurried out the door without giving her time to quiz him.

Idiot. The winter chill bit through his bomber jacket. He scrambled over the rocks and made it to the SUV in record time. He was giving too much away. What was it about her that made Laurel feel so…comfortable? He couldn't afford to like her. Emotions had no place in his world right now. Not when he was fighting an enemy that held all the cards.

He had to get back on track.

By the time he returned to the house with the last of the supplies, the crackle of bacon and a heavenly aroma filled the room.

"I found the bacon in the freezer," she said.

Garrett's stomach rumbled. He hadn't eaten since last night. Without saying a word, he set the groceries on the table and started putting them away. They worked side by side, together. Too comfortably. He sliced a couple of loaves of Hondo's homemade bread. Laurel slid one out of his hands, her touch lingering for a moment. She slathered the toast with butter and popped the slices in the broiler.

"After Molly eats, why don't you distract her?" Garrett said, clearing his throat. "I'll do some looking into your father."

Laurel put down a knife and turned slowly toward him. "How long have you been out of the game?" she asked.

"What makes you think—?"

"At first glance I didn't notice," she said, "but I checked out the equipment a second time while you were gone. Most of it is a couple years old. You haven't upgraded. If you were active, you'd have the latest."

"Molly, time to eat," Garrett called out.

He heard the slap of shoes as she raced into the room. She squealed and sat at the table. "Hairy and I are starving to death." She dug into the bacon and toast, munching down.

"Not a topic for conversation. I get it," Laurel said. "So, you have a favorite football team, Garrett?"

He looked over his shoulder and sighed. "Between your job and your father's career, you have to know sharing information is a bad idea."

"Not much choice. My father is in trouble. So am I. You may be able to help us, but you need me. I have contacts. People I trust. If we're careful they won't be able to trace us back here."

"Really? Even on my *outdated* equipment? Did Ivy trust them, too?"

Laurel hissed at the barb, but Garrett didn't waver.

"I won't apologize. Right now it's all about finding your father. And that means finishing the job your sister started. On our own."

MIKE STRICKLAND SAT in the SUV a block down from the sheriff's office. They'd gotten nowhere searching the man's house. The damn town hadn't had one 9-1-1 call the entire night.

He stroked his stubble-lined jaw. He'd been awake all night, knowing if he fell asleep and missed his chance, his life would be worth nothing.

Strickland couldn't believe Garrett Galloway was actually acknowledged traitor Derek Bradley.

Wasn't his fault the man had decided to take his family somewhere that day. Strickland shoved aside the prickle of regret. He'd gained the boss's confidence with that job. And he'd stayed alive.

He'd also attached himself to the organization the boss had created. Selling guns and secrets to the highest bidder: governments, terrorist organizations, corporations—it didn't matter.

Nothing mattered but the dollars. Loyalty didn't mean squat, and the boss didn't suffer fools. The stakes in the game were too high to risk compromise.

Unless Strickland killed Bradley—make that Galloway—before he saw the boss again, he'd be the next example.

A beat-up truck trundled in front of the sheriff's office. A young deputy jumped out of his truck. He turned the doorknob, then paused.

So, the sheriff was usually in before now.

The deputy dug his keys from his pocket, inserted one into the lock and pushed the door open.

Strickland's phone vibrated. "Tell me you have something," he bit out to Krauss.

"Nothing. Checked out the abandoned house where we triangulated the sheriff's cell signal. Evidence of someone there, but gone. No prints."

"His place?"

"Nothing."

"We're out of options," Strickland said. "I'm going to have a chat with the young deputy." He ended the call, tucked his unidentifiable Glock in his holster, waited for a couple of cars to pass by and stepped out of the vehicle.

He crossed the street and slipped into the sheriff's office.

"Deputy?"

"Can I help you, sir?"

The young man poked his head out from the back room. Strickland could take him out now and no one would have a lead to follow. He ran his hand over the weapon. "Looking for the sheriff."

The deputy sighed. "You and me both. He's not here yet."

"When do you expect him back?"

The kid stiffened, finally recognizing Strickland could very well be dangerous. "I told you I don't know. How can I help you?"

The kid shifted his stance, subtly showing his side-arm.

Strickland flashed his identification badge. "Federal business," he commented. "Contact him."

The deputy's face paled. "Of course." He stumbled to the desk and dialed a number. After thirty seconds his face fell. "Sheriff, a federal agent is here. He needs to see you—"

Strickland grabbed the phone. He lifted the receiver and punched in the erase code. "I didn't tell you to leave a message. Can't risk it."

The deputy stood up, his gaze narrowed, suspicious. "Why are you here?"

"Your sheriff might not be who he says he is, Deputy. I'm here to find out exactly who Garrett Galloway is."

"With all due respect, no way, sir. Sheriff Galloway is the real deal."

"You think so, do you? He ever talk about his past? He ever tell you anything about where he came from?"

"Well, no, but still, he's a good sheriff. Everyone says so."

"Maybe now. My agency has reason to believe he's behind a lot of crimes. Under his *real* name. You recognize the name Derek Bradley?"

The kid gasped. "He's a traitor. Sold secrets to terrorists. Caused a lot of men to get killed overseas. He got himself blown up a couple years ago."

"So the public was led to believe."

The deputy shook his head. "Not Sheriff Galloway."

Strickland leaned in. "Does he trust you?"

The kid nodded. "Yeah."

"He wouldn't leave town without letting you know, would he?"

"No, sir."

Strickland patted the kid's cheek. "Okay, then, here's what I want you to do. If he contacts you, I want you to keep your phone on. Don't end the call." He squeezed the deputy's shoulder. "What's your name?"

"Deputy Lance Keller, sir."

"Well, Lance, are you a patriot?"

The kid sprang to attention. "Yes, sir."

"Okay, then. You do this, and your country will thank you."

The deputy met his gaze. "I think you're wrong about the sheriff, sir."

"Could be. If he's innocent, nothing will happen, will it? And you'll have helped clear him."

Keller smiled. "Yes, sir."

"If he's guilty, you've saved a lot of lives."

Strickland turned and opened the front door. "I'm counting on you, Keller."

He walked back to his truck and picked up his phone. "Kid's clueless."

"You kill him?"

"Came a second away from pulling the trigger, but not yet. Galloway's a straight-as-an-arrow spy. It's what got him into trouble in the first place. He might contact the deputy. And if he does, we'll have him." Strickland paused. "*Then* I kill him."

GARRETT PEEKED INTO the living room. Laurel and Molly were playing hide-and-seek, with Hairy Houdini the key player. He smiled softly. It had been so long since he'd heard that kind of joy.

So many lost memories.

And Laurel. She had his heart beating again. He didn't know if he liked feeling again. A cold heart made it easier to focus on revenge.

She let out a laugh and tackled Molly in a gentle hold. Those two had melted the ice encasing his heart. And Laurel had lit a fire.

He wanted to scoop her into his arms, touch her and hold her until she trembled against him. They could both forget the past and lose themselves in each other. He'd recognized the heat, the awareness in her eyes.

She wouldn't say no.

Problem was, Laurel was a forever kind of woman. And Garrett had stopped believing he had a forever.

The reality made this decision easier. He planted himself in his office chair and picked up the secure line. For a moment he hesitated. Daniel Adams had been through hell, but the man had connections…and he was one of the good guys. These days, men who lived by a code of honor were few and far between. Many talked the talk. Few walked the walk.

He punched in the number Daniel had given him.

"Adams." Daniel's voice held suspicion.

Garrett was silent for a few moments. Daniel said nothing either, obviously unwilling to give anything away.

"It's Garrett Galloway," he finally said.

"If you're calling on this line, it must be serious, and not to request an invitation to Christmas dinner."

"You said to call if I needed a favor. I might. And it's a big one. Just how covert can your *friends* be?"

"Very. What's the situation?" Daniel's voice went soft. A few loud squeals sounded in the background before the snick of a door closing muffled the noise.

"My past is raising a dangerous head, complete with teeth. A woman and her niece are in the cross fire. If I fail, they need new identities and a new life. Untraceable, undetectable."

Daniel let out a low whistle. "I always wondered about you, Garrett."

"Look, Daniel, don't run a search on me. Eyes are everywhere. The minute you pull strings, those eyes will come back on you and your friends. You get me?"

"I played the game," Daniel said. "Do your friends know what they're in for if they disappear?"

"I'll make sure they understand. We're not far from

that gorge you hid out in. How long will it take you to get here?"

"I can have a chopper there in less than an hour."

"I think we'll have to talk about that." Behind him Laurel stood in the doorway, foot tapping. "You're palming us off? Where's that idea of working together, *Sheriff*? I'm not ready to give up on having my life back yet."

Daniel chuckled at the other end of the phone. "She reminds me of my wife. Doesn't take any prisoners. You need me, call this number. I'll have the helicopter on standby."

"No details. To anyone."

"None needed. They know me. You had my back once, Garrett. I've got yours."

Garrett hung up the secure phone and turned around in his chair. He'd know very soon which direction this operation would be taking.

He had a feeling he knew. And that Laurel wasn't going to like it.

NOON HAD COME and gone. Laurel kissed Molly's forehead and quietly closed the door to the bedroom. The little girl had fallen asleep before her usual nap time, but she was exhausted. Even though the weather was brisk, the sun had shone. They'd explored outside, careful to make enough noise to startle any other predators from coming too close. They'd collected pinecones. The moment Laurel had crossed the baseball-sized tracks of the big cat, she and Molly had scurried back to the house. She didn't want to come face-to-face with it again, even with her SIG.

She hovered over the sleeping girl for a few minutes. Molly hadn't mentioned her brother or sister all morning. Laurel couldn't help but worry. When the truth hit, it would hit hard.

She left a small crack between the door and the jamb so she could hear Molly if she woke.

Quietly she exited into the living room. Garrett must still be in his office. She padded across the wood floor and stuck her head through the door.

He sat in front of the wall of electronics, bent over, studying the monitor intently. He typed in a few keystrokes. The screen turned red.

He cursed and quickly pressed a button.

"No luck?"

The chair whirled around. He'd removed his hat and his hair stood up, as if he'd run his fingers through it dozens of times.

"They've closed off most of the loopholes I knew about. Not surprised, just irritated. I let James…" His voice trailed off.

She eased through the doorway. "What about my father?"

For a moment it looked as if he wouldn't tell her. Finally he met her gaze. "I kept a low profile. It was the wrong decision."

"I can help," she said. "Let me do my job. What are you looking for?"

He glanced at the cracked-open door. "Molly?"

"Asleep. Her afternoon naps are usually an hour or so, if her visits with me hold."

"Front door locked?" he asked with a raised brow.

"Dead bolted and chained at the top," Laurel said with a shake of her head. "Ivy said Molly started finding ways out of her crib at just a year old. Once she caught her climbing over the side rail and then just hanging there by her fingertips before jumping down and going after her lion."

"Maybe she'll be a gymnast." Garrett chuckled. "Or a spy." His face turned serious. "I'm trying to identify James's last *official* location, but I haven't found a record of travel, much less any files. His data is locked down tight."

He faced the screen and Laurel bent over him. She rested her hand on his shoulder and leaned in. "I monitor data coming from Afghan tribal leaders," Laurel said. "I might have access to some locations or at least chatter."

"Can you get in from the outside?"

"Are you on a classified network?"

"Secure, not classified," Garrett said. "No way I could pull that off for this long without someone noticing."

"I could get at some information." She gnawed at her lip. "I could end up leading them here, Garrett."

"I know."

He rose from his chair and paced the room. "James said the operation had been compromised. That probably means they'll be looking for my signature."

"He also mentioned Ivy's research."

Garrett tapped his temple with his forefinger. "You know your sister. You know how she thinks. Maybe we can get to her files through you, instead of me or James."

"There's still the problem of leading them here. If I use her name or any identifying information, they'll know it's me. Us."

"You're right." He patted the console. "We do much more here and it'll be the last bit of info they need to come after us."

At the look on Garrett's face, Laurel stepped back,

understanding flooding through her. Garrett *had* learned from her father. Classic James McCallister M.O. "You *want* them to catch you?" She grabbed his shirt collar. "You saw what they did to Ivy. You can't do that."

"You're too damned observant." Garrett scowled at her. "And yeah, I know *exactly* what they might do to me. On the other hand, they won't be expecting me to be ready for them. I'm going to let them think they're getting the drop on me. Surprise is worth a lot."

"It's crazy."

"You think I love this plan, Laurel? If I were planning this op, this would be option Z. But that's where we're at. It's the *only* option. We don't have the insider to help us. We don't know who the traitor is. Your father hasn't contacted us again. We have no choice."

"What about Molly?" Laurel whispered.

"I called a friend while I was retrieving the groceries. He's someone I can trust. Maybe the only person I can trust. He has friends who can hide you and Molly while I go after James."

She could see he'd made up his mind, but there had to be another way. She sat across from him and grabbed his hands, squeezing them tight. "Let me try? We can cut off communication if it's taking too long or if I detect someone tracing us." She met his gaze. "I'm good at what I do, Garrett. Let me try."

"I watch every move. The moment there's feedback, we turn it off and go with my plan. Agreed?"

She was silent for a moment.

"Those are my conditions, Laurel."

"Agreed."

She took a seat and stared at the keyboard. She prayed her abilities wouldn't fail her now.

A LOUD SCREAM yanked James McCallister awake. For a split second he didn't know where he was. Then the pain overwhelmed him. He fought not to cry out.

He shifted his legs, trying to ease the tension in his shoulders. His jailer had shoved him into this dirt-walled prison, clamped a manacle over each wrist and whipped him until he lost consciousness.

James had said nothing.

Footsteps walked down the hallway. James looked up; his eyes widened with shock, and then nausea rose up his throat.

He couldn't believe it.

And yet the proof stood before him.

"I…I wouldn't have guessed," he said through dry lips. "You fooled me."

"Of course I did, but you cost me nearly a billion dollars this month, James. I'm not happy. You know I get cranky when I'm not happy."

A knife sliced down his chest, drawing blood. He hissed, pulling away, but the movement only caused droplets to fall to the floor.

"And Garrett Galloway."

James struggled to keep his heart from racing.

"Oh, yes. I know he's alive. You hid him well. I just wanted you to know that I'm smarter than you are." His captor lifted out a small device.

James nearly groaned. Impossible. No one should have discovered his secret.

"That's right. I can track Garrett Galloway anywhere. He's dead, James. And it's all your fault."

Chapter Five

Laurel leaned forward in the chair, staring at the screen. The disappointment nearly suffocated her.

"It's okay," Garrett said softly. His hand rubbed her back.

"I can't find him." She shrank away from his touch. She didn't want comfort. She'd failed. She'd been so certain. She shoved away from the console.

"Don't do this to yourself." He stood beside her and turned her into his arms. He looked down at her. The expression on his face held too much sympathy.

"I failed my father. I failed Ivy. I failed you." She tried to push away, but he refused to let her go. She shook her head. "I failed Molly."

Laurel couldn't stop the tears from rolling down her face. She'd thought she could do this. She'd believed if she were in her element she could save them all. What a fool she'd been.

"Listen to me. These people are good. I wasn't able to catch them. Neither was Ivy. Or your father. You didn't let anyone down."

He pressed her into his chest. She clung to his shirt, gripping him tight. His warmth seeped through her as the sobs racked her body.

"Shh," he muttered. "It's okay."

Laurel couldn't stop the flood of emotions: the guilt, the pain, the grief. Everything overwhelmed her. She didn't know how long she stood in Garrett's embrace, but when she came up for air, her body was spent.

He rubbed her back awhile longer, whispering soft words of comfort—lies, really. Because nothing would be all right. It couldn't be.

Finally she pushed against his chest and tried to hide her face from him. He tilted her chin up. "You don't have to hide. You just did what I wanted to do from the moment I came to Trouble."

With a swipe of her tears, she cleared her throat. "Doesn't do any good. Now I'm exhausted and fuzzy headed."

"And less likely to crumble under the pressure. Molly will need that strength from you."

"You're going to lay down a trail of bread crumbs, aren't you?"

"Yeah."

"Without backup? You can't."

Garrett brushed aside the chopped hair that didn't feel like hers. "I can't let them use you and Molly as leverage. Not against James. Or me." He closed in on her, his large frame looming. His presence sucked the air from the room. He took her hand in his. "You can trust Daniel, and he has connections. If I fail, they can give you a new life."

She gripped his fingers. "Dad will kick my butt if I let you sacrifice yourself without a fight."

"He'd understand," Garrett said, his face certain, frozen like stone.

"Convince me," Laurel said, placing her hand on his chest. "They could end up using you anyway."

Garrett whirled away from her, stalked across the room and shoved his hands through his hair. "You are the most stubborn woman I have ever had the misfortune of meeting. And that's saying a lot given the work I do. Why can't you just agree?"

"Because I can't let you go on a suicide mission." She followed him, reaching up to his shoulders. Something more was going on with him. She could feel it.

She tugged at his arm, trying to see his face, look into his eyes. When he finally faced her, she gasped at the pain in his expression.

"Why are you doing this, really?" she whispered, leaning into him.

"It's not important." Garrett cleared his throat and then his hand trembled. He cupped her cheek. "You and Molly need to be safe. I can't let anything happen to you."

The air grew thick between them.

"Because of your loyalty to my father?"

His thumb stroked her skin. She closed her eyes. Something had been simmering between them since they'd met.

"Because I can't let anyone else I care about get hurt."

With a groan he lowered his mouth to hers. She clung to him, holding his face between her hands while he explored her lips.

He tasted of coffee, a hint of cinnamon and something uniquely Garrett. With each caress of his mouth, a tingle built low in her belly as if he had a direct line to her soul. A low rumble built within his chest and he scooped her against him, flattening her breasts against his chest.

This wasn't like any first kiss she'd ever experienced. He took her mouth as if he owned her, and she met him more than halfway. When he tried to raise his head she tugged him back down.

"More," she whispered. "Make me feel."

She wanted to lose herself in his touch. She tugged his shirt from his pants and let her fingers explore the skin of his belly, then up to the hair on his chest.

"You're playing with fire," he muttered.

"Then let me burn."

A squeaking door erupted between them. Laurel's eyes grew wide.

"Molly."

"AUNT LAUREL, I'M BORED. There aren't any toys here." Molly shoved into the office, her little arms crossed. Laurel sprang out of Garrett's arms, her face flushed.

"What are you doing?"

Garrett cleared his throat and tried to order his body under control. He glanced down at Laurel. She didn't appear any less flushed. Her cheeks went red and she pulled her hands from beneath his shirt. He regretted the loss, but in some ways Molly had saved them both. He smiled at the little girl. "So, sugar, it's almost lunch-time. How would you like to go on a picnic?"

Laurel stepped back, her expression stunned. "I don't think—"

"What about the big kitty?" Molly asked, her voice tentative.

"Well, I'll be there, and cats usually stay away from people. We'll be fine."

"Absolutely not." Laurel shook her head. "It's December."

"December in West Texas isn't the same as anywhere else," Garrett said. "All she needs is a jacket. And we both need to run off some energy, take in a bit of brisk air." He sent her a pointed glance.

"Oh, please, Aunt Laurel," Molly said, tugging on her shirt. "I wanna have lunch outside and go 'sploring with Sheriff Garrett."

Laurel's face softened, and Garrett could see her indecision. Laurel loved her niece. He liked her fierce protectiveness. Laurel McCallister had a lot of her dad in her. Courage that started with a spine of steel. Courage that made her way too attractive for his peace of mind.

Besides, if they stayed in this cabin, Garrett didn't know how much longer he could resist her. James would take him to the torture chamber if Garrett put the moves on his little girl.

"I need to take a look around and set a few pieces of equipment." Laurel sent him a meaningful gaze. So she'd decided to work with him.

One surprise after another, this woman.

"Yay!" Molly twirled around and around. "We're going on a picnic. We're going on a picnic," she repeated over and over again in a singsong voice.

She skipped around the small cabin.

"Are you sure about this?"

"Do you want to try to keep her inside all day and then get her to sleep tonight?" Garrett arched a brow.

Laurel's gaze fell to Molly's movements, and then she sighed. "I thought she'd grieve more," she said. "I thought she'd be sad." She reached into the box of staples Garrett had brought and pulled out the homemade bread, then grabbed the sandwich fixings Hondo had provided out of the small refrigerator.

"She will be. She'll have a moment when she falls, but right now, something isn't letting her process what happened."

Laurel spread mustard over a piece of bread, then bent over the sink, clutching the porcelain. Her shoulders sagged. For a moment or two she fought the emotion. Everything inside Garrett made him want to hold her, comfort her, but he also knew sometimes grief needed space.

When her shoulders quivered, then shook, Garrett couldn't stay away. He crossed the small kitchen in two steps and placed his hands on her shoulders. He bent to her ear. "It's okay," he whispered.

Molly entertained herself across the room. He turned Laurel in his arms. Tears streamed down her face. She buried her head against his shoulder to hide them.

"I miss Ivy. I miss my family." Her voice had thickened with grief. Garrett rubbed her back, holding her close.

After he'd woken from the coma, alone in a hospital, with a new name, he hadn't had time to cry. God, he'd wanted to, but there was no one left to comfort him or hold him. His family was gone.

He could hold Laurel, though. His arms wrapped tighter around her. He kept his gaze locked on Molly, who'd found an afghan and a small cardboard box and was creating a fort under a beat-up end table.

"Can she see me?" Laurel whispered, her voice thick with tears.

"She's playing," Garrett said.

Laurel trembled against him. Then a calmness flowed through her. She stood in his arms, soft, welcoming.

Comfort shifted to something more, something else.

Something simmering beneath the surface. She cleared her throat and straightened, swiping at her wet cheeks. Through her lowered lashes, she looked up at him. "I'm okay now."

He stroked a tear from her cheek. "You don't have to be."

She glanced over at Molly. "Yeah, I do." Laurel pasted a smile on her face and strode over to Molly, hunkering down. "Whatcha doin', Molly Magoo? Can I come in your fort?"

Garrett turned back to the half-made picnic lunch, thankful Laurel had crossed the room. She and Molly had reawakened his emotions, emotions he couldn't afford to have.

He'd gone against his best instincts when he'd fallen in love with Lisa seven years ago. James had warned him, had told him that there would be secrets he could never tell his wife, lies he'd be forced to live. He'd even said there was a remote chance of danger from the enemy.

The enemy wasn't who'd gotten him… He'd been framed by one of his own. Of that he was certain.

He snagged some bottled water and a juice box from the refrigerator, completing their lunch. "Ready, ladies?" he called out.

Molly scooted from under the blanket and ran across the room. She peered into the makeshift picnic basket Garrett had created using a box. "Cookies?" She blinked up at him, those baby blues innocent and hopeful.

"What's a picnic without Hondo's cookies?" Garrett said. "Can you take this?" he asked Laurel. She grasped the box and he strode into his room. He unlocked the closet and entered a combination into a hidden safe. Quickly, he pulled out his dad's Remington.

He walked over to her. She tugged the box closer. "I'll take this. I like your hands free. In case the big kitty shows up again."

They walked out of the ranch house. The midday sun shone through a bright blue sky. Laurel gazed up. "I've never seen a color like that before."

"Welcome to the desert," Garrett said. "A little different from the East Coast, huh?"

"Considering they started today getting doused in snow, I'd say yes."

Molly bent over and picked up a pinecone. "Ooh. Sticky," she said, dropping it. She skipped around Garrett and Laurel, then ran a bit ahead.

"Molly," Garrett said with a warning tone.

She stopped and turned. "Sorry." She bowed her head and kicked a small rock.

"Just let me go first when we come to a thicket of trees," he said.

"What's a thicket?"

"A big group. Like right here."

Garrett stepped into a small grove. He bent down. "See where the winter grass is bent over? An animal slept here sometime last night or this morning."

He looked around and knelt beside a few tracks, two teardrops side by side. "Deer, probably mule deer in these parts."

Molly crouched beside him. "You can tell that?"

"Everything and everyone makes its mark." He shot her a sidelong glance. "Most everything can be traced or tracked. No one is invisible."

"My job was to analyze data from sources no one can imagine," Laurel said. "I know it's difficult to hide. But not impossible."

"Fair." Garrett stood. "But if it were easy to hide, Ivy would never have found me at all."

The admission didn't come easy, but Laurel needed to understand how difficult her life was about to become.

"There's a small pool nearby. We've had some rain this year, so it might be full."

They climbed over some more craggy rocks to a granite outcropping. The sun had warmed the rock, and below, a large pool of water glistened in the light.

"Just the place for our picnic."

He looked at the surroundings. Safe, and it was clear enough that he had a view where he could see anyone coming.

"Not exactly rolling hills," Laurel said, sitting down with the small box holding their lunch.

"I want to sit by here," Molly said, pointing at a small, flat rock.

"Just your size," Garrett said.

"Nothing rolling or quaint about West Texas," Garrett offered, pulling the sandwiches from the bag.

"It's dramatic," she admitted. "You can see forever."

"I like this spot. I come here sometimes. To think. Nothing small about this land. About seventy-six miles that way is the border with Mexico. North fifty miles and you're in New Mexico. On a clear day like today, you can see one hundred and fifty miles. Can't do that on the coast." He handed Molly a juice box.

"You miss D.C.?"

Garrett bit into his sandwich, swallowing past the lump in his throat, and considered his answer. "I miss the life I had." He missed his family. Every day. He no longer wanted to die along with them. The need for revenge made a body fight. Just to make the guilty pay.

Laurel's gaze fell to Molly. "I understand that. Going back will never be the same, will it?"

"Nothing is ever the same."

Molly crossed her legs and gazed into the water. "Can I touch it?"

"It's cold," Garrett warned.

Molly tiptoed to the edge of the pool, squatted in front of it and dipped her hand into the water. She snatched it back with a yelp.

"I'm not swimming in there." She raced back to Laurel and hugged her legs. "Too cold."

"Molly, do you see this rock?" Garrett picked up a piece of dark granite.

"It sparkles."

Molly's eyes widened as the stone glittered in the sunlight. "Can I keep it to show my mommy when she comes back?"

"You can have it," Garrett said, then lifted a familiar bag from the box.

Molly grinned. "Cookies?"

He set the treat aside. "Of course."

Molly popped a cookie in her mouth. When she finished it off, her leg swung on the side of the rock. "Can I go 'sploring?"

Laurel started to shake her head, but Garrett interrupted, "We've made too much noise not to drive the animals away." He turned to Molly. "Stay in sight. If you leave the clearing, we'll have to go back to the house."

"Cross my heart, hope to die, stick a nail in my eye," Molly said, making a motion across her chest.

A chuckle escaped Garrett. She was so like his Ella.

But so different, too. Molly jumped from the rock. She scampered to the edge of the clearing.

He folded Laurel's hand in his. "She'll be okay. I promise we're making too much noise for the cougar to be interested," he said.

"Bears?"

"Not here. Not enough vegetation and large animals."

Laurel dropped her half-eaten sandwich in the box and stood. She watched Molly. "I'm scared for her."

Garrett rose from the rock. "She's a strong girl. She's got a great aunt. You'll both make it through this."

"What if whoever killed Ivy gets away with it?"

Garrett couldn't stop his teeth from grinding together. No way would he let that happen. Not while he still lived. But he couldn't promise anything. The people after him had no morals, no conscience. If anyone got in their way, they killed them. And they didn't care about the innocent ones who got hurt in the process.

He turned Laurel in his arms and stared into her eyes. "However this goes, I'll make sure you and Molly find a way to be safe."

Laurel lowered her lids. "They might get away with it."

Garrett couldn't deny the truth of her words. Instead, he tilted her chin up with his finger. His heart stuttered at her pain-filled gaze. She'd lost her sister, her brother-in-law, one niece and nephew, and she might have lost her father. She'd lost the life she once had. He wanted to make everything go away, but he might not be able to. "I won't stop until I find them, Laurel."

She shivered in his arms. He tugged her a bit closer, his gaze falling on Molly. The little girl had hunkered down, stacking pinecones. He wrapped Laurel in his arms, pulling her close, and rested his cheek against her hair. Her warmth seeped into his skin, even as the sun shone down on his face.

For one moment he could comfort her. She sighed, leaning against him. "I wish we could stay here forever and the rest of the world would stop," she said.

Garrett closed his eyes, breathing in the fragrance of her hair. He turned and kissed her temple. Her arms tightened around his body. The comfort shifted into something more. Laurel tilted her head, her gaze stopping at his mouth. Garrett stilled, unable to stop the desire flaring just beneath the surface.

"I found a track, Sheriff Garrett," Molly shouted.

Laurel stiffened in his arms. He sighed and touched his finger to her lips. "Sometime soon," he promised. "When we can't be interrupted."

A pang of conscience needled the back of his neck. They were in danger and no one knew what was going to happen, but he couldn't deny the pull between him and Laurel. He'd been so alone for so long. Having her in his arms made him…made him feel hope again.

She squeezed his hand, her gaze warm, her cobalt eyes flaring with a hidden fire. With a sigh of regret, he walked across the small clearing where Molly hunkered down just at the edge.

"What have you found, sugar?"

She pointed a few feet past the row of pines. Garrett stilled. The track was human.

He peered past the trees into a clearing. The remains of a campfire had been hastily shoved aside, but the ash and rocks used to surround the small flames couldn't be mistaken.

Garrett's hand hovered over his weapon. His voice soft and low, he reached out a hand. "Come on, Molly."

"But I found a track."

"And you did well, but we need to go." He scooped her into his arms and strode away from the edge of the trees, one hand still inches from his weapon.

"What'd I do?" Molly whispered. "I didn't do anything wrong."

Laurel met him and he handed over the little girl. "What's wrong?" Laurel pulled the girl to her. "Shh, Molly."

"Company," he said, his voice calm.

Her eyes widened and a line of tension drew her mouth.

Molly squirmed in her arms. "I'm scared."

"Go back the way we came," Garrett said. He tugged the Beretta from beneath his jacket. "You have your SIG?"

She nodded.

"Be ready."

She shuffled Molly in her arms.

"Fire in the air if you see anything or anyone and then head back toward the ranch. I'll catch you. Can you find it?"

She nodded, placing herself at the edge of the clearing, ready to bolt, her hand gripping the weapon.

Garrett pushed through the pines and studied the ground. There were at least two sets of shoes. He sifted the dirt. The fire's remains were cold. They hadn't been watching. The tension in his chest eased a bit.

He glanced over at Laurel. She stood alert, watching everything. She would protect Molly with her life. He didn't like leaving them alone, but he needed to discover who these two people were. He followed the trail. The ground told many truths. One person fell, then scrambled to his feet. Garrett hit some granite rock and the trail vanished, but he picked it back up again on the other side.

Kneeling down, he studied the prints. "Who are you?"

Then he caught sight of a small impression. A kid's sneaker.

Aah. Quietly, he topped a hill. Below, a man hurried his wife and son across the terrain. The guy looked at him, and Garrett knew he recognized the sheriff's uniform, even without the star.

His face erupted in terror, but he didn't pull a weapon. He shoved his wife and son behind him and stared up at Garrett.

Not a great place to cross the border. Especially with a family. Was a coyote nearby? Most of the men who made a living illegally bringing people across the border made Garrett's stomach turn. They charged thousands of dollars to cross into the United States, and if their "customers" were lucky, the coyote got them to civilization. The unlucky ones ended up dead of thirst in the desert.

Garrett scanned the horizon, searching for signs of a coyote, but he didn't see anyone.

With a quick nod to the man, he turned and hurried back toward the clearing. He had to get Laurel and Molly to safety.

They might end up much like that man and his family. Living under the radar.

Unless Garrett succeeded where he and James had failed for the past eighteen months.

Garrett shoved his Stetson on his head. Now, though,

he had to succeed for more than just revenge—he had to succeed to protect two innocent lives.

He wouldn't lose. He couldn't.

LAUREL CARRIED MOLLY back into the cabin. Her niece was way too quiet. The little girl toyed with the collar Ivy had placed around the neck of her lion.

Garrett followed her in. "I'm canvassing the area once more. Lock the door behind me. I'll knock three times when I get back. And keep the gun handy."

"Shoot if someone else tries to get in," Laurel said. "Got it."

"Not if it's me." Garrett shut the door, putting the box of food on the floor.

Molly wiggled from Laurel's arms. "I want to go into my fort," she muttered. "I want Mr. Hairy Houdini to come with me."

"Want me to play with you?"

The little girl whispered into her stuffed animal's ear and shook her head, disappearing beneath the afghan.

Laurel sighed and put away the groceries, keeping a close eye on Molly.

Within a few minutes, the little girl was rubbing her eyes and yawning. It had been a tough few days. Not to mention just getting over strep throat.

Massaging her temple, Laurel scanned the room. They couldn't stay here forever. The only way out was to find who was behind Ivy's murder. And her father's disappearance. And stop them.

Garrett knew more than he was revealing. She believed that, and she didn't know who he was, really. That uneasy feeling at the base of her neck increased the urgency. She needed to *do* something. To protect Molly and herself. Not just for the moment, but for the future.

Laurel checked once more on her niece, but the little girl had zonked out.

Careful not to make any noise, she opened Garrett's office door and walked inside. She propped the door open so she could hear Molly or anyone outside and turned the machines on.

She'd had an idea. Maybe, just maybe, it would work.

Growing up with her father's ability to discover what his daughters were doing, Laurel had become adept at hiding her tracks. She'd joined the computer club at school. Yeah, it had helped her get into college, but more important, it had taught her a few tricks. Tricks that came in handy at her job, and that might come in even handier now.

She risked a lot doing this without Garrett here, but she had to try. It was her last chance or they'd have to go with Garrett's plan.

She navigated to a portal leading into some of the intelligence organization's unclassified databases.

When the log-in came up, she tapped her finger on the keyboard.

If she entered her information, she was starting a ticking clock. Eventually they would know she'd entered the system; they'd know what she discovered.

Garrett still hadn't returned.

She took a deep breath. She had to take the chance.

Her finger trembled typing in the password.

She was in.

Glancing at the time on the computer screen, she quickly

navigated to the travel database. Relatively low priority. She entered her father's name.

Access denied.

Interesting. She backed out, this time searching for Ivy's name, then hers. Finally, with her own name, she received a different screen.

Clicking on a link pulled up her personal data.

Status: Missing, presumed dead.

"What the hell do you think you're doing?"

Chapter Six

Strickland cursed. "Waiting around in this godforsaken town is getting us nowhere." The December Texas sun heated up the SUV and sweat trickled down his neck. He wiped his arm on his forehead. "Garrett Galloway isn't coming back."

"Do you think he knows the boss has found him?" Krauss asked, rolling down the window enough to allow a small crack. A soft, cool breeze flowed in. "I sure wouldn't stick around."

"Could be he ran. Or maybe he's hiding the woman and the girl."

"We're screwed either way, you know." Krauss's tone held nothing but resignation. "The boss'll find out we lost him, and we'll be dead. We're expendable and you know it. We both know it."

Krauss was right. But there had to be a way out. Maybe that deputy… Derek Bradley, aka Garrett Galloway, had lived in this town awhile. Strickland had discovered the people liked him. The waitress at the diner, the deputy, the local motel owner—they all thought the guy walked on water. Though that motel guy had shown Strickland the door too fast when his loopy sister had shown up and started yammering.

Maybe the tattooed freak knew more than he let on.

Strickland drummed his fingers on the steering wheel. "So, Krauss. You think Galloway would come back if real trouble visited Trouble, Texas?"

Krauss slowly nodded his head, a glimmer of hope reaching his eyes. "After what we know about both his identities, yeah. He's just enough of a hero to take the risk...if the bait is right."

"And I think I know exactly who—" Strickland's phone sounded. One glance at the number appearing on the screen and he could feel the blood drain from his face.

"It's the boss, isn't it?" Krauss said, a string of curses escaping from him. "What are you going to say?"

"I don't know." Strickland rubbed the back of his neck and tapped the phone. "Strickland."

"Imagine my surprise when I discovered your current location. Why didn't you tell me you were already in Trouble, Texas?"

At the biting tone of his boss's voice, he shivered, then gulped. He didn't have a good answer.

"Don't bother lying. There aren't a thousand people in that town. You come clean, Strickland, I might let you live...minus a body part or two."

Strickland met Krauss's gaze. The man's expression looked as if he'd scarfed down a large helping of bad fish. He'd seen the boss's handiwork. Missing fingers, missing toes, missing eyes...and worse.

"I—I saw a note Ivy Deerfield wrote when we went to set up the bomb." Strickland couldn't prevent the squeak in his voice as he lied. "She wrote down this sheriff's name. I just wanted to make sure she hadn't given anything—"

"How did you discover the connection between the McCallisters and Galloway?" his boss asked sharply.

"I didn't know about a link. I just had a bad feeling." More truth in those words. Strickland swallowed again. "You ordered us to follow up on loose ends. And to get rid of them."

"Which you enjoy a little too much," his boss muttered. "Okay, Strickland, I'll let you fix your little problem, but if I find out you're keeping something from me—"

"I've worked for you too long, boss," he said. Yeah, long enough to know that if he told her the truth of how he'd had them and lost them, she wouldn't just take a body part—she'd make him suffer and want to die.

Krauss just shook his head.

"Perhaps." The boss paused for a moment. "Well, Strickland, this may be your lucky day. I have Garrett Galloway's location for you. A gift from…a good friend."

The boss gave him a frequency. Krauss entered the number into the small tracking device. A red dot appeared on the screen. "He's in the mountains not far from here," Krauss said. "Rough country."

"Are you sure it's him? Or could this be his laptop or something?" Strickland asked.

A chuckle filtered through the phone. "It's inside him. You track that frequency, you'll have your target."

Strickland scratched at a surgical scar from a rotator-cuff repair a year or so ago. "That's not possible."

"Really? You have an inside track on the latest research and development of the agency, do you?"

Strickland gulped at the disdain in his boss's voice. "Of course not."

"You better be glad the chip isn't widely available. If I'd had one inserted inside you, I have a very good feeling you'd already be paying the price for some extracurricular activities."

The muscles in Strickland's back tensed. The only way out of this mess was clean it up and beg...or find out something he could bargain with.

"Find him, Strickland. And kill him. No mistakes." The phone call ended.

He grabbed the map from Krauss's hand and smiled for the first time since he'd realized the McCallister woman had escaped the bomb. "We have a pointer to Galloway. Which means we have McCallister and the kid, too. They're out in the middle of nowhere."

"Easy to dispose of bodies out there. No one will ever find them."

"Yeah." Strickland stared down at his phone. Now if he could only find a way that he wouldn't disappear either.

AT GARRETT'S BITING WORDS, Laurel's hands froze above the computer keyboard. She winced and whirled her chair around. If she'd thought he might be glad she'd taken the initiative to use her skills, that notion vanished the moment she took in his tight jaw and narrowed gaze.

"I had an idea," she protested. The niggling doubts that had skittered up her spine when she turned on the machine gnawed through her nerves. But what choice did they have?

"You've started the ticking clock." His cheek muscles pulsed.

That she had an answer for. "The clock would have

started anyway. We both know that. I just happened to control the start."

"Explain."

"I set up the signal to bounce all over the world. We're on a ticking clock—like you wanted, but thirty-six hours from now. Maybe forty-eight."

"How certain are you?"

"I wouldn't play with Molly's life like that. Or yours."

He studied her expression, then finally nodded his head. "Then sit down in the damn chair and get us some information. You started this. Let's see what your stint at the CIA can do for us."

Garrett snagged a kitchen chair from the other room and flipped it around, sitting astride the hard wood. She let out a long, slow breath. She knew her business, but her nerves crackled at his constant stare. Leaning forward, she focused on the monitor.

Soon she lost herself in the task, following path after path. She didn't know how long she'd been beating her head up against dead ends when a folder suddenly appeared.

Laurel stilled. "Look. The directory belongs to Ivy, but it's not official."

Garrett straightened in his chair. "Unauthorized?"

She nodded and clicked on the folder. It contained only one file. "It could be a trap."

"You've been at this awhile. What's your gut say?"

"To open it."

"Then do it."

She held her breath and double-clicked the file.

A password box came up.

"You know it?" Garrett asked.

"Maybe," Laurel said. She typed in her sister's anniversary.

Access denied.

Her children's names.

Access denied.

Her birthday.

Access denied.

"One more shot and I'm locked out. I'll have to start over," Laurel said, rubbing her eyes. "I may not even get access to the file again."

A long, slow breath escaped from Garrett. "You know your sister. Most of these passwords require at least one capital letter, one symbol and one number. And once you encrypt a file, if you forget the password, you're screwed. She'd have to be able to remember it."

Laurel drummed her fingers on the desk and sat back in the chair. She closed her eyes. "Ivy, what did you do?"

The room grew quiet, just the fan of the equipment breaking the silence.

Garrett didn't chatter, didn't interrupt her thoughts. She liked that about him. So many people didn't know when to simply be quiet.

"I may have it." She turned her head, meeting his gaze. "Ivy was older than me. She'd just started to date when Mom died. They had this special code. Even while Mom was in the hospital, she made Ivy promise to let her know if she was okay at nine o'clock. If there was trouble, there was a special message she'd leave on the pager."

"What was the code?"

"Mom's name, then nine-one-one, then an exclamation point. But if I'm wrong…"

"What do your instincts say?"

"That Ivy knew she was in danger and that she would pick something I knew." Laurel kneaded the back of her neck, her eyes burning. "She knew there was trouble."

"Do it."

Laurel swerved around and placed her hands on the keyboard. She couldn't make her fingers type in the password. What if she was wrong?

"Trust your gut." Garrett placed his hand on her shoulder. "Do it."

Laurel picked the keys out one at a time, taking extra care. Finally, she bit down on her lip and hit the enter key.

The machine whirred. The screen went blank.

"Please, no." She half expected a message with red flashing lights and alarms to appear stating the file had been destroyed.

A few clicks sounded and the word-processing program sprang to life.

Ivy's file opened. Laurel blinked. Then blinked again.

At the top of the file in bold letters were just a few words.

Derek Bradley is alive.
Alias: Sheriff Garrett Galloway.

THE WORDS SCREAMED from the page. Garrett groaned and gripped the wooden slats of the chair until his fingers cramped. Ivy had found out about him. This couldn't be happening. If she knew…others knew as well.

James's plan had failed. And God knew who he could trust.

Laurel launched out of her chair and faced him. "*You* are Derek Bradley? The traitor?" She backed away, shaking her head.

"Laurel—"

"You caused the deaths of dozens of agents. My father told me. He said you finally got paid back. You died with your wife…and daughter." Her hand slapped against her mouth, and her eyes widened. "It was a car bomb."

"I should have died. My wife and daughter *did* die," Garrett said, his voice holding a bitterness that burned his throat. How many times had he begged to die only to have first James, then the doctors, fight to save him? How many weeks had he lain in his hospital bed planning revenge when he discovered who had taken them from him?

Laurel's eyes were wide with horror. "Like Ivy."

Garrett gave a stiff nod. "I was running late on my way home from the office. I'd promised my wife I'd get home early, but I'd been hell-bent on tracking down an insider. I'd discovered a few hints, nothing concrete, but enough to keep me asking questions, pursuing leads in areas where I had limited need to know." He could barely look at the knowledge in her eyes. She knew what was coming, but he had to get it out. She had to understand. "I was running late, tying my tie. Lisa took my daughter and put her in the c-car." He cleared his throat. "I'd just walked out the door, dropped my keys. Lisa was tired of waiting. She turned on the engine and it blew. I had my back to the car or else the explosion would have taken me out."

"But why doesn't everyone know you're alive?"

Garrett shoved his hands back through his hair. "Your father. I don't know how, but he knew something was wrong at the agency. He'd seen some questionable information cross his desk. I was being framed. He came by right after the bomb went off. Just lucky, I guess, because he fixed it." Garrett raised his chin and met Laurel's gaze. "Derek Bradley died that night with his family."

Laurel's entire body shook. "My father called you a traitor."

"Your father didn't know if I would survive. He knew I wouldn't if whoever set the bomb realized their mistake. So he created a new identity and took me to a hospital in Texas, and I recuperated there. By the time I came out of the coma, I was dead and buried, and Garrett Galloway was born."

"How could no one find out?"

"I was in a coma for months, under another name. James tried to identify the leak, but there were no leads. By the time I woke up the case was closed. I had several months of physical therapy."

"If you're telling the truth, why didn't he warn Ivy?" Laurel's pleading gaze tugged at Garrett. She paced back and forth, her movements jerky, uncoordinated. She swiped at her eyes. "Why didn't my father protect Ivy? He could have told her to quit. She might still be alive."

"I don't know." Garrett stepped in front of her and took her shoulders, tilting his head to force her to look him in the eyes. "I know your father. James McCallister loved his family more than anything. If you want to blame anyone, blame me. I shouldn't have stayed Garrett

Galloway this long. I let your father convince me he was closing in on the traitor, that if they thought I was still dead they'd eventually get complacent. I agreed to let him continue the search."

"Dad could convince someone in North Dakota to buy ice in the winter," Laurel said, shaking her head. "He always thought he knew the best for everyone else."

"He believed I'd take too many risks. He was right." Garrett had to face the truth. "I'm sorry, Laurel. So sorry. If I'd come back, maybe I could have forced the traitor's hand."

She scrubbed her hands over her face and stepped out of his embrace. "This doesn't make sense. Ivy knew about you and your case. She said you were right. You have to know *something*."

"I discovered there was a mole in the organization, but I never figured out who."

"Maybe Ivy did." Laurel's expression turned eager. She plopped into the computer chair and scrolled down her sister's file. Garrett leaned over her shoulder. She'd taken his identity in stride. The more time he spent with James's daughter, the more Garrett recognized the similarities. Smart, tenacious, optimistic. Traits he admired in his mentor. Qualities he liked in Laurel. A little too much.

He shifted closer, aware of the pulse throbbing at her throat, the slight increase in her breathing. He wanted to squeeze her shoulder, offer her encouragement, but he didn't want to distract her either. He backed away, forcing himself to focus on the file. Lists of operations, lots of questions, brainstorming. Ivy had been smart, curious and methodical. And her quest had gotten her killed.

As Laurel scrolled, an uneasy tingle settled at the

nape of Garrett's neck. Every operation involved James somehow. Several involved Garrett; some didn't.

"Slow down," he said softly, his voice tense.

"Ivy had more questions than answers." Laurel shot him a sidelong glance then stilled her hand. "What's wrong?"

That she read him meant he was out of practice. He guarded his expression. "Probably nothing."

"I can see it in your eyes." She snapped the words in challenge. "You've already lied about your identity, Derek. Don't lie about anything else. I deserve the truth. So does Ivy. And Molly."

"I'm Garrett now." He stiffened, but knew she was right. If something happened to him, she couldn't be in the dark. She had to be cautious. Around everyone. "James was involved in all the cases Ivy investigated."

Laurel's back straightened and her expression hardened. "My father is not a traitor. Who else was involved?"

"I didn't say he was—"

"You were thinking it. Tell me."

He couldn't deny the thought had crossed his mind.

"I was involved," he said.

"You know, Garrett, sometimes you have to have faith in the people you love. Even when the whole world seems screwed up, there are people who live by honor out there." She looked over her shoulder at him. "You're proof of that. My father trusted you with his family when he was in trouble. So have I. My father deserves the same consideration. Unless you really are a traitor."

Man, Laurel McCallister went right for the jugular with a few well-placed words.

"Then why aren't you afraid of me? Are you afraid that I might betray you?"

"You would have killed us already. Instead, you saved us. You sacrificed your hideaway. You put yourself at risk. Face it, Garrett, you're a hero. Just like my dad believed." Laurel scrolled to the end of the file. "There's a link here."

She clicked it. Another password. She tried the same one.

Access denied.

After three more attempts, Laurel shoved back from the keyboard with a frustrated curse. "I'm out of ideas."

Laurel shook her head, and he could see the fatigue and disappointment on her face. He kneaded her shoulders. "You're good with that machine. Is there another way to figure out the password? Are you a code breaker?"

"It's not my area, but…" She drummed her fingers on the table. "Maybe I can do one better." She chewed on her lip. "I developed a code-breaking computer program with some friends when I was in college." She winced. "We nearly got kicked out of the computer-science department when our adviser found out. I could run it from here, but it will take a while."

"As in we'll be connected to the network for a long time?"

Laurel nodded, and then her eyes brightened. "Unless I download the file."

At this point, it was worth the risk. "Do it."

Laurel clicked through options so quickly Garrett's eyes nearly crossed. "You never hesitate."

"My dad and Ivy have the gift of thinking on their feet. I do better with zeros and ones."

"Mommy!" Molly screamed at the top of her lungs. "Daddy!"

The terrorized cries pierced the air. The sound speared Garrett's heart. He didn't hesitate, throwing open the door to the living room.

At the same time, Laurel exploded from her chair, racing to her niece.

Molly sat straight on the sofa, her cheeks red, sweat dripping down her face, her eyes screwed up tight.

Laurel sat beside Molly and wrapped the little girl in her arms. "Shh, Molly Magoo. I've got you."

Laurel rocked her back and forth, but Molly refused to open her eyes, shaking her head so hard her hair whipped around, sticking to her tearstained face. She clutched at Laurel.

"Is she still asleep?"

"She's clinging to you. She knows you're here."

Laurel hugged Molly closer. "What do I do? This has never happened before."

Molly's sobs gutted Garrett's heart. Ella hadn't had a lot of nightmares, but she'd watched part of *Jurassic Park* at a friend's house and that evening the night terrors had stalked her. Only one thing had calmed her.

Molly struggled against Laurel. "You took me away," she whimpered.

Laurel's face went pale. The agony in her expression made Garrett hurt for her. "Give her to me," he said.

Laurel hesitated.

"I know what to do," he whispered.

Reluctantly, she handed the twisting little girl to Garrett. He sat down in a large overstuffed chair and held

Molly close to his chest. "It's okay, sugar," he said, making his voice soft and deep and hypnotic. He snagged a blanket and wrapped her like a burrito inside it, one arm tight around her.

He rocked her slowly and started singing in an almost whisper. "The ants go marching one by one, hurrah, hurrah. The ants go marching one by one, hurrah, hurray. The ants go ma-ar-ching one by one, the last one stops to look at the sun, and they all go marching down, in the ground, to get out of the rain."

The melodic, low tone of the song echoed in the room. He rubbed her back in circles. Her sobs quieted a bit.

Garrett sang the second verse, all the while rocking her, rubbing her back, holding her close.

Molly's cries turned to hiccups and finally softened. His chest eased a bit. Just like Ella. He looked up. Laurel's face had turned soft and gentle, and awed.

She hitched her hip on the arm of the chair and fingered Molly's locks. The little girl's eyes blinked. She opened her baby blues, looking up at Garrett, then at Laurel.

"Mommy?" she asked. "Daddy?"

"They aren't here, sugar," Garrett said. "But your aunt Laurel is. She won't let anything happen to you. Neither will I."

Molly bit down on her lip. "There was a 'splosion. Daddy's car burned like in the fireplace."

A tear trickled down Laurel's face. "Yes, honey, it did."

"Are Mommy and Daddy coming back?" she asked, her voice small, fearful.

Laurel glanced at Garrett. He warred with what to do, what to say. He simply nodded. It was time.

He tightened his hold on Molly. Laurel cleared her throat. "Honey, they aren't coming back, but they're watching over you. They're in heaven."

Tears welled in Molly's eyes. "Even Matthew and Michaela?"

"Even them, sweetie." Laurel handed her Mr. Houdini. Molly hugged the lion close.

Tears rolled down her face. "I want them back."

Laurel sank closer to Garrett. He shifted and she nestled next to him. Her arm wrapped around Molly, her cheek resting on the little girl's head. "So do I, Molly Magoo. So do I."

Molly clutched her stuffed animal. She didn't scream, as if the pain was too much for that. She laid her head on Garrett's chest. Fat tears rolled down her cheeks.

"Sing to me," she pleaded. "My heart hurts."

"The ants go marching…" Garrett fought against the emotions closing his throat. Memories too horrible and too deep slammed into him. Nights lying in the hospital bed after he'd awakened, reaching out his hand for Lisa's or for Ella's and no one had been there.

Just anonymous nurse after nurse—or no one at all.

Laurel leaned against him, her shoulders silently shaking. He knew she was crying. She buried her face in his neck.

Garrett held on to them, the children's tune now a mere murmur. Soon Molly went still in his arms.

He fell silent.

Sunlight streamed into the window, but he could tell from the angle it was low in the sky. Late afternoon.

He looked over at Laurel. Her eyes were red. "It breaks my heart," she whispered.

His own emotions raw and on the surface, he gave

a quiet nod. "I should put her in bed. She'll wake up at some point, but she needs the rest."

Laurel shifted away from him and he rose, taking the precious bundle into his bedroom. He pulled off her shoes and tucked her under the covers. He kissed her forehead. "Sweet dreams, sugar."

His arms felt empty. His throat tightened as the past overtook him. His own little girl, afraid. His Ella hadn't known a nightmare would come. Neither had Molly.

He turned and Laurel stood in the doorway watching him, her face ravaged with grief. His own festered just beneath the surface. Part of him wanted to escape the claustrophobia of his bedroom, to run to the top of a mountain and shout his fury. Instead, he walked toward her and she backed up. He stepped into the living room and closed the door softly behind him. The latch clicked.

She said nothing, and he didn't know what to say. Molly's tears had torn away the defensive emotional wall he'd worked so diligently to build over the past eighteen months.

She simply walked into his arms, and he could do nothing but enfold her, cling to her and struggle to contain the dam of feelings that threatened to break free.

Laurel stood there silently for several minutes. Her warmth seeped through his shirt. How long since he'd just let himself be this close to someone?

Much too long.

"Thank you," she said. She eased back and touched his cheek with her hand, her whispering caress soft and tender.

"You handled her well. She'll cry more. It won't be over today, but she'll make it. So will you."

He kissed her forehead and she wrapped her arms

around his waist, hugging him tight. He knew she just needed someone to cling to, but he couldn't ignore the slight pickup of his heartbeat. She was too vulnerable. And so was he. Laurel and Molly's presence reminded him of a pain he'd barely endured. Now somehow he had to find the strength to help them survive.

A small whimpering filtered from his bedroom.

"Go to her." Garrett stepped away. "She needs family."

Laurel gripped his hand and kissed his cheek. "You're a good man, Garrett Galloway." She disappeared behind the door and he heard her softly speaking to Molly.

Once he was certain the little girl was calm, he grabbed his Beretta from atop the refrigerator, where he'd stashed it, and strode onto the porch. The sun had turned red as it set on the western side of the ranch. The face of the mountain had turned light red and purple. Garrett sucked in a deep breath of mountain air. He exhaled, shuddering, and gripped the wooden rail until his knuckles whitened.

He blinked quickly, shoving back the overwhelming emotions that threatened to escape.

Molly and Laurel could rip what was left of his heart to shreds. When he'd come to and realized Lisa and Ella had paid the ultimate price for his job, only the need for revenge had kept him alive those first few months during therapy. He'd buried the grief deep in a hole where his heart had once resided.

Garrett scrubbed his face with his hands. Molly had reminded him of what it was like to protect someone who was truly innocent. And Laurel. God, that woman made him want what he couldn't have. He couldn't even let himself think about her that way. Not until whoever had killed his family—and hers—was no longer a threat.

A rustle in the trees made Garrett still. He focused on the movement. For several seconds he watched. Another slight shift of the pine needles, a scrape. Not the wind.

Someone, or something, was out there.

He gripped his weapon and moved behind the stone pillar at the corner of the house. If a weapon had a bead on him, he needed cover.

Once he decided to move, he'd have only a split second.

A shadow shifted in the fading sunlight. Two eyes peered at him from between the pines.

Garrett stepped off the porch. "So, you're back."

Chapter Seven

Laurel snuggled Molly next to her. The little girl twisted the flannel of her Christmas nightgown. It had been a present from Ivy when she'd realized Molly wouldn't be able to attend the pageant that fateful night.

When Laurel had followed Molly into the cabin's bedroom, her niece had pulled her mother's gift from the duffel and silently handed it to Laurel.

"You can wear my T-shirt, Molly Magoo," Laurel had said, barely able to speak.

"Mommy said Santa would know where to find me if I wore my special nightgown. He'd know I was being a good girl even if I couldn't be an angel." Molly had looked up at her. "Santa can find me here, can't he?"

"Of course he can. He knows you've been a very good girl this year."

Laurel stroked Molly's hair. "I'll have to find Christmas for you, Molly," she said under her breath. "Somehow."

The little girl hugged her lion close, her face buried in its mane. Her breathing slowed, growing even. She sighed and tucked her tiny hand under her cheek. Laurel held her breath, but Molly simply snuggled down under the covers.

Hopefully sleep would bring peace. For a while.

Minutes ticked by. Laurel's heart ached with an emptiness she'd never imagined. She wanted Ivy to walk through the door, tell her it was all a mistake. Tell her this had all been a bad dream, a setup. One of their father's elaborate plans.

A small part of her still hoped that were true, but she knew it wasn't. She'd heard her father's voice on the phone. This had nothing to do with the intelligence game he played. Every moment was real.

Her father was probably dead as well.

She and Molly were alone.

Laurel dug her fingernails into her palm, savoring the bite of pain. She wasn't dreaming—even though she was in the midst of her own nightmare.

Her niece's blond hair fell over her forehead. At least Laurel had Molly. The little girl gave Laurel a reason to not curl up in a ball and disappear. She'd never imagined her heart could feel so empty. That loneliness could suffocate her as if she were drowning.

Garrett had lost his wife and daughter. Laurel couldn't imagine the agony he'd gone through. How had he survived? Alone, with his entire past erased, how had this not destroyed him?

Laurel glanced at the door. She could stay in this room for the evening. Every muscle in her body ached with exhaustion and fatigue. Each time she blinked, grit scraped her eyes, but for the first time in days, she felt safe. At least for the next twenty-four hours.

She should sleep, but Garrett was out there. Alone.

Her father had told her Derek Bradley was a traitor, but the more she recalled the conversations, the more she recognized the inconsistencies. Her father was an excellent liar, no doubt, but he'd been cagey about Bradley. He'd set up the doubts, so she would be able to trust him.

"Derek took too many risks," James McCallister had said last Thanksgiving. *"He paid the price. So did his family. Traitors always get what's coming to them. Eventually."*

Her father had never called Derek Bradley a traitor.

Something from around Laurel's heart eased, and she realized that somewhere deep inside she'd still had doubts. They were gone now. Besides, her image of a man who would sell out his country for money didn't mesh with the man who could sing Molly into calmness from hysteria.

As she'd said to Garrett, at some point you had to let faith lead you. Careful not to jostle Molly, Laurel rose from the bed and padded across the room. The little girl didn't stir. Laurel pressed her hand against the door and slowly turned the knob. She opened it and eased out of the bedroom.

The living room was empty.

She peeked into his workroom, but he wasn't there. The encryption program still ran.

Finally she looked out the front window. He stood on the porch, his back to her, staring out at the sunset. His entire body screamed tension. As if he wanted to be left alone.

Laurel hesitated. She could return to the bedroom for the night, plant herself in front of the computer and wait, hoping the program would find the password, or she could go to Garrett. Except she knew what would happen the moment she touched him. They were both vulnerable. They both needed something only the other could provide.

She opened the front door. The cold gust of wind made her shiver. The last rays of light disappeared behind a mountain and deep purplish-blue painted the sky, rimmed at the horizon with a splash of pink and red. "Garrett?"

He didn't turn around. She glanced down. He held his gun at the ready. She froze.

"In the trees," he said softly.

She followed his gaze. Two piercing blue eyes peered at them, intent and calm.

The cougar.

"He's back," Laurel whispered.

"Cats are curious, but cautious. He won't come closer."

Garrett walked down the steps and picked up a large stone, tossing it toward the animal. The cat scampered off into the trees. "We need to keep Molly inside," he said. "That cat's learned people are a source of food. Probably eating after some of the border crossers left provisions behind."

He shoved his gun into the back of his jeans and escorted her inside the house. "How's Molly?"

"I'd guess out for the night, though she'll probably be up before dawn."

"Which reminds me." Garrett flicked the dead bolt in place, then shoved a chair underneath the doorknob before activating the sensors.

"You think that will stop her?"

"She'll make a lot of noise trying to get that chair out. I'll hear the little Houdini."

Laurel couldn't help but smile. "She's just like Ivy. When we were kids—"

"I would imagine she got you into a lot of trouble."

"Dad would get so furious at us. I tried to take the fall

a time or two, but Ivy wouldn't let me. She was so much fun. I would have never had all those adventures if not for her." Laurel sighed. "I'll always miss her, won't I?"

Garrett double-checked the chair then faced her, his expression solemn. "I won't tell you it gets better. The scab may get a little tougher."

She chanced a glance at him under her lashes. His stance was a bit awkward, as if he didn't know what to say either. Maybe she'd been wrong. She should have just turned in with Molly.

"We'd better check on the computer—" he started.

"I guess I'll turn in—" she said at the same time.

She shifted from one foot to the other. "I just looked at the program's status," Laurel said. "Still running. No answers."

"I see. Then I guess it's good-night."

Something solemn and painful had settled behind his eyes. And vulnerable. She didn't want to leave him. She didn't want to be alone tonight. She crossed to him, her heart rate escalating with each step. She knew exactly what she was inviting. So did he.

She stopped inches away from him, still staring into his eyes. They darkened into a deep mahogany flaring with want, maybe with need.

"What are you doing, Laurel?" His voice had grown deep, husky.

Her touch tentative, she placed her hand on his chest. She needed him. "We're safe for a while," she said. "Aren't we?"

"That's debatable," he said softly.

He covered the hand resting on his chest with his and lifted her palm to his lips. He nipped at the pad then threaded his fingers through hers. "You know this is a mistake," he said, his voice barely audible. "You don't know me. Not really."

A shiver skated down her spine at his words, but the naked longing in his eyes shoved aside her doubts.

She knew him.

"I've watched you. You gave up your safe existence to help me and Molly. You calmed her fears tonight. I know everything I need to know."

"Even though the world thinks I'm a traitor."

"I know the truth." She shook her head, leaning closer, wanting more than anything for him to stop talking and kiss her.

"What if you're wrong, Laurel?" He cupped her cheek and held her gaze captive. Her heart fluttered in response. His thumb grazed her cheek. "What if I'm a man who would do anything to get what he wants? I'm good at keeping secrets. And I'm *very* good at telling lies."

She couldn't stop staring at his lips. "I can tell when you're lying, Garrett. Your eyes grow dark, and the right corner of your mouth tightens just a bit."

Would his mouth be hard or soft, passionate or gentle against hers when they kissed?

"I don't want you," he said softly, his breath whispering against her cheek as he moved closer to her lips.

"You're bluffing."

"You're too trusting." He lowered his mouth to her ear. "But I don't have the strength to pull away."

She smiled. "Now you're telling the truth."

With a groan he fastened his lips to hers and wrapped his arms around her. She didn't hesitate. She clung to him and let his mouth drive away the memories of the past week. For this wonderful moment all she could think about was his touch, his mouth exploring hers, the taste of him.

He lifted his head. "Be very sure, because I won't let you go all night long."

She didn't answer, just pulled his mouth to hers once more. He groaned and swept her into his arms. With a long stride he carried her into the smaller bedroom, closing the door behind them. She didn't notice the Spartan furniture; her only focus was on Garrett. She used the name of the sheriff she'd come to know, not the name of the man he used to be.

"I don't know what the future holds, but I know what I want right now," Laurel said. "I need you, Garrett."

"Not more than I need you." Gently he laid her on the bed, following her down, covering her with his weight.

She didn't resist, but relished the feel of him on top of her. With a groan, he buried his lips against her neck, exploring the pulse points at the base of her throat. Laurel threaded her hands through his hair. Every kiss made her belly tingle with need. She wanted more.

"Please," she whispered. "Kiss me."

"I am," he said softly, nipping at the delicate skin just below her ear.

"Garrett." She couldn't stop the frustration from lacing her voice.

"How about here?" He nibbled the lobe of her ear. "Or here?" He worked his way down, shifting her shirt aside, and tasted the skin just above her collarbone.

Laurel stirred beneath him until finally he raised his head. He tugged at her lower lip. "Or how about here?"

His mouth swooped down and captured hers. He pressed her lips open and she moaned in relief that she could finally taste him. She returned his kiss for kiss.

Her hands seemed to have a mind of their own, exploring the strength of his back through his shirt. She hated the barrier between them. She wanted to touch him, skin to skin. She wedged her hands between them, unbuttoning his shirt and shoving the material off his shoulders.

He stilled above her, looking at her, his gaze intense, hesitant, full of warning. Her fingertips paused when she encountered roughened skin.

Burns. The car bomb.

He let out a slow sigh then moved off of her, lying on his back. "I should have warned you." His shirt fell open and she pulled away. His chest was mostly unmarred, except for a long surgical scar down his midline.

"You think what happened changes anything? It makes me want you even more." She didn't hesitate, but straddled his hips and traced the scar.

He looked up at her and caught her fingertip. "My entire back was turned when the car exploded. There was a lot of damage. I had several rounds of skin grafts. During surgery my heart stopped. I died on the operating table and they cracked me open." His voice was detached, his jaw tight, holding back emotion. "It's not pretty," he said. "It will never be pretty."

"And if I could have Ivy back, you think the scars would make me love her less? You earned these badges of courage." Laurel moved her hands up to his shoulders, venturing a tentative touch on the puckered skin. "Does it hurt?"

"I can't always feel when you touch me. And in some places the nerve endings go a little haywire, but mostly no. It's healed as much as it's going to."

He didn't move, didn't try to pull her to him, didn't try

to kiss her. He simply lay there gazing up at her. "You don't have to do this."

"Neither do you, but you're the bravest man I know and I don't think you'll chicken out now," she said and leaned forward, gently, tenderly pressing her lips to his. "I want this. Now. With you. Tell me if I hurt you."

She lifted her shirt over her head and removed her bra. His eyes hooded as he cupped her breast in his hand and drew his thumb across her nipple. It beaded in response and a sharp tingle lit in her belly. A small whimper escaped her and she gripped his shirt.

He smiled, the defensive expression in his eyes darkening to desire once again. "I can't believe you want me." Garrett tugged her down to him, his palm against the small of her back, rocking her hips against his, his desire evident.

"Can you feel me now?" she whispered, shifting her body, evoking a groan from him.

"Definitely." He flipped her over and threw his shirt off the side of the bed. "You're an amazing woman, Laurel McCallister."

She wrapped her arms around him, blinking back the hurt for him when she encountered the mottling of scars down his back and a few strips of unblemished skin. She yanked him down closer and wrapped her legs around his hips. "Show me how amazing you think I am. I don't want to wait another second."

THEY WERE IN the middle of nowhere. Still.

Strickland peered out the front window. The SUV's headlights broke through the early evening, but a cluster of trees and an avalanche of rocks blocked the path. They'd reached the end of the road.

"Damn it." He hit the steering wheel. "How far is Bradley from here?"

Krauss studied the screen. The red dot was immobile. "Couple of miles, according to this. He's not moving."

Strickland rubbed the stubble on his chin. "Give me the city any day of the week. I hate the West. Too much godforsaken territory to cover."

"We going back to Trouble?"

"Not a chance. Get your canteen," Strickland ordered. "We're going after him. He won't expect us to track him out here."

"We're really heading out at night?"

"You want to tell the boss we're taking the evening off?" Strickland asked.

Krauss muttered to himself as he grabbed the water and his weapon. "This is a mistake. Weren't you a Cub Scout or something? We don't know the country. Anything could be out there. It's easy to get turned around in the darkness."

Strickland tapped the glowing red light on Krauss's monitor. "We've got a beacon to light the way. Besides, we don't have a choice. Now come on."

They exited the SUV and Strickland grabbed an M16, slinging it over his shoulder. "I'll tell you one thing, though. I'm not hauling those bodies down this mountain. Once we kill them, we leave them to rot."

GARRETT COULDN'T BELIEVE Laurel was here, in his bed, beneath him, with her long, lean legs wrapped around him. His body surged in response to her arch.

She grasped his shoulders and her hands moved to his back.

He couldn't believe she hadn't politely said good-night and walked away. Garrett didn't think about the scars on his back that often. Just when he'd rub against something the wrong way and the nerves fired, as if a thousand pins were stabbing him.

Laurel nipped at his ear. "I want you," she whispered. "Now."

No more than he wanted her.

He rubbed his chest against her, reveling in the feeling of their skin touching. With each caress of his chest against her budded nipples, she let out a low moan, shivering against him. He moved again, and this time, she hugged him close, tilting her pelvis into his hardness. God, she was so responsive. She didn't hold anything back. He'd never been with a woman who was so honest about what she wanted.

Her hands worked their way between them to the waist of his pants, tugging at his stubborn belt in frustration.

He lifted away, forcing her legs to release him. He hated she no longer held him captive, but he wanted her wild for him. He wanted to drive them both so crazy that the past and the past week would vanish...at least for a moment.

With a quick flick, he removed the leather belt and threw it to the side of the bed before unbuttoning the waist. She shoved at his hand, but he gripped her fingers. "Not yet."

He lifted her hands above her head, pinning them down with one of his own. He gazed at the rise and fall of her chest. Her breathing quickened beneath his gaze, her blue eyes transformed into cobalt pools. That she trusted him enough to give him control caused his body to throb in response. He let his fingers stroke her cheek and drew her lip down. Her tongue snaked out to taste his finger. He smiled at her and let her suckle for a moment before taking his hand around her jawline, down her throat, where the pulse raced.

Her legs shifted but he trapped her beneath him. With a butterfly-light touch he teased her breasts, circling one nipple, then the other. Her chest flushed; her back arched. He followed a trail, teasing her, relishing in the soft sounds of pleasure coming from her lips.

"Garrett," she finally pleaded. She didn't tug her hands away, though. She wanted more. And he wanted to give her more than she'd dreamed of.

Ever so slowly he explored each delectable inch of skin, first with his fingertips, then with his lips and finally with his tongue. When he reached her waist, tasting the sweetness just above her belly button, she sucked in her stomach. He flicked open the button of her jeans.

Prolonging her pleasure, and his painful desire, he slid down the zipper and eased her pants over her hips. Simple white bikini panties hid her from his gaze.

Garrett tugged at the elastic, swallowing. He throbbed against his zipper. He was going to lose control. He'd been determined to drive her mad, but he was losing his mind.

And his heart.

He rose to his knees and tugged at the elastic waist.

She wrenched her hands from his grip and sat up. "I can't take it anymore," she said. She shoved her jeans and the small scrap of cloth down her legs, leaving her bare to his view.

God, she was beautiful.

Without hesitation she pushed against his zipper. His body surged.

"I'm too close," he said, his voice tight.

"So am I," she countered. "Make love to me, Garrett."

He gritted against the sensitivity of his body as he shucked off the rest of his clothes. He reached into the bedside table and grabbed a condom.

Her legs parted for him and she pulled him to her. She didn't play coy or hesitate. "Make love to me, Garrett. Now."

Unable to resist, with one thrust, he sank deep inside her.

She was ready for him, welcoming, hot and needy. He lost himself in her. The past disappeared, the uncertainty.

She cocooned him in her warmth. With each stroke, she sighed, and then the rhythm built, slowly at first, then stronger, faster, more intense.

His heart raced; his body trembled. He wanted to feel her fall apart in his arms. She tightened around him and he couldn't hold off. He thrust against her and his body pulsed in release. He sagged on top of her, the rhythmic quivering of her body gripping him.

She'd fallen over the edge with him.

For a moment he couldn't move, letting his heart slow, feeling her heartbeat calm.

"Wow," she mumbled, stroking his hair.

He moved off of her, disposed of the condom and spooned her. She felt so good, so right lying against him. He kissed her temple, wrapping one leg around hers, unwilling to let her escape from his embrace.

"Yeah. *Wow* about covers it."

She wiggled her back end against him before settling down. She gripped one of his hands between hers.

"I feel like a boneless jellyfish," she said. "I never want to move from here."

He didn't either. He stared at the wall, just listening to her breathe. In and out, soft and steady. He hadn't planned this. But he couldn't find it inside him to regret.

That in itself made him wince. What had he done?

He toyed with a small curl of hair against her cheek. She was so soft and yet so strong. And so smart. Her fingers had flown across that keyboard and he had seen her analyzing the problem, creating a solution and acting on it.

More than that, she was brave. She hadn't hesitated to protect Molly.

"I can feel you thinking," she said softly. She turned in his arms and looked at him. "What about? Regrets?"

A hesitant expression had settled on her face. He kissed her nose. "No regrets, even though—"

"Don't," she pleaded. "I don't want to think about what's happening. Not yet. Can't we just be, with nothing between us? Just for a few minutes."

"Of course." He wrapped his leg over her hip, pulling her against him, saying nothing.

She played with the smattering of hair on his chest for a moment, then sighed. "But it won't go away. They're coming."

Her hands slowed then stilled. "Do you think Dad is okay?"

"Do you want lies or truth?"

"Truth."

He twirled a strand of her hair. "I don't know. I'd have hoped he'd get word to me by now. Somehow."

"You're worried."

"James has kept himself alive a long time."

"Are you trying to convince me or yourself?" Laurel asked, her voice laced with sadness.

"Both, maybe."

She huddled into him and he wrapped his arms around her. She went quiet for several minutes, and Garrett wondered if she'd fallen asleep. He hoped so. She could use the rest.

"How do we catch them, Garrett?" Her breath kissed his bare chest. "They haven't made a mistake."

The despair in her words touched his very soul. More because he couldn't guarantee anything. Not even her safety. All he knew was he'd do his damnedest to keep her and Molly alive.

His arms gripped her tighter. "Actually, they have made a mistake. Your sister was killed because she identified evidence. Which means—"

"They left a trail," Laurel finished.

"Once you find a way into that file, we could have the answer." Garrett closed his eyes and stroked her hair. An answer to the revenge that had eaten away at his gut since he'd woken up from that coma with his life changed forever.

Lisa and Ella might finally be able to rest in peace. Maybe he would, too. He moved away from Laurel. He unwrapped himself from her and sat on the side of the bed, his head in his hands.

Laurel sucked in a breath from behind him. He'd forgotten about his back. He grabbed for his shirt. "I'm sorry."

"Don't," she whispered.

The bed shifted and she moved behind him. She rubbed the base of his neck. He groaned, feeling the tension that had been sitting there for so long dissipate. Her hands drifted down, in and out of his ability to feel.

Her touch caressed his lower back. "Can you feel me?" she asked.

"Mmm-hmm."

She nipped at the back of his neck with her teeth. "How about now?"

"Oh, yes." He let his head fall forward while she explored.

Her touch danced just beneath his shoulder blade. A sharp prick raced through him and he tensed.

"Did I hurt you?" She yanked her hands away.

"Don't," he said. "Just the nerves going crazy."

"How many surgeries did you have, Garrett?"

"More than I can count. Skin grafts, shrapnel got embedded into my back. I was a mess."

Her fingers returned to his shoulder blade. "I guess that's what happened here. There's evidence of sutures. It's strange—"

A loud beeping sounded from Garrett's phone. He jumped to his feet. "Get dressed. Someone's broken the perimeter."

Chapter Eight

Laurel rolled off the bed and yanked on her jeans, slipping on her shirt as she raced after Garrett. She followed him out of the bedroom and into his office. He flipped on a switch on one of the consoles. A map flickered to life on the screen. Two green dots headed directly to the center.

"They're getting close to the cameras," he said, turning on another switch. Three monitors buzzed on, the infrared images fuzzy.

A few trees, but nothing more.

Laurel slipped on her shoes and glanced down at the computer monitor where she'd been running the decryption program. "We don't have the password yet," she rushed out. "It hasn't finished. What are we going to do?"

Garrett stared at the monitors. Slowly a figure came into view. She squinted, then recognized a man pushing through the trees, his movements jerky, holding a weapon. A second person followed behind him.

He let out a loud curse. "How did they find us so fast?"

"Who are they?"

"*Not* the family I saw earlier today. There were three of them. And no one was carrying an M16. I could rec-

ognize the outline anywhere." Garrett scanned the room
and grabbed a duffel from the corner, tossing it toward
her. "Pack up what you and Molly need. Only the bare
necessities. There's not much time."

At Garrett's grim expression, Laurel's stomach twisted
in fear. She raced from the room and quietly opened the
door to the bedroom where Molly slept. Using the shard
of light piercing through the slit, she fumbled for a few
sets of clothes and toiletries. And Ivy's family's picture.
Everything else was luxury. Except Mr. Hairy Houdini.

She slipped out of the bedroom and back into the office. "Done."

Garrett sat at one of his monitors. "I'm wiping the
entire system. It will disable everything and leave no
trace."

"Are they close?"

"They're making a beeline for the cabin, but they're
still a half mile away. In the dark in the woods. Idiots."

"Do you recognize them?"

Garrett grabbed a control stick and zoomed in. "No.
How about you?"

She squinted at the grainy green image. "I can't
tell."

The computer next to her sounded her college fight
song. Garrett's eyes widened, and she flushed. "We
were…enthusiastic."

She plopped onto the chair. "I've got the password."
She typed it in. "I can download it."

Garrett typed in a few commands on his screen. "Copy
it. We're out of time."

Two figures appeared on the second screen. This
time she could see the second man's gun. Another automatic weapon.

"Military-issue weapons," she said.

"Good eye. They've found us. No telling how many are out there. I'm getting you out of here."

"We should have had another twenty-four hours at least," Laurel said. She looked over at Garrett. "This is my fault."

"Our opponent is better than we both thought."

"Do you have a thumb drive?" Laurel asked.

He opened the drawer and handed her the small device. She stuck the drive into the system, copied the file, then ejected it.

"We're out of time." He grabbed the Remington from a closet, slung the strap over his shoulder and hit a button. The computers started whirring.

"Is it going to explode?" she asked.

"Nothing so *Mission: Impossible*," Garrett said. "Just wiped clean and its components melted down. Can you carry this?" He lifted up a small backpack.

She took it from him and stuffed it into a duffel, zipping it up. She took her SIG and placed it in the back of her pants. She wished she had a holster. Next time she went on the run, she'd remember to bring one.

"I'll carry Molly." He hurried into the spare bedroom. The little girl had sprawled on her back, clutching her stuffed animal. He slid his hands under her body and lifted her up over his shoulder, settling her on one arm and hip.

"Let's go," he whispered, unclipping a narrow flashlight from his belt. "This has a red filter so it doesn't kill the night vision. I'll lead the way. Keep your weapon handy."

He quietly closed and locked the door behind him. Laurel balanced the duffel on her shoulder. They stepped into the darkness. Only the moon lit their way. He pointed the beam of light at the ground in front of him. "Don't veer off this path. You could walk off a cliff."

Taking it slow but steady, they picked their way through the trees, around a series of rugged rocks, careful not to make any noise. Garrett jostled Molly once and she whimpered. He froze. Laurel held her breath. If Molly started crying she could give their location away.

They started off again.

A burst of gunfire in the distance peppered the night.

Laurel hit the ground. Garrett knelt, covering Molly. She yelped in fear. He placed his hand on her mouth. "Molly, listen to me."

Laurel crawled over to Garrett. "I'm here with you, Molly Magoo. We have to be quiet, even if those noises are scary. Can you do that?"

She nodded her head.

Slowly, Garrett pulled his hand away. Molly slapped her hand on her mouth. "Good girl," he said. "You're very brave."

"Will Santa know?" she asked.

"He's definitely watching."

"Do Mommy and Daddy know?" Molly asked, her voice muffled through her fingertips.

"They're very proud of you, Molly Magoo."

"Lay your head on my shoulder, sugar. We're getting out of here."

Laurel could tell, even in the moonlight, that Molly squeezed her eyes shut.

Another bevy of gunfire erupted.

Garrett didn't slow. "It's at the cabin. Keep moving."

A loud curse pierced the night.

"He said a bad word," Molly muttered. "Santa won't visit his house."

"Definitely not," Garrett said. "Hush now."

They trudged forward. It seemed so much farther back to the SUV than it had hiking up to the ranch house. Laurel focused on the ground in front of her. All she needed was to fall.

She stepped on a twig and the dry wood cracked beneath her weight. Garrett stilled. She stopped, her heart quickening. He motioned her forward.

Laurel didn't know how long they walked before she finally recognized the outcropping of rocks ahead. Garrett paused. Laurel stopped as well, listening to the sounds of the night.

In December, not many animals sounded their call. But neither did the men following.

A twig snapped not that far behind them.

"Go!" he shouted. Placing the keys in her hand, he pushed her through a gap in the rocks. The SUV was just feet away.

"Take her." Garrett shoved Molly into Laurel's arms and took off running in the opposite direction.

GARRETT RACED AWAY from Laurel and Molly. How the hell had these guys found them? He slammed through the pine trees, making as much noise as possible. A gunshot echoed in the night, the bullet hitting a pine tree just above his ear. They had night vision. Great.

Garrett took his flashlight and turned the powerful miniature beam on high, then flipped off the filter, shining the bright light in the direction of the fired shot.

A curse of pain sounded toward him. The guy would be blinded for a few seconds. Garrett veered in the direction of the house. Anything to keep them away from Laurel and Molly. He prayed she'd gotten away, that no one else had intercepted them.

"This way!" one of the men shouted. Footsteps pounded at him. They weren't even trying to be quiet. He took a ninety-degree turn away from the ranch, toward some of the cliffs. He had to keep his bearings. A rock outcropping should be coming up to his right.

Sure enough, the strange formation loomed from the ground.

The men following him kept coming.

The sound of a stumble, then a loud curse, filtered through the night. He hadn't lost them. Garrett rounded the rock formation and paused. Fifteen feet away was the edge of a steep hill, its base jagged rocks. Dangerous, deadly and convenient.

He flipped off his flashlight and raced toward the hill. Those guys trailed after him as though they had radar on him.

Was he carrying a GPS? His phone shouldn't be traceable. How did they have a bead on him? He couldn't hear anything above him; a chopper would be crazy to fly at night in these mountains.

No time to figure it out.

He still couldn't be sure if he wasn't walking into a trap, if someone was waiting for him.

"Laurel, I hope you got away."

He stopped in front of the drop-off. They shouldn't have been able to find him, but the two men barreled into the clearing just in front of him.

The red-filtered flashlight one of them carried crossed his body, and they stopped.

A smile gleamed in the moonlight. "Two years late," the man said, lifting his gun.

Garrett dived to the side just as the man charged. The guy tried to skid to a halt, but momentum carried him over the side. He shouted out and disappeared down the hill.

"Strickland!" the second man shouted. Garrett launched himself at the guy and pinned him. "Who are you?"

The man shook his head.

Garrett shoved the barrel of his Beretta beneath the guy's chin. "I'm not playing games."

"Yeah, well, neither is my boss. I'm dead if I say anything."

The man's eyes were resigned. A bad sign.

"How about we make a deal?" Garrett said, easing the gun just a bit. "You tell me your boss's name. I let you go. You disappear out here. You're a few hours from the border."

A flare of hope flashed on the guy's face before a gunshot sounded. A sharp burning slammed into Garrett's back. His gun dropped from his hand. He rolled off the guy and behind a rock, his back screaming in pain. He sucked in a breath and blinked.

His Beretta lay in the open.

Strickland heaved himself up over the edge of the hill and lifted his M16. "Get out of there, Krauss, or so help me, I'll shoot you, too."

Krauss scrambled away. Staggering toward Garrett, Strickland peppered the rock. Dust and shrapnel flew into the air.

If it had been daylight, Garrett would be dead.

Another blast of firepower and he was running out of time.

"You're dying this time, Bradley. Damn you. Your wife and kid weren't even part of the deal."

The words slammed into Garrett's pain-riddled brain. This son of a bitch had killed his family.

"Yeah, that's right. I set the bomb. You want to come out and face me?"

Garrett rolled over, ignoring the pain in his back. Krauss pulled his weapon. This was a no-win.

Then Krauss moved. Garrett had one chance. With a grunt, he launched himself at Krauss and shoved him into Strickland. Garrett's weight forced them back toward the edge.

They all teetered on the precipice. Garrett grabbed a protrusion of rock and stopped his fall. Strickland and Krauss disappeared over the side.

Garrett could feel warmth seeping down his back as he climbed up the few feet. He flicked on his flashlight and peered over the side.

The men lay against a rock, motionless. Krauss's neck was bent at an unnatural angle, his eyes wide-open. Dead.

Garrett moved the beam over.

Blood covered Strickland's face. He wasn't moving. Garrett pointed his weapon at Strickland, but the guy didn't move. He wanted to climb down, be sure. He needed to know the truth.

A wave of dizziness stopped him. He fell down to his knees. A beeping noise just to his side grabbed his attention. He picked up a tablet. A red dot blinked. It was *him*. Damn it, how were they tracking him?

He pulled everything out of his pockets. He'd bought the clothes in El Paso. It couldn't be them.

He didn't have time to figure it out.

He took one last look over the edge—Strickland still

hadn't budged. Garrett stumbled to his feet. He had to make sure Laurel and Molly were gone, out of here. Daniel would help.

Garrett didn't know how bad his wound was, but he had to make sure they were safe, and then he had to get as far away from them as he could. Because whoever had sent Strickland and Krauss wasn't giving up.

THE GUNSHOTS HAD STOPPED. Laurel gripped her SIG, planting her hands firmly along the hood of the SUV.

Molly sat in the backseat, hugging Mr. Houdini close. "Where is Sheriff Garrett? He wouldn't leave us."

"He'll be here," Laurel said. He had to be here. She chewed on her fingernail.

Suddenly a figure came stumbling out of the trees. Her finger tightened on the trigger.

He looked up at her. "Garrett!" she shouted.

"Get in," he ordered and bounded into the passenger seat. "Drive," he said, clearing his throat.

Carefully she backed up and turned the SUV around. "Lights?" she asked.

"On," he said. "Get us out of here fast."

The beams hit the dirt road and she hit the gas.

"Why the hell did you wait for me? What if I hadn't come back?"

"I have the number you gave me." Laurel gripped the steering wheel. "I was getting ready to call Daniel Adams."

"I don't know whether to be relieved you were here or turn you over my knee." The SUV bounced and Garrett took a sharp intake of breath. Laurel flipped on the interior lights and looked over at him.

His mouth was pinched and the light leather of his seat was streaked with red.

"You're bleeding."

"Just drive," he ordered. "Get to the main road as fast as you can. Maybe we'll be lucky and those two were the only ones following us. For now."

She urged the vehicle forward.

Molly stuck her head between the seats. "Do you need a Band-Aid?" she asked. "I have princess ones. You can have my favorite if you want. Which princess do you like the best?"

Garrett smiled at her. "You're my favorite princess, sugar. And don't you worry. It's just a scratch. I'll be fine."

Laurel's knuckles tightened on the steering wheel. He was lying to protect Molly. Tears stung Laurel's eyes. She'd fallen hard for this man. He'd saved them yet again, but this time she really didn't know if they'd make it out alive. Blood kept seeping onto the seat. She had to get him help.

The nearest town was Trouble. She'd seen a clinic there. She could go back. Everyone knew him there. Someone would help.

It took forever to reach the county road leading to Trouble. She finally got to the intersection.

"Turn left," Garrett said through clenched teeth.

"I'm glad you agree. I'm getting you to a doctor."

"I can't now." Garrett leaned his head back on the seat. "Keep driving straight."

After about fifteen minutes he turned his head to her. In the light of the interior his face had gone pale. "There's a dirt road not too far from here. Pull over and let me out."

"No way—"

"Do it, Laurel."

Against her better judgment, she pulled to the side and stopped the car.

Garrett gripped the door handle and faced her. "Here's what you're going to do. Take this road. It circles down some back roads until you reach Rural Route 11. Follow that until you hit this highway again. Get to a phone, even if you have to buy a prepaid cell at a convenience store. Call Daniel Adams. Tell him what's happening. He'll take you to Covert Technology Confidential in Carder, Texas. They'll protect you."

Daniel's employer might be the only one that could hide Laurel and Molly from the agency and get away with it.

She shook her head. "I won't leave you. You're hurt."

"Laurel, they're tracking me. I don't know how, but they are. You have to get away."

He opened the SUV door, but as soon as his boots hit the pavement he collapsed.

She shoved open her door and ran around the car. "At least let me stop the bleeding before I leave. You can't do it yourself."

He closed his eyes, then gave her a reluctant nod. Why did the thing that attracted her so much to Garrett have to be the very thing that could kill him?

"There's a T-shirt in my backpack. And a canteen. Wash off the wound and use the cotton as a bandage. Then you have to go."

"Are you fixing Sheriff Garrett, Aunt Laurel?"

"That's right, sugar," Garrett said with a smile. "I'll be good as new."

Liar.

Laurel fished out the material and the water. She lifted his shirt and he passed her the flashlight. She gasped. Dried blood caked part of his back, but fresh still oozed from the wound. She didn't know how he was still standing.

She ripped the T-shirt in two and soaked half in water. She bathed his back, trying to be gentle. He didn't even wince.

Each pass removed more of the blood, revealing the scars. They weren't all that bad. The horror of what he'd experienced far surpassed this permanent reminder.

She worked her way toward the area that still bled. The bullet had hit him near his shoulder blade, near where she'd seen his previous wound and stitches. He looked as if he'd scraped his back raw on the rocks, too.

"Just how many times have you been shot in the back?" she asked.

"Since I met you?" he asked. "Or altogether?"

"Wiseass."

"Aunt Laurel, that's a naughty word." Molly gasped.

"Sorry, Molly." She frowned at his back. "See what you made me do?"

He chuckled. "I'm going to miss you two."

She ripped the clean half of the T-shirt for a second round and dabbed at the wound.

He could use stitches, and the raw skin had rocks and metal flakes embedded in it. She had to scrub a bit harder. He sucked in a breath.

"Too bad I still have some feeling left right there," he said, his voice tight with pain.

"Almost done."

As she cleaned the last bit, a familiar-looking object became visible. Small, metallic. A chip.

"Garrett? Were you ever fitted with a tracking device?"

"Hell, no. If the bad guys caught the frequency…" His head whipped around. "Is one back there?"

"Yes."

"Get it out. Now."

"It's implanted in your back. You need a doctor to cut it out."

"Hand me my backpack."

She dug into her duffel. He tugged out the nylon pack and retrieved a small medical kit, complete with a small scalpel and forceps.

"Yank it out," he said. "We don't have any time to lose. They could be closing in now."

Laurel blinked, staring at the tracking device. She could do this. Her hand shook, and she sucked in a deep breath.

"It's easy. You said there was an incision? Just follow the scar and pull the thing out.

"I don't suppose you have pain medicine in your bag of tricks?"

Molly stuck her head over the seat. She gasped. "Sheriff Garrett, you have lots of boo-boos. You can use all my princess Band-Aids if you need them."

"Laurel, just do it." Garrett smiled up at Molly. "Why don't you find me those Band-Aids, sugar?"

Molly ducked behind the backseat.

"Now," he said tightly.

"Brace yourself."

He gripped the passenger seat. She leaned over him. Taking a deep breath, Laurel pushed the knife into his back and sliced the skin, revealing the entire chip. He didn't say a word, but when she grabbed it with the medical tweezers, his back tightened. Blood flowed from the wound.

She dabbed at it. "Got it."

"Oh, yuck. That's a really bad boo-boo."

"Not so bad, sugar. Maybe you'll be a doctor when you grow up so you can fix people."

Molly's smile brightened. "I want to fix people." She hugged her lion tight.

"Laurel, clean the wound with the Betadine. Put some antibiotic ointment on it and use the butterfly strips to close it," he ordered.

Molly insisted on adding several of her own bandages. When they'd finished, Garrett turned to Laurel. His face had gone pale.

"There's a clinic in Trouble," she repeated.

"We can't go back there. Where is the chip?"

She picked up the small device with the forceps. He took it from her and turned it over in his hand. His jawline throbbed. "Damn him."

"Who?"

He lifted his gaze and met hers.

"Your father requested these chips. As far as I knew, they were never used, but he had one put into me. He would have been the only one to know the frequency."

MIKE STRICKLAND GROANED and pressed his hand to his head. It came away bloody and sticky. He rolled over. His entire body hurt. He tested each limb. Nothing broken, though his head might explode at any moment. Slowly he sat up.

Krauss lay next to him, his neck obviously broken.

He'd been the weak link anyway. A lot like Derek

Bradley. The guy was a fool. If it had been him, he'd have put a bullet in both men's brains...just to be sure.

Strickland struggled to his feet and glared up the steep incline. "I gotta find that guy."

He searched around. No tracking device. "Damn." He hoped Bradley didn't have it.

A phone sounded a few feet from Strickland. His head pounding as if he had an ice pick stabbed in his ear, he followed the sound and bent down, nearly crying out in pain.

The name on the screen caused his stomach to roil. He vomited all over the ground. He should ignore it.

The ringing stopped, then started again.

"Strickland."

"Don't ignore me again, Strickland."

He wiped his mouth.

"Bradley was moving toward Trouble, Texas, and now his signal has vanished. You failed. Again."

"We have a plan," Strickland lied.

"Oh, really? Now that we can no longer track Derek Bradley, he's an even greater threat. Neutralize him."

"I understand."

"Do you, Strickland? Do you really? Because this is your second mistake in as many days. That's one more than anyone else under my command has made—and still lived."

The phone call ended.

He needed a plan. First to get back to his SUV, and then to find Bradley.

Strickland sank to his knees and emptied the rest of the contents of his stomach next to Krauss's body.

He'd never find Bradley this way.

If he couldn't chase after Bradley, he'd just have to find bait that would attract him.

Trouble, Texas, was the way to do it.

Chapter Nine

Laurel wrenched open the door of the SUV. The destroyed chip lay on the ground, along with her shredded heart. "You're wrong about my father," she said, her face hot with anger. "He would never hurt you like that."

"I know what I saw," Garrett said. "First your sister's evidence pointing to James, and now this."

She scooted into the front seat and gripped the steering wheel. It couldn't be. "He might not have been the perfect father or even around much, but he's a patriot through and through. And he's definitely no traitor."

"Well, neither am I," Garrett snapped. "Yet I'm being hunted. He told lies about me, acted like the heartbroken, betrayed mentor, supposedly to save my life. But now I have to wonder. What better way to hide your true leanings than to throw someone close to you to the wolves and mourn the treason?"

She didn't want to admit the plan sounded good—just simple enough and brilliant enough to have her father's name attached to it. But she wouldn't—*couldn't*—believe James McCallister would do that to Garrett.

"Why did he save your life, then?" Laurel shot back,

desperate to convince him—and herself—that her father hadn't betrayed both of them.

"I haven't figured that out yet."

"If my dad really were responsible for all of this, he wouldn't have kept you alive. He wouldn't have given you your new identity." Laurel put her arm on the back of the seat and faced him. "And Dad sure wouldn't have—" she glanced back at Molly "—caused the explosion in Virginia," she said under her breath.

The little girl's wide eyes went back and forth between them, her lip trembling.

"You're making me cry. I don't like fighting."

Garrett's eyes softened. "Sorry, sugar. Your aunt and I didn't mean to scare you."

Molly hunkered back in the seat, hugging Mr. Houdini close. "Mommy and Daddy fighted about her job all the time."

Laurel twisted in the car. "I didn't know that. What did they say?"

"Daddy wanted Mommy to stay at home with me. I wanted her to stay home, too. Now she'll never stay with me." Molly hugged the stuffed animal and picked at its neck. "She said she was doing something 'portant and couldn't stop them."

"I'm sorry, Molly." Laurel shot Garrett a glare. "We won't fight anymore. Will we?"

He shook his head. "I'm not lying to Molly, because we're going to disagree about this." He gave Molly a small smile. "But, sugar, we'll promise to discuss things more quietly next time. Okay?"

Laurel sighed and started the engine. "Fine. Then

where do we go now? Because I need another look at those files."

"To the next town," Garrett said. "I'll pick up a cell phone."

Still disgruntled, she pressed the accelerator and the SUV took off on the lonely Texas highway. "I still can't believe you, of all people, would assume my father is guilty. They made you out to be a traitor, too."

Garrett didn't say anything at first. "I don't want to believe it. But those chips... James had them developed. He wanted to tag each operative. That way he'd know where they were."

"Seems reasonable. If you were captured—"

"It *was* reasonable, except that we already knew there was a leak in the organization. So he ended the program. No one else had access to the technology, yet I was tagged after the explosion. Now someone is trying to kill us. What would you think?"

"What about the person who designed the chips?" Laurel challenged. "Or the organization that funded the program? My father is ops, not administration."

Garrett stroked his chin, where his beard had grown in since they'd left town. It gave him that outlaw look that Laurel, as a CIA analyst on the run for her life, shouldn't find sexy. But she did.

"Interesting," he said. "I always thought of the killer as ops, but you're right. There are too many layers. That requires redirecting funding and resources. Administrative skills and the ability to hide funding transfers." He drummed his fingers on his knee. "But how do we follow that string to this whole conspiracy?"

"What about Fiona?" Laurel said. "She's got to be

going crazy with James missing, and she'd know who has that kind of power."

"I didn't want to involve her, but we're out of options," Garrett said. "It might be time to bring her in. We're running out of leads. And time."

"And we need someone on the inside, Garrett. You know that." They'd eaten up miles of West Texas roads with not a pair of headlights to be seen. Laurel began to relax. Just a little. Still, they needed communication equipment.

"Let's wait and see if the file has something more." Garrett scanned the pitch-dark horizon. "If not, we'll call her."

"I need access to a computer to look at the file."

"We've gone far enough. Find a place to pull over out of sight. With the chip gone, we should be safe. We'll sleep until daybreak, then head for a public library. That's our best shot of opening Ivy's file."

DARKNESS SURROUNDED THE SUV. A gust of wind shook the vehicle. Garrett shifted his shoulder, seeking relief from the pain. The wound hurt, but he'd had worse. Laurel had rounded the car, slipped into the backseat and cuddled Molly next to her.

She might never forgive him, but what was he supposed to think? Who else could possibly have planted a chip in him after the explosion but James?

Laurel and Molly huddled together, looking less than comfortable, but they couldn't risk going to a motel or even going through stoplights in some of the larger towns. People didn't realize how many cameras watched them. Big Brother really did have an eye on them all the time. Especially when whoever was after him had known his location until a few hours ago. The longer they could stay off the radar, the bigger the search pattern the enemies would require.

And the greater chance of a surprise…if Ivy had found something more than Garrett had discovered when he was doing his digging.

He inched open the door and eased out of the front seat. Laurel had been defiant in defending James. Garrett didn't blame her.

If he hadn't seen Ivy's notes and the telltale design of that chip, he wouldn't have suspected James either. But Laurel was smart and made good points.

Fiona had always had James's back. She'd orchestrated difficult ops with knifelike precision, even those deemed impossible. She almost always found a way for the agents to succeed. She would know *all* the players. Maybe she was the person James had pulled in when he'd told Garrett he was getting close.

Laurel was right. They needed an insider. No matter the risk. He let his gaze rest on her, her eyes shadowed while she tried to sleep. Laurel McCallister was one fierce mama bear when riled. He found that quality strangely attractive. She would need it.

But before he called Fiona, he had to put his backup plan into action. Once he called her, his phone would be tracked.

He dialed a number.

"Adams."

"Daniel. It's Garrett. I definitely need your help."

"Thank God you called. What the hell is going on in Trouble?" Daniel barked like a drill sergeant. "I received a call from your deputy a few minutes ago. I guess he kept my number from our last little adventure.

Evidently he's been taken hostage. Along with Hondo and his sister. The men who took them said he'd better find the sheriff. They left an ultimatum."

"What kind?"

"Come to Trouble. Bring the woman and the girl, but no weapons." Daniel paused. "You have an hour left, Garrett, or they start killing people."

A loud curse exploded from Garrett. "It'll take a majority of that time just to get there."

"Then I'd start driving as soon as you can. I'll meet you there."

Garrett looked through the car's window at Laurel and Molly. Innocent, caught up in a deadly game because of James. Now made worse because of Garrett. That scared the hell out of him. He looked at his watch. He needed a few minutes out of their earshot.

"Daniel, do your *friends* from CTC have contacts in the intelligence community?"

"Oh, yeah."

Garrett cleared his throat. "I need help cleaning up a crime scene. There are two guys at the bottom of Guadalupe Gorge."

"You've been busy."

"There's something else." Garrett paused. "You need to know if you're going to help me. My real name is Derek Bradley."

Daniel didn't say a word, but Garrett could tell from the silence Daniel had heard his name before. "I didn't do what's been said about me. I'm no traitor, but I understand if you decide to back out."

"You don't have to convince me. I've seen you in action. A traitor would have turned his back on me and my wife. A traitor would be living on his own island in the Caribbean, not marking time as a sheriff in a place barely passing for a populated town in West Texas."

A baby's cry sounded in the background. Garrett heard the soft voice of Adams's wife, Raven, speaking to the twins, and then a door closed softly.

"Daniel, think long and hard about Raven and those kids before you commit."

"I am. They'd be dead without you. Besides, I believe you. I've seen what men in power can do to protect themselves." He paused. "I can help you, so shut up and tell me what I need to do."

Garrett let out a long, slow breath and made sure Laurel and Molly were still asleep in the SUV. He walked a few more steps away. "First off, I need protection for two witnesses with a target on their backs. I won't lie, Daniel. It's dangerous."

"Why aren't you going back to your organization? There must be someone there you can trust. Someone whose loyalties you're certain of."

"Maybe one person, but the truth is, I can't tell anymore. The man who saved my life could be keeping me alive as a decoy or a weapon." Garrett hadn't said anything to Laurel, but her father had been the best Garrett had ever seen at deception. A month ago, Garrett would have done anything for James. If his mentor had told him that he'd found evidence of who had killed Garrett's family, he would have exacted justice. Swift and uncompromised justice.

"I don't want anyone at the organization involved," Garrett said, scuffing his boot on the dirt. "I need an independent group that has the contacts to keep Laurel and Molly safe if something happens to me."

"You've got it," Daniel said. "When and where do we meet?"

"No other questions?" Garrett asked.

"Like I said, you saved my life, not to mention my wife and daughters. No questions needed. I know what loyalty means, Garrett. You've earned mine. Now, time is passing quickly. What's your plan?"

"I can't leave my witnesses alone. One is a five-year-old girl. I can't watch them all the time and do what needs to be done."

"I understand," Daniel said. "We'll be there, but it'll take more than the hour you have."

"Then I'll make do until then. I don't know who else will be waiting for us, but meet me in Trouble as soon as you can. I can't let anyone else die because of me."

"Wheels up in ten. See you soon."

THE SUV TURNED a corner, waking Laurel. She blinked her eyes against the hazy light of dawn. She glanced at the back of Garrett's head from the backseat. "You shouldn't be driving. You need rest. And a doctor."

Garrett glanced around at her, then at his watch. "No choice. We're going back to Trouble."

He refocused on the road and pressed down the accelerator, lurching the SUV forward. At the urgency in his actions and his tone, Laurel straightened in her seat. She met his gaze in the rearview mirror. "What's happened?"

"Someone tracking us has taken hostages." Garrett's jaw tightened. "My deputy, Lucy and Hondo. They gave us an hour and time is almost up. They're going to kill the hostages one by one."

"Oh, God." Her hand covered her mouth and she kept her voice low. Molly didn't need to hear this.

"I can't let anything happen to them, Laurel. You understand that."

She nodded, wanting to hold Molly even tighter. This couldn't be happening.

Garrett glanced back at her and Molly. "The problem is, the caller who has the hostages wants all three of us."

"Why? I don't understand. What is it that we've done that's so threatening? Especially Molly?"

"The world thinks we're dead, and we potentially know too much. It's safer and easier to eliminate the witnesses."

"I've seen a lot of evil during my time with the CIA, but this— She's just a little girl." Laurel shivered. "We both know if someone wants you dead, eventually they'll succeed. It's too easy. Tampering with brakes, a car bomb, a sniper shot from a thousand feet away."

"Unless they can't find you." Garrett pressed harder on the gas.

Laurel looked over at Molly. "What's the plan for the three of us?"

"I don't know."

"You're lying."

"I'm running options through my head. It will depend on who is waiting for us, how many. Wish I had a sitrep." The SUV sped up and he glanced at his watch. "They'll call in the next five minutes to set up a rendezvous point. I want to try to surprise them. Hopefully it's not too many."

"I can help, Garrett. I may not have field experience, but I'm a good shot. You know I am."

"You need to protect Molly. I have help coming."

"But will they be here soon enough?"

"I don't know."

"Another lie."

"It's not good that you can read me so easily. I'll have to work on that."

"I'm watching your back, Galloway, so get used to it."

A BRIGHT LIGHT blasted into the midnight-dark prison room. James blinked as the beam burned the backs of his eyes.

He tried to squint through the glare, but he could barely see.

"You should have told us about the chip sooner. It might have saved your daughter Ivy and her family's lives. Too bad she had to start digging and learned too much."

James squeezed his eyes shut tight. God, no. Not Ivy. Not the kids. What had he done? He didn't remember revealing anything, just the shot from a hypodermic needle.

A chuckle from across the room lit a fire of hatred. James jerked up his head, not caring how much it hurt. "You won't get away with this."

"I already have. My reputation is impeccable. I'm trusted. People come to me because they know I'll find a way to get them money, resources, equipment. You knew that, too."

"Which *should* make them suspicious of you."

"People see what they want to see, even in the intelligence community."

His captor pulled out a gun and sauntered over to him. The barrel pressed against his temple. "I should kill you now. You're a loose end."

James knew he wouldn't come out of this alive. For

now, he had to try to get a signal to Garrett. There had to be a way.

"Do it."

"You'd like that. Well, it won't be so easy, James." A quick flick of the wrist brought in a beefy man with eyes cold and dead as a snake. "Find out what else he hasn't told us."

James swallowed. The inflamed scar on the man's face was obviously the result of recent burns. He carried an iron rod with him. "Make it easy. I can't stop until you give me something," the man said, touching his cheek.

The man walked over to a heating element and flicked on a switch. A gas flame roared to life and he stuck the tip of iron in the flames, rotating the bar slowly, evenly. After a few minutes the man pulled the red-hot iron from the flame and walked toward James.

"You don't have to do this," James said. "We could leave together."

He let out a harsh laugh. "I just tried. My daughter was killed in a car *accident* yesterday, along with her boyfriend and two others. I have a wife and son, and I've been told what will happen to them if I fail. I won't try to leave again."

He bent over James. "Now tell me something. Anything. Because I *will* protect my family. Even if you have to die for me to do it."

James closed his eyes. He'd already lost one daughter. Just like this man, he would die to protect Laurel. "I can't."

Scorching heat set fire to his skin. James couldn't stop the scream. Blistering pain, unlike anything he'd ever known.

Suddenly it was gone. James sagged in his chair. He caught his breath.

"Tell me," the man said. "I can't stop."

From outside his prison cell, his captor's words filtered through the bars. "You've arrived? Excellent. Strickland failed twice. You know what to do. Kill Bradley and Strickland. I want this hole plugged up today."

THE BUILDINGS OF Trouble, Texas, were one story and far apart. Dawn had come, and the dim light brought with it visibility. For better or worse.

Garrett couldn't afford to drive any closer on the highway. He turned onto the flat desert plain. "I'm not going in through the main drag. I'll drive through the plains and come in on one of the side streets."

"What about your *friends?*"

"They'll be here soon."

"But not before your meeting." Laurel leaned forward. "You need backup, Garrett. You're one of the walking wounded right now."

She was right, but he had to think of Laurel and Molly first. "You have to watch your niece. She can't afford to lose anyone else."

Laurel hugged the little girl closer.

His cell phone rang.

With a quick movement, Laurel tugged at his wrist. He frowned, but eased the phone from his ear so she could hear.

"Galloway."

"You should have answered *Derek Bradley,*" the voice said. "Traitor."

Garrett cursed under his breath. No one knew about Daniel, so that information had to have come from James.

"I don't know what you're talking about."

"Don't play dumb, *Sheriff*. How close are you to your office?"

"Fifteen minutes."

"Five minutes before I'm scheduled to kill your deputy. You're cutting it close. The poor kid just broke into a sweat."

"I said I'll be there."

"You have the woman with you?"

Garrett didn't respond.

"If I don't have your word that I'll see her outside your office in fifteen minutes, the deputy dies now."

He glanced at Laurel. She nodded.

His lips tightened. "She'll be there."

"And the girl?"

"For God's sake, she's only a child."

A shotgun pump sounded through the phone.

"Damn it. All right, Molly will be there, too."

"Excellent. Look, Sheriff, you play this right, and I *might* let the woman and girl live. But you try to double-cross me and I won't hesitate to kill them. I've done it before." The man paused. "I hear you have a lot of scars from the bomb. Too bad it went off before you were in the car with your wife and kid."

"Strickland? You're dead."

"Guess we're both hard to kill."

The phone went dead.

Garrett's mind whirled. He *still* hadn't killed the bastard. What had he done?

Laurel rested her hand on Garrett's shoulder, but he shook her away.

"Strickland killed my family and I let him leave that ravine." Garrett couldn't think, could barely feel. He'd failed. Again. This time Laurel and Molly might pay the price.

"He won't get away with it," Laurel said. She set her SIG on the front seat. "He killed my family, too. He'll pay. Together, we'll make sure of it."

A BLACK ESCALADE pulled two blocks down from the sheriff's office.

"There's Bradley." Shep Warner looked over at his new partner. Léon had an accent Shep couldn't place, but he had some serious skills. The boss wouldn't have brought him on otherwise. "I worked with him. He was good. Too good, I guess."

"The boss wants him dead."

Shep looked through a pair of Zeiss binoculars. "Someone's in the backseat. Two people. A woman and a kid."

Léon stiffened. "No one said anything about killing a kid."

Shep took a quick image with his camera. "Boss will want to know about this."

He hit Send and waited.

Immediately the phone rang.

"Where did you take this?" The computer-filtered voice always gave him a chill, with its inhuman tone. He had no idea who his boss was, just that his bank account was a lot more robust since he'd started the job. It was just business.

His new partner, Léon, unsettled him. Shep couldn't quite pinpoint what felt wrong. He certainly was a surly bastard, like a robot. Well, if he didn't work out, the boss had a means of making more than one person disappear, particularly when the government had already named anyone missing or disavowed.

"Trouble, Texas. She and a kid are in the target's car."

"Strickland's third strike. Our source here isn't talking. Kill them, too, and dispose of the bodies."

"Won't there be questions?"

"Just make them disappear. In the eyes of the world they are already dead."

Léon turned to Shep. "What's the plan?"

"Leave no one alive. Including Strickland."

"The girl?"

"Even the girl."

Chapter Ten

Two blocks from the sheriff's office, Garrett let the SUV idle. Trouble's Christmas lights knocked against the light poles.

The place looked deserted, causing the hairs on his arms to stand on end. He had a bad feeling about this whole thing. Too many unknowns.

He needed a diversion, and with Daniel and CTC still an hour away, he had no choice about who he had to choose. It tore him apart he'd have to put Laurel in danger.

"We're out of time," Laurel said.

"I know." Garrett let out a sigh. "How's Molly?"

"Resting now." Laurel stroked the girl's forehead. "I gave her some acetaminophen. Her temperature popped up last night, so maybe she'll sleep longer. I need to get her checked out by a doctor."

"Hopefully this will be over soon." Garrett studied the sheriff's office. No one was behind the building. Thank goodness. "I have a way to sneak into the back of the building and get to a stash of weapons, but I need a distraction."

"I'll drive," Laurel said, "and park in front of the

sheriff's office. Hopefully they don't have a bazooka in their arsenal."

"Don't even joke about that, Laurel."

"If I don't joke, I'll run screaming from town, Garrett. I'm terrified for Molly."

He turned in his seat. "And I'm scared for both of you.

"When you hear things go bad in that building, you take off to Hondo's place, the Copper Mine Motel. It was on the right as we headed into town. Daniel will be there soon."

"What about you?"

"If it goes well, I'll get to Hondo, Lucy and the deputy. I'll meet you there with the name of the person who ordered these hits. Let's switch places."

Garrett exited the vehicle, leaving the car running to ward off the nippy morning. He rounded the car and Laurel slipped into the front seat. He knocked on the glass and she cracked the window.

"Give me five minutes before you round the corner. Until then, stay down."

She nodded, but tears glistened in her eyes. "You're a good man, Garrett Galloway, so go kick some bad-guy butt and come back to me."

"I promise I want to." He touched Laurel's cheek, then looked over at Molly. "You're going to do great with her," he said.

Her eyes darkened. "That sounded a lot like goodbye. Please don't let it be."

"You know I need to do this."

"For your family," she whispered.

"And for you." He kissed her lips lightly, lingering for just a moment. "For you and Molly and me."

Garrett eased into the alleyway. He took one last

look at Laurel and lifted up a silent prayer. *Please, let them be okay.* He had to focus on the job at hand: take Strickland out, hope he hadn't brought a ton of friends and save Keller, Hondo and Lucy. Not to mention Laurel and Molly.

He scanned the area. He didn't see anything unusual, then paused. One vehicle stood out. The Escalade had to be Strickland's.

Garrett checked his watch. He didn't have time to hesitate. In less than four minutes Laurel would pull the SUV in front of his building.

He rounded the sheriff's office. He had cameras inside and outside, but they required a password to access. He hadn't even given the code to his deputy. Garrett ran his fingers along the bricks at the back of the building. He pulled out a loose one. Inside was a latch to the emergency entrance. Garrett had always thought the whole setup bordered on paranoia, but now he thanked his overly cautious predecessor. Of course, the man had been right, just not careful enough. He was serving twenty for drug trafficking.

Praying Strickland had kept his deputy in the main room, Garrett entered the digital code and the lock clicked. Slowly he eased the door open.

He heard one set of heavy footsteps pacing from the far room to his left, near the jail cells. Had to be Strickland. He wouldn't allow anyone to be moving around.

"Your sheriff is cutting it close, Deputy," Strickland snapped. The footsteps stopped. "You ready to die for a traitor?"

"Sheriff Galloway is on the up-and-up. I'll never believe he did what you said."

"Damn straight, you cow dung," Hondo hollered, rattling the bars of the cage. "He's twice the man you'll ever be."

Hondo should know better. What the hell was he doing? If Strickland lost his temper, he'd start shooting. Garrett had no doubt that if Strickland had his way, no one would be left alive. Not Laurel or Molly. Not Keller, Lucy or Hondo. And certainly not Garrett.

He glanced at the wall safe, opened it and pulled out an extra set of keys to the jail. If nothing else, he needed to get those keys to Keller or Hondo so they had a prayer of escaping.

A loud clatter rang out. Hondo let out a curse. "You trying to break my hand?"

"Shut up," Strickland said. "Or I'll kill you first. I may choose you anyway. You're too damned annoying."

"No, please, no. Now, Lucy, it's going to be okay."

"Make her stop that sniveling, or I take her." Strickland stomped away, toward the front of the building. "Someone's pulling out front."

That had to be Laurel.

Which meant Strickland had his back to the jail.

Garrett hurried outside the emergency exit to the side of the jail. A small window ledge was the only opening. He lifted himself up, then dangled the keys in front of the glass. He grabbed a diamond cutter from his pocket and within seconds had opened a hole. He set the keys in reach.

Garrett tapped lightly.

Keller jerked his head up. His eyes widened. He sidled over to Hondo. The man slid a subtle glance toward Garrett and gave a nod. At the right moment, they'd grab the keys.

Garrett had to trust the ex-marine to get Keller and

Lucy out safely. He returned to the secret entrance and pushed back inside. The easiest thing would be to shoot Strickland in the back of the head. The man deserved it. Garrett had been dreaming of killing the man since he'd woken up from his coma, but that would silence the only lead Garrett had to the identity of the mastermind behind a decade's worth of death and criminal activity.

And Strickland's death wouldn't protect Laurel and Molly in the long run.

That made his job that much more difficult. He needed Strickland alive, which made his every move that much more dangerous.

Hondo hadn't budged. Good man. Playing it smart. Lucy was tucked up on the end of the cot, rocking away. Easy to see how Strickland had gotten the drop on Hondo. Deputy Keller… Well, Garrett would be having a talk with him.

Strickland held an M16 in his hand. He peered through the front window, stepped aside and opened the door.

"The McCallister woman and the girl. But where's Bradley?" Strickland shifted his M16.

"Guess Bradley didn't believe me when I said one of you would die." He pointed the gun at Lucy.

Now or never.

Garrett launched himself at Strickland, knocking the man's weapon from his hand. Garrett landed on his shoulder and nearly cried out in agony even as he grabbed Strickland by the throat. He pressed his forearm against the man's trachea. "I should have killed you."

Strickland grinned up at him. "But you won't, because

someone will keep coming now that the boss knows you're alive. You can't kill me."

The bastard was right.

Garrett pressed harder, blocking the man's air. "Who do you work for? I want a name."

Strickland glared up at him. "Let me go."

"Let me out. Let me out," Lucy shouted.

Out of the corner of his eye, Garrett saw Hondo pluck the keys from the ledge and unlock the door. Lucy raced from the jail cell the moment Hondo opened it.

With that second's distraction, Strickland thrust his arms against Garrett's chest and twisted his body. He broke Garrett's hold and leaned back just in time to avoid Garrett's killing blow to his windpipe.

Strickland leaped to his feet, grabbed Lucy by the hair and dragged her to the front door.

Garrett raised his Beretta. "You won't get out of here alive."

"Stay still, Lucy," Hondo pleaded with his sister.

The poor woman started crying. Strickland's trigger finger flinched.

"What are you going to do now, Sheriff?" Strickland grinned. "Looks like I'm back in charge. Drop your weapon."

Garrett cursed. He had no choice. He slid his weapon over.

Keller circled around Strickland. The man didn't hesitate. He let a bullet fly. Keller went down, his shoulder bloody.

"No more games. Get McCallister and the girl inside, and we'll finish this."

Before the words left his mouth a gunshot echoed through the room.

Lucy screamed.

Strickland fell to the floor, unmoving.

Hondo ran to his sister and cradled her in his arms, turning her away from the dead body. "I was only bringing the deputy cookies," she babbled.

"Everyone down." Garrett raced to the open front door. He stood in the doorway, Beretta drawn. Molly was ducked down in the backseat. Laurel had squeezed under the SUV. "He's dead," Garrett said.

Laurel's eyes widened; she crawled toward him, rose and threw herself into his arms.

"Did he say anything?" she whispered. "Give us any information?"

Slowly Garrett shook his head. "I'm sorry."

"I understand."

But her voice held a resignation that Garrett didn't like. She, too, realized the implications. If Ivy's file didn't give them the name of the person responsible, they were at a dead end. That could cost all three of them their lives.

THE BLACK ESCALADE backed out of sight of the sheriff's office. Shep shoved the gear into Park and glared at Léon. "You should have taken the shot. Strickland was easy, but Bradley was in your sights twice. First when he orchestrated that harebrained scheme with the keys, then through the front door. You could have taken them both out."

His new partner shook his head. "The deputy would have been collateral damage. Plus, I saw movement inside through that front window."

"So what?"

"The boss doesn't want too many bodies that can't be explained. I need to be able to take them out quick, and we have to move in and grab them...or they need to disappear."

"I didn't hear that order."

"Well, I was told when I was brought on board to keep every job out of the papers and low-key. Killing a bunch of people in a sheriff's office will make the news. Trust me, that's how the boss wants it."

"Then how do you expect to get the job done?" Shep asked. This new guy was really starting to bug him. And his accent irritated the hell out of Shep.

"I've got an explosive in the back of the truck that makes C-4 look like Play-Doh. Nothing for forensics to find. We follow them, get them together, blow the car and leave. It'll burn so hot nothing is left. It's cleaner. And we get rid of them all at once."

Shep drummed his fingers on the dash. "Explosives. That's why the boss brought you in. Léon, I may like your style after all."

"Then we're in agreement." Léon peered through his binoculars. "Hmm...looks like we won't have to make Strickland disappear. Our friendly neighborhood deputy's hiding the body."

"Maybe he's taking it to the morgue."

Léon shook his head. "Wrapped the guy in a blanket and dumped him in a pickup. They're getting rid of the body."

"One less task for us to finish."

"One more reason to do this job right, because I refuse to be made into an example of my new boss's desire for perfection."

HONDO'S MOTEL ROOMS were simple, but comfortable. Laurel took a long, slow breath, but her nerves refused to settle. At least the chaos from outside had disappeared.

The group of CTC operatives who had arrived had taken over the motel and the sheriff's office and pretty much secured the entire town. No one went in or out without CTC knowing it.

They'd searched for the man who'd shot Strickland, but the only lead was an unfamiliar black Escalade that had raced out of town. An expensive car carrying a sniper with a good eye.

They'd be back.

Laurel couldn't feel completely safe, even with the armed guards at the door. The two men originally tailing her might be dead, but they'd been replaced. Someone wanted her, Molly and Garrett dead, not to mention they still hadn't heard from her father.

Laurel shifted backward and let her spine rest against the bed's headboard. Molly crawled into her lap, resting against her chest. With a sigh, Laurel hummed the addictive ant song Garrett had sung the night before.

Everything around this room seemed peaceful and safe, but Laurel could feel the tension knotting at the back of her neck. Her gut urged her to run, but she had nowhere to go.

She had to trust Garrett and his friends.

Molly picked at Mr. Houdini, rocking him slightly. She'd gone way too quiet after the latest attack. Would Molly ever be the same? Laurel knew she wouldn't.

Molly snuggled closer and squeezed her lion tightly, playing with its collar.

A knock sounded at the door. Molly jerked in Laurel's arms as the door opened. Laurel palmed her SIG and aimed it at the woman with black hair who stood on the motel's porch. Behind her, Laurel recognized one of the CTC operatives standing guard.

"Who are you?" she asked.

"Raven Adams, Daniel's wife. May I come in?"

The man Garrett trusted so much. One more leap of faith.

Laurel nodded and lowered the SIG, but kept it within reach.

A large reddish-colored dog panted beside Raven. "How about my furry friend, Trouble?" She tilted her head toward her canine companion.

Molly straightened a bit in Laurel's lap and stared closely at the dog, which seemed to smile.

"Come in," Laurel said.

The moment Raven crossed the threshold, Trouble bounded toward Molly, but he didn't jump on the bed. He simply tilted his head and stared at the little girl, then put his big head down on the bed and looked up at Molly with sad brown eyes.

"Your dog's name is Trouble?" Laurel asked.

Raven smiled. "It's a long story. He gets more people out of trouble than into trouble, though."

Molly bit her lip and scooted off of Laurel's lap. "Can I pet him?"

"He'd like that," Raven said. "He especially likes getting his ears rubbed."

Molly reached out a tentative hand and patted Trouble's head. The dog's tail thumped.

"He likes me," Molly said. She moved her fingers to his ears and scratched. The big dog leaned into her and practically groaned with pleasure.

Molly slid off the bed. "He's big." Her lion in one arm,

she wrapped her other around the big dog and hugged him. "I like you."

Raven held up a bag. "Have you had some of Hondo's cookies? He likes you a lot, Molly, so he gave me a few cookies just for you."

Molly's ears perked up even as she rubbed Trouble's nose. "Chocolate chip?"

"Is there another kind of cookie?" Raven opened the bag and passed a cookie to Molly. "Daniel and I wanted to invite Molly to take a ride on a plane and visit my house. I have a swing set in the backyard. It's too big for my little girls, but it might be just Molly's size."

Trouble rolled onto his back and Molly giggled, rubbing the dog's belly. The smile that lit her eyes made Laurel's heart ache.

"She'd be safe with us," Raven said.

Laurel leaned down and patted Trouble. Then she stroked Molly's hair. "When are you leaving?"

"Daniel and Garrett are discussing their plans."

"Really?" Laurel crouched down in front of her niece. "Molly Magoo, I need to go speak with Sheriff Garrett. Do you want to stay here with Trouble?"

Molly nodded.

"Do you mind watching her for a few minutes?" Laurel asked Raven. "She's had a rough time. If she needs me, I'll be right outside."

Laurel started toward the door. Raven took one of Laurel's hands. "You can trust Garrett. He's one of the good ones."

Laurel studied the woman's eyes and recognized the tortured memories of events gone by. Raven had seen things. Laurel looked back at Molly.

"I'll take good care of her. I almost lost my girls. I

don't take their safety for granted." Laurel hesitated. "Look, I know you don't know me from any woman off the street, but Garrett and Daniel saved my life and the lives of my children. There's no one else I'd want in my corner if I were facing the devil himself."

Laurel met Raven's gaze. "We're in a lot of trouble. What if it follows Molly to you?"

"More of Daniel's organization will be stationed at my house. She'll be well guarded. And Trouble will be there, too."

Laurel bit her lip. "I'll think about it."

She walked out of the motel room. Several men with serious faces and equally impressive weapons prowled the area. One tipped his cowboy hat at her. "Ma'am. The sheriff's in the next room over."

Laurel walked in. Garrett sat next to Daniel Adams at a small table near the window, studying the screen of a laptop, deep in conversation.

She strode over to them. "What have you found out from Ivy's information?"

Garrett lifted his head, but the guilt in his eyes gave him away. "We should talk about this later."

"I don't like the secrets," Laurel insisted. "Tell me."

He turned the laptop around and Laurel read through the first page. "This can't be true."

"Ivy's file makes a direct connection between your father and almost every agency leak. It connects gun running, selling of top secret documents and the movement of over a billion dollars into overseas accounts."

Laurel snatched the laptop from him and sat on the bed. She took in page after page. Her shoulders tensed at each new, damning word. "I don't believe Ivy wrote this." Laurel raised her gaze to meet Garrett's. "This is the file I downloaded?"

Garrett nodded.

"She's wrong. She has to be. If anyone saw this—"

"Your father would be convicted of treason."

"He wouldn't do any of this. And I'm not just being naive." She lifted her chin and stared at Garrett.

He knelt beside the bed and held her hand in his. "I don't think so either, but I do believe someone else within the agency is setting him up. Just like me."

"What can we do? Strickland is dead."

Daniel cleared his throat. "After I spoke with Ransom Grainger, the head of CTC, about you, he let me in on some sensitive information. CTC has a contact buried deep in a covert operation within the agency. Ransom had been asked to investigate some irregularities within their overseas operations," he said.

"By who?"

"Let's just say it's someone at the very highest levels of the government. There was a whistle-blower involved."

"Who?" Laurel asked.

"James McCallister."

"Dad?"

"I think this is why he hoped to solve my case," Garrett said.

"Daniel, can you help us identify who wants us dead? Maybe even find out what happened to my father?" Laurel asked. "Can CTC?"

The CTC operative frowned. "Our informant hasn't met face-to-face with the highest level in the organization yet. Evidently, whoever's in charge keeps things very secret, so it's delicate. Any contact with our operative and we risk his life. Too many questions and he'll disappear. Others have."

"So, what do we do until then?" Laurel asked, rubbing the back of her neck to try to get rid of the headache threatening to escalate into agony. "Eventually that sniper will find a way to us. We can't hide forever."

Garrett rose and looked down at her, his expression warning her she wouldn't like whatever he was going to say. "That's why I want you and Molly to disappear for a while with Daniel and Raven."

Laurel took in Garrett's grim face. "You'll come with us, though. You're in danger, too."

"I can't, Laurel. I'm going to—"

"Get yourself killed," Laurel finished.

"I think I'll leave you two to hash this out." Daniel disappeared out the door, closing it behind him.

Garrett plucked the laptop from her and brought her to her feet. He touched her cheek. "I'm going to find James and take this guy down, but I can't focus on the mission if I'm worried about you and Molly. I don't want you hurt, Laurel. Your father would want you out of the cross fire."

"That's playing dirty." She scowled at him, knowing exactly what he was doing and hating him for it.

"I'm telling the truth." He bent down and gently touched her lips with his own. "It has to be this way. For Molly. You know that."

Garrett laced his fingers with hers. She liked the way they intertwined, as if they were one. They'd known each other just a few days, and yet she felt as if they'd been together always. She didn't want to lose him.

"I don't like it."

"But you'll do it." Garrett squeezed her fingers. "For Molly."

"For Molly."

With a soft peck on her lips, he walked to the door and opened it. "Daniel, I need transportation."

Daniel slipped a phone from his pocket. "To D.C.?"

"That's where this thing started. That's where I'll end it."

"Give me a couple of hours to get a plane here. You guys have been up all night. Rest. We'll take care of things for a while."

"Thanks, Daniel. I owe you."

"We're even now," he said. "I'm going to find my wife."

Daniel closed the door on them and Garrett faced Laurel. She could hardly breathe. "I don't like this. It feels wrong. I came to you. I caused you to lose everything."

Without hesitation, Garrett tugged her back into his arms. "You're wrong. You brought me back to life, Laurel."

He stroked her arms, warming the chill that had settled all around her with the knowledge that this might be the last time he held her.

"I'm afraid. For you."

"All I want is for you to be safe. That's all James would want. This is your chance."

She could barely breathe. "Hold me, Garrett. Tight. Please."

"I'll do more than that." Garrett lowered his lips to hers and pressed them open.

With a low groan she wrapped her arms around his waist, pressing her ear to his chest, listening to the strong beat of his heart, memorizing his scent, the feel of him, taking in every moment, terrified that soon it would be over. Soon he would be gone and she would have only this moment to cherish.

When Garrett pulled back slightly, she couldn't stop the moan of protest. But he didn't let her go. He cupped her face this time, the kiss so very sweet, so very loving. So very scary. Like a goodbye.

Without words, he scooped her into his arms and laid her down on the bed, spooning against her back.

He threaded his fingers with hers, breathing in deeply. "If things were different, I would take you away. I would disappear with you. Believe that."

She brought his hand to her chest and squeezed tight. "I'm terrified. For you. For my father. So many people have died." Laurel turned in his arms and touched his cheek, taking in each line of tension, each fleck of gold in his brown eyes. "I don't want to lose you now that I've found you."

"I'll do everything I can to bring your father home, Laurel."

"And you, too. I want you back, Garrett." She clutched the front of his shirt. "You made me feel something these last few days. I've always believed I could only rely on myself. My father taught me that. But you— I feel like I can count on you. I want and need you in my life. Don't die on me."

"I have a whole lot to live for these days," he said softly. "I don't want to leave you." He pulled her closer, and she realized he'd never made a promise that he'd come back. For the first time, the easy lie didn't trip off his lips.

She felt the truth in every word.

GARRETT WATCHED LAUREL sleep for two hours. The rise and fall of her chest, the gentle smile on her face. He wanted nothing more than to take her away and make a new life for all of them, but he knew better. This would never be over, Laurel and Molly would never be safe, his family and Laurel's family would never be avenged until the traitor in the organization was stopped.

Garrett had said goodbye with every kiss, every touch, every caress. Knowing it might be for the last time, he slipped out of the bed with a sigh, pulled on his boots and walked out of the room.

Laurel wouldn't be surprised to awaken and find him gone, but she'd be furious. He knew they were lucky to have survived the past few days. Luck didn't last forever.

He closed the door quietly. Daniel stood on the porch of the Copper Mine Motel in a small pool of sunlight, Raven folded in his arms, a blanket wrapped around her.

Several armed guards nodded at them. Daniel nodded back.

"Any strangers in town?"

"None. And no sign of the Escalade. It looks clear. For now."

"And Molly?"

"Playing on my tablet, using Trouble as a pillow," Raven said with a smile. "She's a tough little thing. Not to mention a girl after my own heart, with her fondness for Hondo's chocolate-chip cookies."

"How are Hondo and Lucy? And Keller?"

Daniel frowned. "Lucy isn't handling it well. Doc gave her a sedative. Keller's going to recover, but he's got a lot of questions."

"Poor Lucy. She's been through hell. You know, I spent the last year in this town playing the waiting game when I wanted to be in the action. Now I've hurt the people who gave me their trust when they shouldn't have. I don't know how to make it up to them."

"You can catch whoever's responsible and make them pay." Hondo's harsh voice came from around the corner. The big man looked devastated.

"Hondo." Garrett stilled. "I'm so sorry about you and Lucy—"

The motel owner raised his hand. "You didn't bring them here. They came after you. Lucy knows better than anyone that evil exists. Her ex-husband's beatings damaged her brain and left her with a childlike innocence. Then a few months ago she was shot and nearly killed. She sees the truth now, though." Hondo handed over another bag of cookies. "Give these to Molly. Lucy wants her to have them. She wouldn't let herself sleep until I brought them out here."

"Again, I'm so sorry."

"Sheriff, you want to make it up to me? Take care of those men, then come back. Obviously Trouble needs a lawman who knows how to handle more than just old man Crowley's drinking binges. We need good men around here, and that's what you are. So get it done."

Hondo disappeared back behind the screen door, then closed and locked it.

Garrett exhaled slowly, shoved his hands into his pockets and looked at Daniel. "I left everything I know about this case on a disk in the top drawer in the hotel room. If I don't come back...use your best judgment."

Daniel nodded.

"Strickland and Krauss are gone, but there are more coming." Garrett pulled Strickland's phone from the evidence bag. "Once I turn this on, sooner or later someone will track it, or the traitor at the other end will call."

With a solemn nod, Daniel rubbed the back of his neck. "Then press the button and let's get this damned thing over with."

GARRETT DROVE THE TRUCK several hours from Trouble before he pulled off to the side of the road. He didn't want anyone being led to Laurel.

He dozed, dreaming of lying next to Laurel and cuddling her warm body with his. Afternoon sunshine filtered into the pickup. The phone hadn't revealed the blocked number, so his only choice had been to wait for the call. He'd signaled Daniel with a text, and CTC would triangulate the signal.

Just past twelve-thirty the phone rang.

"Derek Bradley, I assume?"

Garrett immediately texted Daniel: The tracking began.

"Strickland and Krauss are dead, I understand. That must feel good, Mr. Bradley, considering Strickland blew up your family right in front of you."

"Not particularly. But then again, I don't get off on killing people."

"Should I even ask what you want, Mr. Bradley? Or should I call you Garrett?"

"A bargain. For the lives of Laurel McCallister and Molly Deerfield. They walk away. No one follows them and they're left alone."

More silence, and a prickle of unease rocked down Garrett's spine.

"That could be possible. Ivy Deerfield was a better detective than you were, Garrett. She infiltrated my organization farther than I would have expected. She collected information I wish returned to me. Returned and destroyed."

"I have her evidence." Garrett waited for several moments. He had to keep the traitor on the phone.

"Your proposition has merit."

Interesting. Whoever was on the other end of the phone felt vulnerable.

"I can come to you," Garrett offered.

"It may very well be time we meet. Then you might begin to understand."

Anticipation coursed through Garrett's blood. He knew he was walking into a trap.

It didn't matter.

"Tell your friends that their attempt to triangulate my location won't work. Besides, you don't have to guess where I'll be, Sheriff. Come to James McCallister's home. Alone. It's a fitting spot for our…reunion. You have until midnight tonight to be here. Or I *will* finish my original plan and eliminate Laurel McCallister and her niece."

Chapter Eleven

Laurel awakened without warmth next to her. She stretched her palm across the motel-room bed, but the sheets were cool to the touch. She didn't have to call out to know Garrett was gone.

Keep him safe.

The silent prayer filtered through her mind. She tucked her legs up. Her skills hadn't brought them the answer. Ivy's investigation had done nothing but incriminate their father, just as he seemed to have done to Garrett. Which was probably why Ivy had thought about leaving the organization.

Garrett would never stop trying to prove his innocence and avenge his wife and daughter, though. And he wouldn't stop now to protect her and Molly.

He was that kind of man. A hero, but the kind of man who could get himself killed in the name of justice.

There had to be something they were missing. That Ivy had missed.

Laurel sat up and rubbed her eyes. How long had she been out?

She slipped on her shoes and opened the door. Daniel stood near her room, his body watchful, his weapon at his side.

"Molly?"

"With Raven and Trouble next door. She's fine."

"I need to see her," Laurel said.

"Sure thing." Daniel took a scan around and met the gaze of a CTC operative at the other end of the motel. "Go on."

Laurel rushed the five feet to the next room and opened the door.

"Aunt Laurel!" Molly grinned, gave Trouble a pat, grabbed her stuffed lion and raced over. "Trouble and me are bestest friends now. Can I have a dog like him? I'll take good care of him and feed him and give him water, and take him for walks, and pick up his poop." She wrinkled her nose. "If I have to. Miss Raven said you were resting. I'm glad you're done. Where's Sheriff Garrett?"

Raven sat cross-legged, hosting a makeshift picnic on the bed.

Laurel fingered Molly's blond hair, able to breathe for a moment, knowing her niece was safe. "He left, Molly Magoo."

Everything within Laurel longed to assure Molly that Garrett would be back soon, but the words simply wouldn't come. Laurel not only couldn't be certain; she feared the worst.

Molly stilled; a frown tugged at the corners of her lips. "He didn't even say goodbye. That's not polite. And I wanted to show him my star. I kept forgetting before. It's just like his when we first met him."

"You have a star?" Laurel asked in confusion.

"Mommy put it on my lion."

Molly held out Mr. Houdini. Laurel stared at the small charm hanging from the lion's collar. She dug into her pocket and retrieved the charm bracelet that her father had sent to Ivy. No charms were missing from it. Every other silver shape had meaning—a seashell representing the last vacation with their mother, a horse for when they'd learned to ride, a ballerina from the terrifying lessons both girls had endured before their mother let them quit.

But a sheriff's star. It had no meaning in their lives.

Except in reference to Garrett.

"When did she put this on, Molly?"

Molly's forehead crinkled in thought. "The day I got sick. She said it was a special star. Grandpa sent it and I had to protect it 'cause I was a brave girl just like the man who wore the star. That's Sheriff Garrett, right?"

"Yes, I think it is." Laurel could barely speak past the thickening of her throat. "Can I borrow it, honey?"

Her niece's face went solemn. "You'll give it back?"

"I promise, Molly Magoo."

Laurel slipped off the lion's collar and returned the animal. She opened the door and motioned Daniel over. "Do you have a magnifying glass or a microscope?"

Daniel's brow rose. "What's up?"

"Maybe nothing. Maybe an answer."

Daniel rounded the back of one of the black vehicles swarmed in the motel's parking lot. He dug into a duffel bag in the back. "Raven is always telling me I carry weird stuff in my bag." He handed her a small magnifying glass. "I've had it since I was a kid. My father taught me to build fires with it."

Laurel sat down at the table in the motel room and laid the charm down. She studied it closely. Molly had carried that lion everywhere. She'd almost left it behind in Virginia when'd they run that very first night.

After studying one side and seeing nothing, she gently turned it over and there it was.

"A microdot." She looked up at Daniel. "We have to find out what's on it, fast. It could save Garrett. And my father."

LAUREL SAT CROSS-LEGGED on the bed, staring at the computer file that the CTC technicians had pulled from the microdot.

Page after page of all the proof she needed that Garrett and her father were innocent. Except for one thing—the true identity of who was behind all the transactions.

But why had her father and Ivy kept it secret?

"Oh, Ivy, where do I go from here? Who were you going to give this to? If only Garrett were here. He might see something unusual."

She opened the motel-room door and called out to Daniel. "Any word yet?"

He shook his head. "They haven't broken radio silence. They will as soon as they can. All I can confirm is that they landed in D.C. a few hours ago."

"D.C.? No. Garrett's walking into a trap." She frowned at Daniel. "You know that."

Worry creased Daniel's forehead. "You have to trust him. I've looked into who Garrett used to be. The man was very good at his job."

Laurel scrubbed her face. This wasn't the same situation. He was a known traitor to the rest of the world. The moment law enforcement recognized he was alive, if someone killed him, not that many questions would be asked.

The answer was in that file. Laurel had to decipher

it. She had to save him somehow. She needed someone who could help her see what she was missing.

She closed the door on Daniel and paced the motel room. She wanted him here, with her. Safe. She longed for him to hold her in his arms, to talk this over with him. She had to call in her last resort.

She toyed with the phone in her hand. Garrett had wanted to keep Fiona out of it, but with the new information from the microdot, Fiona might be the only other person who could help. She could put the word out Garrett was innocent, and that her father was innocent. Save their lives.

Maybe even help Laurel decipher something hidden in the file—something Ivy and James had known about, but that Laurel couldn't identify. Then Garrett wouldn't have to go through with whatever risky plan he and his CTC friends had come up with.

Her finger paused over the numbers. Garrett hadn't wanted to trust anyone else, but even he had recognized Fiona's knowledge. With a deep breath, Laurel dialed Fiona's personal number. No way Laurel could risk her call being recorded.

"Fiona Wylde." The woman's voice was pleasant, welcoming. As it always was. This woman could very well marry her father someday.

"Fiona, it's Laurel."

The woman gasped. "But…I thought… Oh, my God, James and I thought you were dead."

Laurel's knees buckled and she sagged onto the bed. "You've seen my father. Is he okay? Is he safe? I've been so worried about him."

"Oh, honey." A sob came through Fiona's voice. "He's been through hell, but he escaped yesterday and found his way home. We thought…" She could barely choke out the words. "We thought we'd lost everyone."

Laurel's hands trembled. "Can I…can I talk to him?"

"Of course." Laurel heard fierce whispering in the room. "I'll put it on speakerphone. His hands…have been injured. He's weak, but it's all okay now."

"L-Laurel?"

Her father's voice sounded tired, hoarse.

"Dad. Oh, Dad. You're okay?"

"I've been better." He let out a chuckle, then started coughing.

"I have proof you aren't a traitor, Dad. And neither is Garrett."

"But how?" Fiona asked. "We've been trying for so long. I thought we'd have to leave the country. I couldn't find anything but horrible corroboration that your father was dealing with terrorists."

"I-Ivy. You know what happened—?"

Fiona cut Laurel off. "I'm so sorry, Laurel. Look, your father is hurt. Badly. And he has to lie down, but we need to talk—"

A grunt sounded through the phone, then a crash.

"James!" Fiona shouted. "Laurel, your father just fell. I have to go to him." Muffled whispers filtered through the receiver. "James, darling, stay still. You've torn the stitches."

The phone went silent. Laurel gripped the cell tight. "Fiona, is Dad okay?"

"For now. I've had to treat him myself." Worry laced Fiona's breathless voice.

"Garrett Galloway is going to Washington. He needs help. Please."

"I have to get back to your father. I don't know what

I can do. We felt it better to keep James's reappearance and Galloway's identity a secret. I could make it worse. Things don't look good at the agency."

"But if you looked at the file, maybe we can discover who is doing this."

"You have the file? With you?"

"Yes. Please, Fiona."

"Don't send it to me," she said sharply, all business now. "Come to his house, Laurel. I have someone I trust who can bring you. Are you still in the U.S.?"

Laurel took in a deep breath. "I'm in Texas."

"What are you doing—? Oh, Garrett."

"You knew about him?"

"Of course. James and I share everything. But we had to keep it quiet."

"I wish I'd known."

"I understand. Listen to me, Laurel. I *have* to get off this phone. It's been almost three minutes. We can't risk surveillance. I'll send a plane for you. Your father needs to see you." She lowered her voice. "And, Laurel, don't tell anyone where you're going. Anyone. Do you understand? Not until we end this. Once and for all. Trust no one but me."

THE BLACK ESCALADE idled on the side of the road. Shep glared at Léon. "You got us lost. Do you know what the boss does to people who make mistakes?"

"I watched you blow Strickland's head off," Léon snapped. "I get the picture."

"We should have taken out the woman and girl first?"

Léon fiddled with the GPS receiver. "Do I need to explain this in small words, Shep? Galloway's the hard target. We kill him first. He's the biggest risk."

Shep thrust his fingers through his hair. "Well, we're pretty close to finding him right now, aren't we?"

The device in Léon's lap beeped. He smiled. "Maybe I just saved the day."

The tablet blinked on again. Shep let out a curse. "Are you going to be able to fix that thing or not?"

Léon tugged out a small tool set. "I'll fix it. Be patient."

"Tell that to the boss."

The phone sitting between the two men rang.

"Are we bugged?" Shep pressed the speakerphone button. "Yeah, boss?"

"I have a job for you."

"Kill our three targets and dispose of the bodies," Shep repeated.

"No. I want you to pick up your targets just outside of Trouble, Texas, and bring them to me. I'll give you the location."

"We could dispose of them more easily here."

"Are you questioning me, Shep? Strickland started using his brain—that's why you had to blow it away."

"Of course not."

The boss rattled off a rendezvous point. "I want them both alive. I need them unharmed. At least for another few hours." There was a slight pause. "After that, you can use them as target practice."

JAMES MCCALLISTER'S VIRGINIA home appeared deserted.

Garrett glanced at his watch one more time. Five minutes to midnight. He looked over his shoulder. Rafe had parked a second vehicle down the block. They both recognized this was a trap, but they also knew it was important that the mastermind behind this plot believe Garrett had come alone.

He'd taken every precaution he could, because he wanted to survive. He wanted to see if what he'd experienced with Laurel was real. It felt real—almost too good to be true, which made Garrett distrust it all the more—but, oh, how he wanted it to be real.

He'd never thought he could love anyone again, not after his heart had been destroyed when he'd lost Lisa and Ella, but Laurel had put her faith in him, despite the doubts that had to have raced through her mind more than once since they'd met.

They hadn't known each other long, but Garrett had been dead inside long enough to know what he felt. He had two very good reasons to make it out of this op alive.

He glanced at his watch. One minute before the agreed-upon time.

Garrett slammed the door on the vehicle and walked up the concrete sidewalk. When he reached the familiar front porch he hesitated. He might never come out. And he hadn't told Laurel how he felt. He'd tried to show her, but he hadn't been able to say the words. If he died tonight, he didn't want the words haunting her, but right now he wished he'd said something. He prayed she knew how special she was, how much she deserved to be loved with all a man's heart and soul.

He wanted her to know what was between them meant something more than two people seeking comfort. She truly was an amazing woman, and he wanted to see her again. He wanted to tell her he loved her.

Garrett pressed his finger on the doorbell.

The front door slowly opened. His shoulders tightened. Silence greeted him from the house. He stepped inside. Behind the door, tears streaming down her face, Laurel McCallister had let him in.

"What the hell are you doing here?" Garrett reached out to her, but Laurel stepped back.

"I invited her."

Garrett turned around.

"Fiona?"

Fiona Wylde. James's lover. A woman he knew well. Strike that. Based on the gun she had drawn on him, Fiona was a woman he'd *thought* he knew well.

"You're a difficult man to kill." She nodded at a man standing in the shadows. "Disarm him, Léon."

A man gave a quick nod. He walked over to Garrett, patted him down and removed the Beretta from his back, the knife from his ankle holster and the small pistol hidden within his boot.

Léon met Garrett's gaze and patted his other boot, right over where a second knife was hidden. What the hell?

"Cuff him and bring them both downstairs. We'll have a family reunion."

Garrett slid a glance over at Laurel. "Damn it. Why are you here?" She was supposed to be safe, with Daniel, with CTC.

"I found a microdot Ivy left. It contains proof of your innocence and my father's, too," she said, her gaze resigned. "I called Fiona thinking she'd help us."

"Oh, darlings, after tonight, you'll never have to worry again." Fiona led them down to the basement. She hit a code in a panel on the concrete wall. A door to a small room opened up.

James McCallister sat slumped over in a chair, his arms and legs tied in place. He couldn't lift his head.

Garrett saw the flicker of James's eyes, but his clothes

were in tatters, his face bruised. Burns smoldered his pants.

"Dad," Laurel shouted.

"Aunt Laurel?" Molly's cries sounded from behind a door. "Let me out! Please, let me out!"

"Tie them to the chairs," Fiona ordered. "We end this today."

Léon shoved Garrett toward a steel chair and pushed down on his head, indicating for him to sit. The man took nylon rope and secured his hands and feet. A second man did the same to Laurel.

"Why do this, Fiona?" Garrett asked, clenching his muscles against the ropes. He needed room to work if he was going to escape and get Laurel, Molly and James to safety.

"I'm not having a reveal-my-inner-motivations conversation with you, Garrett, because there are none. I'll make it simple. I did it for the money. A *lot* of money."

"He's secure," Léon said. "What about the little girl in the closet?"

"Leave her."

Fiona stalked up the stairs, then whirled around. "I don't want any evidence left behind. Everyone in that room is dead or missing. They aren't to be found." She paused. "And, Léon, this is why I smuggled you into the country. Those explosives should take the house down. Get it down so it's too hot to find even a fragment of bone."

"Where's your loyalty?" Laurel shouted. "To my father, if no one else. He loved you."

"Ah, love and loyalty. How quaint. Almost as heart-warming as Léon's amusing use of handcuffs." Fiona looked down from her perch on the stairs. Her eyes hardened. "Haven't you learned there is no loyalty? The powerful feed off the powerful. And heroes die for nothing. The only thing you have is yourself and your needs. You should have remembered that, Laurel."

Léon and his friend followed Fiona up the stairs. The door closed behind them.

Garrett palmed the key that Léon had placed in his hand. Twisting his wrists, he maneuvered free of the handcuffs, then pulled out of his other boot the knife... the one Léon had left.

Laurel stared at him. "How?"

"Daniel's inside guy. We don't have much time."

Garrett cut through the zip ties around Laurel's wrists. She ran to the door.

"I'm here, Molly."

"Aunt Laurel, help me!"

She tugged on the doorknob. Locked.

"Molly, step back from the door, honey. Hide in the corner."

Garrett gave the lock a hard kick and the door broke free. Laurel scooped up Molly.

"I'll get your father," Garrett said.

Above them an explosion roared. Glass shattered; timbers fell. Laurel raced up the stairs and put her hand on the door. "Fire. Smoke's starting to come through. We're trapped."

"If Léon set the charges, I hope to God he gave us extra time." Garrett knelt in front of James and shook him. "Tell me you followed your own advice, old man. Where's the escape route out of here?"

Laurel hurried down the stairs.

"James, we don't have much time."

The old man blinked. "Behind their mom's picture." His voice croaked.

Garrett spun around, but he didn't see a painting of a woman on the wall. "Where is your mother's picture, Laurel?"

"There's only the mural she painted."

The starry night sky covered one wall.

Murky smoke began to filter into the room. "Get washcloths from the bar area and wet them," Garrett shouted. "Use them to breathe through."

His eyes teared up from the smoke. "Where is it?" He ran his fingers along the brick wall. Finally, at the Big Dipper, he felt a notch at one star. He pressed the button. The brick gave way. He pushed the concealed doorway open.

"It was good of Fiona to have our meeting at midnight. Darkness will help hide us."

Garrett paused at a weapon safe in the corner. He grabbed a hunting knife and a rifle. "Laurel, here you go." He shoved an old Colt .45 at her. "You couldn't have had an Uzi in here, could you, old man?" He pulled a Bowie knife from a drawer and pressed it into James's hands. Even with his injuries, he gripped the weapon.

"Get them out," James choked. "Leave me." He passed out.

"Not on your life." Garrett heaved James over his shoulder in a fireman's carry. "Laurel, let's go."

She clutched Molly to her and followed him out through a short passageway leading up to a tunnel. The gradient rose.

A dim lighting system lit the narrow path. Garrett struggled with James's weight. At the end of the tunnel there was a small door. A key dangled at the edge.

"Thanks, James." Garrett grabbed the key and unlocked the door. It led into what looked like a storage shed. Garrett recognized it from his previous visits.

"I never knew this passageway was here," Laurel whispered.

Garrett didn't turn the light on. He laid James on the ground and propped him up against the rough wooden wall. Garrett peered through a small window in the shed.

Laurel stood at his side, her entire body stiff with resolve.

Flames erupted from James's house, searing through brick and wood. Loud crackling overwhelmed the quiet neighborhood. Smoke billowed into the air and the fire painted the midnight sky red.

Another explosion rocketed through the house.

"That one waited for us to get out," Garrett whispered to her. "Not bad, Léon."

"He's on our side. He can help."

"Rafe Vargas is out there, too." At Laurel's questioning glance, Garrett added, "Another CTC operative. We aren't alone."

"If they haven't been caught," Laurel said. "What's the plan?"

"I'm going out there. Fiona's not getting away with this."

He gripped the old Remington hunting rifle he'd snagged from the safe. "Stay here," he ordered Laurel. "Protect them."

She gripped Garrett's arm. "Be careful. Come back to me."

He gave her a small smile. "Count on it." Then his gaze turned serious. "Have you got your weapon?"

She pulled out the Colt. "I know what to do with it."

He kissed her quickly. "I love you. I should have told you before." Garrett raced out of the building.

A lone figure, carrying an M16, emerged from the smoke. Fiona pointed the weapon at Garrett. "I don't leave witnesses."

Garrett didn't hesitate. He raised his weapon. Before he could get off a shot, a bevy of bullets tore across his body.

He blinked and looked down, then sank to his knees.

Chapter Twelve

A spray of bullets sounded from outside, and then another volley came a moment later. Some pierced the shed. Laurel dragged her father to the ground and covered Molly with her body.

The little girl cried out in fear.

Laurel's heart raced. Garrett hadn't had an automatic weapon.

Please, God, let him live. "Molly," Laurel ordered. "Get over by Grandpa. Hide in the darkest corner."

Molly crawled over toward James, and Laurel quickly stacked a wheelbarrow and other tools in front of them. "Stay here. Take care of each other."

She slipped some metal spikes and a small scythe next to her barely conscious father. It was all she could do for weapons.

"Back up Garrett if he's still—" Her father paused and looked at Molly. "You can't let Fiona escape. Do what needs to be done."

Laurel grabbed the old .45. Handguns were hard to shoot accurately. She'd need to get close.

She opened the shed door slowly, only to see Fiona standing over Garrett's prone body. Behind them, the bodies of her two minions lay on the grass near the burning house.

Fiona pointed her weapon at Garrett again. "You've been damn tough to kill, Bradley, but this head shot ought to do it."

Laurel didn't hesitate. She aimed and fired. Once. Twice. And again, until the gun was empty. Fiona jerked, but she didn't go down. "Stupid woman," Fiona taunted. "Never heard of Kevlar? You're going to pay for that."

Laurel dropped her weapon. She had one chance. If she could get the right angle—

"Aunt Laurel, Aunt Laurel. Come quick. Grandpa's not moving." Molly ran into the yard.

Fiona met Laurel's horror-struck gaze. The woman smiled and swept her gun around, pointing it at the little girl. "Guess the rug rat's next."

Just as Fiona was about to squeeze the trigger, a shot rang out from behind her. The bullet struck her in the head. She hit the ground hard, the wound fatal.

Molly screamed and cowered on the ground.

Laurel's eyes widened. Garrett's arm shook and he dropped the Remington. "She's not the only one who's heard of Kevlar." He coughed. With that, his head dropped to the grass. Laurel grabbed Molly and raced over to Garrett.

Blood pooled at two gunshot wounds.

He glanced down at the red seeping through his shirt. "I needed a bigger size." He looked up at Laurel. "I'm sorry."

Sirens grew louder in the distance.

"Garrett, you're going to be fine. Just hang on. Help is on the way," she said softly, then gasped as his eyes fluttered closed. "Garrett, no!"

"Sheriff Garrett?" Molly whispered. "Please don't go away."

"I'll try, sugar." He coughed.

Laurel leaned down closer. "You told me you loved me, Garrett. You can't leave me now. I love you, too."

There was no response. His chest barely rose.

"Oh, God, no." She didn't know what to do. The vest might be stanching the blood. She needed help.

Suddenly, a crush of police cars, fire engines and ambulances skidded to the curbs. Various personnel carrying hoses, guns and medical equipment came around the house. Laurel yelled to them, "We need help here. A man's been shot!"

She clutched Molly tightly as tears streamed down their faces.

Two paramedics rushed over. "Move back."

Laurel jerked away, hiding Molly's face against her own chest. "My father is in the shed over there." Laurel pointed out the small bullet-ridden structure. "He's badly hurt. Please help him, too."

The paramedics called another of the backup teams to check out the shed.

The yard was complete chaos. The firemen futilely fought the blaze, but whatever had been used to blow up the house did not back off easily.

"Another injured," a cop shouted. "Guy's pinned under a wall."

Men raced around the house. The police hovered over the paramedics, watching them work on Garrett. Others checked the gathering crowds. Still more hurried to where Fiona and the other two bodies lay.

"Hey, this one's alive," someone called out, bending

over one of the men lying near Fiona's body. "I need a medic, quick."

Laurel couldn't tell if it was Léon. She hoped so.

"Please, Garrett. Please make it," she said, clutching Molly to her.

More responders dragged gurneys across the grass to the injured. Laurel stood back, holding Molly, her attention split between Garrett and the activity in the shed. She prayed her father wouldn't come out in a black bag.

What seemed an eternity later, Garrett, her father and Léon were all loaded into different ambulances.

Laurel carried Molly over to the back of the one carrying Garrett and tried to get inside.

"You can't, ma'am."

"Why not? That's my father and Garrett is my...my... fiancé."

A police detective walked up beside her. "Lady, as the only person still standing on a field with multiple dead bodies, you have a lot of explaining to do. I can see the gunshot residue on your hand. We're not letting you near anybody. The kid will have to go with Child Protective Services."

Laurel panicked and held Molly close. "No, she may not be safe without special protection. Please, she's been through so much. Let me call a family she trusts to come take care of her."

"Aunt Laurel," Molly cried. "I want to stay with you. Don't make me leave."

Laurel knelt down in front of Molly so they were face-to-face. "Molly, honey, I have to go with these policemen for a little while to tell them what happened. It's not a place for children."

She shook her head. "You said you wouldn't leave me. Not like Mommy and Daddy."

Laurel couldn't control the tears. "I'm going to call Daniel and Raven. You can stay with them. You could play with the twins, too, and their doggy."

Molly bit her lip. "I like Raven a lot. She gives me cookies. Daniel's nice, too." Then she shook her head. "But I want you and Sheriff Garrett."

Gripping Molly's hands in hers, Laurel met the little girl's gaze. "Please, Molly Magoo. Can you be brave for me one more time?"

"Like Sheriff Garrett?"

Laurel squeezed her niece's hands. "Like Sheriff Garrett. Go to Daniel and Raven."

"You'll come back for me. Promise?"

Somehow she would. "I promise." Laurel looked up at the officer. "Please, let her go to them. You'll understand what's going on soon enough. I cannot have her put through any more trauma."

The detective's brow furrowed. "I got kids of my own," he relented. "Give me the family's info and I'll check them out. Otherwise, the girl goes with CPS."

THE POLICE STATION reeked of the sights and smells of nighttime indigents and criminals. Molly wouldn't let go of Laurel's hand.

She desperately wanted to pace the walkways of the police station, but she had to shield Molly. She glanced over at a tired-looking woman standing in the corner, ever watchful. If Daniel didn't arrive soon, CPS might just take Molly away. Laurel's heart broke at the idea of being separated from her niece.

How could she explain everything that had happened? Would the cops even believe her?

Finally, the door opened and Daniel strode inside, along with another man wearing a patch over one eye, who looked as if he'd been on the wrong end of a fight. She recognized him from somewhere. He walked over and had a few words with the officer assigned to watch Laurel. Her interrogation would start as soon as Molly left.

Laurel finally placed the man's face and scowled. "Exactly *who* is your friend?"

Daniel looked back at the man who was now approaching them. "Laurel, this is Rafe. He's part of CTC, the organization I work for. He was stationed outside the house, but got buried by a wall."

"Is there a problem?" Rafe asked seriously.

"I don't know," she said, her voice full of suspicion. "I saw you driving the ambulance with that man, Léon, inside. You didn't go the same direction as the other ambulances. Why?"

Rafe lowered his voice when he spoke. "Léon is one of ours, too. I took him to some medical facilities that were a little more…discreet. His recovery will take a while and we wanted him safe."

"Great," she snapped. "What about Garrett and my father? What about keeping them safe?" She knew she sounded like an ungrateful witch, but no one would even tell her if Garrett and her father were alive or dead.

"Garrett and your father are alive," Rafe said, "but in critical condition. We have guards both inside and outside their doors, as well as throughout the hospital, keeping watch for intruders. My boss is trying to keep the feds and agency people out of this so they don't have access to Garrett. If they identify him as a fugitive before we prove his innocence, the government will claim him."

Laurel rubbed her face with her hands. "They're alive." Her knees shook.

"I've brought enough evidence that you should be out of here soon, Laurel. Just be patient. I'll take Molly now, and Rafe will wait and handle bail or whatever comes up. He won't let you down, Laurel. I swear it."

Tears filled Laurel's eyes as she hugged Molly and sent her off with Daniel. "Please keep her safe."

"Daniel would give his life for Molly. He'll guard her well."

Just then, a policeman walked over. "Ms. McCallister, it's time."

FROM SOMEWHERE FAR OFF, Garrett heard a sweet female voice calling to him.

"Garrett, please wake up."

He felt a gentle touch on his forehead, but couldn't make much sense out of the soothing, soft words being whispered in his ear.

The dreams had been haunting him again. Strange dreams, where Lisa and Ella were running to him, holding him close, but suddenly they were waving goodbye. *No! Don't go.* Something was wrong. It was very wrong. He fought his way toward consciousness.

The dream changed, colors swirling and spinning in his mind, and this time he was reaching out for Laurel and Molly. He tried to reach them, but they were so far away. They were leaving, too. Sadness in their eyes. The gray returned and pulled him back into the darkness.

The whispering continued, more urgently this time.

The voices were louder. Why wouldn't they leave him alone?

"Garrett. Wake up."

He strained to understand, but each time he tried to open his eyes, they didn't respond at all.

"Come back to me now. You can do this."

Laurel? Was that Laurel trying to get him to do something? He struggled again, forcing the fogginess in his mind away.

A firm hand gripped his, as if to will him to do something. His eyelids were so heavy, but somehow he forced them open for the briefest second. The blaze of sunlight burned his eyes and he groaned, flinching from the light. Even that slight movement sent a spear of fiery pain through his chest.

"He moved!" Laurel yelled. "His eyes opened for a second. Get the doctor in here fast." A firm hand gripped his. "Come on, Garrett. Open your eyes."

"Hurts," he rasped.

"Shut the blinds and turn off the lights. It's too bright," Laurel ordered, then suddenly laughed. "Oh, my God, Garrett. You're waking up. I thought I'd lost you. I love you so very much."

Laurel's voice pulled him from the darkness. He needed to reach her. He had to reach her. He fought with everything inside to open his eyes.

A halo around beautiful brown hair slowly came into focus. He blinked again. She was beautiful. Like an angel.

"Laurel?" His voice sounded strange, hoarse, and when he tried to raise his hand, that blasted pain speared through his chest again.

"Don't move and don't try to talk, Garrett. They just

took the breathing tube out." She put the tiniest ice chip on his tongue to soothe his throat. "You've been in a coma. But you're going to be okay."

Visions came back to him. A little girl holding Laurel's hand, so small and scared. Then outside, in the darkness, an AK-47 pointed at her. "Molly?"

"She's safe. You saved her."

"Fiona?"

Laurel's face went cold. "Dead."

"Good." His eyes closed. "You're all safe." Everything went black and this time he didn't fight it.

LAUREL SAGGED IN the chair when Garrett lost consciousness again.

The doctor strode in.

"The nurse said the patient moved." The man's voice was skeptical. "He looks pretty out of it now. What happened?"

Laurel stood. "He woke up. He spoke to me. He knew me. He remembered some of what happened the night he was shot."

"I didn't expect that much, so it's a good sign. He's been unconscious for two weeks, so don't expect him to go dancing anytime soon." The neurologist leaned over Garrett and checked his vital signs, then his bandages. "The bullet wounds to his chest are healing nicely. His latest MRI showed the swelling has gone down."

"I knew he'd come back to me."

The doctor smiled at her. "Family often knows best. The more you stayed and talked to him, the more you kept his brain stimulated. He may not have known what you were saying, but even in a coma, there is some level of communication happening, especially among loved ones. Your dedication has been important to his recovery. You're going to make him a great wife."

Laurel gulped. She'd never cleared up the misconception that Garrett was her fiancé. The hospital staff never would have let her stay as often or as long as she had.

Legally, she and Garrett weren't family, but in every way that mattered, Garrett had become an integral part of her life. So much had happened. She prayed he'd still want her when he awoke and he could make different choices than the ones she hoped he would.

A short time after the doctor left, Laurel gripped Garrett's hand. If what the doctor said was true, had Garrett heard all the times she'd told him she loved him? There hadn't been time before. But she could no longer imagine life without this man.

"Laurel?" His eyes fluttered open again. With the lights off and window shades drawn, he was able to keep his eyelids somewhat open. "I thought I dreamed—"

His voice gave out and Laurel quickly gave him another ice chip. Several more, spread over the next five minutes, finally allowed him to speak without too bad a rasp to his voice.

"Did James make it?" he asked, watching her warily.

She smiled. "Yes, but he's hurt badly. The burns were…" Laurel stopped, unable to speak further.

"Is he still in the hospital?"

"No. Not this one, anyway. The authorities took him away for a debriefing. I don't know when I'll see him. Your friends at CTC are working on it."

"I'm sorry. You haven't heard anything?"

"Nothing specific, other than that they're angry that he lied about you under oath. It will take time for him to win back anyone's trust. At least my sister's evidence cleared you both of the treason charges. The story has been all over the papers. You're a hero."

"Yeah, right. I almost got you all killed."

"No, Garrett," Laurel insisted, "Fiona almost got us all killed. I've been afraid to take any chances ever since my mother died. My father drilled into Ivy and me that we were only to rely on ourselves. Not anyone else, and sure as hell not him." Laurel hesitated. "Yet a few weeks ago I found myself relying on a man I didn't even know, and every time you proved yourself worthy of trusting."

"You mean when I wasn't lying to you or sneaking out without telling you."

"Yeah, well, we can work on that."

"It was always for your own good," Garrett said.

"Like I said, we'll work on it. Don't push your luck, Sheriff. I was giving you the benefit of the doubt, and you're blowing it big-time."

"Come here." He pulled her gently toward him.

Laurel closed her eyes and leaned forward on the bed. Afraid to jar the wound on his chest, she rested her head gently on Garrett's arm. She longed for those arms to surround her again; she longed for him to hold her close and just talk, just to hear his voice tell her again that he loved her. She wanted to hear him sing that silly ant song once more to Molly in his deep voice. The one that made her feel safe down to her soul.

He stroked her head with his hand. "Why didn't you leave? You didn't have to stay watching over me."

Had he changed his mind about her? She couldn't stop the tears from falling down her cheeks. "I didn't have anywhere else to be," she said. "I figured hanging out in a hospital with you would be a good way to spend Christmas. It's already decorated for the holidays and

Molly's having a wonderful time at Daniel and Raven's. The I-want-a-puppy hints are coming fast and furious. I think a dog is even beating out the princess palace she asked for all year."

Garrett blinked. "Wait a minute. Back up. It's Christmas?"

"Not quite, but close. It's next week."

His eyes went wide. "How long have I been out?"

"Thirteen days, seven hours and twenty-three minutes, but who's counting?" she said, trying for a nonchalance she did not feel.

"You should have left me here," he said. "Molly's so afraid Santa won't be able to find her this year. She needs some normalcy back in her life. She needs you."

His words pierced her heart. Laurel pulled back. "You don't want me here?"

Garrett swallowed and looked at her. "I...I want what's best for you. And Molly."

"You are what's best for me. Can't you see that?"

"I didn't protect you," he said. "You could have died because I didn't plan well enough ahead."

She laughed incredulously. "Garrett, I'm the one who contacted Fiona. If I'd trusted you—"

He gripped her hands. "If we'd trusted each other."

Laurel rose from the bed slowly. "Is this really where we are? Fighting over something this stupid?" She stepped closer. "I am going to give you an ultimatum. Answer it wrong and I will walk away forever."

He struggled to sit up in the bed. "Wait. What are you talking about?"

"I'm talking about us. I love you. Do you hear me? No doubts, no questions on my side. You once told me the same thing, but you thought you were going off to die."

"Laurel—"

"I am not done, mister. Not by a long shot. Derek Bradley's name has been cleared, so if that's the life you want, you can go back to the clandestine, lonely life you led before. But you have a choice. The mayor of Trouble says that you can continue as the sheriff."

Garrett sat staring at her. "The mayor? The mayor hates me because I'm onto his tricks."

"Oh, Daniel had a little talk with that mayor, and he resigned. Hondo took over the job, and he said you can be sheriff as long as he's in office."

Garrett chuckled, then turned serious. "Is that the end of the options available to me? Because it's not a hard choice." Laurel could barely breathe. "Do you think I'd choose anyone or anything but you, Laurel? Where's your faith?"

She couldn't stop the smile from spreading across her face.

"Say the words. When guns aren't blazing and you're not running off to certain death. I need to hear it."

Garrett met her gaze, unwavering, serious. "I love you, Laurel McCallister. I will always love you."

She quivered against him and laid her head on his chest. "I won't ever let you go."

Epilogue

Garrett sat on the floor and placed the last fake flower in the garden of Molly's princess palace.

Laurel walked up to him and handed him a cup of coffee. "You shouldn't be drinking this."

"I won't tell the doctors if you don't." He took a sip of the dark brew and nearly groaned in pleasure. "Some assembly required? That's what the box said. How long have I been at it?"

"Six hours." Laurel chuckled.

"I just hope she likes it. Molly needs some joy."

Laurel knelt down beside him. "She feels safe with you, Garrett. And loved. That's all she needs."

The chime of the clock sounded through the house.

"It's six o'clock."

Garrett struggled to get up off of the floor. Laurel held out her hand to steady him. "Take it easy," she said, putting her hands on his waist. "I just got you back."

He kissed her lips, drinking in the taste of her. He stroked his hand down her cheek. "Have I told you lately that you've made my life wonderful?" Her cheeks flushed. "I'm serious. You didn't just love me—you brought Christmas back. You brought joy into this ranch house."

"I could say the same about you, Garrett Galloway."

Laurel wrapped her arms around him, taking his lips. Garrett let himself get lost in her touch. If it weren't for the fact that this was Christmas Day, he'd drag her back to their bedroom and stay there all day long.

A soft knock forced him to raise his head. "Who is that?"

Garrett walked to the door, pulling his Beretta from atop the refrigerator. Slowly he opened the door.

A thin man in a red suit stood on the steps.

"Santa?"

Molly's sleepy voice came from just outside the living room.

The man walked inside.

"Dad?" Laurel whispered.

"Grandpa!" Molly raced to her grandfather.

He swung her up in the air with a grimace. "Molly Magoo!"

She wrapped her arms around him and hugged him tight. "Grandpa, I thought you were gone to heaven like Mommy and Daddy. And Matthew and Michaela."

James hugged Molly and met Laurel's and Garrett's gazes. His eyes were wet. Molly touched one of his tears. "It's okay, Grandpa. They're watching over us all the time. Aunt Laurel and Sheriff Garrett said so."

"I know." The old man cleared his throat. "Hope there's room for an old man on Christmas morning."

"It's Christmas!" Molly wiggled until James put her down. She looked around the room, past the princess palace. Her head dropped. "My letter didn't reach him."

Laurel knelt beside Molly. "Look at the beautiful princess palace. Santa knew exactly what you wanted."

"It's beautiful," she said, tears streaming down her face. "But I wanted to change my Christmas wish list."

Molly's tears broke Garrett's heart. "What do you want, sugar?" he asked gently.

"I want a family," she said, her voice small. "I know my mommy and daddy can't come back, but I don't want to be alone."

Garrett picked Molly up into his arms. He kissed her temple. "I think I can do something about that wish." He walked over to Laurel. "Wait right here."

He walked out the door and within minutes returned with a wrapped gift the size of a bread box. "Sit on the sofa, Molly. You, too, Laurel."

Garrett's nerves were stretched thin. James stood in the corner, a satisfied grin on his face. The old spy knew too much.

With his hand bracing himself, Garrett eased himself down on one knee. "Open the box, Molly."

She lifted the lid and peeked inside. A smile lit her face. A russet-and-white puppy poked its head out.

"For me?"

"You need a friend on this ranch, don't you think?"

Molly hugged the puppy to her. The mixed breed licked her face. "What's his name?"

"Whatever you want it to be, Molly."

She stroked his soft fur. "I love him, Sheriff Garrett."

"What do you think, Laurel?"

Her eyes were wet with tears. "I love him as much as I love you."

"Then maybe you should check out what's around his neck?"

Laurel grabbed the squirming bundle of fur and looked

at his collar. A ring swung back and forth. She stilled. "Garrett?"

"I love you, Laurel. I love Molly. Will you marry me?"

"Yes!" Molly shouted, hugging Garrett around the neck. "We want to marry you. Right, Aunt Laurel?"

"Right." Laurel's voice was thick with emotion. "I do."

"So we're going to live here forever and forever. You, me and Aunt Laurel. And Pumpkin Pie?"

"Who?"

"My doggy. His name is Pumpkin Pie. He told me."

"Yes, sugar, we'll all live together. Sometimes here, but sometimes in town. In Trouble, Texas."

Molly grinned up at them. "I think my daddy and mommy in heaven would like that. They told me almost every day that I was an angel always looking for trouble." She flung herself into Garrett's arms. "And we found it."

Garrett met Laurel's gaze over Molly's head. "Okay with you? If we're a family?"

She slipped the ring on her left hand and kissed his lips gently. "A family for Christmas is the best present ever."

* * * * *

"What's going on? Who are you really?"

Nick's face was stoic. His jaw set. Determination creased his forehead now dark with ash. "You're in serious trouble."

"Start talking or I'm going to scream." She crossed her arms over her chest. "Or, better yet, take me home."

"No can do. And you needed help."

"Damn it, Nick, you're creeping me out. You have to give me something more." She didn't know why he'd shown up. Nothing made sense. "At least tell me where you're taking me. I deserve to know what's happening."

He kept one eye trained on the rearview mirror as he reached in his pocket and pulled out a badge. "I'm a US Marshal."

All those times he'd stopped in the bakery and led her to believe he was flirting with her caused a red blush to crawl up her neck. A piece of her had enjoyed his attention, too. What an idiot. Was he monitoring her situation the whole time? "You're a radiologist."

His lips parted in a dry crack of a smile. "You don't believe me."

"Why didn't you mention this before?"

"It would've blown my cover."

WITNESS PROTECTION

BY
BARB HAN

MILLS & BOON

Published in Great Britain 2014
by Mills & Boon, an imprint of Harlequin (UK) Limited,
Eton House, 18-24 Paradise Road, Richmond, Surrey, TW9 1SR

© 2014 Barb Han

ISBN: 978-0-263-91380-4

46-1214

Harlequin (UK) Limited's policy is to use papers that are natural, renewable and recyclable products and made from wood grown in sustainable forests. The logging and manufacturing processes conform to the legal environmental regulations of the country of origin.

Printed and bound in Spain
by CPI, Barcelona

Barb Han lives in North Texas with her very own hero-worthy husband, has three beautiful children, a spunky golden retriever/standard poodle mix and too many books in her to-read pile. In her downtime, she plays video games and spends much of her time on or around a basketball court. She's passionate about travel, and many of the places she visits end up in her books.

She loves interacting with readers and is grateful for their support. You can reach her at www.barbhan.com.

My deepest gratitude goes to the men and women of the US Marshals Service for their many sacrifices.

A heartfelt thank you to my editor, Allison Lyons, and my agent, Jill Marsal, because you make dreams come true. I'm still pinching myself. Brandon, Jacob and Tori, you guys inspire me every day.

I love you with all my heart.

To my husband, John, you are the great love of my life. And this is one heck of an adventure.

Chapter One

A clink against the back door of the bakery sounded again. Sadie Brooks lost her grip on the twenty-five pound sack of flour she'd held. It struck the floor and a mushroom-shaped cloud of white powder formed over the bag's lip.

Creek Bend, Texas, was a far cry from Chicago, she reminded herself. No one from her past knew where she was. No one could hurt her. No one cared. And she was no longer Laura Kaye.

It was four-thirty in the morning in a town that rolled up the streets by eight. The noise was most likely a cat rummaging through trash. No big deal. Nothing scary.

"Only you and me are crazy enough to be up this early," she said to her two-year-old rescue dog, Boomer, while forcing air in and out of her lungs. He didn't so much as crack an eyelid. "And I think we both know I mean me."

Working when everyone else slept suited Sadie just fine. She'd had very little use for daylight or people ever since she'd been kidnapped two years ago.

Yes, she still flinched at every noise. Constantly checked over her shoulder at the slightest peep. But she was always ready. Always expecting the worst. Always on guard. And yet, the past year had been peaceful. There was no reason to believe anything would change save for the all-too-real feeling in the pit of her stomach screaming otherwise.

Being constantly on alert felt a lot like parking and then leaving her high beams on. Pretty soon her battery would run out.

Boomer whined in his sleep. Her protector? Now that was funny. She'd rescued a big dog for protection. She got the Scooby Doo of golden retrievers. All he wanted to do was eat, and he wouldn't scare away a cat. But he did make noise and his low-belly bark sounded fierce. Sadie figured it was good enough to make anyone think twice.

As she bent over to pick up the sack of white powder, another noise sent a chill skittering across her nerves. Boomer's head cocked at the unmistakable snick of a lock. Her heart drummed against her chest.

Using the lock was good, right? That meant someone with a key was most likely standing on the other side of the door. She thought of Claire, her very pregnant boss who was her only friend. With her baby due any day, she would be asleep right now.

Boomer, shackles raised, stalked toward the stock-room to investigate.

"It's okay, boy." She scoured the area looking for a weapon just in case. Was there anything she could use to defend herself? To protect Boomer? She moved toward the nearest counter.

A sparkle caught her attention. Light reflected from the blade of a knife. Her fingers shook as they curled around the black plastic handle.

Then everything went dark. No lights. It was too much of a coincidence to think the breaker could've been tripped. This blackout was on purpose.

Boomer's low throaty growl nearly stopped her heart. It

was the same noise he made when a stranger approached the lake house. Boomer had found an intruder. And they weren't familiar.

His barks fired like a machine gun, rapid and ear-piercing.

Sadie's adrenaline kicked into high gear. Her fight, flight or freeze response jacked through the roof. Every instinct inside her screamed, "Run!"

But she couldn't.

She wouldn't leave Boomer defenseless. Could she signal to him without giving away her location? No.

What about help? Her cell? Good luck finding her purse in the pitch-black.

She crouched and felt her way behind a rack filled with pastries. A hand covered her mouth. Her fingers, which had been curled around the knife handle, flexed cold air. She had been disarmed with frightening ease.

"Shh. Don't say a word or they'll hear you. Be very still." A second ticked by before she recognized the voice as Nick Campbell's. Why in the hell would a radiologist show up at the bakery in the middle of the night?

The last time a man took her by surprise she ended up spending two weeks in the ICU with facial lacerations and cracked ribs.

Determined to break free this time, she ignored the shivers running up her arms and bit Nick's hand.

"I said, 'be still,' and don't do that again," Nick said. His deep, quiet tone was different. Dark and dangerous. Experienced. And she knew instinctively not to push him.

With a total stranger somewhere in front of her and Nick's big frame behind her, she was trapped.

"I won't hurt you," he whispered.

What on earth was he doing here? And how had he gotten in without her noticing?

Boomer's barks mixed with growls and intensified.

Before she could wrap her brain around what was happening, Sadie felt herself being hauled toward the front door. The recollection of being snatched in daylight two years ago flooded her. His behavior brought up horrible memories. No way would Nick Campbell abduct her. Not a chance.

But what, besides a feeling that she could trust him, did she know about Nick? His brown eyes and black hair were almost always covered by a ball cap and shades. His shoulders hunkered forward, masking his true height. She hadn't fully realized his lethal potential until he stood behind her, his masculine chest flush with her back. She was five-foot-seven and he dwarfed her. He had to be more than six feet tall. Maybe six-one?

Neither his height nor his mannerisms had intimidated her before. She'd felt a sizzle of attraction, but then most of the women in Creek Bend seemed eager to get to know him better. With his forearm locked like a vise grip around her waist, she suddenly realized just how strong and buff he truly was.

"What do you think you're doing?" she whispered, choking down the anger rising inside her.

"No time to explain."

Hell if she'd wait. She wasn't about to be caught with no means of self-preservation again. She wasn't defenseless as she'd been before.

The first principle of judo was never to oppose strength to strength. Sadie shifted her weight enough to kick off the wall. She bucked, trying to throw him off balance while bracing herself to land on the painted concrete floor.

Didn't work.

Strong as an ox, he'd anticipated the move and counteracted by placing his feet in an athletic stance and tightening his grip. "I'll drag you out of here kicking and screaming if I have to, but we'll most likely both be killed."

"I can't leave my dog. Boomer's back there," she said, hating how her voice quivered and got all shaky with fear. She'd sworn no man would make her feel defenseless again. She realized, on some level, he was there to help, but she could walk for herself.

She kicked and wiggled. His grip was too tight.

It surprised her that a nerdy work-at-home radiologist knew how to counteract her martial arts moves. He also knew the back of the bakery well enough to navigate in the dark. She couldn't even do that without bumping into something and she'd worked there for a year.

Fighting was no use. She would bide her time and break free the second the opportunity presented.

"I'll go back for him. Once you're safe in the truck," he said. "Trust me."

She snorted. "Why? Because I know so much about you?"

"I can explain everything. Once you're out of danger."

Bright Christmas lights lit a cloudless sky. Once they were out of the building, she could see. Nick's expression was that of soldier on the front line.

He tucked her in the truck and then closed the door. The lock clicked. Trust him?

The door handle didn't work. She rammed the door. All that did was hurt her shoulder. Try again and there'd be a nasty bruise. There had to be another way. She banged on the window. "Hey!"

She tried to pop the lock. Nothing.

Spinning onto her back, she used a front kick to drive

the heel of her foot into the door, praying she could find
the sweet spot. No good.

She scrambled to the front seat. By the time she
gripped the handle, she heard a horrific boom from the
alley. The bakery caught fire. She couldn't catch her
breath enough to scream.

The world closed in around her, and her stomach
wrenched. Boomer!

Shattered glass littered the sidewalk. Thick black
smoke bellowed from every opening.

What was left of the front door kicked open and out
strode Nick, coughing, with her hundred-pound mutt in
his arms.

As soon as she got a good look at him saving her dog,
her heart squeezed and a voice inside her head warned,
Uh-oh.

Out of the ashes and burning timber, he moved toward her, carrying her dog as if Boomer weighed nothing. Nick opened the back door of the truck and gently
placed the dog on the seat.

"What's going on? Who are you really?"

There was something about his compassion with the
animal, something nonthreatening about him that kept
Sadie's nerves a notch below panic.

His face was stoic. His jaw set. Determination creased
his forehead now dark with ash. "You're in serious trouble."

Icy tendrils closed around her chest. "What are you
doing here showing up out of nowhere like that? Who
was coming in the back door?"

He started the ignition.

"Start talking or I'm going to scream." She crossed
her arms over her chest. "Or, better yet, take me home."

"No can do. And you needed help."

"Dammit, Nick, you're creeping me out. You have to give me something more."

His determination was written all over his squared jaw. He had obviously saved her life. He wasn't there to hurt her. She didn't know why he'd shown up. Nothing made sense. "At least tell me where you're taking me. I deserve to know what's happening."

He kept one eye trained on the rearview mirror as he reached in his pocket and pulled out a badge. "I'm a U.S. Marshal."

Her brain scrambled. Where was Charlie? He was her handler. And what did Nick mean he was a U.S. Marshal? All those times he'd stopped in the bakery and led her to believe he was flirting with her caused a red blush to crawl up her neck. A piece of her had enjoyed his attention, too. What an idiot. Was he monitoring her situation the whole time? She needed to call Charlie and find out what was going on. For now, it was best to ignore her embarrassment and play dumb. "You're a radiologist."

His lips parted in a dry crack of a smile. "You don't believe me."

"Why didn't you mention this before?"

"It would've blown my cover."

ANGER FLASHED IN Sadie's big green eyes as her gaze darted around the vehicle. Her phone was her only connection to her handler, and it was just as lost as she looked. She turned her attention to him, glaring as if this was all his fault.

"Sorry about your cell." He pulled a new one from the dash and handed it to her. The movement called attention to the bruise she'd put on the inside of his forearm when she'd tried to kick out of his grasp earlier. The memory of her slim figure and sweet bottom pressed against him stirred an inappropriate sexual reaction. Her flour-dotted pale pink V-neck sweater and jeans fit like a second skin over a toned, feminine body. Her fresh-baked-bread-and-lily scent filled the cab. "I didn't have time to retrieve your purse."

She looked at the phone as if it was a hot grenade. "Why should I trust you?"

Nick couldn't blame her. Her world was about to be turned upside down again, and he sensed she knew on some level. "You don't have a choice. I apologize for that."

She recoiled, most likely remembering being forced away from the only life she'd known in Chicago two years ago. His surveillance told him she'd made a home in Creek Bend and a friend in her new boss. The two had become close. Claire and her baby were a surrogate family to Sadie. He didn't like taking it all away again. He bit back frustration.

"Where are you taking me?" The fear in her voice was like a sucker punch to his solar plexus.

"Somewhere safe. Charlie's dead."

She gasped. Her shaky hand covered her mouth.

"How do you know? Did you…?"

"No. Of course not." She'd been taught not to believe anyone but Charlie. He had no idea how she would react now. He'd have to keep a close eye on her during the ride. "I know this is a lot to digest."

She sat there tight-lipped, looking as though she'd bolt if given the chance.

"This is real. You're in danger. I'm here to help."

Her angry glare trained on him. "Prove he's dead."

"Can't. Not tonight, anyway."

"Why? Shouldn't there be a news report? A U.S. Marshal dying should make the headlines."

"It's complicated."

"Then explain it to me slowly." She clenched her jaw muscles. Impatience and fear radiated from her narrow-eyed glare.

With her wavy brown hair pulled off her face in a ponytail, she could pass for a coed. Her lips were full, sexy. Not that they were his business. "He was found in his bed. A bullet through his brain. The agency is keeping his death under wraps."

"Oh, God. He was a nice man."

Nick bit out a derisive snort. "Good guys don't get in bed with the enemy."

"Are you saying what I think you are?" she asked incredulously.

"Yes, ma'am."

"I don't believe you. He brought me here. Set me up with this job. He would not help them."

He arched his brow. "Because he did a few nice things for you, he can't possibly turn into one of them?"

She stared at the road in front of them. If she bit down any harder on her bottom lip, she might chew right through it. "Don't twist my words. I know he was a family man. He cared about his work. I knew him better than you did. He wouldn't turn on me. Not now. Not after two years. Besides, what would he have to gain in hurting me?"

"Malcolm Grimes has been broken out of jail and someone on the inside helped. Your handler showed up at the prison two days before he escaped."

Her tight grip on her nerves shattered. Just like when a rubber band broke, Nick could almost see the pieces of rubber splintering in all directions. Her eyes closed. Her fingers pressed to her temples. Her body visibly shook. "He's out? Just like that?"

"I'm afraid so."

Her eyes snapped open and her gaze locked on to him. "How can you let that happen? Now he's free to come after me?" Her voice shook with terror.

"That's why I'm here."

"Let me get this straight. Grimes is out, and you automatically suspect Charlie? Wouldn't he be alive right now if he'd helped?"

"Not if he crossed Grimes. He was executed in his own bed. Someone was making a statement."

Weariness crept over her face as she gripped the phone, closed her eyes again and rocked back in her seat. "The first thing Grimes does after killing Charlie is come after me? Why? Wouldn't he figure you'd be waiting for him?"

"Your file's missing from Charlie's place."

She drummed her index finger on the cell.

"I'm supposed to tell you 'Pandora.'"

The tension in her face eased slightly even though she didn't speak. Her movement smoothed, timed with her calmer breaths. She stopped tapping on the cell. The safe word resonated. "Any idea why my boss chose Pandora as your safe word?"

"Yeah."

"Care to fill me in?" It wasn't as if he was asking for her Social Security number.

"Not really." A solemn expression settled on her almond-shaped face. "The bakery. Did they blow it up because of me?"

"Most likely."

"That was all Claire had to support her baby and now it's gone. Why didn't they just shoot me straight out?"

He tightened his grip on the steering wheel. "Good question. My guess is they were trying to ensure there'd be no mistakes. Easier to just blow up a building with you in it. Also has the added benefit of looking like it was an accident. It's tidier. Leaves less of a trail."

"So, it's over. Just like that. I walk away from everything I know one more time because of these jerks. I'm on the move again?"

He nodded.

"I didn't do anything wrong," she said fiercely.

"I know."

"Is this what I can expect the rest of my life? Because some guys want to murder and maim me?" She drummed her hands on the dash. Her tension was on the rise again.

"It shouldn't happen to good people."

"Save the speech. I've heard it before. 'Nice folks deserve better than this, but we have to do what we can to protect you. It's not your fault. Sometimes the system doesn't work.'"

"It's true."

She pressed her lips together. "Yeah? Well, your system sucks."

He could appreciate her anger. When his youngest sister was kidnapped and beaten by a crazed ex-boyfriend, Nick had hunted the teen down and nearly ended up in prison himself. His mom intervened while his grandmother called 911 to stop him from meting out his own justice. Sadie's haunted expression reminded him of his kid sister.

Under the circumstances, Sadie was doing well. Damn that his own anger rose thinking about the past. He already felt a connection to Sadie. His protective instincts flew into high gear the moment someone breached the bakery. He shouldn't care this much about a witness. "It'll keep you alive if you let it."

A beat of silence sat between them.

He risked a glance in her direction. A ball of fury formed in his throat at the tears streaming down her pink cheeks. From what he'd observed in the few weeks he'd been in Creek Bend, she worked hard. She was always on time. By all accounts she did a great job. He already knew about her resilience and courage. She seemed decent and kind. She deserved so much more.

He might have to take away her home again, but he would keep her safe.

Rather than debate the quality of the WitSec program at the U.S. Marshals Service, he dropped his defenses. The experience of growing up with four women under the same roof had taught him a thing or two about the point at which he'd lost a battle. He didn't need any of his experience to see this one was long gone. He raised his hands in the universal sign of surrender then dropped them right back on the steering wheel. "I didn't say any of that to upset you."

She folded her arms. "It's fine. I guess you're right. The program probably helps a lot of people. Just not me. I get to be the exception. I might be the unluckiest person on the planet. Even a program meant to help people makes my life miserable."

"For what it's worth, I'm truly sorry."

She looked at him long and hard. Her green-eyed stare pierced him. "Your boss, Mr. Smith, said whatever I stepped into opened a Pandora's box because they started fighting to take over Grimes's territory."

"Sounds like something my boss would say." He clenched his back teeth. "It did. Violent crime shot through the roof after we put Grimes away."

"Doesn't seem like I helped by having him locked away."

"Testifying was still the right thing to do. You saved a lot of innocent lives."

"Did I? Not mine. And what about Claire? Now I've ruined the business of the one person who I could count on as a friend."

"She'll receive money. I guarantee it. Citizens are safer with these guys off the streets."

"But they aren't, are they?" she snapped. "I wasn't even the one Grimes wanted. They kidnapped me by mistake. The woman they were after moved away and disappeared. She was smart. Not me. I believed your boss. I testified. Look at me now. Shouldn't you check in with him or something?" She palmed the cell, scrolling through the names in the contact list with her thumb.

It didn't take long.

There were only two. Nick Campbell. William Smith.

They were the only two people in her world for now. Nick couldn't imagine being that alone.

"Nah. There's only one reason I want you to call that number. Anything happens to me, don't hesitate. Make contact. Smith will tell you where to go and what to do."

Her grip tightened on the cell phone. "But you're with me. Anything happens to you and we'll both be dead."

"Nothing's going to happen to either of us. I promise. I only gave you the number to ease your concerns."

"If one U.S. Marshal's already dead, our odds don't seem all that great." Her words came out raspy and small.

The back windshield shattered. The truck swerved as he slammed the brakes.

A truck rammed his left bumper, sending his vehicle into a dangerous spin. He grasped the steering wheel, turning into the skid.

Chapter Two

Cold blasted Sadie. "Boomer!"

He'd never been good at car rides. She glanced in the backseat. He was practically plastered to the floor mat. His fear might've just saved his life.

"Get down." Nick's tone changed to a dark rumbling presence of its own.

Rocks and dirt spewed from under the tires as he navigated the vehicle back onto the roadway.

Sadie curled into a ball on the floorboard. "That the same person who was trying to get through the door at the bakery?"

"No."

She flashed her gaze toward him. "How do you know?"

Oh. Right. He'd killed him. The soot on his face outlined the scratches he'd collected. Looking at this guy—this new Nick—she believed him capable of doing whatever was necessary to get the job done. The transformation from the old one still shocked her. The once almost nerdy-looking facade a stark contrast to the battle-weary expression of this warrior. If he drove as well as he hid his identity, she had no doubt he'd get them out of this.

The truck swerved and jolted her thoughts to the very real threat screaming toward the back bumper.

The image of Nick calm and collected despite the danger brought her panic levels down.

He aimed a revolver out the back and fired a round.

The squeal of tires, the crunch of metal against a tree, and she knew another bad guy was dead.

Nick floored the gas pedal. He had the wheel in one hand and his weapon in the other.

An invisible band tightened around her rib cage.

Nick looked at her, his expression serious and reassuring. "We're okay."

"I know."

With one hand on the wheel and his eyes on the road, he placed the gun on the seat between them and offered a hand up. She pulled herself up onto the bench seat.

He turned the heater on high and then shrugged out of his leather jacket. "This should help."

She realizing for the first time her teeth were chattering. Wrapping the coat around her shoulders, she was flooded with the masculine scent of leather.

"I'm not going to let anyone hurt you." He was sweet to make the promise even if they both knew he didn't have control over what happened to her.

Even so, her heart rate slowed a notch. "Th-thank you."

With the gun next to her, prickly heat flushed her neck and face. An overwhelming fear pressed down on her body, making her limbs heavy.

Concern wrinkled his charred forehead. "What's wrong?" His gaze shifted from the firearm to her face then back to the road. "This? Does seeing my gun bother you?"

"It's okay. I have to get used to it, right? This is my life now." She heard how small her voice had become, hating that she'd lost her power by looking at the piece of cold metal.

"Not today." He slipped the weapon into an ankle holster and tugged his jeans over it.

She'd barely noticed his legs until that moment. Her gaze moved up to the line of his muscular thighs pressing against the denim material of his jeans. A black V-neck T-shirt highlighted a broad chest and arms as thick as tree trunks.

An electric current swirled inside her body. This strong man looked more than capable of protecting her. He seemed able to handle anything that came along. She realized why she'd never noticed how adept and strong he'd been before. There had been no reason to. He'd played the work-at-home radiologist to perfection. Most of the women in Creek Bend had noticed his seriously good looks and lucrative career, while she'd spent the past year trying to avoid everyone—especially men. She'd closed her eyes to anyone she'd dismissed as a nonthreat.

Odd as it sounded, she would miss seeing Nick come into the bakery right before her shift ended. Different didn't begin to describe the change in him. She'd already been introduced to his powerful chest and lean, muscled thighs when her body had been pressed against his earlier. Forget about his strong hands around her and the sensual current they had sent through her body.

This close, she could see his almost overwhelmingly attractive facial features. His brown eyes had cinnamon copperlike flecks in them. His jawline with two days' worth of stubble a sharp contrast to full, thick lips—lips she had to force her gaze away from. His dense, wavy hair was as black as his shirt. The combination made for one seriously hot package.

She thought about how fast the bakery had gone up

in flames. Her boss and only friend who had become like family would have to start over. Claire had worked hard to build her business. The building would be burned to the ground by now. A little piece of her broke at the thought of never seeing Claire's baby. Her only real friend was out of her life forever.

Friend? Sadie almost laughed out loud. What kind of friend didn't even know her real name?

A sign that read Now Leaving Creek Bend filled the right corner of the window.

She thought about the town Christmas party she wouldn't attend. About the baby she would never meet. About the family of her own that was so out of reach. About all the things she would never have.

Burning tears rolled down her cheeks.

A feeling of loss anchored in her stomach.

Straightening her back, she clicked on her seat belt. Let those bastards get inside her head, and they won. "There are a few knickknacks back home I wish I had." She glanced at her taupe boots with teal outlay and sighed. "At least I get to keep these."

Nick's gaze intensified on the road. "I already sent someone for your things."

"Seriously? Isn't that against the rules or something?"

He shrugged. "We'll keep 'em somewhere locked away until it's safe to retrieve them."

"I don't know what to say. That was very kind of you. I was told everything had to be left behind when this happens."

"It's not the way I work." His gaze intensified on the stretch of road in front of him. "You deserve to have your clothes at least."

Appreciation washed over her. She knew not to trust

it. "This is the second time I've thanked you since we've been in the truck."

Sadie forced herself to remember other positive things as she reached in the backseat to pet Boomer. Not losing everything was a huge blessing.

Besides, the alternative—giving up—was never an option. All she could gain there was depression. Feeling sorry for herself wouldn't change her circumstances. Alcohol? A drinking problem didn't sound like the worst demon to battle at the moment. But, no, she'd never really taken to the taste other than an occasional glass of wine.

She turned toward the stranger beside her as he pulled the truck off the main road. "Is Nick Campbell your real name?"

"Yes," he said with the voice that was like a caress on a cold winter's night. He arched his dark brow.

"Are you telling me the truth?"

"You deserve that much from me."

A traitorous shiver skittered across her nerves. It was chilly outside. Now that the window had shattered, there was nothing keeping out the frost. The shiver came from being cold, she told herself, and not the sexual appeal of the man next to her. "This can't be the work of Grimes alone, can it? Is he big enough to take out a U.S. Marshal?"

"It's stupid to come after you. The agency has been keeping a close eye on everything since his escape. Smith and I were hoping he'd leave you out of this. And, yes, there's more to this than we know as of now. But we'll figure the rest out."

"Doesn't sound good for me. Maybe he wants revenge badly enough to risk everything?"

"He didn't get where he is by being stupid."

"He's been out for a month? Timed with when you showed up?"

"We received intel something was brewing. My boss wanted to make sure our bases were covered. I came out a few days before he broke out."

The Christmas party invitation she'd received flashed in her mind. A small town holiday scene complete with four-foot-high snowdrifts piled on either side of the road. There were glowing street lamps. The scene reminded her very much of Creek Bend sans the snow. Sadie's boss had all but made her promise she'd show. "What would make him risk his safety to find me? He can't possibly want to go back to prison. I mean, why me? Why now?"

His jaw muscle ticked. "Revenge."

That one word packed more power than if she'd been struck with a fist. "I was upset before. I didn't mean to insult the agency. I honestly appreciate everything you guys have done to keep me alive so far."

"Our failures are putting your life at risk."

And keeping her on the run. Creek Bend would start its day perfectly timed to the sunrise in another forty-five minutes. Life would go on without her.

Claire would have her baby. Sadie would never hold the little girl she'd anticipated for so long. Claire had become more than a friend, she'd become like family. And now everything was gone.

At least she still had Boomer. He was tucked safely in the backseat. "None of this has ever made sense to me. I didn't do anything wrong and yet I'm the one slinking out of town in the middle of the night."

SADIE'S SADNESS WAS PALPABLE. Worse yet, she put up a brave front.

One look into those haltingly green eyes, transparent like single perfect gemstones, and Nick might forget his real reason for being there. Protect his witness without getting overly involved. Not generally a problem for him. Discipline was more than his middle name. It was his life's creed.

Nothing and no one had threatened his ability to focus. Or could.

This was different. Her circumstance reminded him too much of his little sister's. The thought of another woman being targeted by a man hell-bent on revenge when she was innocent ate at his insides. Many of the people in the program he came across could use a fresh start. Giving them a new job and home also provided a new lease on life. Not Sadie. What had she done wrong? Nothing. By all accounts, she should've had a promising future with a business consultant in accounting. She'd be well on her way to two-point-five kids, a big house and a Suburban.

None of *this* had been invited into her life. A crazed criminal had sent her to the ICU.

People called her lucky for living.

Luck wasn't her gig. She'd had enough courage to defy the odds and enough spunk to fight when her future was bleak.

What she had was a hell of a lot better than chance.

And yet, seeing her now, she looked small and afraid. Chin up, she was determined not to give into it.

He'd give anything to ease her concern and put a smile on her face. Wanting to protect her and needing to were two different things.

Why was he already reminding himself of the fact?

He pulled the truck onto a narrow dirt road. "I have better transportation stashed here. Besides, we won't make it five miles without drawing attention with the condition of the truck."

Winding down the lane wasn't a problem. Turning off the lights and navigating in the dark was a different story. He'd memorized the area easy enough. But he hadn't had time to make a night run.

A thunk sounded at the same time they both pitched forward. The air bags deployed. Sadie gasped and Boomer yelped as he banged against the back of the driver's seat.

"Hold on, boy," she said.

Nick focused on Sadie first. "You okay?"

"Fine."

He hopped out of the truck and opened the door to the backseat of the cab. Running a hand over the frightened dog, Nick didn't feel anything out of the ordinary. He checked his hand for blood. Relief was like a flood to dry plains. "Shook him up a bit."

She struggled to work herself free from the airbag, and then climbed over the seat. "But he's fine, right?"

"Yep." Nick owed the big guy upstairs one for that.

What caused the wreck? Had he misjudged the road?

He circled to the front of the cab. His eyes were adjusting to the dark. The sight before him pumped his stress level fifty notches. A tree blocked the road.

He seriously doubted nature had caused the barrier. Had someone found his hiding spot?

A branch snapped to his right. Could be an animal evading, but he wouldn't take unnecessary chances with his cargo. He moved to the truck. "We can't drive through. We'll have to go on foot."

Sadie nodded, coaxing Boomer to follow.

Nick shouldered his backpack. They had enough

supplies to last a couple of days. He hadn't expected to need them.

"Where're we going?" Sadie's eyes were wide and she blinked rapidly. Fear.

"There's a place about a day's hike from here. If we can make it by nightfall, we'll have safe shelter."

Her gaze locked on to the barrier behind them. "That wasn't an accident, was it?"

He shrugged his shoulders casually, not wanting her to panic. "I'd rather not take anything for granted."

The crack and crunch of tree limbs on the ground grew louder.

Boomer faced the woods on the opposite side of the truck. His shackles raised, and he growled low in his belly.

Nick reached for Sadie's hand, and then wound his fingers through hers.

"We have to go. *Now.*"

Chapter Three

Nick pulled Sadie into the woods at a dead run. Branches slapped her face and arms, stinging her skin.

Boomer quickened his stride, keeping pace by her side step for step.

They could've been banging drums for all the noise they made. No chance they'd slip through the brush unheard. Nick seemed more intent on moving fast. Another reason her pulse kicked up and her anxiety levels roared.

Her thighs hurt. Her lungs burned. She pushed forward, determined not to complain.

He stopped at the edge of a lake. She collapsed to the ground, gasping for air. Her ears were numb, frozen. Every other body part overheated.

Sunlight pushed through the trees, which meant they'd been on the go at least forty-five minutes. Her lungs felt as if they'd explode, whereas Nick hardly seemed affected. Of course he was in shape. His job—his *real* job—would demand excellent physical conditioning. She forced her gaze away from the way his muscles expanded against his jeans when he walked.

The rustle of leaves and bird whistles were the only noise. "Is it safe to take a break?"

He stood, listening. Then he scanned the area. "We can take a minute."

"What about the racket we made?"

"I made a few shortcuts that made it harder to track us." He opened his pack and handed her a bottle of water, taking one for himself. "Let me know when you think you can move again."

She could barely open the lid. Tired and dirty, her stamina waned. The cool liquid was a godsend to her parched mouth. "So what's the plan?"

"Shelter. But it's a ways ahead," he warned. "It isn't much, but it'll get us through the night."

"No. I mean ultimately. Where is all this hiding going? Surely no one expects me to keep this up forever."

"If you're tired we can stop."

"I don't mean now."

His face tensed. His glare intensified. His slack jaw became rigid.

"What? No answers?"

"You want the truth? We catch him, figure out who else is involved and why, and get your life back." He turned to face the lake.

"I doubt that," she huffed. "What good did it do me to testify? I never got my life back. His men kept searching for me. I've had two homes in two years. Now, he's out. Hunting me. I'm running for my life. Again. Your boss made promises he didn't keep."

Nick bent down and poured water on his palm, allowing Boomer a drink. When the dog was hydrated, Nick took a swig of water. "He shouldn't have done that."

"It was all well and good when people wanted me to help them." She pulled her knees into her chest. "I'm sure it didn't hurt his career to be able to put a man like Grimes away."

He whirled around on her. "What's that supposed to mean?"

"How much do you trust your boss?" Anger had her bating him into an argument.

"Smith is fine. You're tired."

"Is that right?"

"I hope so because if this is your personality, it's gonna be a long night."

"You think this is funny? Forgive me if I don't laugh along with you."

Nick cleared his throat. "I never said that. I'm not here to hurt you. In case you hadn't noticed, I'm trying to help."

"For how long? You can't watch me the rest of my life. Maybe I should go after him for a change." What she'd said was the emotional equivalent of raising a red blanket in front of a bull. She had two choices. Fight or cry. She'd rather fight.

"Now you're being crazy."

Tears welled, but she'd be damned if they were going to fall. "First I'm tired. Now I'm crazy. Which is it?"

"I get why you're…freaking out."

"Do you? You think you already know what's going on inside my head? Why don't you tell me, then, because I'm confused." She shot daggers at him with her glare. Fear pushed away the cold air, replacing it with heat. Her body vibrated from anger, her defense mechanism for not losing it and crying.

She stood and took a step toward him. She expected to see anger or confusion. Instead, he faced her with his whole body. His hands were open at his sides. His relaxed gaze moved smoothly from her eyes to her mouth and back. His lips softened at the corners in a smile.

She steeled her breath, but nothing prepared her for the warmth of his big hand on her shoulder.

The fight drained from her.

"We have a long walk ahead. You should save your energy."

Her chest deflated. She plopped onto the cold ground. Boomer nuzzled his cold wet nose on her neck.

"Give me a minute. I'll be fine."

THE LAST THING Sadie looked was fine. If he'd learned one thing from having two sisters, the word *fine* didn't mean good things. He'd give her a minute to regroup even though he'd feel a lot better if they kept moving. They'd put some distance between them and whoever was following, but for how long? "For what it's worth, my sisters tell me I'm stubborn. If I were in your situation, I'd be crazy, too."

She rewarded him with a smile warmer than a campfire. "Smart women."

"Don't tell them that." He bent down on his knee, fighting the urge to provide more comfort than his words.

"Do I detect a case of sibling rivalry?" Her brow arched.

"No. But I do have two younger sisters to keep track of."

"You must be exhausted."

"Not really. They can take care of themselves mostly. Both work in law enforcement. They humor me, though."

She relaxed a little more. "Bet I could learn a thing or two from them."

"I doubt it. You're a survivor."

"How do you know?"

"You've made it this far."

"You never told me where we're going. Do you have a hunting cabin or something out here?" she asked.

"Guess I didn't adequately fill you in. I'd apologize but I'll just do it again. My sisters tell me I tend to get in a zone then information comes out on a need-to-know basis."

"Does that mean your brain can act and speak at the same time?"

He laughed. "It's possible. Words are empty, though." He could hear his grandmother's voice in the back of his head echoing the same sentiment. "Actions are better."

She'd also taught him to be grateful for what he had instead of sorrowful for what he'd lost. Some lessons were easier to catch on to than others.

Sadie's laugh had the same effect as the first spring flower opening. "You've been surrounded by a lot of smart women in your life, haven't you? You're lucky."

"Not sure if you would hold on to that thought if you spent more than five minutes with them."

Her gaze focused on the water and she absently picked at a leaf. "I'm afraid I don't have a big family to draw experience from. It's just me. Has always been just me."

He nodded.

She glanced at him. "Right. You already knew that didn't you? You probably know everything about me, don't you?"

"The agency gave me your intel. For what it's worth—"

"Don't apologize. You'll just do it again when you need information about someone." She half smiled.

"True."

"I know you were doing your job. I'm not blaming you personally. It's just surreal to me that there's some file out there with my life history in it."

Silence sat between them.

"It's been me, alone, for so long, I can't remember what it's like to have a real family. It was just me and my parents growing up. I never had more than that. They were always working. I wouldn't know what to do with siblings who watch over me."

"A big family sounds like heaven in theory. In real life, not so much. Add my mom and grandmother into the mix and I've had four women constantly telling me what to do for most of my life." He chuckled.

"Sounds like the promised land to me right now."

"Mom had a lot of mouths to feed when my dad disappeared. She'd come home beat, but tried not to show it. I became a handful. My dad leaving didn't do good things to my head. But then I saw how much pain I added to my mom. She was already devastated. Being the oldest, I got a front-row seat to her pain."

"From the looks of it, you turned out okay."

"That's still up for debate."

"You're a U.S. Marshal. You change people's lives with your work. I'd be dead right now if not for you. I'm sure dozens of other people would say the same thing."

He tightened his grip on the water bottle as he screwed on the lid. "Think you can walk?"

"I'd like to hear more about your family." Her voice hitched on the word *family*. Was she thinking about his family, or the husband and kids she should already have with the accounting consultant in Chicago?

A twinge of jealousy heated his chest. He ignored it. "There isn't much else to tell. I have two brothers."

She rolled her eyes. "Are you focused again?"

He couldn't help but smile. "Not intentional. I'm thinking about getting us both through the night."

She straightened her back and glanced around. "Any chance they gave up and went home?"

"They've come this far. They won't stop looking."

"You said there's a place we can stay?"

He nodded.

"That the best idea? I mean, shouldn't we get out of here altogether? Maybe call for backup?"

"Afraid we're on our own this time." A warm sensation surged through him when he thought about the implication of being alone with her in the small cabin all night. One bed.

She turned and his gaze drifted down the curve of her back to her sweet bottom. Another time, different circumstances, he could think of dozens of things he'd like to do with her on that bed. This wasn't the time for inappropriate sexual fantasies.

"Why are we on our own?"

"Smith made the call. I agree. Can't risk anyone on the inside knowing your status or whereabouts in case there's a leak. We have to consider the fact this might be bigger than Charlie."

"How many people in the agency know about me?"

"Now?"

She nodded.

"As far as we know, me and Smith. We'd like to keep it that way."

"Then what are you afraid of?"

"If Grimes found a way in with Charlie, I wonder what other connections he made. We think we're the only two with your intel, but we can't be sure. Your file was with Charlie. Now it's missing. Did he tell anyone else about you before he was killed? We have no clue. There's too much uncertainty."

"I know what they did to me, but what other crimes are they responsible for?"

"Grimes is well-connected. Has his hands in contract

killings, loan sharking, gambling, bribery—to name a few. His channels run from South America to Canada, and straight through Chicago."

"Sounds big-time."

"Ever play the game Six Degrees of Separation?" He looked at her.

"Yeah. Sure. Why?"

"He's the Kevin Bacon of crime."

She shifted her weight and looked at him. "Or he was..."

"Until you put him away, which started a war. Now that he's out, we have no idea what to expect."

"Pandora's box?"

"Armageddon."

"Still doesn't explain what he wants with me. Except good old-fashioned revenge, I guess." Sadie stood and wiped the dried leaves clinging to the back of her jeans.

"He's not exactly a nice guy. He's capable of doing a lot of damage on his own. We can't underestimate him or his connections."

"Lucky me."

Nick closed the water bottles, zipped the pack and shouldered it. The winds had picked up and the air had a cold bite. "We'll catch him. Or the marshals, or the feds will."

"You believe that, don't you?"

"It's my job. The system isn't perfect. Sometimes it fails. I see it succeed ninety-nine percent of the time."

She stared at him incredulously. "You don't need to tell me about the system. I'm living proof it doesn't work."

Nick didn't offer a defense. Sadie was the exception. He inclined his chin and powered forward.

The best thing he could do for her was give her a half-decent night of sleep in a comfortable bed. A hot shower and warm bowl of soup would defrost her and revive her energy.

"You good at what you do?"

"The best."

"Excellent. I wouldn't want to be stuck out here with an amateur." She turned and made kissing noises at Boomer, who dutifully followed.

Nick kept a brisk pace until they reached the small cabin before dark, only stopping long enough to eat a Power Bar for lunch. Sadie followed close behind; the crunch of tree branches under her boots and her labored breathing the only indication that she kept going.

The first thing he did when they got inside was to fill a bowl of water for her dog. Boomer trotted over as though they'd become best friends. Maybe they had. They had a common bond. Protecting Sadie. Nick scratched the big red dog behind the ears.

"Shower in the bathroom works. Water's warm."

"Sounds like paradise."

"This place isn't much, but it'll get us through the night."

Her gaze moved around the one-room cabin, stopping on the twin bed. "Rustic, but has everything we need. Is it yours?"

"Belongs to a buddy of mine. Keeps it for when he wants to be alone. There's nothing and no one around for miles."

"He knows we're here?"

"Doesn't need to."

"How do you know he won't come walking through that door any minute? Or, worse, in the middle of the night, and scare us to death?"

"He's out of the country right now. We met in the military. He's career." He walked to the bathroom and back, delivering a dark green towel. "He'd look me up if he was on the continent."

"Fair enough."

"This place isn't exactly the Ritz-Carlton, but it serves our purpose for tonight."

She tugged the towel from his hand. Her green eyes sparked with her smile as she studied the gold shag carpeting, a relic from the '70s. "I had no idea the government paid so well. Maybe I should consider enlisting."

"They can be generous."

She glanced from the carpet to Nick. "No one can accuse this place of being boring. That's for sure."

"And we have the added benefit of being completely off the grid."

"Right. I almost forgot. The whole part about trying to keep me tucked away and alive." Her smile faded.

Instead of taking a shower, she sat on the edge of the bed. "So what happens next?"

"You clean up. Then, I'll take a turn." He knew what she was asking. Problem was he didn't have an answer.

"I'm serious."

"You want the honest truth?"

"Yes. Of course."

"I keep you alive tonight. Tomorrow, we'll figure out the rest. Find a good place to tuck you until this mess blows over and we fit all the puzzle pieces together." He ground his back teeth; didn't like this any more than she did, as evidenced by her frown.

"We? Does this mean you're staying with me?"

"I think it's best for now. With any luck, Smith will find Grimes, arrest him again. It'll turn out to be that simple, and you'll get a new home before sunrise."

She released a heavy breath. "I don't want a new home. Just a plain old home. I feel like I've been running so long

I can hardly remember who I was before all this started." She stood and walked, pausing at the bathroom door. "I guess it's only been two years."

He could see the anguish darkening her green eyes, the frustration and loss causing her shoulders to sag. "Twenty-four months can feel like an eternity."

"I got too comfortable in Creek Bend. Started to think I might actually build a life there." She closed the door behind her.

Everyone deserved a stable home, a base. Speaking of a life, Nick had almost forgotten about his. His grandmother's birthday party was in a couple of days. He'd been so busy with work he'd forgotten. Not that his sisters would've allowed him to be late. He'd have to ask why they weren't riding him about what present he planned to bring. They generally started a month early. For reasons he couldn't explain, a very big part of him wanted to make sure Sadie spent time with a real family.

Could he take her home with him?

Being with his family definitely qualified as *special*. He just wasn't sure she was ready for the whole clan. Besides, he'd be breaking protocol.

He rubbed the scruff on his chin. No. There had to be another solution. He moved to the kitchenette and emptied his pack. He made two sandwiches and heated soup. They had a few more minutes before the sun completely disappeared. They couldn't risk using electric after dark.

Sadie walked into the kitchenette after her shower. She'd changed into the shorts and T-shirt he'd left in the bathroom. Did her long legs feel as soft and silky as they looked? She stopped so close he could smell her shampoo and notice the freckle on the inside of her thigh. He looked up and his gaze followed a water droplet rolling down her neck and then onto her shirt. Full breasts rose and fell as lust swirled through him, pulsing blood south, which couldn't be more inappropriate.

He forced his gaze away, handing her a cup of heated soup before she could see the effect she was having on him. Stray beads of water anywhere on or near Sadie's body weren't part of this assignment.

He wrapped a peanut butter sandwich in a napkin. "I made sandwiches. It's not much but should keep your stomach from growling."

She accepted the food, looking far more excited about it than he expected. "Good protein. I used to love PB&Js."

"This is just a PB. Hope it works."

She took a bite. The moan she released wasn't his business, either. But it still stirred a feeling. "I'll just grab a quick shower. I already fed your dog. He should be good until morning. Save mine for when I get out."

Boomer was already curled up on the bed.

"Will you leave me your gun?" Her voice rose and shook.

"I thought it scared you."

"It does. To death. Even so, I'd rather be prepared in case I need it."

An emotion that felt a lot like pride swelled in his chest. "Do you know how to use one?"

"I took a class. After…"

He set the weapon on the bed. "Anybody comes through that door, aim and shoot."

Chapter Four

Sadie stared at the gun. Her body trembled. Her hand shook as she held on to her sandwich. Boomer moved to her side. His gaze trained on her. His hackles raised. His sixth sense on high alert.

She didn't have enough saliva to manage a good spit. Every bite of bread and peanut butter was the equivalent of rubbing sandpaper in her mouth. She set down her PB sandwich and picked up her water bottle, taking a sip to ease the dryness in her throat. She picked up her sandwich and took another bite, ignoring her racing heart.

She could do this. She could sit near the gun. She could finish her meal.

Every instinct in her body screamed *run*.

But she'd learned long ago her body and mind couldn't always be trusted. They'd played tricks on her since her ordeal two years ago, making her afraid of little noises and shadows. Since then, it didn't take much to sound off her alert systems and kick her adrenaline into high gear.

Calming breaths generally did the trick to help her relax.

She took a few.

Another bite of sandwich and she'd be fine.

There were times when life called for taking one minute at a time. This minute, she could handle life. She could take another bite.

Another minute passed and she managed to keep it together.

She didn't know if she should thank her judo instructor or hug her yoga coach, but right now she appreciated them both.

A few more minutes ticked by and she heard the water in the shower stop.

Nick didn't take long to towel off.

He came out of the bathroom wearing jeans low on his hips. He tucked the gun in his waistband. The sight of him shirtless sent a warm flush up her neck.

With him in the room, she didn't have to remind herself to take slow breaths anymore. He brought her nerves down by the sight of him, capable and strong.

Her tense muscles relaxed as he moved to the kitchenette and picked up his PB sandwich.

A few freckles and a raised line with deep ridges curved below his left shoulder blade. A scar?

She shivered thinking about the ones she'd collected. "I've been thinking about something. Why didn't they just wait for us at the car? They could've surprised us. Why block the road?"

He shrugged, causing his muscles to stretch and thin, his movement smooth and pantherlike. "Didn't think we should stick around long enough to find out. I stashed a backup vehicle not far from the site. There was only one way out. They must not've wanted us going anywhere in case we got past them."

Heavy pressure settled on her chest. "So, we're exactly where they want us?"

He took a bite of a sandwich, chewing as he turned. "I wouldn't say that. I doubt they figured we'd have another escape route. This cabin is too out of the way for them to know about. It's the reason we walked all day. I didn't want to be anywhere near where they'd expect us. That being said, we still have to be careful. No lights after dark."

Sadie shifted her position, stretching her sore legs. "I have proof of all the walking, too. Right here in my calves."

"Sorry. A good night's rest will help. A few stretches will do wonders, too."

Night would fall soon and everything would be black. The small space felt intimate. She pushed off the bed and walked into the kitchenette. "You did everything else. Kept us alive. The least I could do was walk to safety."

"We'll have a few more miles of hiking tomorrow. Part two of my backup plan."

"Any chance you have a horse or a four-wheeler stashed out there? I don't think my legs can take another round of Goldilocks tromping through the forest."

The corners of his lips curled. He took the last bite of sandwich. "Boomer here will keep the wolves away. Won't you, buddy?"

Boomer craned his neck and his ears perked up.

"I doubt that." She didn't see the need to explain her dog's deficiencies when it came to being badass.

"I can help with sore calves." Nick placed his hand on the small of her back, urging her to the bed before dropping down on one knee in front of her. He took her calf in his hand, rolling his thumbs along the muscles. An electric current shot up her leg.

She picked up the water bottle and squeezed, praying electricity wouldn't be conducted. The current ran hot enough to singe her fingers. His hands on her leg felt as if they belonged there.

"You know I'm going to find him, right?"

"Then what? Put him away and start the process of relocation all over?"

"Lock him away for good this time."

"And if he gets out again? What then?"

"We'll throw away the key this go-round. I know you don't trust the law. Hell, I can't blame you. But it works most of the time. And when it does, everyone is safer."

"You said this might be more complicated than you originally thought. What does that mean?"

"All we know for sure is that the case involves Grimes and your old handler. We don't know how the two are connected aside from you. Is he out for revenge? Or is it something more?"

"So you think this could be a lot bigger than Charlie and Grimes?"

"Yeah. I do. All I have to go on so far is gut instinct, a dead marshal and an escaped convict. You're the only link I have."

"Sounds like a mess. How on earth did you end up stuck with me?"

How DID NICK explain he'd practically volunteered for the case?

"Smith asked my professional opinion about your case. He needed someone he could trust. He was leaning toward pulling you. I wanted to give you a chance to stay put." Those were the basic facts. All she needed to know. Besides, he couldn't explain to her what he didn't understand. From the moment he'd picked up her file and saw her picture a warning bell had fired and his heart stirred. He hadn't heard that sound or felt that feeling since the first time he saw his high school sweetheart, Rachael.

Hadn't heard it once since her death. Nick figured

he was broken now and she'd taken that piece of him with her.

"Where do you even start looking for a man like Grimes? Someone with enough power to get to a U.S. Marshal?"

"He runs a tight operation. No one talks. We never would have convicted him without your testimony."

"At least I won't have to go through another trial. See him again, hear his voice…" Her entire body shuttered.

"No." He didn't want her to relive the experience, either. "His conviction still stands. If anything he's made appeal impossible. I'm sure his lawyers are frustrated. We'll get him and keep him locked up this time."

"You said he moves illegal stuff from South America to Canada. To do that, he must have connections in both. Maybe I'll get lucky and he'll leave the country."

He issued a grunt. "You don't trust me to catch him?"

She laughed. Her smile broke through the worry lines bracketing her mouth. "It's not you."

"Oh, we're going to have *that* conversation. It's *you* and not *me*." His attempt to lighten the mood was met with another smile.

His cell vibrated. He glanced at the screen. A text from Smith.

Deputy Jamison is missing.

Nick pinged back, asking if this was somehow connected to Sadie's case.

Smith responded that he couldn't be sure, but his contact had said he'd been spotted with one of Grimes's men several times in the past couple of weeks.

Nick could feel Sadie watching him as he absorbed the news that a supervisor in the U.S. Marshals Service might be involved in the case. Was Jamison in league with Grimes? With Charlie?

"What is it?"

"A supervisor inside the agency is being investigated." The reality staring at him from his three-by-four-inch screen startled him. Grimes's involvement with the agency could very well move up the chain. Sadie had never been more in danger.

"Whoever is doing this, I screwed with his livelihood. A man like that isn't going to forget, now is he?"

"Not likely."

"Then he'll keep coming at me until I'm dead." It wasn't a question.

"Not if I can get to him first."

"But there's more than just him involved."

He set his cell on the floor, and added pressure to the muscle in her silky calf. "When he was in jail, his business was the most vulnerable. His men were busy keeping rivals from taking over. Now, everything's changed. With him out running free, he can focus on what he wanted to get done. And, yes, his plans most likely involved leaving the country at some point. I'd almost hoped he was going to do that before because it meant he wouldn't be coming after you."

"I'm just unlucky, I guess." She clasped her hands. Subject closed.

He could see fear in her green eyes and it ate at his gut. He shouldn't want to be her comfort.

"I noticed a scar on your back. Mind if I ask how you got it?" She turned the tables.

"A stint in the army."

"Did you serve overseas?"

"One tour in Afghanistan was all it took to figure out

military life wasn't for me. I got out when my number came up. Decided to fight the bad guys at home instead."

"We're lucky to have you here."

He cracked a smile, trying to break the tension. "*You* are not lucky."

"That's the understatement of the century." She rolled her eyes and almost smiled. "In a weird way, this is kind of…nice. I'm not used to being able to talk about being in the program. It's hard to hold everything in all the time. Pretend to be someone you're not."

He nodded.

"I kind of like not having to lie to you about my background or who I am. I feel like I'm deceiving nice people all the time. Worse yet, I'm always afraid I'll slip and introduce myself by my real name. I've always been a terrible liar. I walk around feeling like a fraud."

"I can imagine."

She looked straight at him. "What happened to the witness who disappeared? Do you know?"

He hesitated for a second. "We tracked her into Canada. There wasn't much we could do when she crossed the border with her husband and kids. They had dual citizenship, so they didn't come back. Not that it would've done any good. No one can be forced to testify unless they have something to lose."

"What happened? I mean, she was obviously ready to go to trial at one point. What changed her mind?"

He looked at her deadpan. "She heard about what happened to you."

"Can't say I blame her." Sadie's eyes grew wide as she stifled a yawn. "No offense to the U.S. Marshals office."

"None taken. I get to walk away from most cases feeling good about the job I did. Then there are those rare ones like this."

"Thank you."

"For what?"

"Not calling me lucky."

He smiled warmly but didn't say anything.

"I try to be grateful no matter what. But after everything I went through it's hard sometimes," she said.

"I have a superstitious grandma who drilled that whole gratitude bit in my head. I dreamed about catching bad guys when I was little. Hell, who am I kidding? After my father disappeared, I did my level best to become one of them. Life sucked. I wasn't grateful for much of anything."

"Were you angry?"

He nodded.

"Your family help you get through it?"

He nodded again. "Not sure where I'd be without them."

"Sounds like you have a lot to be grateful for."

That much was true. "Remind me of that the next time I want to pull my hair from them driving me nuts."

She laughed and he could feel her relax in his hands. He couldn't touch her much longer without giving away the effect. He needed to think about changing the oil in his car or caulking the tub when he got home. Anything besides the way her milky-soft skin felt pressed against his thumbs and how she flared his instincts to protect her that went way beyond the badge.

"Besides, you can decide for yourself if you like them when you see them."

Chapter Five

Sadie's jaw went slack. "You're taking me to *your* house?"

"Not exactly. We're going to my grandmother's ranch. I grew up there. I've given this a lot of thought and it's the only place I can guarantee your safety."

She shook her head fiercely. "Not a good idea."

Concerned wrinkles bracketed his full lips as he stood, then sat next to her. The mattress dipped under his weight. "Why not?"

"You seem nice. It sounds like you have a terrific family. So, don't take this the wrong way, but I'm not going." She folded her arms and turned her back so he wouldn't see the tears welling in her eyes. No way would she drag sweet, innocent people into her personal hell. Whoever killed Charlie and infiltrated the U.S. Marshals Service wasn't someone to take lightly. She still had her doubts Charlie would turn on her but she couldn't ignore the evidence.

"I don't plan to give you a choice."

"I won't do it. You can't force me. I know my rights. I can walk out of the program anytime I want." She stood and then folded her arms.

"Talk to me. Tell me why this is a problem. It's my grandmother's birthday. There'll be lots of people around. You'll blend right in."

He came up behind her and brought his hand to rest on her shoulder. Her resolve almost melted under his touch.

She rounded on him, shooting daggers with her eyes. "Well, then, I'm really not going."

"Give me one good reason."

She didn't know how to be around a real family, that's why. "Because I don't want to go. I'd rather hide somewhere on my own while you do your family stuff. Maybe it's best if I strike out on my own, anyway. Especially if the Marshals Service has been compromised."

"You leave this program and you won't live an hour. I'm trying to do what's best for you."

His words nearly released the flood of tears threatening. He was right. She wasn't ready to relent. "Without including me in the decisions?"

"Of course you have a say. We can talk about options. I care about what you think, Sadie."

She rubbed her arms. Crying wouldn't change her mind. "It wouldn't be fair to put innocent people at risk because of me. That's why I don't think I should go to your family's place."

"All of my sisters and brothers work in law enforcement. You don't have to worry about them. They know how to handle themselves."

"Then I'm sure your wife has other plans for your family holiday than to hide me." Why did the word *wife* sit on her tongue so bitterly?

"I'm not married. And once you get there, you might change your mind about calling my brothers and sisters innocent." His steel voice warmed her as a wry grin settled over his dark features.

Being this close, she could see the depths of his brown eyes. The cinnamon copperlike flecks sparkled. He was attractive and fired off all her warning systems by being this close.

Her fight, flight or freeze response kicked in, escalating her pulse.

She didn't like danger. Danger caused her chest to squeeze. Danger had her waking up in the hospital in the ICU, and then on the run from everything familiar.

She focused on Boomer, who had moved to her side, and scratched him behind the ear.

Besides, she felt a little too relieved hearing the news Nick wasn't married. A man like him had to have someone waiting at home. If not a wife, then a girlfriend. Sadie needed to remind herself of that fact because when his dark gaze settled on her, places warmed that had been cold and neglected far too long. This close, he was almost too attractive. Nick was one seriously hot package. Why was she surprised by this admission?

Hadn't she been a little bit interested in him before?

An attraction now couldn't be more inappropriate. Her mind was grasping for a distraction, she reasoned, not wanting to admit Nick's true effect on her—her body.

She held up her hand, palm out. "I'm not agreeing to anything. But if I do decide to go to the ranch, what will you tell your family about me?"

"My first thought is to tell them we're a couple."

"And they'd believe you? Just like that? I thought you guys were close."

"We are. Which is why that wouldn't work. They'd see right through it. Besides, I've never lied to my family and I have no plans to start now. Momentary lapse in judgment on my part."

The suggestion of her and Nick being a couple should repulse her. The thought of most men touching her sent her straight to nausea. Not him. What had changed?

Nick.

He was strong and capable and gorgeous. She also felt as though he was the first person who had her back in a very long time. Charlie had done a good job. But she had been part of his work, his job, no more or less. With Nick, it felt personal.

But could she trust him?

There were too many sleepless nights under her belt to convince her to let her guard down. The few private judo lessons she'd taken had helped ease the nightmares. She'd even convinced herself to keep a gun in the house, although the sight still made her chest hurt and the air become thick around her. There was something about having the wrong end of one pressed to her forehead that made her heart race every time she saw a sleek metal barrel. She couldn't even watch those popular cop shows on television.

Had she gotten comfortable recently? Become sloppy?

There was a good reason. Creek Bend had started to feel like home. She had a new life and a dog for company. There were even nosy neighbors to round out her small-town experience. She'd settled into a rustic cabin near the lake that, against all evidence to the contrary when she'd first arrived, had become her safe haven. She loved her job at the bakery, even the zany hours. And some day, maybe, she'd learn to trust men again.

Nick the radiologist had rented the lake house adjacent to hers, and had made a habit of coming by the bakery in the mornings as soon as it opened and her shift ended. She could hardly fathom the muscled man sharing the cabin was the same Nick. Then again, it was his job to go unnoticed when it served him best. So, why did she feel betrayed?

She hated all the lying. Could she continue this facade

of a life? Lie to Nick's family? Deceive more people? "Can't we just be straight with them?"

"If I could tell them the truth, I would. I need to think about it first. They're law enforcement and Smith gave me strict orders not to risk exposing you."

"I already told you I'm a bad liar."

"The past couple of years have trained you better than you think. The whole time I watched you in Creek Bend, you didn't give yourself away. If I hadn't known in advance, I wouldn't have figured it out."

"My life depended on hiding my secret." She blew out a breath and then inhaled. The warmth of his body standing so close and the scent of citrus soap washed over her in a mix that was all virile and male. "Besides, I don't know if I could pull off pretending to be someone's girlfriend if I had to."

"Why not?" He seemed offended.

"I know you're here to help, but strange men still scare me."

"Maybe we should change that." He placed his hand behind her neck, leaned forward and pressed a kiss to her lips that made her body hum.

He pulled back first, leaving Sadie swirling with an emotion that felt an awful lot like need.

"We're not strangers anymore." He stretched out on the bed, clasped his hands behind his head and looked up at the ceiling. "We have all night to get to know each other better. Let the talking begin."

"WHAT DO YOU want to know first?" Nick had to repress the anger rising, burning a hole in his chest. He'd felt Sadie tremble when he'd touched her. His offer of comfort had had the opposite effect on her. Yet, it was something else that sizzled when they kissed.

When he'd put his hands on her calves, he'd felt her relax. He'd even felt a spark of something else. But he'd been on the floor in a less threatening position. When he sat beside her or stood next to her, he seemed to overwhelm her.

"Where'd you grow up?"

"Texas. In a small town outside Dallas on the ranch." He'd been grasping at straws when he offered to pretend she was his girlfriend. When he really thought about it, he'd never be able to convince his sisters she was his girlfriend. Not with his history. It was a desperate thought. His family would be very keen to figure out how Sadie had done what no other woman in seven years could. Make Nick fall in love again. He wouldn't bring a casual fling to the ranch.

"Did you have a lot of friends?"

"I had a lot of family. Not much time for anything else."

"Tell me about your brothers and sisters."

"You already know I have two brothers, Luke and Reed. My sisters' names are Meg and Lucy."

Sadie eased onto the edge of the bed. "And you're the oldest?"

"Correct. But that doesn't mean they listen to me." He chuckled. "I'm afraid they all have strong wills and minds of their own."

"And everyone works in law enforcement?"

"True. I guess we all felt the call to serve. Luke's FBI and Reed's Border Patrol."

"What about the girls?"

"Lucy works for the sheriff's office and Meg is a police officer in Plano. She's married to Riley and he works for the department, too."

"I take it they met through work."

He nodded. "You guessed right."

"What else should I know about you?"

"I can't think of much else." He'd always been there for his family, his mom. His other relationships were a bit more complex. After watching his mother's pain, seeing how much agony someone could go through when the one they loved walked out on them, a piece of Nick had closed off early on in life.

"What do you do when you're not working?"

"The usual guy stuff. Watch the Cowboys in football season. I like to work a good steak on the grill."

"Steak sounds like heaven about now." Her smile was the nearest thing to heaven he figured he'd get in this lifetime.

"I can't argue with that logic."

"What about school?" She turned on her side, facing him, and propped herself up on one elbow.

His eyes had adjusted to the dark and he could see her green eyes clearly. "Finished it as fast as I could and joined the military. I was the oldest, so I guess I felt the most responsibility for filling my dad's shoes. I tried to ease the financial burden for my mom best as I could. We were broke but we stuck together."

"Sounds like you made the best of a bad situation."

"We banded together. We joke around a lot, tease each other, but we're a close bunch. Mess with one of us, and you mess with us all."

She lay back and stretched out, absently running her finger along the top of the comforter. "Sounds like you gave each other a soft landing. What about the rest of your family? Did any of your brothers or sisters serve in the military?"

"Luke served before joining the FBI. War changed him. He lost his whole unit. Came back a mess. Ended up divorcing his wife. He doesn't talk about it much, but I know he hasn't gotten over it. He stopped our youngest brother from even thinking about enlisting."

"I'm so sorry. Sounds like you guys have had to overcome a lot."

"Doesn't everyone?"

She nodded solemnly. Her beautiful green eyes filled with sympathy.

His fingers itched to reach up and touch her face. To move her lips closer to his. To taste her sweetness…

He stopped himself right there.

His thoughts needed to stay clear to keep them both alive. He sighed harshly.

She had brought up an excellent point earlier. His family would see through a lie. They deserved to know the truth so they could understand the risks. He would have to be up-front with them. "On second thought, taking you home with me is riskier if I'm not honest with them."

"You mentioned your boss earlier. Didn't he tell you not to trust anyone?"

"No choice. Besides, they're law enforcement. They'll understand. Maybe even chip in their advice. The more minds we have on this, the better. Plus, they'll be able to keep you safe while I disappear to chase any leads we get on the case. The ranch is our best bet."

"Sounds like the best way to go."

Boomer faced the door and growled his low-belly growl. His hackles stood on end.

Nick jumped to his feet. He palmed his weapon and pressed his index finger to his lips.

Crouching low, he covered the distance to the door in a few strides. Anyone came in, they'd regret it. He turned and motioned for Sadie to follow.

She was already on the ground, comforting the dog.

Good. Last thing Nick needed was for the men outside to hear barking. Someone had found them. Could be Grimes's men. Now the trick would be slipping out alive. It was dusk. He'd hoped to give Sadie a chance to rest. No luck. She'd have to make do on what she'd gotten so far.

Another thought crossed his mind. They'd have to leave what little supplies he'd brought with him. He shouldered his backpack. At least there was water inside.

The door handle jiggled.

He braced himself, waiting for the bang against the door or the cheap wood to splinter. Whoever was out there wouldn't wait long.

He glanced at Sadie. She sat there, fear and desperation in her eyes. Something inside him snapped.

"C'mon," he whispered, urging her to stay low and move toward him.

The sound of footsteps on the porch made his stomach muscles tighten.

"The door's locked. Want me to break it down?" A muffled voice came through the door. There had to be at least two guys out there, maybe more.

Boomer was quiet for now, but his ears were laid back and his body stiff. A low growl rose from his belly. He'd bark any second.

Nick ducked and rolled, keeping his profile low. "We have to go. I know you're scared. I won't let anything happen to you. Stick close by me." He pressed a reassuring kiss to the top of her head. "Don't think about them. Focus on me."

NICK'S REASSURANCE UNLEASHED a flood of butterflies in Sadie's chest, and she breathed a notch below panic.

The voice outside was familiar. "I know him."

"Is it one of Grimes's men?"

"Y-y-yes." Her throat tried to close from panic. She refused to buckle and let them freak her out.

"I'm here. Nothing's going to hurt you this time." He slipped on his T-shirt and work boots, the motion pulled taut skin over thick ridges of pure hard muscle. His movements were fluid, almost graceful, as he found his way back to her and wound their fingers together.

Boomer growled his low-belly growl again. The rapid-fire barks bubbled just below the surface.

Nick's gaze moved from her dog to her. "You think he'll keep calm?"

"As long as my hand is on his back, he knows not to bark." At least she prayed he would. It had worked in training, but this was real-world. And nothing about this situation could be simulated in training mode. Besides, he wasn't some German shepherd or pit bull ready to lock jaws on an intruder the second they showed their face. This was Boomer, her sweet dog who was meant to be her companion.

"Then keep it there." Nick slid her boots on for her.

"It's okay, boy." She hated that her hand trembled on Boomer's back. Hated how helpless she'd felt when they'd abducted her the first time.

Not again.

Not now.

Not like this.

She was stronger now.

Besides, she had two very important assets this time that she didn't have the first go round…Boomer and Nick.

He released her other hand and moved stealthily along the windows, his weapon drawn, checking each one for sounds outside.

"I'm not sure how many others there are to contend with. We know there are at least two," he whispered.

"How did they find us?"

"That's the question of the day."

These guys were good. They knew how to track the movements of a U.S. Marshal. That couldn't be a good sign.

A foreboding feeling came over Sadie, eating away at her insides.

Grimes was important, smart...but this savvy?

He was also devious, and that scared her almost as much.

She watched as a shadow moved around the room. Thankfully, her eyes had adjusted to the dark a long time ago so she could see clearly.

A blast shattered the window near the bed, sending shards of glass splintering in all directions.

Chapter Six

The plywood door blasted open, smacking against the wall. An imposing man burst through. The tall, burly figure aimed a gun at Sadie.

Boomer fired rapid barks, holding his ground in a low stance between her and the intruder.

Sadie scanned the room for Nick, didn't see him.

The crunch of glass breaking sounded from behind. She spun around. A male figure framed the window, sealing the other exit. He had streaks of blond in his long hair and the build of an athlete on steroids. There was no place to run or hide.

Boomer surged, his collar slipped through Sadie's fingers. He lunged at the man coming from behind, startling him enough to back him off. The reprieve would be short-lived and Sadie knew it.

Nick lunged from a corner. He disarmed the burly man breeching the door. Burly head-butted Nick, causing him to spit blood. A savage look narrowed Nick's dark eyes as he shoved Burly's face against the wall and twisted his arm behind his back. "I'm Marshal Campbell. And you're under arrest."

Burly twisted free at the same time a shot fired from the window area.

Sadie's heart lurched.

Had the bullet hit Boomer? Nick? Her?

Relief flooded her when she saw a red dot flowering on Burly's shoulder. The bullet meant for Nick had been a few inches wide. Boomer launched another attack toward the window. Steroids ducked.

Nick's gun lay on the floor in between her and Steroids. Could she dive for it in time before he popped up again and got off another round?

She tried to move but her limbs froze. Doubting herself for even a second gave Steroids the opportunity to fire another round. She resolved not to let that happen again. Her body had to move, fear or not.

The second bullet lodged in the bricks near Burly's head. He grunted and dropped to his knees. If Steroids had a second longer to aim, Nick would be dead. He cuffed Burly's hands behind his back.

In one swift motion, Nick dove and rolled, coming up with his gun and firing a round before Steroids could pull the trigger again. Nick's body was a shield between Sadie and the gunman. Nick took aim. Steroids disappeared under the window frame. Nick fired a warning shot and then motioned for Sadie to run.

She bolted toward the door.

Burly had managed to maneuver his hands in front of his body. He grabbed her foot before she reached outside. She twirled and kicked, but his grip was too strong to break away from by herself.

Boomer's shackles raised and he stalked toward Burly, barking wildly and focused on his target. He bit, clamping his jaws on Burly's forearm.

He grunted. "Get that mutt off me or I'll choke him."

Sadie pivoted. Burly released her boot and clasped Boomer's throat. His yelp cut through her.

Her shrill scream split the air.

She gripped the doorjamb with both hands and thrust her boot at Burly's face. The pointed tip connected with his jaw. A satisfying crunch, then blood spurted from his mouth.

Pivoting right, she stomped her foot on his face, her heel connecting with his nose. More blood spouted.

He grunted, "You bitch!"

Dismissing the nausea and pounding in her temples—the mother of all headaches raging at her heels—she stomped her foot another time.

Burly groaned and loosened his grip enough for Boomer to escape.

Sadie hopped out of reach, glancing back in time to see Nick firing his weapon. No doubt he was trying to keep Steroids from shooting again while she got away. She hesitated on the steps but Nick was already behind her, urging her toward the woods.

She made kissing noises at Boomer and he broke into a run beside her. Thank God he listened. Thank God he wasn't hurt. Thank God neither were they.

Running in boots cramped her feet and rubbed her blisters raw, but protected her legs from being cut by underbrush.

Boomer easily matched her stride, sticking beside her as Nick set a blistering pace.

They ran until her thighs burned and her lungs screamed for air.

Nick halted at the sound of crunching branches in front of them. He pressed his index fingers to his lips and scanned the woods. More broken stick noises came from behind. Rapidly. Push forward and they'd run into whoever was there. Going back wasn't an option, either.

"What do we do?" Sadie whispered.

"Follow me. We'll find a hiding spot and wait them out." Nick led them across a shallow five-foot-wide creek.

The sun had gone down, and the moon lit the evening sky filled with a thousand stars. A chilling breeze blew. There'd been no time to put on more clothing and the cold pierced through her T-shirt. Her teeth chattered.

"Wish I'd had time to bring something to keep you warm. I didn't have a chance to grab my jacket," he whispered, leading them farther east.

The memory of his smell mixed with leather assaulted her senses.

Another noise sounded ahead. More tree branches crunching under the weight of someone or something sizable. More people?

Nick stopped, listened. He looked as though he needed a minute to get his bearings. "This way."

She followed him as he zigzagged through the trees, branches slapping her in the face.

Faint voices grew louder. For all she knew they were running in circles. In the dark, it would be impossible for Nick to know which way they headed.

He stopped running and she took a moment to catch her breath.

The voices grew louder.

Nick searched around for something. But what? Where could they hide? At this rate, they might walk into a trap set by the men chasing them.

He stopped twenty feet away and waved her over.

"This ditch should hide us. Jump in," he whispered.

Boomer led the way into the four-foot-by-five-foot hole. Sadie hopped down and crouched low.

Nick disappeared, returning a moment later dragging several large tree branches. He used them to cover the opening. "This should buy us some time."

"Any chance you have matches or a lighter in that backpack to make a fire later?" Sadie gripped her cold knees, her chest heaving. She rubbed her hands together and blew on her fingers to bring the blood flow back. At this rate, she'd have frostbite before the sun came up again. Her eyes were adjusting to the blackness and she could see the outline of Nick's face.

Boomer's panting slowed as she stroked his back.

The only other sounds came from the men closing in on them and the insects surrounding them.

The sound of footsteps came closer.

The three of them stilled. Sadie kept her hand on Boomer's back to calm him.

One of the men muttered a curse. "When I find that bitch who kicked me, I'll kill her with my bare hands."

Burly? Hadn't he been shot? Must not have been enough of a wound to stop him. Should slow him down, though. Even if he found them, maybe she could out-run him?

Another man, most likely Steroids, made a shushing sound.

Their footsteps came closer.

Sadie's pulse raced. She bit her lip to keep from panicking. If Boomer so much as growled, he'd give away their position.

She squeezed her eyes shut, willing her teeth to stop chattering and him to stay quiet. Her hand didn't move from his back.

Nick's hand closed on her shoulder, radiating warmth and confidence she didn't own.

"Keep moving. They have to stop somewhere. When they do, we'll get 'em," Steroids said, disdain deepening his tone. He spit again. She presumed more blood.

A full minute of silence passed before Sadie exhaled

the breath she'd been holding. Washed-out, weepy and running through a whole host of other emotions, she leaned back against the cold hard dirt, wishing for safety, a cup of hot tea and a warm bed.

"Here. Squeeze closer. You'll lose all your heat through the ground." He scooted behind her and pulled her onto his lap.

His powerful thighs pressed to the backs of hers, sending sensual shivers rippling through her. A powerful urge to melt into him and allow his body heat to keep her from freezing surged through her.

Or was it something more she craved?

His body pressed to hers reminded her just how long it had been since she'd been with a man. Arousal flushed her cheeks. She was relieved he couldn't see her face. Her physical response couldn't be any more inappropriate under the circumstances.

His arms encircled her waist. Impulses shot through her. She pressed her back against his virile, muscular chest and all she could hear was a whoosh sound in her ears.

Boomer put his head on her leg. "You've been a good boy today," she said.

"He's special." Nick's words came out low and thick.

Sadie tried to focus on Boomer to distract herself from the sexual current rippling up her arms, her neck. On Nick's lap, she could feel his warm breath in her hair and it spread like wildfire down her back. Heat moved through her body, pooling between her thighs.

SADIE SHIFTED IN Nick's lap, her sweet bottom pressed against his crotch, and his tightly held control faltered. Why did he already have to remind himself this wasn't the time for rogue hormones?

Hell. It was as if he didn't already know that. He was a grown man, not a horny teenager who got an erection every time he was close enough to smell a girl's perfume. Sadie's hair hinted of flowers and citrus. He needed to ask Walter why he had flowery shampoo at his man retreat.

First, he needed to get a message to his buddy about the cabin.

Nick made a mental note to circle back to this subject when he had Sadie tucked away somewhere safe. He liked the idea of taking her to the ranch even more when he thought about how much reinforcement he'd have there. Between his siblings, someone could keep watch 24/7.

She shivered and he instinctively tightened his arms around her. He expected her to move away from him, but she didn't. Instead, she burrowed her back deeper against him. He didn't want to get inside his head about why that put a ridiculous smile on his face.

The last thing he wanted to think about was how two thin strips of cotton kept them from being skin-to-bare-naked-skin. At least her teeth had stopped chattering. He didn't care whether or not he was warm. He'd survive a few nights of cold. She wouldn't. Not in those cotton shorts he'd given her to sleep in.

He could see through the tops of the branches. The winds had picked up and the temperature had dropped a good ten degrees in the past fifteen minutes. The sky was blue-black. Exactly the way it looked when a cold front blew in.

They needed shelter and food. Neither of which were in his possession. Nor were the means to get any anytime soon.

Sadie shifted position, her curvy bottom grinding against him. He half expected her to push him away, but she didn't. Instead, her hands squeezed in between his. Her fingers were near frozen. He rubbed his hands over hers, warming them.

"Thank you. That's better already," she whispered.

She wouldn't thank him if she knew he mustered all the control he could to sit there with her and not slip his hands inside her shirt and caress those pert breasts the way his fingers itched to do. Needed to do? She wouldn't thank him if she knew how unholy his thoughts were about those taut hips. And she sure as hell wouldn't thank him if she knew how badly he wanted to spin her around in his lap and do things to her to remind her she was all woman and he was every bit a man.

He needed to redirect his thoughts. What other home projects needed addressing when he got back to the apartment? Wasn't there a small leak under the kitchen sink that needed attending to when he'd been called away last-minute for duty?

He was sure there were about a dozen other projects around the house that needed fixing, as well. And yet, his thoughts kept wandering back to how good Sadie felt in his arms. How he'd remember the scent of her—citrus and cleanliness—that was all hers long after this assignment was over. Didn't take a rocket scientist to see she affected him. He just hoped she wasn't offended by the growing erection he couldn't contain. She had to have felt it. Because blood pulsed south every time she moved, and so did his ability to think rationally.

He dismissed it as going too long without sex.

He'd fix that when this assignment was over. He'd have sex with the first beautiful and willing woman he could find. Hadn't there been a few? No woman from his past could erase the naked image of Sadie from his mind; the one where her legs were wrapped around his waist and he was buried inside her.

"Better now?" he practically grunted.

"Much. I can feel my fingers again."

The sweet purr in her voice had him wanting to stay exactly where he was. But he couldn't be sure they'd be alone for much longer. He couldn't risk sticking around. "We'd better head out. I slowed those two down, but there could be more."

"One of them was bleeding. He was shot in the shoulder. Won't he need to go to the hospital?"

"Depends on how deep the wound is and how prepared they are. His injury might slow him down or buy us a few hours. Unless they sent more than two men. We don't know how big the team is. Either way, they located us at the cabin, and that's bad. We're on foot and it's getting cold out. We have limited supplies. They'll expect us to camp nearby, which is why we have to keep moving. I disabled GPS on our phones for obvious reasons, so we need to keep moving until I see something familiar. If I can give our location to someone back home, they'll come pick us up."

"Okay."

She made a move to get up and it took a minute for him to send the message to his arms that he had to let go. She felt a little too right snuggled against his chest.

No woman, not since Rachael, had felt more right inside his arms.

Chapter Seven

Sadie and Nick walked for hours before his brother messaged that he was close. Headlights were a welcome sight to her after walking in the cold black night in her boots.

Nick squeezed her hand. "I'll have you in a warm bed in two hours." He cleared his throat, seeming to catch how the last part sounded. "What I mean is—"

"It's okay," she said on a half laugh. "I know you didn't intend to say it like that." Remembering his powerful thighs and chest against her body had her thinking she might not mind waking up snuggled against a strong, warm body like his. Those brown eyes with cinnamon flecks and hair blacker than night made for a package most women would consider beyond hot. Sadie wouldn't argue.

That she was crushing on her handler also reminded her how ridiculous she was being.

When was the last time she'd allowed herself to notice a man? Or relax at all. There was no laughter in her life. No humor. No friends. No sex. Okay, where'd that last bit come from?

It was true, though. There hadn't been any sex in far too long. And nothing was funny anymore. She missed the simple pleasures of feeling warm skin against her back when she slept, or laughing at an inside joke.

If she was being brutally honest, she couldn't remember the last time she really laughed at anything. She could blame her hollow existence on this whole ordeal. Was that accurate?

Sure she'd had to lie and keep people at a safe distance in the past two years. What about before then? Her boyfriend, Tom, had wanted to get engaged. Start a family. And yet she'd kept putting off the conversation. Her skin had itched and the air had become thick at the thought of making the two of them more permanent. She'd had to abandon the notion before she could really consider it.

In the past two years, she could've been almost anyone or anything she wanted. What had she chosen?

A baker.

Someone who works in the middle of the night when everyone else slept.

Did a little part of her shrink at the idea of becoming close to anyone because of the pain of rejection she still felt with her aunt?

And yet with Nick, everything was different. She didn't have to lie. She didn't have to pretend she was someone else. She didn't have to fake a relationship. He was her new handler. It was his job to keep her safe. He was proving capable of the task. So much so, that she was starting to feel more like herself than she had in months.

But was letting her guard down a good thing?

Before she could get inside her head about what that meant, a dual cab pickup truck pulled up.

Nick braided their fingers. A slow smile spread across his almost too perfect lips. "Our salvation has arrived."

The passenger's-side window rolled down, revealing an attractive man in the driver's seat. Right away she could see the two were related. The driver had the same sturdy, muscular build. He was similar in size to Nick.

He had the same nose and smile. Other than that, his hair was lighter and he had dimples when he smiled.

"This is my little brother Luke." He introduced the two, motioning toward the cab as he let go of her hand to open the door for her.

"Little?" Luke scoffed. He flashed perfectly straight, white teeth. "I'm second-youngest. And way better looking than this guy."

"Keep believing it, and maybe it'll be true someday," Nick grunted. "You're as modest as ever, I see."

"Beautiful dog," Luke said, as Nick coaxed Boomer into the backseat.

"Thanks," Sadie said. "He's been pretty brave today."

Nick pulled himself inside the warm cab after her. She was so cold she couldn't stop shivering.

"I can see my brother didn't prepare well enough for this trip. You're an icicle. What are you trying to do, freeze your witness into testifying?" He cranked up the heat and pulled a blanket from the backseat, spreading it across Sadie's lap for her. "This should help. Or you could scoot a little closer and I could put my arm around you. You know, body heat and all." Another show of perfect white teeth greeted her. Luke seemed to be greatly enjoying teasing his brother.

"She'll warm up fine without your paws on her," Nick said quickly, folding his arms.

"This is fantastic." Sadie pulled the blanket to her chin and leaned toward the vent. "Thank you."

"Where we headed?" Luke put the gearshift in Drive and handed a steaming foam cup to Sadie. "I brought hot chocolate for you."

"You've got to be kidding me. This is heaven." She gripped the drink with both hands and took a sip.

"Take us to the ranch," Nick said.

Luke cocked a dark brow, looking as though he needed a minute to rationalize the location before he spoke. "Darlin', do you want the radio on while I talk to my crazy brother?"

"No. I'm fine," she said. Besides, she wanted to see if sparks were about to fly.

"You just let me know if there's *anything* I can do for you, you hear?"

Sadie was certain she blushed. Good looks and charm must seriously run in this family. "I will."

"You didn't tell me the package I needed to pick up was this beautiful." Luke chewed on the piece of gum in his mouth.

Being so close to him, Sadie could smell the cinnamon.

Nick made a disgusted noise from his throat. "Don't you have a girlfriend somewhere?"

Luke didn't immediately speak. What flashed in his eyes? Hurt? Anger?

An expression crossed Nick's features that Sadie couldn't quite put her finger on. Was it regret? Did Nick wish he could take those words back?

She braced herself for more bantering. Instead, Luke's smile morphed to a serious expression, and he gripped the steering wheel tighter. "Nope. You're looking at a free man."

"Lucky for single women everywhere," Nick said, easing the tension.

She made a mental note to ask about that later.

"Aren't you on a case?" Nick glanced at Sadie when he said, "Luke works for the FBI."

"Coffee's for you, by the way." Luke held out a cup toward his brother.

Nick took it and held the cup to his lips for a few seconds before he took a sip. "Thanks, man."

"No problem. I'm around until after Gran's birthday. Do I need to be checking the rearview or did you ditch the son of a bitch who redecorated your face?" All the charm in his features returned full force.

"Just a couple of bumps and bruises. Nothing permanent, like a bullet hole. I think we walked far enough out of the way. No one should be able to track us."

Sadie leaned into Nick for warmth.

Luke's expression turned serious again, all cute playboy disappeared, when he asked, "What are we dealing with here exactly? I take it she's one of yours in the program."

Nick nodded. "Except she wasn't mine before. I inherited her when her handler was killed."

"And this guy being killed put her at risk?"

"She was relocated two years ago after testifying against Malcolm Grimes and assigned to a marshal by the name of Charlie."

Luke clenched his jaw muscle. "*The* Malcolm Grimes? One of the biggest crime figures in Chicago?"

"The very one."

"I read about that case, but I don't remember you being involved in that one."

"I wasn't," Nick said, taking another sip of coffee. He leaned his head back and closed his eyes for a moment. "That's good. Really good."

"Isn't that case old news?"

"It was until Grimes broke out of jail and her handler was found murdered."

"That's not good. Sounds like a mess. And an inside job. Does everyone at the U.S. Marshals Service check out?"

"Nope. This case has a stench so strong even my boss wants away from it just in case our channels of communication are dirty," Nick said. "A supervisor who was spotted with Grimes's men has now gone missing."

"Damn. Okay, so she testified and put the bad guy away. Why come after her now? They have to know the agency would be watching."

"You'd think. My predecessor relocated her after the trial twice, the last of which was to a small town where she should've been able to live out her life in peace."

"Until her man breaks out of jail and comes after her with reinforcements."

"Exactly," Nick agreed. "Possibly with her handler's help. And, worst-case, a supervisor's."

"That stinks to high heaven."

"Don't I know."

"And you think you can help her if…" Luke let his sentence die. He was silent for a minute, chewing on more than his gum. "Even so, taking her to the ranch?"

"I know what you're about to say."

"Then you know you can't break protocol. Not even to keep her safe. And you also know I mean this in the best possible way. God knows I invented doing things on my terms. But stashing her with us? Not a good idea." Luke turned to Sadie and said, "No offense."

"None taken. I agree with you," she said.

"True," Nick interjected. "Here's the thing. Everywhere I take her, these guys show up. They're barely a half step behind. The man power they have is staggering. I thought about staying on the run. And I can. But what do I do when I need to investigate a lead? Leave her exposed, alone in a hotel room? I don't have backup on this. And these guys are one step behind me out in the open like this."

"From the looks of your face, they've been catching you, too."

Nick pressed the heel of his right hand to his forehead. "It's been a problem."

"What about your boss?"

"He told me to go on Graco protocol, which basically means do whatever it takes as long as it's legal."

"I can see your problem. No one in the agency knows about the ranch."

"I've thought about every other possibility. The ranch is the only place I can keep her safe while I find Grimes. I can't leave her vulnerable in some random motel. I need backup I can trust, which means no one from my agency. I'm counting on you guys. I need everyone's help on this."

Luke didn't hesitate. "You know I have your back. I have a hot case but you have every other minute of my time."

"Chasing corporate spies again?"

"Nah. I got a serial killer on the loose in The Metroplex."

"The one in the media? Ravishing Rob?"

Luke rocked his head. "He's my guy."

"I appreciate your offer of help, little bro. I'll get back to you on that. Let's get through the next few days, and we'll see where we're at after Gran's party. You've got an important case of your own to work on."

"Nothing's too important for family. Besides, I'm a half hour outside The Metroplex on the ranch."

"Don't you mean forty minutes?"

"Not the way I drive."

The two bumped fists. Sadie's heart filled with warmth at the obvious affection these brothers had for each other. Their love came through even when they teased each other. And they were taking care of her, too. Not even

Tom did that and she'd almost married him. Heck, when she'd caught a cold that turned into pneumonia, she'd asked if he could pick up her medication from the pharmacy and bring soup. He didn't show up for hours. When he finally came through the door, she was exhausted and in tears.

He'd asked what was wrong.

She'd said she was starving and had waited for him.

He'd given her a shocked look and had said, "You know I always play poker with the boys on Thursdays."

Where her relationship with Tom lacked in spark, he made up for in dependability—and he could be depended on as long as she didn't ask him to upset his normal routine. She'd also learned that depending on others was the fastest way to get her heart broken.

Sadie didn't let herself go there about how nice it would be to have a family supporting her. At least she had Boomer.

"You know I appreciate it," Nick said.

Luke glanced at Sadie. "Sounds like a mess. But don't worry, darlin'. I'll do what this guy can't. Keep you safe."

"I'd be dead already if it weren't for him." She wasn't sure why she felt the need to defend him against his brother's teasing. Or why her heart squeezed when Nick smiled his response.

Luke cocked an eyebrow. His gaze shifted from Sadie to Nick and back. He placed his wrist on top of the steering wheel and drove.

Sadie leaned her head back.

She woke with a start, and realized she was still in the pickup.

"Sorry about the bumps. Need to fill the potholes. Gran ran out of gravel, so more's on the way," Luke said.

Nick's eyes opened, and his hand came up to his forehead. Using the heels of his hands, he pressed against his eyelids. "Means we're home."

"I must've fallen asleep." She stretched and yawned. "It's been a long night."

She couldn't see much except for shrubs lining the winding path. "I'll be okay. Just need a boost of caffeine and then we can talk through our next steps."

"Your immediate future holds a hot shower and warm bed."

And leave her out of the important stuff? No way. "You have to let me help. It's my life we're talking about here."

Nick started to protest, but she cut him off. "Look. I listened to the Marshals Service before and, with all due respect, I'm on the run again with no home and men chasing me with guns. I deserve to be included in any plans that involve me and my life. Clear?"

Nick emphatically shook his head.

Luke parked the truck and deadpanned his brother. "The lady has a point."

"Damn right," she said, grateful for the support. "And if you don't let me be part of the solution, then I'm out of here first thing in the morning. I'll figure out my own way. I can hide. I've gotten pretty good at it." She wasn't stupid enough to follow through on the threat. Her options were nil. She had no other leverage.

"Not a good idea. Promise me you won't disappear on me," Nick said. The worry in his tone almost shredded her resolve.

She had to be strong. Depend on him and she might as well roll up the tent because as soon as this assignment was over, he'd be gone. And she'd be left to pick up the pieces of her life again. Alone.

She glanced at Boomer.

Not completely alone. At least she had man's best friend as comfort. He'd shown himself to be not only a dedicated companion but a force to be taken seriously, as well. No more Scooby Doo nickname for this guy. His new moniker would be Cujo.

She folded her arms. "Fine. I'll agree to let you know when I decide to leave. And you owe me a promise, too."

"I'll include you. But you need to remember I'm the professional here. This is my job. I do this for a living and I'm trained. Not to mention I'm damn good at what I do."

"I've seen that already," she said. Then felt the need to point out, "We're alive but someone seems to anticipate our every move."

His downturned lips at the corners of his mouth told her everything she needed to know about how much she'd just insulted him. She wasn't trying to get into a fight. She wanted to be dead clear about her intention to be involved in her own future. She'd relied on the U.S. Marshals Service to keep her alive for the past two years. In that time, she'd also picked up a few survival tricks on her own. She wasn't as naive as when she'd first joined the program, wide-eyed, believing every word that came out of Charlie's and his supervisor's mouths.

Charlie.

Her heart still hurt at the thought he was killed most likely because of his involvement with her. If a criminal was powerful enough to get to a U.S. Marshal, what chance did she have? Even with Nick watching her back, there weren't any guarantees. He'd done an excellent job of keeping them safe so far, but the government wouldn't pay him to stay by her side 24/7. Surely he had other cases to work on.

Even if he was dedicated to her, how long before Grimes caught them? His men seemed to be one step behind so far, which blew her mind. Plus, life had already taught her that depending on others brought nothing but heartache.

"I understand you think my agency let you down. But from where I sit, they've also been the one thing that kept you alive."

"I won't argue that. I have a feeling if they'd sent any other deputy, I'd be dead right now and not here in this truck."

He ground his back teeth. Didn't argue.

Sadie knew she was right. "So, you won't mind if I take more of an interest in where I go and what I do next."

"What I say goes." Nick palmed the empty coffee cup. "You don't do anything to get yourself killed."

"I'll agree to consider your opinion but from now on I make decisions for myself. Whether you like it or not."

Nick crunched the cup in his hand.

She made kissing noises at Boomer and he lumbered out of the backseat. "I don't see the problem with sharing information with me."

"Can't tell you what I don't know." Was it frustration deepening his pitch?

He had a point. Admitting he had no idea where Grimes might strike next seemed to darken his bad mood. Everything was uncertain in her life. "When you do find out where he is and what he's doing, you have to promise to keep me informed. I get to know everything, including your plans for apprehending him."

"As long as you agree not to do anything stupid that could jeopardize your safety or mine," he whispered, toeing off his shoe at the doorstep.

"Why would I do that?" she snarled, angry at the accusation. She deserved to be in the loop. It wasn't like she was asking to be sworn in or anything.

"Just making sure we're clear."

"I'm not confused. Are you?"

He blew out a sharp breath. "You don't leave without telling me first. I don't make a move without informing you. Sound about right?"

"Yes. Break your promise and all bets are off."

"Got it."

Even with the lights off, she could tell she was being led into a ranch-style home.

Despite the bickering, Nick twined their fingers. He led her down a dark hallway with Boomer on her heels. Her faithful companion. He'd done well today.

When the chips were down, he'd stood his ground and growled.

Precisely what she planned to do from here on out.

Chapter Eight

By the time Sadie cracked her eyes open again, she could tell by the amount of light streaming in through the window that noon had come and gone. When was the last time she'd slept that well? Her queen-size bed, shaker-style, with a matching chest of drawers next to it made the room feel cozy.

The decor was simple. The white sheets were soft. The bed had four thick, plush pillows. A handmade quilt with alternating patterns of deep oranges and browns had warmed her through the otherwise chilly night.

Boomer lay snoring at her side. He didn't budge when she sat up.

Poor baby. He must be exhausted after all the walking they'd done in the past two days.

"You did good, buddy," she said in a low voice.

He didn't budge.

There was clothing folded on top of the five-drawer chest. She slipped out of the covers quietly, so as not to disturb her hundred-pound hero who was now growling and panting in his sleep. No doubt, he was reliving the ordeal from last night.

Sadie placed her hand on his side and soothed him until his breath evened out and he snored peacefully again. She moved to the dresser and examined the clothes. Jeans and a T-shirt suited her just fine. Her pink silk bra and panties had been washed and folded neatly in the pile. Red heat crawled up her neck at the thought of Nick handling her undergarments. Warmth flushed her thighs. Because it wasn't so awful to think of him touching her personal things…and she knew instantly she was confusing her feelings for him.

Feelings was a strong word.

She appreciated his help. He was her knight in shining armor, ripping her out of the hands of killers. Who wouldn't be wowed by that? What she experienced was gratitude. Nothing more. So why did she feel the need to remind herself of the fact?

One thing she knew for certain was that she'd been so tired last night she scarcely remembered taking a shower or changing into bedclothes. Nick had brought them in while she was showering, saying he'd borrowed them from one of his sisters. She didn't even want to think of the current running through her at the realization she was completely naked behind the shower curtain not five feet from him.

How long had it been since she'd been held by a man? Two years.

The last time she and Tom were together they'd had their usual Friday night movie at his place. He'd ordered deep-dish pizza from their favorite restaurant on the corner just as they had every week for the entire year and a half they'd been dating. If anything, Tom was consistent. Boring?

Where did that come from?

To be fair, her ex was a little too predictable, but he was also decent. There were no surprises when it came to Tom, and Sadie appreciated him for it. Wasn't knowing she could count on someone a good thing?

Why did it suddenly feel as though she'd been settling?

Her aunt had been unpredictable, and look how their relationship had ended. Sadie had felt no need to visit the woman one last time before she'd left Chicago.

The time she'd stopped by after her first semester of community college, her aunt had practically blocked the door. Sadie's excitement at having made good grades shriveled inside her at her aunt's reaction to seeing her. She'd expected a warm greeting, and chided herself for being foolish when she didn't receive one.

When she pressed to come inside so she could pick up a few of her things, her aunt had turned on the tears. She'd complained of not having space or enough money for rent before delivering a crushing blow. She'd sold all of Sadie's belongings.

Her heart broke that day.

She'd left many of her prized possessions behind until she got settled in her new place. Between work, class and study, she hadn't had time to stop by and retrieve them once the semester hit full stride.

Gone was her mother's wedding ring. Gone was the baby blanket her mother had crocheted for her when she was born. Gone was her father's revered vintage coin collection.

Everything from her parents had been sold, stripped away from her.

She'd stood in the doorway, feeling raw, exposed and orphaned all over again.

Her stomach twisted, the pain so very real. Even now.

Tom could be unyielding, but he would never have done that to her.

Did he make her pulse race the way being around Nick did? No. She and Nick ran from bullets and murderers. Of course her blood would be pumping and her adrenaline surging. And he did so much more to her on the inside. Her heart fluttered when he was close. Electricity pulsed between them. Her thighs warmed.

The comparison to Tom was apples and oranges. She loved Tom. Didn't she?

Not the same thing, a little voice told her. She ignored it. When this blew over, she would still end up alone with a new identity, a new lie. *If she survived.* Grimes seemed intent on making sure she never had to hide again. Or breathe.

She pushed aside those heavy unproductive thoughts and slipped on the jeans. They fit well enough. She cinched her waist with the belt and pulled on the T-shirt.

After dressing, she moved down the hall toward the sounds of voices, her heartbeat climbing with each step closer. There had to be at least six or seven people in the room. She followed the chatter, stopping at the door to the kitchen where a handful of people sat around the table. Her nerves stringing tighter with each forward step.

Nick stood at the kitchen sink, looking out the window.

The oldest woman, the one who had to be Gran, sat with a large pair of scissors and a stack of cloth. She met eyes with Sadie first. "C'mon on in, dear. Take a seat. Nick will get you a cup of coffee."

Nick had already begun pouring.

When attention turned toward Sadie, she wished she had the power to shrink. She knew all of two people in the Campbell family. Nick and Luke. And Luke wasn't in the room. She tentatively stepped inside, her back plastered against the door frame. Her heart pounded her chest and her breath came out in short bursts. She almost turned back and retreated to her room, offering an excuse about needing to go to the bathroom. Families were scary.

"Go ahead and sit, dear. We're a loud bunch, but we

don't bite." Gran motioned toward the chair next to hers. She looked younger than her years. Her white hair was in a tight bun positioned on the crown of her head. She wore jeans with a blouse, and a turquoise necklace with matching earrings.

Sadie eased onto the edge of the chair, wishing she could crawl out of her skin and disappear for all the eyes on her, staring. "Good morning. Uh, I'm sorry to sleep so late. We got in pretty late last night."

"I'm glad you're here. Feel free to call me Gran just like the others. And don't worry about what time you get up around here. I bet you're starving."

"I'm on it," Nick said, handing her a cup of fresh coffee. "How'd you sleep?"

"Fine. Better than fine actually. I almost forgot who I was."

He gave a knowing glance before diverting his gaze to the hallway. "How's Boomer? Still asleep?"

"He didn't even budge when I got out of bed."

"I can feed him as soon as he wakes," Nick said. Then tension lines bracketing his mouth told her he hadn't forgotten about their discussion last night.

She needed to soften the message, set things right with him, but she already felt as out of place as celery in cherry-flavored yogurt.

Although, looking around, everyone seemed so at ease with each other. The vibe in the room was comforting.

Nick returned a moment later with cream. "Pass the sugar, Meg." He turned to Sadie. "This is my sister Meg, by the way."

"Nice to meet you."

"Pleasure. I'd stand, but…" Meg, with a cute round face framed by cropped brown hair, leaned back from the table far enough for Sadie to see a round pregnant belly. "I'm due soon."

Sadie's heart squeezed. Her thoughts snapped to Claire and the baby she would never see. "When?"

"Any day now." A tall, blond, attractive man with a runner's build moved beside Meg and planted a kiss on the top of her head. His affection toward his wife could melt a glacier. "How's your back today?"

Meg's cheeks turned a darker shade of red. "It's better."

"What can I get you? Another pillow?" he asked.

"Nothing. I have everything I need right here." She smiled back up at him and patted her big belly.

Sadie had to tear her gaze away. The tenderness and love between them brought a flood of tears threatening. She sniffed back her emotions and took a sip of the hot coffee as a pang of self-pity assaulted her. Had Claire gone into labor? Was her little girl swaddled in her arms? Did the sweet baby have her mother's honest blue eyes? Her father's dimples?

The tall man interrupted her moment of melancholy, introducing himself as Meg's husband, Riley.

Sadie took his outstretched hand, praying he didn't feel hers shake. She wished Nick was closer. He was the only thing familiar to her in the room. He stood at the stove over a pan of eggs.

A figure cut off Sadie's line of sight. She stared at the hand being stuck out toward her. "I'm Lucy."

"Nice to meet you." Sadie shook the hand being offered, surprised at the strength coming from someone who couldn't be more than five-foot-four-inches tall. The term "cute as a bug in a rug" had to have been invented for Lucy. She had curly brown waves that fell past her shoulders, big brown eyes and Luke's dimples.

Luke came through the back door. A six-foot-two version of the Campbell men followed. "I see you've met the clan. Except for my brother Reed." Luke motioned toward his younger brother. "Our mother will be here tomorrow."

Reed tipped his black cowboy hat and smiled. His cheeks were dimpled, too. "Ma'am."

Sadie smiled, trying not to show her nerves, and turned to Gran. "You have quite a beautiful family." Her voice hitched on the last word. Truth was, she had no idea how to interact with a family. It had only been she and her parents when she was a child but they both had worked long hours in the small trinket store they'd owned. She was lucky if she saw them for more than a half hour before bed every evening.

"We're blessed." Gran beamed.

Nick delivered a plate of food, and the earlier chatter resumed. Sadie was thankful the spotlight wasn't on her anymore. As it was a rash had crawled up her neck. A few deep breaths and she might be able to stop it from reaching her face. She focused on the food. The eggs were scrambled with chopped red pepper and onion. A couple of homemade biscuits smothered in sausage gravy steamed. This was heaven on a stick.

Sadie wasted no time devouring her meal.

Nick had taken the seat across from her. "Guess you were hungry. I have more." He made a move to stand.

"No. Don't get up. I'm fine." Sadie's cheeks heated when she realized he must've been watching her eat the whole time.

The satisfied smile curving his lips warmed her heart more than she should allow. She couldn't risk getting too comfortable. She wondered just how much everyone knew about her aside from Luke. He knew enough.

"Meg's on leave until the baby's born. She and her husband work for Plano P.D. And Lucy works in the Victim Advocate Unit for the sheriff's office."

Was he reassuring her everything would be okay? Maybe he'd misread her tension.

Luke and Reed stood at the kitchen sink, eating fresh cut watermelon.

Gran's gaze narrowed on the outline of weapons in their waistbands. "I hope I don't have to remind either of you about the 'nothing that fires is allowed in the house' rule."

Luke shot a concerned look toward Nick. After picking them up last night and hearing the threat, Luke seemed more comfortable keeping his weapon as close as possible. He seemed to be waiting for acknowledgment from Nick that it was okay to leave his gun outside.

Nick barely nodded.

"Go on. Don't make me repeat myself." Gran shooed them toward the door.

"Sorry, Gran." Luke glanced back in time to see Nick smoothing his hand down his ankle.

His slight nod said he understood. Nick was telling him where to hide his weapon.

A boulder would've felt lighter on Sadie's chest at the reminder of just how much danger she was still in. To be in a room full of law enforcement out on a country road, and still need to have weapons within reach at all times didn't say good things for her situation. Plus, being in a room full of well-intentioned strangers shot her blood pressure up. At this rate, she'd have hives before she finished her coffee.

"I should check on Boomer." She made a move to stand, but Nick held his hand up to stop her.

"I got this." He picked up her plate and set it on the counter before disappearing down the hallway.

Lucy looked at her intently. "So, how'd you get my brother to come back home?"

"Now, Lucy, that's none of our business, right?" Gran shooed her away, winking at Sadie.

Apparently, not everyone knew the real reason she was there.

Nick returned a minute later with her hundred-pound rescue trailing behind. Boomer's ears perked up as soon as he saw Sadie and he trotted over to her side, tail wagging.

"Sweet boy. Did you get some rest?" Sadie asked, grateful she had something familiar to focus on besides Nick in this room full of strangers.

Nick's hand grazed hers as they scratched Boomer's ears and her skin practically sizzled where he made contact. An electric current raced up her arm.

She stood. "He probably needs to go out." She practically ran through the opened screen door to find a place where she could think straight.

Boomer's nose immediately scanned the ground. He stopped at a tree and hiked his leg.

The screen door creaked and Nick bounded down the porch stairs holding a plate. "Don't have any kibble, but I figure he won't object to biscuits and gravy." He set the meal down on the ground.

Sadie rubbed her arms to stave off a chill even though the thermometer displayed a number in the high seventies. "Darnedest thing about living in Texas. Never know what the temperature's going to be this time of year." She turned her back to Nick and looked out on to the wide-open sky.

"Supposed to be a storm blowing in tonight. It should be plenty cold later. Remind me to give you an extra blanket."

She turned to face him, unsure of the right words to tell him she needed to go. She rubbed her arms to tamp down the goose bumps—the chill she felt from deep within encasing her heart. "Thanks. For all this. But I think we both know I don't belong here."

"Sure you do." He moved closer, took off the shirt he was wearing and wrapped it around her shoulders. Even through his undershirt, his broad, muscled chest rippled when he took in a breath. "What makes you say that?"

"I just don't. This is your family." She gripped the top of the fence, turning her face away from him, not wanting him to see how much it hurt to say those words. "And I'm grateful for everything you're doing for me. But I'd rather stay at a motel where I'd be out of the way."

"We're just normal people. There's nothing special about us."

She looked out across the landscape. The way they loved each other seemed pretty special to her. "You have a gran and sister with a baby on the way. This is a family moment and I don't feel right intruding."

"Did anyone say anything to you? Lucy? She can be quick to judge, but she means well."

"No. No one had to. I can see with my own eyes. This is a special celebration. Your gran is sweet. She deserves to have all the attention."

"You don't know Gran. Don't get me wrong, she loves for us all to be together. But she doesn't need to be the center of attention. She's content right here with all of us running in and out. If she had her way, not one of us would've moved out. We'd all still be here, tripping over each other."

Sadie glanced around at the yard that seemed as if it went on forever with the low shrubs and mesquite trees, then toward the blue skies with white puffy clouds. "I can think of worse places to be. It's beautiful here. This where you grew up?" She leaned her hip against the fence.

"Yeah."

"Where do you live now?" she asked.

Boomer loped over, sniffing around as though he tried to get his bearings. This was a far cry from his home at the lake house. Was he as lost as she felt?

"Dallas. I have an apartment in The Village. But, I'm never there. I guess it doesn't really feel like home."

"Why'd your sister say you don't come around here anymore?"

"Who? Lucy?" He paused. "Must've been her. Everyone else has been briefed." The muscle in Nick's jaw pulsed. "Sorry about that. I'll fill her in."

Why did he dodge the question? There was more to the story and her curiosity was piqued. She told herself it was because it would be nice to know one thing about him that didn't have to do with how well he did his job. "So you get to know everything about me and I don't get to return the favor. Is that it?"

"Afraid so. Besides, some subjects are out-of-bounds."

"Oh, that's great." What was the big deal? Did she hit a nerve?

"Tell me about the accountant."

"Who?" She had to search her memory for a second. "Tom?" She'd almost forgotten about him, being this close to Nick. Even so, what right did he have to ask about Tom? Indignation squared her shoulders. "He's none of your business."

"All indicators show you two should be married by now, planning for your kids' college funds."

Anger simmered. He didn't have a right to judge her life, past or present. Besides, none of those normal things were in her outlook anymore.

"Kids? Me?" She laughed out loud. It came out as a choked cough. "That's about the most ridiculous thing I've ever heard. How exactly am I supposed to have time to push around a stroller while I'm being chased by a man who won't stop until I'm dead? How selfish do you think I am?"

He stood there as though words wouldn't form. Did he regret his tone?

It didn't matter. Tears had already boiled over and spilled down her cheeks. A family had never been more out of the question for Sadie. And when could she ever stop running? What was her future going to be like? Relocate every six months? No friends? No roots? No home?

Sadie couldn't stop the sob that racked her shoulders. Or the flood of tears that followed. Before she could fight, Nick pulled her into his chest where she met steel wrapped in silk muscles. His strong arms wrapped around her and he spoke quietly into her hair. "It's going to be okay. You're going to be all right."

"You don't know that." She needed to get tight and stop feeling sorry for herself. She'd been strong so far. This was not the time to unravel.

"I'll find Grimes and anyone else trying to hurt you, and lock them up. I have help here. We don't have to do this on our own anymore."

"You already said this is your job. And I'm glad you're good at what you do. But this is my life. And it sucks. I never get to be me again. I always have to play the part of someone else. Those bastards took it all away. Everything." Tears fell freely now. Sadie had no power to stop them. It had been two long years of being strong.

Twenty-four months of lonely nights, freaking out every time a creak sounded, and a lifetime on the run to look forward to. She could never stop or slow down for fear one of Grime's gang members would be right behind her, lurking, waiting.

And Tom?

Did Nick really want to know the truth about Tom?

Did he need to hear that Tom was stable and that was about it? He provided all the things she'd been missing in her childhood? His life was about order, routine and ties that matched his suits. Where he lacked in excitement, he made up for in stability. He was the kind of guy who would stay the course, no matter what. And she'd almost agreed to marry him for it.

And yet, she now realized that with him she'd be living a different lie. Because she never felt *this* good in Tom's arms. Never wanted so desperately to feel his bare skin against hers. Never wanted any man this much. Nick was a safe haven in a storm.

A temporary shelter, a little voice said.

NICK STOOD THERE, holding Sadie, and for a split second in this mixed-up crazy world everything felt right.

He ignored the danger bells sounding off in his head. The ones that threatened to end his career. "We'll figure this out."

His cell buzzed. He fished it from his pocket. "Smith."

He answered the call and put it on speaker. "What's the word?"

"My source has been able to identify a dozen real estate holdings. There's a couple you'll be the most interested in that were bought by a dummy corporation. One of which has had a lot of activity."

"Let me guess, this company is licensed out of the Caymans," Nick practically grunted.

"You guessed it. Word has it that Jamison could've been in business with Grimes all along."

"If Jamison was involved with a known criminal, he'd have a lot to lose if someone could identify him."

"This might explain why they've come at Ms. Brooks so hard. It could be more than revenge. He might need to make her disappear to bury his involvement."

Nick focused on the floor intently as his free hand fisted. "They can't be thrilled I'm alive, either."

A sigh came across the line. "I agree, which is why it's more important than ever to keep you off the radar. I'd initially thought we were dealing with one rogue deputy. Charlie. But, this? A supervisor? To be honest, it scares the hell out of me that one of our own could be in on this."

"I agree. It also explains how they keep anticipating my moves."

"They must've narrowed down her location. It doesn't appear that they have Charlie's file, but anything's possible. And, now, I believe you're a target." His solemn tone sent a shiver down Sadie's spine.

"Explains why they seemed so eager to run me off the road before," Nick agreed. "They would have known we were watching her."

"Another thing bothers me and makes me believe what I'm hearing about Jamison could be true. They didn't seem particularly bothered that a U.S. Marshal was involved," Smith said.

"No, they didn't." Nick paused. "If he's involved, it explains how they knew where to look for us."

"It does make their job easier."

"What did you say a minute ago about those holdings?"

"I've narrowed down two locations as possibilities.

One in Houston and one in Dallas. We can't find any information on these. I can't send anyone else to check them out. Can't risk word getting to Jamison."

Nick took out a small notebook and pen from his back pocket. "I'll do it. Give me the addresses."

"1495 Oliver Street in Houston and 2626 Brenner Drive in Dallas," Smith said.

The Dallas address wasn't far. He'd look it up on Google and pinpoint the exact location. "Got it."

"Report back as soon as you know what's in there."

"Will do, Chief."

He ended the call and turned to Sadie. Big green eyes stared back at him. The hurt, loneliness and disbelief he saw there was a knife to his chest. He wanted to take it all away. Make her world safe again.

The only way to do that was to make sure Malcolm Grimes didn't hurt her again.

Protecting Sadie just became his number one priority.

Chapter Nine

Evening had fallen quickly. Now, after everyone had said their good-nights and the house was dark, everything was quiet, save for the crickets chirping outside Sadie's window in the middle of the night. The stillness reminded her of the lake house. The place had been eerie when she'd first moved from the city. There was no hustle and bustle. No horns honking. No sounds of the L train running. Everything about living in Creek Bend had felt foreign because of her Chicago upbringing.

And yet, she'd felt an almost instant connection to the place. To the people. To the slower pace.

Sadie rolled onto her left side and glanced at the alarm clock again. A whopping three minutes had passed since the last time she'd checked.

She didn't even bother to close her eyes again. Wouldn't do any good. They'd just bounce open again, anyway. The winds had kicked up and there was a storm brewing outside.

It was four in the morning. Normally she'd be leaving the house for work at this time. An ache pressed into her chest. The small bakery had become her second home. She missed everything about it. The smell of dough leavening. The first sip of coffee she took once inside the quiet shop. All the little tasks that added up to a productive day.

Working in the bakery made her feel as though she contributed something positive to the world. There was something primal and satisfying about feeding people.

And having a routine. She missed the comfort of a schedule.

The wind outside howled. A gust slammed into the window. Her gasp made Boomer stir. *It's only the wind.*

Her morning coffee ritual would have already started. Wouldn't she kill for a double shot latte with extra foam about now?

She missed the feel of dough in her hands. The weight of it. The warmth.

She always started by mixing and weighing it. Baguettes were first, and then the sourdoughs since they took the longest to ferment. As Claire neared her due date, there had been only one specialty bread on the menu. A mini cranberry panettone.

Another blast of wind rocketed and a dark shadow crossed her window. *A tree branch. It's only a tree branch.*

While dough mixed, she'd hand-laminated croissants for the day, rolled out tart shells and mixed muffins and cookies. Some breads needed to be knocked back as much as three times before being left to ferment until just right for scaling. Each loaf had to weigh an equal amount, or they wouldn't bake at the same rate.

Tap, tap, tap on the window. *Raindrops finally fell.*

The timer had become her new best friend. She'd learned that small batch bread-baking was so much about timing. Ten minutes early or twenty minutes late made a huge difference in the quality of what came out of the oven. *So much in life was about timing.*

By now, Sadie would have been preheating the ovens. Helping wake the town with handmade treats after it had been so good to her felt right. After all, there were no strangers in Creek Bend, or so they'd said. At first, she'd thought it was their way of being nosy. She soon realized, they'd meant it. Neighbors popped in to check on her and see if she needed anything. When she'd brought Boomer home, it wasn't long before baskets of treats with cards started showing up on her doorstep.

Her heart ached for the friendly faces she'd never see again.

Time to move on.

On her agenda?

A new town. A new job. A new start.

If—and it was a big if—Grimes was found and locked up, how long before he got out again? He seemed to have connections in high places. Would he ever stop looking for her? Would his men ever move on?

She doubted it.

Another boom of wind blasted against the window, causing her to jump. Could someone be out there? Lurking? Using the storm as cover?

She slid out of bed and moved to the side of the window, trying to gather enough courage to peek outside. She thought about the guns in the shed. How easy would it be for someone to locate them? Her throat suddenly felt dry, and her heart hammered her ribs. She quieted her thoughts and listened intently.

Had she heard something? No. Couldn't be. No one was awake. Her imagination was playing tricks on her. No one dangerous knew where Nick's family lived. And they were all asleep.

She peered through the window. Nothing.

The sound of a board creaking outside her door sent

her heart into her throat. Had someone slipped inside the house? Were they sneaking down the hallway? Her pulse kicked up another notch even as she knew her imagination was most likely running wild. What she needed to do was chill out.

If anyone was up, they were probably making a night run to the bathroom, she reasoned. With a pregnant woman in the house, middle-of-the-night bathroom trips weren't out of the question.

The weather had Sadie skittish, looking for things hiding in dark shadows.

She couldn't think of pregnancy without picturing Claire. Her belly had been so round the last time Sadie saw her friend. She'd wobbled when she'd walked and said her ankles were lead weights. Was Claire awake feeding her little angel? Changing her diaper? Crying over the loss of her bakery? She probably thought Sadie had died in the fire.

Oh, no.

Claire would be told Sadie was dead. Her heart squeezed thinking Claire would be mourning when she should be celebrating. Was there any way to get word to her friend?

Not without putting her in danger.

Now she really couldn't go back to bed and close her eyes because she'd picture a sad-faced Claire.

Sadie's heart ached. Dwelling on it was only making the pain worse. Claire, her baby and the bakery were all part of the past now. Time to pick up and move on. And what about Tom? What did it say that he barely crossed her mind anymore?

When she missed a man's arms around her, she thought about Nick.

Startled at the realization, Sadie eased out of bed. She needed to get to the kitchen to get a glass of water.

Questions raced through her mind. What was her next move? How long would it take before Grimes found them at the ranch?

They couldn't stay long. She wouldn't put his sweet family in danger, no matter how much he insisted. Whether Nick liked it or not, she would move on soon. She'd need to change her appearance again. Maybe she wouldn't look too bad as a blonde?

And her name.

She would need a new name. Maybe she could pick her own this time? What about Elise? Or Brittany? Or Ann?

She hadn't taken two steps into the kitchen before Luke poked his head in.

"Everything okay?" he whispered.

"You mean aside from the small heart attack I just had?"

He chuckled before glancing down the hall, and waving someone away. "Doesn't pay to walk around at night in a house full of law enforcement officers."

"I'm sorry. Who was that?"

"Reed, Riley, Lucy and, of course, Nick."

"Oh, great. Now I've gone and forced the whole house out of bed. I'm sorry. I was thirsty." She pulled a glass from the cupboard.

"No trouble. I'll let everyone know." He disappeared down the hall before she could thank him.

She poured water and took a sip, not ready to go back to bed. She hadn't meant to interrupt everyone's much-needed rest, even if relief washed over her knowing an intruder wouldn't get through those doors unnoticed.

She didn't realize she'd pulled out a mixing bowl and located a bag of flour until she looked down. A lamppost streamed light through the kitchen window. It was enough to see what she was doing. Her actions at the bakery had become so routine she could do them in the dark if she needed to. She mixed yeast into the flour, then added butter and water. When she'd beaten them thoroughly, she dumped the contents onto the counter. Pressing her palms into the mix, folding it over, kneading it, brought a sense of sanity and calm over her.

Luckily, the bedrooms were on opposite sides of the house. She could only hope to work quietly enough so as not to disturb anyone again, and least of all Boomer. If he started barking, the whole house would be up faster than she could say *quiet*.

Sadie pressed her palms into the dough, rolled and repeated until her shoulders burned.

Doing something familiar had her almost forgetting about the scary men chasing her and their ability to find her almost everywhere she went.

She turned on the oven and left the dough to set on the counter.

The feeling of eyes on her gave her a start. She turned to the doorway and caught a glimpse of a male figure filling the door frame. She knew exactly who it was. "Nick? I'm sorry if I woke you."

"You didn't. I couldn't sleep." He stood there all shirtless man and muscle, his jeans hung low on narrow hips, one arm cocked in the doorjamb and a grin on his face that made him even more handsome if that were possible. "What are you making?"

His words traveled across the room as soft as feather strokes.

"I got bored. Thought I would do something useful and bake a loaf of bread." She motioned toward the counter. "That should do it. Needs to sit for a while."

"Can't wait," he said, pulling up a stool and taking a seat. "You're used to being up all night, aren't you?"

"Yeah," she said on a sigh. She thought about how different he was now. Women had lined up in Creek Bend to talk to him. But they'd had no idea what was really underneath the ball cap and sunglasses he'd worn. He'd always stood to the side, awkward. If he hadn't been so shy she feared he would've asked her out on a date. Feared or hoped? The question had to be asked.

She'd almost convinced herself that she didn't need anyone. Her past certainly had taught her the same lesson. It would be a long time before she'd be ready to spend her Saturday nights with a stranger. And yet, didn't he awaken a tiny piece of her that she'd tried to ignore far too long?

It would be easy to lie to herself now and say she hadn't given him a second thought before. But what good would it do? Sure she'd been interested. She knew then as much as she knew now that she would never allow herself to get caught up in feelings for a man. She wasn't ready.

There'd been a time when she thought she had it all figured out. She'd been dating someone nice, decent and reliable. She and Tom were on track to walk down the aisle. He'd hinted about making the relationship more permanent. She'd made it clear she wasn't ready. Yet. Plus, she'd figured he was working up the nerve to ask her officially.

A case of mistaken identity had changed everything about her life.

She'd escaped with her life and nothing from her past. Her testimony had put Malcolm Grimes away for what was supposed to be a very long time.

Nick moved behind her and encircled her waist with his arms, covering her hands with his, entwining their fingers.

"You sure I can't help with anything else?"

She shouldn't allow him to get this close to her, but her body screamed *yes*.

Bad idea. She ducked out of his hold and moved to the sink, filling a glass with water.

"After Gran's celebration tomorrow afternoon, we'll dig deeper into the case again."

The mention of family caused the muscles in her shoulders to bunch. Her skin felt as though a thousand tiny ants were biting her. She straightened her back. "Your gran is very sweet, so don't take this the wrong way. There any chance I can sleep through the festivities?"

NICK WATCHED SADIE'S movements intently as she folded her arms and hugged them into her chest. "I can tell she likes you if that's what you're worried about. Everyone does."

"Not everyone. Did you see the way your sister Lucy looked at me earlier? What was that about?"

"She's protective." He stopped himself before he explained that they were all most likely shocked beyond hades he'd brought a woman into the house again. Even if it was for professional reasons. "Don't pay any attention to her. She doesn't mean anything."

Sadie looked ready to crawl out of her skin. "I'm sure. But I think I'd be more comfortable leaving you to your family celebration while I take a walk outside with Boomer or something."

Her cold shoulder made the room feel as if the temperature had dropped twenty degrees in the past second.

He thought about her past. How overwhelming a big family can be for anyone and especially someone who'd lost theirs. He needed to ease her into his. "We can figure out something. I didn't mean to make you uncomfortable—"

"It's fine. Don't worry about it. Really." She checked a timer and put the ball of dough on a baking sheet. She slid it into the oven, put a pan of water underneath and closed the door. Then she turned off the heat so the dough would rise faster. "What do we do next? We can't stay here forever. It probably isn't safe to stay here past tomorrow."

"I thought about that. Smith sent a text on my throwaway. He believes Grimes is still somewhere in Texas. The locations of the warehouses are perfect for moving merchandise from the Gulf all the way to Canada."

Sadie covered her mouth.

"Reports are saying he wants to stay close to the Mexican border so he can escape quickly if need be. It'd be easy for him to slip across the border and get lost if he feels the heat. Except we can't trust intelligence."

"There any other possible reason for him to be here other than me?"

"Smith isn't sure. The Dallas warehouse is leased to his company. He might be using it to move…product."

"What does that mean?"

"Guns, money, illegals. Whatever he needs to move through the country. These guys adapt their business quickly, keeping pace with what's selling."

"So we start looking for him at the warehouse?"

"I agreed to keep you informed. I didn't say you could come with me to follow a lead. I plan to leave tomorrow night after midnight." He actually planned to leave at eight o'clock, but he had no plans to share that information with her. He figured he'd find her sitting on the hood of his truck if she knew the real time.

"Fine."

"There's a dangerous word coming from a woman."

"What do you want me to say? Do you need me to beg? I will." Her green eyes were pleading. "I want to go. I want to be included. I want to be part of this 'sting' or whatever you call it."

If he wasn't so frustrated, he'd laugh. "There's no sting. I'm just going on a fishing expedition."

"You need someone to watch your back."

"True."

She folded her arms and tapped her foot. "Okay, tell me. Who else is going with you?"

Perceptive. "Luke. As you can see, I have all the backup I can handle."

"You said you're leaving at eleven, right?"

Was she testing him? He drew his brows together. "I'm pretty sure I said midnight. And I'm even more sure you heard me the first time."

"My mistake." She turned on her heel. Before she left the room, she said, "Throw the bread into a loaf pan and turn on the oven when it's ready."

SADIE'S BRAIN WAS way too active to sleep. She needed a little space to be able to think clearly and that was increasingly difficult to do with Nick around. It was all too easy to get lost when he was near. With him close, she started thinking about a future that might involve children and a husband. She knew herself better than that. Sadie would never knowingly put someone else in her situation.

She curled on her side, trying to ignore the sounds outside her bedroom window. Her imagination could go wild with every snap of a tree branch.

Closing her eyes did no good. All she saw were the

faces of her abductors. The sounds of their voices would haunt her forever.

She curled on her side and counted sheep. On the tenth round of that joy, she surrendered.

What was the use?

By six o'clock, she was ready to crawl up the walls.

She didn't want to go in the other room, but boredom got the best of her and she was getting hungry, too. The scent of her fresh loaf filled the air. Someone had finished the job for her.

After getting dressed, she followed the noise coming from the kitchen hoping she'd find Nick there so she could ask him what their next steps were. She froze when she saw Lucy sitting at the table.

In fact, no one was in the kitchen but Lucy. Well, this just got awkward.

If Sadie turned around like she wanted to, Lucy might catch her sneaking away and that would just be embarrassing. So, she didn't. Better face down the raging bull. Besides, she'd be out of there soon and Lucy would never have to set eyes on her again. Her heart squeezed. She would be long gone and into a new life—a life without Nick.

"Morning."

"Hey."

Great. Didn't seem as though Lucy wanted to talk to her any more than she wanted to talk to Lucy. "That coffee I smell?"

"Yep. Cups are in that cabinet." She pointed next to the sink.

Sadie gripped a mug and shot a weak smile. "I'll just grab a cup and get out of your way."

"No. Stay. We should talk."

Oh, glory. Sadie filled her mug and took a sip. At least she had coffee. "What's up?"

"Sit." Lucy motioned to the table.

Sadie took the seat opposite her. "Are you an officer?"

"Yeah. It's in the blood, I guess."

Could a second tick by any slower?

Lucy leaned her weight to one side and tucked her foot underneath her. "My brother's had it rough."

Should Sadie know what Lucy meant by that? She shrugged. "I'm afraid I don't know much about him."

"He didn't tell you about his past?"

"Afraid not." Sadie sipped the steaming brew, welcoming the burn on her lips. "Why would he?"

Lucy's eyes widened in surprise. "I just thought…"

Sadie leaned back in her chair, trying not to look as if she was hanging on Lucy's every word. The truth was she would like to know more about Nick. He already knew so much about her. She felt at a complete disadvantage.

"Did he at least tell you why he went into law enforcement?"

"Nope."

"Wow. I overestimated the situation, then." Lucy looked even more surprised by this revelation.

"All I know about your brother is that he works for the U.S. Marshals Service. He is my handler while I'm on the run from men who want to see me dead. But you already know that, right?" It was more statement than question.

Lucy nodded.

"So, if there's something you want to tell me, I'm all ears. But I don't like playing games." Sadie was being bold, and she knew it. But Lucy would not intimidate her, dammit.

Lucy's jaw went slack. A beat passed. She sat up stiffly and said, "I knew there was something about you I liked."

The pair burst into laughter, shattering the tension that had been between them.

Sadie spoke first. "If there's something you think I should know about Nick, tell me now."

Chapter Ten

Lucy shifted in her seat. Her expression darkened and her gaze focused out the window. Sadness overcame her once-bright features. "I can be protective of my brothers, but especially Nick. I owe him my life."

Sadie leaned forward and gripped her mug with both hands. "He said you two were especially close. I can see the bond your family has. It's sweet."

Lucy's eyes brimmed with tears, but she didn't immediately speak.

Sadie took a sip and waited. She knew what it was like to try to recall a painful experience.

"I don't normally bare my soul to strangers, but my brother told me a little bit about what happened to you. I think you of all people will understand."

Thinking about what Grimes and his men had done to her still elicited a physical response. Her heart rate increased, and she found it hard to swallow. Sadie forced herself to stay calm. "I was in the ICU for a couple of weeks after what those jerks did to me."

"It takes a strong person to survive something like that. You're really brave. I know firsthand what it takes to keep going after someone hurts you."

"That why you work at the sheriff's office as a victim's

advocate?" Sadie asked, realizing her initial assessment of Lucy had been all wrong.

Lucy nodded. "When I was young, my ex-boyfriend became obsessed with me. Didn't think much about it at first. I was dumb enough to think it was cute. That it showed how much he cared. So I didn't tell anyone right away. Let it go on way too long. Then, it got weird. For weeks he'd show up unexpectedly. We'd already broken up. Time to move on for me. He had other ideas."

"The people you care about shouldn't want to hurt you."

Lucy nodded in agreement. "Tell that to a young girl. They don't always listen." She took a sip of coffee. "It got worse. He started threatening my guy friends and stalking me."

"I can't see your brothers putting up with that."

"Which is exactly the reason I didn't tell them. They'd outright hurt him, and I thought I could handle my own problems. Figured this was my fault somehow. It was on me to finish it. I had no idea what was he was truly capable of." Tears streamed down her cheek. "Sorry. It's been years. And, yet, it still gets to me when I think about it."

Sadie patted Lucy's hand. "I can see it's still hard to talk about it. We don't have to keep going if you don't want."

"It's okay. Just especially emotional lately for some reason," Lucy said quickly. "Guess we have a lot going on in the family right now. Anyway, the experience made it hard for me to open up to anyone and especially men."

Anger burned Sadie's chest. No woman deserved to be intimated by a man, but especially not a young girl. "How old were you when this all happened?"

"Sixteen. He was my first love. I was so dumb."

"You were young," Sadie corrected.

"And stupid."

"Naive, maybe. But you're not capable of being stupid."

Lucy half smiled, kept her gaze trained out the window. "He kidnapped me. Planned to rape me and then kill me. Said he didn't want another boy touching me. That I belonged to him."

"Sounds like he was a very sick boy."

"I can't believe I didn't see it before. He was a little jealous at first. I thought it was cute. When I wanted breathing space, he got worse."

"You couldn't have known. Grown women get themselves in worse situations. I hope you don't blame yourself. You didn't ask for any of this." Sadie noticed a small scar above Lucy's eye. Did that bastard do that to her?

"I tell people the same thing all the time. Strange how hard it is to believe for yourself." She paused a beat. "My family didn't like him to begin with. I was being defiant, sneaking around dating him behind their backs. I should've listened in the first place. I could've saved myself a lot of heartache. He wasn't even my type. I guess his bad-boy image hooked me. I figured he was good underneath. Learned the hard way not every person is."

"We all do things as teenagers we regret later. No one's perfect. We learn. It's part of growing up."

Lucy shifted her gaze to Sadie, turning the tables. "I just want you to know I understand your fears. What you went through was hell. And my brother told me it was all a mistake. You weren't involved in any criminal activity. They grabbed the wrong woman."

If Lucy was trying to make Sadie feel better, she was succeeding. "Crappy things happen sometimes. We don't always get to control everything."

Lucy's ringtone sounded. She held up a finger and answered the call, lowering her voice.

Sadie tried to block out the conversation, focusing instead out the window and on the beautiful yard.

Lucy ended the call with, "I love you, too." She stuffed her phone back in her pocket, turning her attention to Sadie again. "He's the reason I finally decided to go to therapy. I don't want to lose him."

"Sounds like a good guy. You better hang on to him."

"Yeah, he is. His name is Stephen, by the way." Lucy sipped her coffee. She grinned. "I don't know where you come from, but there's no shortage of good men around here. If it weren't for Nick…"

"Don't get any crazy ideas about me and your brother. I'm his work, remember?"

Lucy held her hands up in surrender.

"Good." Why did her heart race at the mention of Nick?

Seeing the warmth and love Lucy had for her brother, for all her family, hit Sadie in a deeply emotional place. She had no doubt if one Campbell was in trouble, the rest would step up. Her heart opened a little more.

Sadie pushed aside her heavier thoughts, allowing the sun to shine through the opening in her chest. "Can I be honest with you?"

Lucy nodded.

"I didn't think you liked me at all."

"It's not you. I was thrown off when my brother brought another woman home. He hasn't since his girlfriend died."

He didn't say anything about that. "What happened?"

"It was a long time ago, but to look at the way he's still suffering you'd think it was yesterday. He doesn't talk about it."

"What happened?"

"She didn't see her twenty-second birthday."

"Oh, no." Sadie pressed her hand to her chest to stop her heart from hurting for him.

"They hadn't actually made their relationship official…" She cast her gaze around the room and fidgeted. "He always gets a little down this time of year because of it."

Talking almost seemed irreverent. Sadie let the words hang in the air.

"She was killed by a drunk driver," Lucy said.

"I had no idea." Is that why he sounded so bitter at the mention of her fiancé? Or having a family? Sadie couldn't imagine losing the one person in the world she loved. Her heart ached for Nick. To lose his one true love. She couldn't fathom it. And yet, hadn't she lost hers? What she and Tom shared was different. Was it earth-shattering, world-ending love? No. Their relationship was more mature, she lied.

Had she been sad when she'd walked away from Tom? Of course.

Heartbroken?

No.

This explained a lot about Nick's reactions. Was it also the reason he broke protocol to collect her things in Creek Bend? He understood loss.

Nick obviously held his emotions inside. Had he learned to do that when he was a kid, watching his mom suffer?

"I'm so sorry."

"He was a mess for a while. Got out of the military when his time was up, and eventually got his head screwed on straight again. Started dating. He's been out with lots of women since then. No one seems to measure up to her. I haven't heard about him seeing anyone in the past year. I was afraid he'd given up. Even though she died years ago, he's never been the same—"

The sounds of feet landing on the tile floor stopped Lucy midsentence. She stood and half smiled. "I'll catch up with you later."

"Morning." Nick grunted the word as he passed Lucy on his way to the coffeepot. Boomer trailed behind, wagging his tail as if he were home.

Nick's black hair was tousled and he wasn't wearing a shirt.

Sadie's heart squeezed. She stood and walked to the back door, making kissing noises at her dog as she opened it. "C'mon, Boomer. You need to go outside."

He trotted past her unceremoniously.

She followed him. Not because she had to stand over him while he did his business, but because she needed air. Her heart ached for Nick, for his tragic loss. Maybe he did understand the feeling of losing everything.

She breathed in the crisp air, inviting it into her soul.

The grass glistened, still wet from the storm. The birds chirped their morning songs. The sun, a warm glow, rose just above the trees. Everything about the ranch was perfection. How could a place she'd never been before feel so much like home?

This must be what heaven is like.

Or maybe it was the love she felt from the moment she saw the Campbells together. Even though Luke teased Nick that first night in the truck, she felt an unspoken, unbreakable bond between the brothers. She imagined they could get away with teasing each other, but let someone else try. No doubt they'd rally for one serious fight.

A little piece of her heart opened.

Being on a ranch seemed to suit Boomer, too. He ran

toward the fence and then cut a hard left a second before crashing into it.

The place wasn't extravagant. The barn needed a good coat of paint. And yet, it was a beautiful, serene place.

This would have been a great place to grow up.

Boomer returned to her side with a stick clenched in his teeth.

He dropped it at her feet. She picked it up, red paint dotting her fingers. No. Not red paint. She examined the stains closer, fanning out her fingers...blood. She released her grip on the stick, sending it tumbling to the ground.

Boomer lurched toward it.

"Leave it." The command came out harsher than she'd planned.

He froze.

She kicked the stick, launching it into the air while distracting Boomer with kissing noises.

She scanned the tree line, the barn, the fence. Her heart jackhammered her ribs with painful stabs.

Where'd the blood come from? Boomer's mouth? Maybe the stick had jabbed his gums and caused them to bleed. She bent down to get a better look in his mouth and opened his jaw flaps. "You okay, boy?"

She examined her fingers. His saliva mixed with blood. "Did you cut your gums with that stick?"

Her warning bells sounded. She stood and glanced around one more time, ignoring the chill racing up her spine. Could someone be out there? Waiting for the right moment to strike?

The explanation was right in front of her, on her hand. The sight of blood still goose bumped her flesh.

She opened the door to see Nick standing near the coffeemaker. Seeing him there had a similar effect to feeling morning sunshine on her face.

The door creaked closed behind her and she turned long enough to lock it.

"Everything okay?" Nick asked, studying her expression.

"Yeah. Fine." She didn't want to tell him every shadow made her jump. Being cautious was one thing. Letting her fear get the best of her was something totally different. She washed her hands and poured a bowl of water for Boomer before setting it on the floor. "I need to pick up dog food. Anything around here he can eat until I can get to a store?"

"I can make a trip into town later. I'll find something for him in the meantime." He turned and searched the pantry. A minute later, he poked his head out. "The bread turned out to be pretty amazing. I had to fight my brothers to save a piece for you." He pointed to the counter by the stove. "I missed waking up to that smell first thing in the morning."

A chunk had been neatly wrapped for her and placed on the kitchen island.

Sadie peeled open the Saran wrap and took a bite after pouring a fresh cup of coffee. "You finished it?"

"We make a good team." Nick stepped out of the pantry. "Nothing in there for our boy to eat."

She liked the sound of the words *our boy*.

Luke strolled in, rubbing his eyes. "I'm going in this morning for supplies. What do you need?"

"Food for Boomer," Sadie said then frowned.

"What's wrong?" Luke asked.

"I just realized that I don't have any way to pay for food or anything else. I lost my wallet along with my purse when the bakery caught fire."

"You don't need money." Nick bent down and scratched Boomer's head. "You hungry, boy? I got something around here for you." He moved to the fridge and pulled out enough meat to fill a small pan. "I'll cook up something for him. He'll like this better, anyway."

A look passed between Nick and Luke.

"What's going on?" Sadie asked.

Neither spoke.

"I deserve to know." She stood her ground.

Nick stood and folded his arms. "I don't want my brother in town buying dog food all of a sudden. We can't break with routine. Otherwise we'll alert people to our presence. I can't have anyone stopping by unexpectedly or asking too many questions."

"He's right," Luke interjected, watching Sadie as a wall of emotion descended on her with more force than a rogue wave. "I'm surprised he let you keep the dog this long."

Panic crawled through her veins and she forced back the urge to cry. "I'm not going anywhere without Boomer. He needs me."

"I understand, but you have to think of it from our perspective. He's a liability," Luke said apologetically.

"He saved our lives," she said. Her gaze flew to Nick.

He nodded agreement. "He's a good boy, don't get me wrong. It's just the other team already knows about him. He might give us away at a critical moment."

On some level, she knew he was right. Yet, the thought of being without her constant companion was almost too much to handle. "I hear what you're saying, but no. I can't do this without him. You have to let me keep him. Please."

"I didn't say you had to get rid of him, did I? I just

don't want to wave a flag in town that we're here." He patted Boomer's head.

Luke disappeared down the hall.

She couldn't pinpoint the emotion darkening Nick's features. She'd seen it before in the truck moments before he'd said he sent someone to pick up her personal things from the lake house. A shared sense of loss? A kindred spirit? A person who truly understood her dog was the only family she had left? She didn't care. He was agreeing to let her keep the one thing she loved the most. She took a step forward and wrapped her arms around his neck. "Thank you."

She could feel his heartbeat against her chest, his rapid rhythm matching hers. His arms encircled her waist. His body, flush with hers, caused sensual heat to pulse through her.

She wouldn't argue that she felt drawn to Nick from the start, even when she thought he was a nerdy radiologist. Getting to know him better was only deepening the attraction.

"Don't mention it," he said, his low baritone vibrating over her already sensitized skin.

Sadie took a step back, trying to get her bearings and erase his warm body and citrus soap scent from her thoughts. He was masculinity personified. Her mind tried to wrap around the fact the air could be charged with so much chemistry and heat in such a short time.

She suddenly remembered Luke could walk in any second. Embarrassment crawled up her neck in a rash as she glanced around.

She focused on Boomer. "He did good yesterday."

Nick cleared his throat. "Sure did. He's not the only one. He'd make a good officer, wouldn't you, boy? We'll figure out a way to keep him."

Sadie should feel relief. She was getting what she wanted. Or was she?

The past few minutes had her suddenly wanting more…she wanted the whole package. Would she ever have a house with the white picket fence and the perfect man to go along with the dog? Was Nick that perfect man?

Whoa. She was seriously getting ahead of herself.

There was an undeniable sexual current running between them. But real feelings? Wasn't it way too early to tell?

A short, well-kept curly-haired woman who looked to be in her late fifties walked in the back door. "Boys, come help me get bags from the car."

Luke didn't make eye contact with Sadie or Nick as he walked by, and out the door. He'd already said his piece about Nick breaking protocol to bring her to the ranch. Now she was practically throwing herself at him in front of his brother.

Nick introduced Sadie to his mother—she had the same thick black hair as him. Hers curled around her ears. She couldn't have been more than five foot four. Her arms were filled with grocery bags. Her wide brown eyes took Sadie in for a minute before she spoke. "You must be Sadie." His mom looked her up and down with a smile.

"Nice to meet you," Sadie said. "Let me help with those."

"The pleasure is mine, sweetheart. I'm looking forward to getting to know you better." Her gaze honed in on Nick. "I brought the supplies. Grab your other brother and help unload the truck so we can give Gran the celebration she deserves."

Nick relieved his mother of the bags she held. As soon

as her arms were free, she wrapped them around Sadie in firm hug. "It sure is nice to meet you. Call me Melba."

"It really is nice to meet you, Melba." Sadie didn't shrink at the older woman's contact. Instead, she had an unexplainable feeling of being right where she belonged. It was a temporary feeling at best. Sadie hadn't felt as though she belonged anywhere in her entire life. Even when her parents were alive, they'd never made her feel this safe.

The memory of when she was twelve flooded her. She'd had to stay after school for choir practice. She lived too far away to walk home. Her parents had had to work but promised to be there to pick her up by six o'clock.

Choir practice ended and she went outside with the other kids.

The carpool line was long.

She watched each car go past, smiling parents picking up their children.

The choir teacher gave her an annoyed look.

She'd told them her parents would be there any minute. She prayed they hadn't forgotten like they did her school play.

They were so wrapped up in their business, their own lives, Sadie wondered if they'd cared about her at all.

She never knew what to expect from them.

The choir teacher marched her inside after waiting forty minutes at the curb and told her to call her parents. He took that moment to remind her they'd had to sign a slip at the beginning of the school year saying they understood the commitment they were making.

They didn't pick up the phone.

Sadie lied, saying she suddenly remembered they'd wanted her to walk home.

The teacher reluctantly agreed, saying they were supposed to send a note if other arrangements were needed.

She'd sworn to him they'd be fine with her walking.

He let her go.

Anger and humiliation had her stalking toward home. Then she realized she'd have to walk through a dicey part of town to get there.

Fear assailed her when she heard music thumping from a boom box. Cars with missing parts were parked on front lawns.

Sofas were used as porch furniture.

Midway up the street, several men stood around the cars, downing forty-ounce cans of beer.

The anger that had brought her there turned to apprehension. When one of the men catcalled her, apprehension gave way to fear.

Her heart thumped so loudly she was certain people could hear it from a block away.

She kept her head down and crossed the street.

One of the men, the one who whistled at her, followed.

In that moment, Sadie realized what true fear was. And how someone could instill it in her in five seconds flat.

The other men goaded him on.

Sadie broke into a run.

A voice from behind her, nearing, called to someone in front of her. A man four houses down stepped onto the sidewalk. The look on his face, the grin, was still etched in her memory.

Her twelve-year-old self picked that moment to scream.

"No one can hear you," the man behind her said, his hand on her shoulder. To this day, just the thought of his touch gave her the willies.

She slapped it off.

"Someone's feisty."

The man in front of her closed in.

"This one's spunky."

Fear and anger and abandonment welled inside her. Where were her parents when she needed them?

Yes, it had been stupid to think she could walk.

Anger had her doing that when she shouldn't.

This was too much to handle.

She had no means of escape and one of the men touched her ponytail. His hands were dirty.

Sadie shivered, glancing around wildly.

She was trapped.

"You better think twice before you touch that little girl again." An unfamiliar man's voice to her left said.

She hadn't noticed the couple standing on their porch until just then.

"I push one more button on this phone, and the police'll be here before you can count to three. I doubt your parole officer would be real impressed, Sean." The woman held up a phone.

The man they addressed as Sean, the one who'd touched her, hesitated before holding his hands up in the universal sign for surrender. "No harm here. We was just having a little fun, wasn't we?"

His gaze flicked to his buddy before settling on the couple again.

The woman had handed the phone to her husband and moved to Sadie's side. The older woman's arms around Sadie marked the first time she'd felt safe. "You best keep your fun on your side of the street if you don't want to serve the rest of your time in prison."

Melba's arms around Sadie gave her that same fleeting feeling of comfort as the strangers' had. They'd asked her if her mother knew she was alone in the neighborhood and, embarrassed, she'd said no.

Sadie searched her memory for a time when she'd felt protected by her parents and came up empty.

They'd been frantic when they'd found out what had happened.

Were they a perfect family?

No.

She didn't question their love for her. Work always came first. They'd always told her the best way they could secure a future for her was to make sure she had enough food in her mouth.

Even so, she couldn't help but wonder if they'd notice if she was gone.

Nick's mom patted Sadie's back before letting go.

She gave a quick smile and then clapped her hands together once. "You boys ready to get started? I've got a new bread pudding recipe I've been dying to try out. I've been looking up recipes for the last week."

"All we need are a few good steaks for the grill," Nick said, smiling.

The warmth on his face at his mother's reaction to Sadie put a wide smile on his face.

Luke walked in the back door, bags hanging from his arms, and winked. "You better run while you can get away, Sadie. Or she'll put you to work, too."

"Sadie's quite a talented baker. She might teach us a thing or two if we let her loose in the kitchen," Nick chimed in.

Was he beaming when he said that?

Nah. Couldn't be.

Sadie had to be seeing things.

She'd seen Nick Campbell survive bullets, lead her

through underbrush and trees to safety, and outsmart dangerous men. He was most definitely not the type to beam.

Boomer, tail wagging, walked circles in front of Melba.

"And who is this baby?" Melba acknowledged, as Gran and the others filed into the kitchen.

"He's mine." Sadie smiled, despite feeling like the odd man out in the room. And yet, everyone in Nick's family had made her feel welcome in some way.

Maybe, someday, when all this was behind her and she had a normal life again, she'd live on a ranch like this one.

The image of children running outside, drinking Kool-Aid on a hot summer's day, pierced her thoughts.

What did she think about having children?

For so long, she thought she'd marry Tom, and they'd start a family two years after the wedding. He'd wanted to give them a chance to adjust to being husband and wife before they added to their family.

Part of her thought planning everything out was a good idea. Another side to her railed against the notion. She, of all people, knew how life had a way of charting its own course for people, and especially her.

In her life, if she planned an outdoor vacation, it was sure to rain.

She'd learned years ago not to fight it. Things tended to work out best for her if she found a way to relax and go with the flow.

Tom had been order and plans and spreadsheets.

Miraculously, his plans seemed to work out. The sun even knew when to cue for him if he'd planned their getaway. She had no idea how he'd managed it, but it had worked out.

He'd wanted to graduate from college before he got a job. He did.

He'd planned to work for a company that was willing to pay for his advanced degree so he could save for a wedding. Check.

His last year of graduate school, he expected to date the woman he planned to marry. They'd met Valentine's Day of that year.

He planned to get engaged after dating for two years. He'd already started laying hints.

The marriage part? Well, that didn't work out quite so well for him.

Sadie glanced around at people milling around the room.

She only hoped she could survive the next couple of hours surrounded by all the people Nick loved.

Chapter Eleven

The special occasion plates had been washed and put away in the china cabinet. Everyone had settled into the family room to watch a movie. The sun was beginning its descent. Nick figured he could zip out relatively quietly.

He borrowed Luke's keys and slipped out back.

Most people confused Nick for his brother at a distance, anyway. The safest way to slip out of town unnoticed was to be mistaken for Luke.

Sadie wasn't expecting him to leave until midnight, so he should be good there. She'd excused herself to go lay down after supper, no doubt her body was still on bakery time. Adjusting to being awake in the daytime would take a few weeks.

Dallas was a good forty-minute drive. What was Grimes doing with a warehouse downtown? The obvious answers? Funneling weapons. Human trafficking. Or using it to store product.

As he opened the door and then slid into the driver's seat, his internal warning bells sounded. He drew his weapon, turned around and yanked the blanket from the floorboard.

"Dammit, Sadie. What do you think you're doing?"

She didn't respond.

"You didn't answer my question," he said, immediately withdrawing his weapon and tucking it in the back of his jeans.

"Um, I guess there's no point pretending it's not me." She gave the universal sign of surrender and smiled.

She was kidding around? Trying to make light of the situation? He didn't think so.

"I don't appreciate this at all. What kind of relationship will we have if I can't trust you?" He immediately realized just how hypocritical he sounded.

She gave him a "go to Hades" look that could set ice on fire. "My thoughts exactly."

"Point taken," he conceded, offering a hand up. "How'd you know I was leaving early?"

"I wasn't sure. I guessed. Why? What does it matter? I'm here. That's the most important thing." She hopped over the seat and eased onto the passenger's side.

"No. It isn't." He deadpanned her. "You're not coming."

"Yes, I am. Please. I promise to stay in the truck." Her green eyes pleaded, and his heart stuttered.

"No, you won't." He let out a suppressed laugh. Not a good idea to let her affect his decisions. He'd crossed a line with her physically. Couldn't say he was especially sorry for holding her in the kitchen. But that's where it had to end. When it came to his investigation, there was no give-and-take. She might jeopardize his information-gathering mission.

"I will. Just let me come with you. I'll do whatever you say."

He could think of a few interesting suggestions with their bodies this close. None of them involved work. "Give me one good reason not to haul you out of this truck."

"Because I'm scared something will happen to you if

you go alone and you said Luke was coming. Because my conscious wouldn't be able to handle knowing you'd gone alone. Because maybe I can help."

She was concerned about his safety? "That's three."

"I'm scared."

In a split second, she scooted next to him. Before he could argue, her lips found his. All rational thought as to why he shouldn't allow this to happen flew out his brain when he tasted her sweet lips.

With her mouth moving against his, wasn't as if he could stop himself. He took hold of her neck and positioned her head exactly where he wanted her. Desire was a current running through him, seeking an outlet. This close, the scent of her flooded him. His body so in tune with hers, he was already getting excited. Blood pulsed thickly to the erection growing in his jeans.

He laid her back against the seat, his heft covering her. Her tongue battled with his in the best war he'd ever waged. She tasted sweet, and he wanted more. Now. Not a good idea.

With great effort, he disengaged. "You sure this is what you want?"

Her hands slipped inside his shirt, feeling their way up his chest in answer.

She tasted better than the fresh-baked-bread-and-lily scent he'd first been attracted to. He hadn't forgotten the brief kiss they'd shared at the cabin. He'd had to break apart too soon for his liking.

He cupped her full breast and groaned when her nipple beaded in his palm. A little voice in the back of his head said he shouldn't be doing this. He should take a step back. Analyze the situation. *Like that was about to happen.*

He'd wanted, no needed, to feel her milky skin against

him. It had been too long since he'd had sex, and he was already growing hard as her fingers outlined the muscles in his chest. Her hands came up to his shoulders, pressing deep.

His body ached to feel her naked and positioned right where he wanted her underneath him. Then again, he wouldn't complain if she decided to take charge and climb on top, either. She wrapped her legs around his hips, denim on denim, and he thrust his hips deeper inside the V of her legs.

His tongue slicked across her lips and he swallowed her moan.

Much more and he wouldn't be able to quit.

To hell with that. Another second and his control would be shattered.

Every bit of his body battled against his logical mind. He pulled on all the restraint he could muster to break away from her. "You make one hell of an argument, but if you don't stop this right now, I won't be able to. Your lips are the sweetest things I've ever tasted."

"Then what's stopping you?"

"I don't want you to regret anything you do with me, for one."

The sun was an orange glow in the distance.

She looked up at him, all big green eyes and full pink lips. "Then don't stop. I want you to make love to me right here. And then I want to go with you."

The first part? No problem.

The second presented the hiccup. He had no plans to take her with him. And yet, all he had to do was give her a quick nod, and he'd be in paradise in the time it took them to strip.

He had no doubt it'd be the best sex of his life.

But then what?

Their physical connection would be built on a lie. Not exactly the way he'd planned to start their relationship.

Relationship?

Whatever this was. No good could come of deceit.

She looked up at him, desire darkening those incredible green eyes. Didn't seem as though she planned to make this easy. Did she have any idea how easy it would be to rip open the condom in his wallet and show her how sexy and desirable she was right then and there? He wanted nothing more than to thrust himself deeper inside the V of her legs without all that denim getting in the way…to allow her to wrap those naked silky legs around him.

The heat had been building between them since he'd broken into the bakery to save her.

If he was being honest, there'd been sparks from the second their eyes met the month before. That spark had grown into a raging fire. He wanted her more than he wanted air.

But he couldn't let her make a mistake she'd regret. "I'm not trying to punish you by keeping you at the ranch. I'm trying to keep you safe."

"The only way you can guarantee that is to keep me with you. Besides, you've waited too long to kiss me. Is there something wrong with me? Don't you find me attractive?"

She shifted her weight underneath him, and his erection throbbed.

If she wasn't going to stop this, he should. He wanted to make love to her. Just not on the bench seat of a pickup truck. He wanted to take his time and kiss that freckle on the inside of her thigh until she moaned.

"Finding you desirable is not the problem. You sure you want to make love with me?"

She nodded.

His resolve fractured. "You just gave me an even better reason to march your butt in the house. But I guarantee we wouldn't leave anytime soon. I plan to take my time. And I need to follow up on this lead. Make sure those men can't hurt you anymore."

Her smile made him want things he shouldn't. Threatened to open old wounds, too. More alarm bells sounded, but these had to do with a totally different danger. His heart. He ignored them, dipping his head one more time to taste her sweetness.

With every bit of his strength, he pushed himself up on his arms. "So, you have to go inside."

"We have an agreement. Remember? You don't make decisions without me."

"I didn't violate—"

"No. You didn't. And I don't plan to, either. But take me back in there and I'll be gone before you get back."

He searched her eyes to see if the threat was hollow. He'd suspected it was when she'd made it earlier after they'd first arrived at the ranch. Where would she go? Just run off into the night? She had to realize she didn't have a bargaining chip in this poker game. She wasn't stupid. On the other hand, her back was against the wall. Would she be desperate enough to follow through with her threat? She was smart, sexy and stubborn.

She watched him intently as he processed the information. The minute she figured out she had him, she smiled.

He had no choice but to let her come with him. He didn't want to risk her leaving, even though somewhere inside he knew she was bluffing. Calling her on it would take away what little power she had left. He didn't have it in him to do that. He could make this work. Stash her in the truck and keep her a safe distance from the warehouse. That way, even if she did try to find him, she wouldn't be able to.

"Are you considering taking me?" Her smile melted what was left of his resolves.

"Yes."

She rewarded him with another sweet kiss that was gently pressed to his lips, which almost had him thinking bedding her right then wasn't such a bad idea.

"That kiss is to be continued later. And, sweetheart, I don't plan to be in a hurry when I peel off your clothes and kiss every inch of the silky skin on the inside of your thigh." He pressed his hand to the inside of her leg. "Or your stomach." He ran his finger along the waistband of her jeans, barely touching the sweet skin there. "Or your neck." He dipped his head and skimmed her breastbone with his lips.

She let out a sexy little moan through ragged breaths. Her jewel-toned eyes glittered with need. "I sure hope you're a man of your word."

A big piece of him cursed the timing of the drive to Dallas. He'd be a lot happier if he were back at the ranch. With her. In bed.

The thought sobered him as he took the driver's seat. He patted a spot next to him. "Buckle up."

She scooted over and leaned her head on his shoulder. "You know, if you'd asked me out on a date back in Creek Bend, I most likely would've gone."

"I couldn't. Against the rules. There were times when you looked like you could barely stand to be in the same room with me. Thought for sure I'd scared you off more than once."

"Everyone freaked me out but you. There was something about you that put me at ease. I guess it's all your training. It worked."

His gaze moved to hers and intensified. "Darlin', flirting with you was the only time I wasn't acting in Creek Bend."

He put the truck in Reverse and backed out of the lot. He maneuvered onto the highway with the all-too-real notion his feelings toward Sadie were growing. She'd put a chink in the armor surrounding his heart. This wasn't part of the plan.

What he needed to do was focus on the job ahead.

Grimes was out for revenge. They had no idea where he was but believed him to be somewhere in Texas. He'd partnered with her handler, and quite possibly given up his supervisor. Grimes wouldn't let up until he erased the woman Nick was falling for.

Hold on there.

Was he admitting she'd become so much more than a witness to him? The sexual chemistry between them could light a fresh-cut log on fire. But his heart? Not on the table.

His cell buzzed. He fished it from his pocket and handed it to Sadie, instructing her to put the call on speaker when he saw the name Smith on the screen. "You're on speaker with me and Sadie. What's the word?"

"I have good news for you, Sadie. Evidence points toward Charlie's innocence. Looks like your handler was clean. And there's a pretty good chance he hid your file before he was murdered."

A mix of relief and sadness played across her features.

"Thank you for telling me," she said.

"I figured you'd want to know that first."

Nick kept his gaze trained on the yellow stripes in front of him, leading the way to Dallas. His headlights slashed through the darkness descending around them.

This turned his theory upside down. "What else did you find out?"

"I have it on good authority Jamison is the one who set Charlie up. He threw Charlie under the bus to appease them, since Jamison wasn't having luck finding information on Sadie's whereabouts."

Nick muttered a curse.

"Worse yet, Jamison wasn't their lackey. He was their partner. My source discovered—"

"Don't tell me. Let me guess. Money in a Swiss bank account." Nick grunted the words.

"Close. Jamison had a weakness for the Cayman islands."

"So, Jamison was on the take? The greedy bastard got a good agent killed to pad his own retirement fund?"

Smith coughed. "My sources say it's worse than that. Two hours ago, a list of all Texas deputies and their personal information surfaced."

The words hit Nick like a sucker punch.

His mind snapped into focus. He knew exactly what that meant. The ranch was no longer safe. He had to get word to Luke. His brothers would know how to handle any threat. It wouldn't be safe for Sadie to return, either. He hated to think of her reaction when he told her she couldn't go back for Boomer. They couldn't go back to the ranch now.

He glanced at her. She held up the phone. Didn't say a word. He could almost hear the wheels cranking in her mind.

"Nick."

"Yeah." He was still trying to get his head around this last bit of information.

"I won't stop until I find him." His voice was nothing but steel resolve.

"Any chance Charlie stashed her folder somewhere safe?" He gripped the wheel. "Never mind that question. They wouldn't have found her."

"I'm going to send some pictures. Sadie, I need you to look at them. If you can identify him, I'll be able to get a warrant to search his house."

Sadie sucked in a breath. She must've realized the implication. "One of the guys who abducted me might be a U.S. Marshal."

There was dead silence.

"It would certainly explain why they're coming at you so hard," Smith said. "You said in your statement that you'd seen their faces."

They'd been relentless so far. It also made sense why they seemed to understand how Nick would work. How they anticipated his moves or had had someone on his heels at every turn. A man with the same training would have a better idea where to look.

Nick took the next exit. "Send the photos."

He ended the call and located an abandoned lot. He parked and flipped on the cab light.

Sadie's grip on the phone had turned her knuckles white. Her hand shook and her skin had gone pale.

Nick gently pulled the cell out of her hand and kissed the tips of her fingers. "I need to warn Luke."

His brother picked up on the first ring.

"Bad news."

A yawn came through the line. "You didn't wreck my truck, did you?"

"Nope. Much worse. We've confirmed our suspicions. This case involves some of my own."

The line went dead quiet.

"That's not good."

"My involvement in the case has most likely caused

them to target me," Nick said, his gaze on Sadie the whole time. She was afraid but brave.

"That's really not good."

"No, it isn't."

"Any chance they know about the ranch?" Luke asked.

"A list just turned up with Texas deputies' personal information on it."

Luke let out a string of curse words.

"So far, I know one supervisor was involved. He got a deputy killed to protect his healthy bank account on the islands," Nick said.

"Hard to believe someone would turn on their own for a few bucks, but to each his own, I guess."

"He's a jerk."

"One I'd like to be alone with in a room for ten minutes."

"Agreed. Problem is, because of him a good deputy was killed and many more are at risk."

Luke grunted.

"My boss is sending over pictures for Sadie to look at, so I can't stay on long. We're certain all the deputies in Texas have been identified for Grimes and his men."

"Bastard."

"Agreed. Get everyone off the ranch, just in case."

"Will do. I'll have Reed take them to Galveston. Everyone except Meg and Riley. They'll have to stick around to be close to her doctor. I'll stay at my place in Dallas. Can't get too far from The Metroplex while I'm working on my case."

"Sounds like a plan. Make Meg and Riley promise to have their place watched. Better yet, do Riley's parents live in Fort Worth?"

"I believe so."

"Any chance you can get them to agree to stay there?

I don't want to take any risks with her so close to her due date."

"I'm on it," Luke said. "I'll get the others out by tonight. Don't worry. And I'll make sure Sadie's dog is taken care of, too."

"Boomer," Sadie said in almost a whisper.

"I'll take care of him while you're on the go. You got a safe house, man?" Luke asked.

"Yeah. I'm heading to Richardson after a little trip downtown. I might need a favor while Reed's down south."

"Yeah?'

"Grimes has a real estate holding in Houston. I need someone to check it out for me. Dig around. See what they can find."

"Wish I could go myself." The telltale adrenaline that hit before a big assignment deepened Luke's tone.

"I wish we could go together. I like my odds better if I have someone I can trust backing me up."

"I'll tell Reed. Text the address."

"Will do."

"When this is over, you should come on over to our side. FBI needs more good people they can trust," Luke said, using his sense of humor to lighten the mood.

"Believe me, after this assignment, I'd almost consider it."

"If we were smart, we'd leave our day jobs and work for ourselves."

"Another tempting idea. Have Reed give me a call as soon as he gets to that warehouse."

"Can I give him a heads-up on what he might expect to find?"

"Wish I could help."

"That close to the border, Grimes might be moving product in through Galveston," Luke said.

"Yeah. I have no idea what to expect. All I know is he has a straight line up to Canada."

"You've found the right man for the job if they're hauling stuff through the Gulf," Luke agreed.

"His department might find something interesting. He'll need a reason to search the place officially."

"Reed can be damn inventive when he needs to be." Luke paused. "Keep me in the loop."

Nick agreed and ended the call. He had eight text messages waiting. He opened the first and showed the picture to Sadie.

She shook her head.

The second received the same response.

The third, fourth and fifth had the same affect.

When he opened the sixth and glanced up, he saw recognition stamped all over Sadie's features. Her pupils dilated and her breath came out in a gasp.

"That's him."

Chapter Twelve

"This guy looks familiar?" Nick asked. Anger rose inside him as he watched a tremor rock her body.

Her chin came up, and she locked gazes. "Yes."

He fired off a confirmation text to Smith.

"He was one of the guys who abducted me," she said, her body shaking. "I'd been grocery shopping. I was putting the bags in my car when all of a sudden this van pulled up behind me, blocking my car. I didn't think much about it. I mean, I lived in a relatively safe suburb. I actually thought the driver was about to ask for directions when this man came out of nowhere from behind the van. He put some kind of cloth over my mouth. I couldn't scream. I couldn't fight. I couldn't believe this was happening to me in broad daylight. The smell of whatever was in that cloth burned my nose and eyes."

Nick's fists clenched and released. He was more determined than ever to stop whoever was after the woman he was falling for. Forcing Sadie to remember such a heinous experience went against every fiber of his being. He'd buried his own bad memories so deep hell itself could rise up and not find them. Except remembering might just save her life.

Causing her more pain ate at his gut. Everything she'd been through was totally bogus.

She was in trouble. So was he. His feelings ran deeper than he should allow. He still wasn't sure what the hell to do with them. No one since Rachael had touched his heart so deeply or threatened to crack his tough veneer and he still hadn't figured out why he'd kept her ring in his pocket for a year. He figured something inside him didn't work right after watching his mom's pain and deciding love was about the cruelest thing that could happen to a person. He assumed that part of his heart had been closed off forever. "The whole scenario had to be scary as hell."

"Yeah, panic didn't cover it. I felt so helpless. Next thing I knew I woke up in the back of the van, and that guy was staring at me."

Nick didn't say the agent must've expected to kill her if he let her see his face. "You're safe now. That's the important thing."

A car pulled into the lot.

Nick checked his rearview mirror, started the engine and drove away, spewing gravel from the back tires.

He didn't want to press Sadie to talk but if she remembered something, anything, they might be able to pinpoint a location. He'd talk to her about it more when they arrived at the safe house later. Right now, he had a warehouse to investigate.

They'd been driving a good twenty minutes before either spoke again.

"Where are we going? Sadie asked.

"Brenner and Harry Hines. Near Love Field."

"How convenient to have a warehouse so close to an airport."

He exited Stemmons Freeway onto Walnut Hill and then turned right onto Shady Trail. "It's regional. But, yeah, it would be handy. If they needed to go farther, DFW's twenty minutes away depending on traffic."

He parked the truck in a small lot next to Old Letot Cemetery. The cemetery was the size of a half-decent backyard encased in a four-foot-high chain-link fence. Getting to Brenner would be an easy walk from there.

Leaving a beautiful woman like Sadie in the truck in a bad neighborhood—even locked—was riskier than taking her with him. Besides, he doubted she'd stay put, anyway. He could keep a better eye on her if she went with him.

"We'll need to keep quiet."

She seemed to catch the word *we* quickly, and perked up at the realization she was coming. "Not a problem."

"Anything happens to me and you'll need a way to protect yourself." He pulled his .38 caliber from his ankle holster.

Her hand shook as she reached for it.

"You okay?"

To her credit, she nodded and gripped the gun.

"Stick close behind me. I stop too fast, I want to feel you run into my back. Got it?"

She nodded again.

"Then, let's do this."

She scooted out his door, exiting the truck right behind him. Apparently, she had every intention of taking his request to heart. Good. He wanted her so close he could hear her breathe.

He hopped the fence and helped Sadie over. They cut across the small cemetery so he could investigate the warehouse from the back first. He crouched low behind the Dumpster in the back parking lot and watched.

There was no activity in the row of warehouses. A handful of vehicles were parked in the small lot—two vans and a couple of flatbed trucks. Everything was quiet. He didn't hear any traffic. He located the numbers 2626 on top of the metal sliding door.

They'd wait and see if there was any activity. He needed to ensure no one came or went before he and Sadie made a move to get closer.

So much of this job was about patience.

Twenty minutes passed and nothing moved except for a raccoon in the trash bin that almost made Sadie jump out of her skin. She'd kept her cool.

"Stay right here while I check out the vehicles."

Her eyes were wide, but she nodded.

Nick kept a low profile as he moved across the small lot, squat walking, just in case someone was waiting in one of the trucks. He'd learned to expect anything in these situations. Someone could be there asleep. At least he was sure no one was getting lucky in the backseat. He hadn't seen the telltale fog of the windows. Near Harry Hines, anything was possible. In his years with the agency, he'd pretty much seen it all.

He touched the hood of each vehicle. Cold.

None of them had been driven lately.

One by one, he checked the cabs.

Clear.

Good.

He returned to Sadie. "Ready to move to the front?"

She nodded again. She was either scared to the point of being mute or a good listener. He hoped for the second. He could work with that.

"Let's move."

He was almost surprised when she followed him. Meant she was coherent. Another good sign.

The strip of warehouses was encased by wrought-iron fences out front. He hoped none of them were hot. He could scale the six-foot barrier easily with one hand on the top rail, but Sadie wouldn't be able to. He picked up a rock and tossed it at the fence.

No telltale crackle of electricity.

The sounds of tires turning on pavement caught his attention. Two dots appeared down the street. The headlights were moving toward them.

He grabbed Sadie by the hand and climbed over the fence. She dropped to her hands and knees and crawled behind him.

The headlights moved closer.

Adrenaline thumped through his veins. He couldn't guarantee Sadie's safety. Didn't especially like the feeling gripping him that he'd compromised her security by bringing her along.

Wouldn't do any good to second-guess himself.

She was there.

He was there.

He'd make sure they both made it out alive.

Brakes squeaked the car to a stop two buildings down. Nick made out an older model Lincoln. There was a driver and a passenger. The passenger moved over to the driver's side and the seat flew back. Both of them disappeared.

Nick watched carefully for the overhead light to come on in case someone was exiting the vehicle. An experienced criminal would know to turn it off before slipping out. Neither Grimes nor the U.S. Marshals searching for them were amateurs.

Nick waited another five minutes, his gaze intent on the dark sedan.

"I'm moving closer to check it out. You stay right here," he whispered when enough time had passed. He had to crawl across the empty parking lot to get close enough to see what was going on. No one had left the vehicle as far as he could tell.

A light came on in the third building as he neared the halfway mark across the lot. The warehouse was right next to him. He froze, making himself as small as possible.

Nothing but stillness surrounded him.

He inched closer to the Lincoln. Made it to the corner where his lot and the one for building number two met. The car wasn't a hundred yards away. He was close enough to see the windows fogging up and hear the shocks creaking. Lovers? Not likely. Not at this time of night on this road. But they were having sex.

Nick had a problem on his hands. He could flash his badge and get rid of the prostitute and John, but possibly call attention to himself and Sadie. Or he could wait it out. His back already hurt like hell.

The light flipped off on building number three.

He had to assume whoever was there had gotten what they came for. They must've used the back entrance, which made the most sense if they were loading supplies. He didn't have time to care why a person would be here at this late hour.

Even though he knew exactly what was going on in the car, he had to make sure. Getting close enough to get a visual would be right up there with his least favorite task of the night.

On closer assessment, the pair was doing exactly what he suspected.

Nick crawled across the lot. Relief flooded him that Sadie was exactly where he left her. Not having his eyes on her for even a second did all kinds of crazy things to his insides, to his heart. This didn't seem like an appropriate time to get inside his head about what that meant.

She leaned so close he could feel her breath on him. "What could they possibly be doing over there? I freaked when they pulled up, thinking the worst, but no one's getting out of the car."

He couldn't wipe the ridiculous grin off his face. This wasn't the time to be charmed by her innocence. "You don't want to know."

"What does that… Oh." With the dim glow of a street lamp, he could see her cheeks flush with embarrassment. "What do we do now?"

"Wait."

Fifteen minutes passed before the passenger's door opened and a tall skinny girl crawled out.

Sadie reached out to Nick, placing her hand in his. Hers seemed small by comparison. And soft.

He squeezed her fingers for reassurance. A few more minutes and they'd get what they came for.

The door slammed shut and the Lincoln pulled away, squealing its tires.

Skinny tucked something, presumably cash, in her bra and stumbled away, either drunk or high, or both.

Nick didn't like the idea of her or anyone else being around or the possibility they could be seen. Her presence also most likely meant there were others like her wandering around, searching for their next twenty dollars or fix.

His warning system flared up that anyone else could see them or identify them at the scene. Especially since he had no idea what this warehouse was being used for.

He had to prepare himself for any possibility.

Damn that anyone could signal inside or send up a red flag, alerting Grimes's men to their presence if anyone was there.

"Stick close by me."

Sadie nodded.

He had to make sure Skinny was far enough away, and there was no pimp nearby working this end of the street.

Nick kept to the shadows, with Sadie right behind him every step of the way.

He followed Skinny back to Harry Hines, where she met up with a few similarly dressed women.

Relief flooded him as he backtracked the couple of blocks to the warehouse.

Instinct told him they needed to get the information they came for and get the hell out of there.

Chapter Thirteen

As expected, the front and back doors were locked. Sadie hadn't expected a man like Grimes to leave his inventory, or whatever he kept in there, unprotected.

"We can't break one of the windows up front, can we?" she asked.

"I don't want to raise suspicion we were here." Nick moved to the dock door, bent down and examined the lock. He fished a small Swiss army knife out of his pocket and went to work with his flashlight and small pick-looking tool. "I can manage this one easily enough."

"Can you do this?" Sadie asked, shocked. Surely he wasn't planning on breaking and entering. Wasn't that a felony offense? He'd lose his job. Possibly even go to jail.

He deadpanned her. "Not legally. Anything we find won't be admissible in court. But they've involved my family. I'll do what's necessary to protect them."

The way he clenched his jaw left no doubt he meant every word.

She tamped down the emotion tugging at her heart. The air stirred around them. With the way he watched over the people he loved, Nick would make an amazing father someday. He was exactly the kind of man she'd want to father her children someday.

The shock of her realization she wanted kids was only dwarfed by the one that said she wanted to be with Nick.

"What do you think we'll find in there?" she asked.

"Could be anything from guns to illegals. It's dark and quiet inside. Whoever takes care of the shipments has gone home."

Images of poor, hungry people packed inside trucks without air-conditioning popped into Sadie's mind. Since she'd been in Texas, she hadn't gone a month without seeing something in the news about human trafficker raids or inhumane conditions.

A snick sounded, and she knew he'd cracked the lock. He closed the tool and stuffed it in his pocket.

He rolled up the door enough for them to squat down and slip inside. "I'll go first and make sure it's clear."

"Okay."

A few seconds later, he told her it was fine.

She ducked down and crawled into the opening.

Nick pulled the metal door closed, drew his weapon and picked up the flashlight he'd set down.

The thin beam skimmed the large room, exposing a line of twin mattresses on the floor spanning two walls. Some had pillows and blankets, others had nothing but a towel on them. Looked as if they could pack fifty illegals in there at one time. The place smelled like sweat and fear.

Other than that, the place was empty save for shipping evidence like boxes, tape and a small forklift.

Every indicator pointed toward this place being used for moving illegals through the country, and God only knew what else. "Can you call the police? Have them arrested? It's obvious criminal activity is going on in here."

"Not without proof."

"What about those beds?" She pointed before she remembered he couldn't see her in the dark.

"Circumstantial. Plus, I can't use evidence gathered without a proper search warrant."

Seriously? "Isn't it obvious what they're doing?"

"Yes. But courts, judges and juries want indisputable evidence and an appropriate paper trail before they send people to jail. A good lawyer would shred this case to pieces."

"Seems like a pretty screwed-up system if you ask me."

"From where I stand right now, I wouldn't argue. But that's the structure. It isn't perfect, but it does keep innocent people out of prison."

"It shouldn't be so hard to get guilty people off the streets."

"Agreed." Nick ran the stream of light up a stairwell to what looked like a second-story office.

Hope bubbled. "Maybe there will be something in there we can use."

She followed him up the narrow steps.

The wood door was locked. She had no doubts that Nick could pop the door open with one good bump of his shoulder, but he wouldn't.

Instead, he pulled out his tool and jimmied the lock. This one took even less time to crack.

The flashlight beam skimmed over the room. There was a solid mahogany desk with a leather executive chair tucked into it.

Nick moved to it. The top was clean. He tried to open the drawers of the desk. They didn't budge.

"Whatever they're doing must pay well," Sadie said, taking in the expensive-looking leather sofa against one wall, and the opulent chairs positioned across from the desk.

"Tells me something else. The big boss works from here."

"How do you know that?"

"They wouldn't approve spending this much money on furniture for a captain. And Dallas is a great place to locate his headquarters. We have the worst jury pulls. Even if we gather enough evidence to arrest them, it's harder to get a conviction here. Criminals know it. Grimes knows it. Everyone in the agency would, too."

"Grimes. Here?" She glanced around. A band of tension tightened around Sadie's chest.

"Yes." Nick moved to a filing cabinet positioned against the wall behind the desk. "Might find something useful in here."

He opened drawer after drawer while Sadie helped flip through folders.

She pulled one out. "What is this?"

Nick focused the beam on the piece of paper she held. "An invoice for silk scarves."

Sadie hauled out another one and held it under the light. "And this is for Chinese footwear."

The rest of the contents of the drawer yielded similar results.

Her heart stopped at the sound of a car pulling into the front parking lot. "What do we do now?"

Nick turned off the flashlight and held her hand. "We wait."

She had to remind herself to breath.

Was this another paid late-night tryst with the prostitute they'd seen earlier or one of her friends? Sadie couldn't allow herself to consider anything worse. Like

Grimes returning. If he found her this time, would she and Nick be dead?

Minutes ticked by.

A siren blast followed by squad car lights split the darkness.

Sadie thought she could hear her heart pounding in her chest as they waited for the cop to pull away.

Five minutes later, everything was dark out front.

Nick flicked on the flashlight.

Sadie held up another useless invoice. This one was for bracelets. "We aren't going to find anything, are we?"

"Don't give up yet." He pulled the file cabinet away from the wall.

"What are you doing?"

"I learned this trick a long time ago." He felt along the back of the wood then produced a manila folder. "Taped to the back."

"Oh, my gosh." He'd found something.

They moved to the desk. Nick opened the envelope. He dumped the contents out. There were a few documents, pictures and, holy cow, Sadie's personal information. They had the name of the bakery where she worked, which she already knew they'd discovered, and a picture of her lake house.

She gasped at the picture of her and Nick in the truck, escaping from the bakery. Whoever took it must've been with the person who'd followed them.

Her pulse quickened with every new picture. Luke. Reed. Meg. Riley. Lucy. One by one, each of Nick's family members appeared.

Nick fanned out the photos from the deck and grunted a foul word.

She'd been thinking the exact same one.

The message was clear. No way did they plan to leave his family alone.

NICK SPLAYED THE pictures and documents from the envelope across the desk after making the call to his safe house contact. He pulled out his camera and took photos then texted the new information to Luke. "I'll forward this to Smith once we get to the safe house. We can examine these more closely there, as well."

Nick figured it would be easy to hide Sadie in Richardson's Chinatown among the strip malls.

He pulled onto Greenville Avenue, located Dim Sum, the restaurant, and parked in the dark behind it. Paul Huang's new Japanese import was parked under the street lamp.

Nick flashed his headlights and Paul zipped past him and out of the lot, slowing down enough for Nick to follow. His contact was about as far away from the U.S. Marshals Service as he could be. No one knew about Paul.

A cold front was due, and Nick would at least give Sadie a solid roof over her head tonight.

Winding into a neighborhood behind the shopping mall, Paul pulled in front of a house and jumped out of his car, motioning Nick to park on the pad in front of the house.

"My man, Nick," the Asian said, twin plumes of smoke rising from his nostrils.

They shook hands and bumped shoulders in a man greeting.

"It's been a long time. How's your mom?" Nick asked.

"Ah, you know her. She slaves away in the kitchen. I finally have enough money to give her a decent retirement. I don't need the help. She can relax. What does she do? Work. She's so stubborn."

"Probably wants to feel useful," Nick offered.

"That's true. She worries about getting too old."

"You have any more trouble at the restaurant?" Nick had intervened on several occasions on Paul's behalf when gangs tried to move in on his block and force him to pay protection fees or risk having his livelihood burned to the ground.

"No. Thanks to you. They didn't come back." Paul stood staring at Sadie, waiting for an introduction.

Nick shook his head. "Better if you don't know anything on this one."

Paul, a middle-aged Asian with white hair dotting his temples, nodded his understanding. He popped the butt of his cigarette in his mouth and puffed on it while he stuck the key in the lock. He opened the door. "It's not a big place but it's clean. You hungry?"

"Nah. We're okay for the night."

"You need anything, you take it. I stocked the fridge as soon as you called." He tossed a key onto the counter next to the one he'd used to open the door a moment ago. "The restaurant is behind you. This yard backs up to it. Hop the wall and you're there. If you don't find what you need here, go there."

"I appreciate you letting us use your relatives' place for a few days. We won't be here too long."

"Nothing's too much to ask from you, my friend. You saved my life. My aunt and uncle are out of the country, anyway. Went back to China. I don't know why. I told them there's nothing back there I forgot." He laughed at his own joke and shook his head. "They don't need to use this place right now. It's no trouble at all. I put fresh sheets on the bed for you." His gaze moved from Nick to

Sadie. "If not for this guy, I'd have nothing. Those thugs almost ran me out of business. Out of town. But this guy. He stopped them." He gave Nick a friendly tap on the shoulder. "You didn't let them push around the little guy."

Nick smiled. "Glad to help."

"He's a good guy," Paul said, winking at Sadie. "He'll take care of you."

SADIE STOOD BY the door as Nick thanked Paul again.

The place was tight, but had everything they needed. From the front door, she could see the living and dining rooms, as well as the kitchen. There was a flat-screen TV on one wall and a hunter-green recliner sofa positioned in front. Pictures of family covered most of the white space on the walls.

She excused herself to the bathroom and starting filling the tub while she undressed. A warm bath sounded like heaven. Besides, she needed a minute to process what they'd brought from the warehouse.

A soft knock at the door startled her.

"Come in. I'm covered." She sat on the side of the tub with a bath towel wrapped around her.

The door barely opened, and she could see a sliver of Nick's face. "I don't want to bother you. Just wanted to give you an update. Smith has the information."

"It's fine. I was just sitting here thinking. If there's a U.S. Marshal involved, then no one's safe, are they?"

"You are. I am. My family is on their way to Galveston right now. No one knows about our place there. They sure as hell won't get to us here." He opened the door a little more and leaned against the jamb. "I just spoke to Reed, by the way. Boomer's doing fine. It's probably best for him to be with them right now."

She nodded, ignoring the ache in her chest. "I do realize that. I wouldn't want to do anything that would put his life at risk. And especially not just so I can have him with me. He has to come first."

"He's lucky to have you."

"He's in good hands with your family."

"Gran might fight you for him later." He smiled, and it brightened his whole face. He held out two beers. The label read Tsingtao. "I found these in the fridge. They're actually pretty good. Best of all, they're cold. Want one?"

"Do I? Yes. I would very much like a cold drink."

He opened the bottle of beer and handed it to her.

"Don't worry. We'll figure this out. We're getting closer to uncovering the truth. Knowing who's involved is a huge plus for our side. Now we have to gather enough evidence to put the jerk away."

His words provided a small measure of comfort. There was something about his presence that calmed her rattled nerves. He was just this amazingly calming man. She could get used to this, to him.

"I'll be in the other room if you need anything else. I promise not to peek, but do you mind if I leave this cracked?"

"Not at all. In fact, I'd feel better knowing you could hear me."

He disappeared and she set her beer down, slipped off the towel and eased into the warm water. The tension from a long day evaporated, similar to boiling water turning into steam.

She picked up her drink. Beads of water dripped down the longneck bottle as she curled her fingers around the base. The light taste and cool liquid refreshed as it slid down her throat.

Seeing her abductor's face again had brought up painful memories. She was exhausted. Her mind was spent, her body drained. She calculated how long it had been since she'd slept. Her body screamed *too long*

Sadie leaned her head back and closed her eyes.

After a good soak in the tub, she washed herself before stepping out and hand-washing her clothes in the sink. The shower rod was as good a place as any to hang her garments to dry, so she did.

There was toothpaste on the counter. She squeezed some from the tube and finger-brushed her teeth. It was better than nothing. She tightened the towel around her, and moved into the hall, closing the door to the bathroom behind her.

Nick sat on the couch, flipping through TV channels. He did a double take when she stepped into the room wearing only a towel.

She stopped in the living room, completely aware of how naked she was underneath the towel. His reaction had set off a small fire inside her.

"You, uh, want to sit down?"

If she wasn't so tired, she would've experienced a thrill that her femininity seemed to rob his ability to speak clearly. "Okay."

She curled up on the other end of the sofa.

"You want the remote?" He held it out toward her, but his gaze didn't leave hers. He pushed off the sofa and disappeared into the bedroom, returning a minute later holding a comforter. "This should keep you warm."

The blanket was thick, warm and soft. She pulled it up to her neck and thanked him. "This is perfect."

He stood there for a long moment and raked his fingers through his black-as-night curls. "I, uh, should probably go get cleaned up."

Sensual heat vibrated between them. "I found a towel for you and folded it on the counter."

He double-checked the locks on the window in the living room and kitchen. "You want this?" He held out his weapon.

The sight of a gun sent her body into a full-on shiver. "Yeah. I should be prepared. Just in case."

"No one will find us here. I trust Paul. No one in the agency knows about him." He hesitated outside the bathroom door. "I won't be long. You need anything, yell. I'll be here in a snap."

The image of him naked, wet, muscled, lit another small fire. Combine the two and the blaze could get out of control quickly.

True to his word, he wasn't ten minutes in the shower. He strolled into the living room with a towel secured around his hips. Beads of water trailed down his muscular chest.

Now it was Sadie's turn to flush.

"Found these." He held up toothbrushes still in their wrappers.

She turned off the cooking show she'd been watching and joined him next to the sink in the bathroom.

He handed one over, and she opened it immediately, put toothpaste on it and scrubbed her teeth. "This is heaven."

They hovered over the sink, their heads so close they almost touched as they took turns under the faucet.

"I can throw your clothes in the wash with mine." He picked up his jeans and shirt.

"You found a washer?"

"In the hallway leading to the bedrooms."

"Wouldn't hurt to run them through a cycle." She made her way back to the sofa as he turned on the washer. Was there anything sexier than a half-naked man who knew how to take care of himself and everyone around him?

She didn't think so. She couldn't imagine Tom washing his own clothes. Everything had to be sorted by color, placed in the correct bins and dropped off at the cleaners who knew exactly how he liked his things washed and pressed. She was almost embarrassed to remember that he had his summer shorts ironed. He had good qualities, she reminded herself. Manly? Not so much.

Nick, who was nothing but all-man and muscle and smart, walked into the room. Her gaze dipped to his towel and the line of hair from his navel to…the trail ended at his towel. His raw sensual appeal lit another little fire.

"You can change the channel if you want. There wasn't much on earlier excerpt for crime shows."

"I don't mind watching whatever." He settled next to her. His thigh touched hers and the power of that one touch ignited little blazes all down her leg.

She pulled the blanket over her and turned the cooking show back on.

"Want to share?"

His gaze intensified on the screen. "I'm, uh, okay."

Did he feel it, too?

He must have. He'd never had so much trouble putting together a string of words before. Another trill of excitement rushed through her at the thought she had the power to affect such a beautiful man. His body was perfection on a stick. He didn't seem to realize or care, and that just made him even sexier.

He put his arm around her, and she settled into the hollow of his neck. His body radiated warmth.

It would be a mistake to get too comfortable in his arms. The reasons were clipped onto the waistband of his jeans most of the time. His gun. His badge.

Two excellent reasons to keep her emotions under control and not fall into the trap of thinking this could be any more than what it was right then.

Nick was her handler.

It was his job to protect her.

Making her feel safe was part of his assignment. Making her feel sexy wasn't. He stirred another part of her she shouldn't allow.

Sadie didn't want to think about that tonight.

The cooking host sliced an onion in half, running the blade through each side again and again until it was chopped.

The sounds from the TV in the background couldn't drown out the beating of Nick's heart.

She burrowed deeper into the crook of his arm and closed her eyes.

Chapter Fourteen

Sadie woke to the smell of fresh coffee. She sat up and realized she must've dozed off on the couch last night. Naked save for a towel wrapped around her. Embarrassment sent a rash crawling up her neck. She immediately checked to make sure all her body parts were covered.

The blanket still covered her.

Nick sat at a desk that was tucked into the corner of the small dining room. His back was to her, his face toward the screen. She glimpsed cold metal from the waistband of his jeans—a constant reminder he lived in a violent world—one she might never get used to. His job was dangerous.

She pushed the thought aside, preferring not to think about many reasons they would never be able to be a couple. Even though there wasn't exactly an offer of a relationship on the table. The draw she felt to him was unexplainable. Then again, he was one seriously hot guy who was strong to boot. Who wouldn't be attracted to that?

"That coffee I smell?"

He held up a foam cup. She hadn't even heard him get up or go out.

"It is. And good morning to you."

"You didn't happen to buy two of those, did you?"

He turned to face her, and her heart stuttered. His black hair disheveled, stubble on his chin, only made him more irresistible. Damn that he was gorgeous in the morning. In the afternoon. In the evening. Hell, he looked good all the time.

He was also a man with a gun and badge.

"As a matter of fact, I did." He grabbed a small paper bag from the desk and removed another cup. "And I picked up food. Breakfast tacos. I got one with bacon and one with sausage. I wasn't sure which you liked."

Scrambled eggs with cheese, bacon and salsa rolled in a warm tortilla. A Tex-Mex treat she'd grown to love since living in Texas. "That smells amazing. I'm all about the bacon. Definitely bacon. On second thought, this is too good to be true. You're probably just a hallucination, a figment of my overtired imagination. Am I even awake yet?" She blinked, taking the treasures from him. "If I am, I should get dressed."

"It's real." He bent down and kissed her forehead. "I'm real. I happened to like what you're wearing. But if you don't stop looking so damn adorable, you're going to find out just how very real I am."

"Oh."

"So you better distract me by telling me how well you slept last night." He smiled and stroked her cheek.

"Best night of sleep I've had in a long time." The fire he'd lit last night blazed to attention again. She half remembered his body curled behind hers, and the feeling of everything being right in the world while she was nestled against him. She'd never felt like that in another man's arms.

There was something special about Nick.

Did she just blush again? "How about you? Did you get any sleep or did you stay awake all night at that computer?"

"And miss out on feeling your body against mine? Hell, no. I was right there all night." He pointed to the space behind her. "And I slept like a rock."

She took a sip of coffee, welcoming the burn. "Let me guess, job hazard?"

"Yeah. It'd be dangerous for me to let my guard down." His smile tightened. His gaze focused on a square on the carpet.

Based on the change in his expression, she had the very real sense they were about to talk about a heavy subject.

They hadn't finished their conversation from yesterday. He would most likely want to know more about the man in the picture. And what he'd done to her. Her body shuddered, thinking about it. She didn't want to relive the past. She'd much rather stay in the present, the here and now. A primal urge had her wanting to trace the muscles of his back with her finger, follow the patch of hair from his navel down to where his blood pulsed.

First, she'd enjoy her meal. "Have you heard from your family this morning?"

"Luke called first thing. Everyone agreed to check in every few hours until this is over and he's heard from everyone but Lucy. Said she's probably tied up on a case. He says Reed took Boomer out for a run this morning."

"I bet he loved it. I used to take him out back and throw the ball. Half the time he'd end up splashing in the lake. What was supposed to be a quick outing turned into an ordeal. Muddy paws. The smell of lake water. I'd have to give him a bath before I could bring him back inside."

She took a bite of her taco, washing it down with a sip of coffee. The warmth felt good on her throat.

"I'm sure he misses you. I know I would."

The statement made tears prick her eyes. Not being with Nick? Her stomach lurched at the thought. Yet, there would come a time when this case was over and they'd go their separate ways. Her heart squeezed and she couldn't deal with thinking about it right now. "What about the others?"

"Meg and Riley are in Fort Worth with his parents, so they're good. She's started contractions."

"Oh, how exciting for them. They must be thrilled." Thoughts of having a baby tugged at her heart. Would she be around to meet the little one? She hoped so. If not, maybe there could be a special arrangement worked out. "I'm so happy for them both. That's going to be one lucky little kid."

"Yeah, they'll be great parents."

"They sure will. This little one will also be surrounded by an amazing family. I can imagine spending summers out on the ranch with Gran. The place would burst with people on the weekends with cousins, aunts and uncles. And there'd be food everywhere." It was exactly the environment she'd want for her child, if she ever had one.

"I like the sound of that."

His smile warmed her heart.

"For now, they sounded nervous as hell. And my little tough Meg in the background sounded like she was in pain." He chuckled.

"She'll do great. It'll all be worth it when she holds that baby in her arms."

"Doc says a first labor can go on for days before the baby comes." He shrugged. "I'll make sure and check in with Meg later. Almost forgot. Luke said the last time he spoke to Lucy she said there's some big news about her and Stephen but they won't say what it is until we're all under the same roof and can celebrate together."

"Are you thinking what I'm thinking?" She took another sip of coffee anticipation lightening her heavy heart.

"I'm guessing they're announcing an engagement."

Sadie was genuinely happy for Lucy. "I hope so. He did say it was good news, right?"

Luke's smile reached his eyes that time. "Yeah. They also said it was scary. Marriage can seem that way. So I've heard."

His brown eyes sparkled. He got that glittery look of pride every time he talked about his family. His love for them was written all over the sappy smile on his face and the pride in his eyes. His smile might be sentimental, but the way those lips curled at the corners was sexy, too.

She didn't want to ruin his mood, or make him think about the past but curiosity was getting the best of her. "What about you? Ever have any plans to take the leap with anyone?"

NICK COULDN'T EXACTLY pinpoint why he wanted to tell Sadie about his past, but he did. Whatever the hell it was, it must be the same driving force making him want to share details about his family. Something he rarely ever did with anyone. "Yeah. There was someone once. It was a long time ago."

"Do you mind if I ask what happened?" She offered him her coffee.

"No. Ask me anything." He paused long enough to take a sip and hand her cup back to her. "I was young. Thought I had life all figured out. What did I know? She and I had been going together for years already."

"Was she your high-school sweetheart?"

"How'd you know that?"

"I hope you don't mind. Lucy told me a little bit about her."

"Lucy is the most protective of me. I'm surprised she told you anything. She's the quiet one in the family."

"I sensed you two were close. She told me about what happened to her."

A set of surprised eyes stared at her. "That she told you anything about me is shocking. I have no words for her telling you about what happened to her. I can tell you this, though—when that bastard hurt her, I nearly lost my mind. I wanted to kill him with my bare hands."

"If I'm being honest, I'm surprised you didn't. Your family stopped you?"

Tension had him grinding his back teeth. "Thankfully. When he went to trial, I sat in the courtroom and listened to his testimony. All I could do was sit there, helpless, trying to figure out how many punches I could get in before the bailiff could pull me off him."

"But you didn't."

"Not with Gran sitting next to me, holding on to my arm. She knew exactly what I was thinking."

"I've said it before and I'll say it again. Smart woman."

"It almost killed me to let the courts handle him. I was young and angry. The world pissed me off, and I was ready to take out my frustration."

"What happened?"

"I signed up for the military, ready and willing to fight just about anyone. Rachael didn't want me to go to war. She wanted me to go away to school with her."

"But you didn't."

He intensely focused on the patch of carpet at his feet. "Nothing like nonstop fighting for four years to screw your head back on straight. Before my tour was up, I'd planned to ask her to marry me. I'd sent money home to help Mom and Gran take care of the others. I had a little tucked away for college. Rachael wasn't thrilled I didn't listen to her before, but I thought we had it worked out. She had no idea I was about to surprise her with a ring."

"And then…"

"We argued about where the relationship was going. She decided to party with her friends on New Year's Eve instead of spending it with me. A drunk driver crossed the median and hit her car head-on."

"I'm so sorry."

"The crazy thing was I'd had that ring in my pocket for a year. For some reason, I didn't ask. I held on to it. Even though she'd made it clear she wanted me to. Guess I thought I had plenty of time. Or maybe I had my doubts about taking the plunge. Marriage seemed so permanent. When I finally realized I wanted to ask, I wanted everything to be perfect. Maybe make up for not asking before. I had it all planned out. I was going to ask first thing New Year's Day…"

He heard Sadie mumble a few words meant to comfort him, like *I'm sorry,* and *Life can be so unfair.*

This was the first time he'd spoken about Rachael with anyone outside of his family. Hell, he didn't say much to his family about the topic.

God, it felt good to finally talk about it. To get it off his chest. He'd been holding everything in for so long, erecting an impenetrable barrier around his heart.

Sadie got up, stood in front of him, her arms around him. He leaned forward, resting his forehead on her stomach, holding on to her around her waist.

"I can't help thinking if I'd asked her sooner, somehow things would have turned out differently."

"You don't have a crystal ball."

He still felt the burden of wishing he could go back and change the past. "My timing sucked."

"You couldn't have known what would happen."

"Maybe if I'd asked her the night before, she would've been with my family celebrating instead of going out with her friends."

"That might not have changed the outcome."

He clenched his fists. "Yeah, well I'll never know now. I could've been the one to run into her for how responsible I felt after."

"It wasn't your fault."

Those four words were more effective than a bullet, piercing the Kevlar encasing his heart.

He sat up, keeping his gaze on hers the entire time, waiting, expecting her to tell him to stop or give him a signal this couldn't happen.

Instead, her tongue slicked across her lips and he couldn't tear his gaze away from the silky trail.

"Do that again and I won't be able to stop myself from doing things I'm not convinced you're ready for."

He could see her heartbeat at the base of her throat. It took everything in him not to lean forward and press his lips there.

"You didn't try to kiss me last night. I thought you'd changed your mind about making love to me."

Damn, she was sexy with her big green glittery eyes staring at him. "I don't flip-flop. I just wanted you to be sure you're ready for this—this changes things between us."

"Are you telling me you've never had sex for sex's sake before?"

"Sure, when I was young and stupid. I'm a grown man now, and I like to know I'll be welcome back before I go down that road. I don't do one night."

"I like the sound of that."

"Then make sure you're good and awake because I want full awareness for what I plan to do to you."

She sucked in a little burst of air. "Hold that thought."

She disappeared down the hallway, and he could hear the sink water running in the bathroom and the swish of her toothbrush.

He clasped his hands together and rested his elbows on his knees. The debate about whether or not this was a good idea was a lost argument at this point.

Nick wanted Sadie more than he needed air.

His pulse hummed when he saw Sadie standing there. Her wavy brown hair layered around her shoulders, wearing nothing but a towel wrapped around her and tied at the top.

"You want me, Nick?"

His chest hurt for how bad he needed to be inside her. His erection was already painfully stiff. "I think you already know the answer to that question."

"Then I'm all yours." She untied the knot in one quick motion, and the towel pooled at her feet.

Chapter Fifteen

The pure beauty of her body, her sensuous curves, kept him rooted to his spot as she walked toward him. Her gaze never left his as she walked him to the couch and nudged him to sit down.

She stood in front of him then gripped his shoulders and pushed until he pressed against the backrest. "Dammit, Sadie. Are you determined to finish this before it gets started?"

She grinned, looking as if she understood and enjoyed the effect she had on him. "Something wrong?"

"Abso-freakin-lutely-not. Everything in my view couldn't be more perfect. But I do want this to last and you're making that very difficult for me."

She straddled him. "How about now?"

"Heaven." He gripped her waist as she rocked back and forth, fighting the urge to drive himself inside her. He needed to remove his jeans, but she felt so damn incredible, he didn't want to move. Plus, truth be told, he liked allowing her to set the pace.

She leaned forward, her bare breasts skimming his chest, and he breathed in her floral soap scent.

The image of her in those boots, wearing jeans and her pale pink sweater, broke through his thoughts. He'd been wanting, no needing to touch her ever since that moment in his truck. Hell, if he was being honest, ever since that first day he'd met her at the bakery.

He smoothed his palm over her flat stomach, and then wrapped it around her sweet bottom. Electric impulse drilled through him. The need to be inside her caused an ache in his chest.

Patience.

"You're an amazing woman, Sadie," he whispered, "and incredibly beautiful."

A pink flush rose to her cheeks. Her green eyes darkened. Desire. "Then make love to me."

Better-sounding words had never crossed those pink lips in the time he'd known her.

He pressed a kiss to the hollow of her neck. Then, he lowered his head to her breastbone and feathered kisses there, making his way down to her pert breasts.

Kissing the tip of her breast, he slid his tongue up to her neck. He feathered a kiss on the small mole on her cheek. He found her mouth and groaned when she teased his tongue into her mouth. She nipped his bottom lip.

Little did she know, it was her turn to squirm. He slid his tongue in her mouth. He palmed her breast. With his other hand, he drew circles on her sex.

She moaned.

He pulled and tugged at her pointed peak.

Her eyes opened and the power of that one look almost knocked him back. She didn't need words to tell him she wanted him inside her. Right then.

"Patience."

Her cheeks were flush as he gripped the dimpled spot above her sweet bottom.

With her naked and warm body pressed up against him, he realized just how perfectly she fit him.

The feel of her bare, clean skin was enough to drive him to the brink even with his jeans on.

But he would force himself to wait, to savor every second of this until passion couldn't be held at bay anymore.

He thrust his tongue deep in her mouth, needing to taste every inch of her. She returned the intensity of his kiss.

With one arm wrapped around her waist, he pulled her body in tight against his until her heat pressed against his stomach. His hands wandered over every inch of her stomach until they rose to her full breasts. Her skin was soft.

Her wet heat was so close to his erection, his body hummed.

Patience.

He pushed up enough to sit, picked her up and carried her into the next room, where he placed her on the bed and dipped down to kiss her. She gripped his neck and pulled him on top of her.

He trailed kisses down her neck until his mouth found her breasts, roaming, as the tip of his tongue flicked the crest of her nipple before taking it in his mouth.

She moaned and gripped his shoulders.

"Just a minute," he said. His hands went to the button on his jeans, but her hands were already there, hungry, tearing button by button. Damn, he got so caught up in the moment, he almost forgot something. "Hold that thought."

He retrieved a condom from the wallet in his back pocket, then let his jeans drop to the floor.

"This is insane. I've never been with a more beautiful woman." With both knees on the bed, he leaned forward and his lips crushed down on hers.

He broke free long enough to rip open the condom

package. Her hands were already around his shaft as he rolled the condom over his tip and moaned as she stroked him.

"I want you. Now."

"Then take me," she said. Her hands were on him again. Her fingers traced his jawline, down his chin, along his Adam's apple. "I have never wanted a man like I want you right now."

He eased her onto the bed. Before he could make another move, her legs wrapped around his midsection. He tensed as she guided him inside her.

He thrust, her body taking him in, and his control nearly shattered. He plunged deep inside her again and again, slowing his pace every time he neared the edge.

She greedily clutched at his back, pulling him deeper into her as their bodies molded together.

He thrust. Surged.

When her muscles clenched, released, exploded around him, he pumped harder as she bucked her hips and said his name over and over until he detonated.

He collapsed on top of her, careful not to overwhelm her with his weight, needing to stay inside her, with her, in this moment, for as long as he could.

NICK'S BODY STILL glistened with beads of water when he returned from the shower with nothing but a towel wrapped around his waist.

His cell buzzed. He located his jeans and retrieved it from his front pocket. "It's Meg."

"You better take the call." She patted the seat next to her, reaching out for his free hand.

He twined their fingers and took a seat.

"How's she doing?" He asked into the phone. His gaze locked on to Sadie's. "It's Riley."

She nodded.

"How far apart?"

"Fifteen minutes," Riley said.

He heard Meg in the background groaning and clamped his back teeth. "And the doctor doesn't think she should go to the hospital yet?"

"We're leaving my parents' house now. I don't care what the doctor says. Fort Worth is a long drive from Plano."

"Which hospital?"

"Presby."

Nick glanced at his watch. This time of morning traffic shouldn't be too bad. "I can be there in twenty minutes."

"I'll meet you there."

"Okay, man. Meg is saying she doesn't want you to come."

"Did I say I was planning on asking permission? Besides, what she doesn't know won't hurt her."

"Feel free to take your life in your own hands." Riley chuckled. "I'll call you as soon as we get there."

"Hell, I'll be waiting at the front door."

Sadie squeezed his hand before disappearing into the other room.

He presumed to get dressed. He could think of a few things he would've liked to have done while she was still almost naked on the couch. His hormones were overriding rational thought again.

When it came to Sadie, he had little control over either.

He ended the call with his brother-in-law.

Could he and Sadie have a future when this was all over? The very real notion she had a U.S. Marshal whose career, hell, life, depended on her not being alive to identify him pressed down on Nick.

Sadie stepped across the hall and he could see that she'd put clothes on and left the bathroom door open as she brushed her teeth.

If Nick could protect her, he might just be able to think about having a relationship with her. Or could he? She was scared to death of his constant companion, his Glock, and he wore a badge. The very badge he loved also prevented him from getting involved personally with her.

And yet, she'd broken through the shield protecting his heart. She'd cracked the armor…and he couldn't say he was especially sorry.

Chapter Sixteen

"Change of plans today. I picked up a few supplies when I was out. Put these on." Nick held out a sweatshirt, wig and sunglasses. "Meg and Riley are on their way to the hospital."

"That's so exciting." Sadie tried on the black cropped hair, tugging at the sides until it felt right. "How do I look?"

He grinned, wrapped his arms around her waist and kissed the hollow of her neck. "Not bad."

He thrust his hips forward and she could feel his arousal.

Need welled deep inside her.

"I don't think you should start something you can't finish," she teased, enjoying the feel of his lips on her skin.

"You're probably right, but I wouldn't mind trying." His sexy smile tore at her heart. And her better judgment. Memories of those lips taunting and teasing other places on her body warmed her. And the feel of his arms around her. She could get used to him. Dangerous thinking for a woman who wanted a peaceful life in the country. No guns. No scary men. No hiding. And yet, he made her think having kids and a husband might not be such a bad idea someday. Maybe she could get another dog to keep Boomer company, too?

The life that everyone else took for granted made her heart ache for how badly she wanted it. Kids, a husband… a stable life were a world away.

A painful stab, like a bullet piercing bone, slammed into her ribs.

Seriously? Hadn't she learned to protect her heart any better than that? If her own family constantly disappointed her, wouldn't Nick do the same? She thought she'd gotten pretty darn good at keeping everyone at a safe distance. But here she was falling hard for Nick. The icing on the cake was that he wore a gun for a living.

Didn't she have any more sense than to fall in love with a man whose job would ensure many late nights of her wide awake worrying about him? A lifetime of fear?

And, yet, looking into those cinnamon, copperlike eyes melted her reserves every time.

They'd had incredibly hot sex. She couldn't argue that. Clearly, the bedroom would not be a problem for them.

But most of life was lived outside the sheets.

The big question would be did they have what it takes to make a relationship work with their clothes on? Or would two very important pieces of equipment get in the way? A badge and a gun.

She already knew the answer. Her body shook every time she was near either one.

What if he left the Marshals Service and got another job? a little voice inside her head asked.

And take away everything that was Nick?

No way would she ask. He was too good at what he did to think about him in another line of work. He saved innocent people. She would never be so selfish as to ask him to change.

She straightened her wig. "Ready?"

He groaned, nuzzling his face in her neck. "Just give me another minute."

"Okay, but you might miss the birth of one very important little person."

"You're beautiful when you're right." He skimmed his lips across her collarbone. "And you're sexy when you're thinking about others." He feathered kisses where her heart beat at the base of her throat. "And especially when you're looking out for me." His lips found hers, and he pressed a sweet kiss to her mouth.

She wanted to dissolve in his arms.

Bad idea.

He'd regret not being there for Meg.

"Keep this up and we won't get out of here," she said.

He grumbled, mumbled a curse word and pulled back. "We'll get back to this later."

"I'm planning to hold you to your word." She returned his smile.

"You, a couple of steaks on the grill, a cold beer and I might never want to leave." He finished getting dressed. He dipped his head under the running faucet to wet his hair then finger-combed it. He put on a ball cap and shades.

Her heart stuttered.

This was the Nick she remembered from the bakery.

The one who'd first piqued her interest.

"Heard from Lucy yet?"

"No. I left her a voice mail. I'll check in with Luke once we get to the hospital."

Sadie slid her feet into her boots. She should hate them by now. Her heels might never recover from the blisters. But the hard leather was beginning to give. She was starting to wear them in and, heck, they were too awesome not to adore. They fit her to a T. Once the leather was worn in, the blisters would go away, too. She could definitely see herself becoming a Texan when this whole ordeal was behind her. Okay, she'd learned "real" Texans were Texas-born, but she could be a transplant. One of those people who may not have been born in Texas but got there as fast as they could.

Nick put on his shoes, twined their fingers and led her outside to the truck parked on the pad out front.

Sadie glanced down the street, her usual habit, checking for anything or anyone that looked out of place. Would there ever come a time when she didn't instinctively do this?

Two years of training had her watching shadows, checking cars and searching strangers' faces.

At a house four doors down there looked to be someone in the driver's seat of a small blue sport-utility. Could be nothing. A friend waiting outside for someone to run inside their house and grab something they'd forgotten.

Being snatched from the grocery store parking lot two years ago had taught Sadie to fear what was out in the open more than anything in the dark.

She squeezed Nick's hand and inclined her head toward the parked vehicle. "Think we need to be worried?"

"I saw that. We'll keep an eye on him," he reassured.

Traffic on Interstate 75 was almost at a crawl, but picked up once they merged onto President George Bush Turnpike, heading west. Nick took the Dallas North Tollway exit, heading north to Parker Road. Once he exited there, he made a left. A small white building came up quickly on the left. To the right was a strip mall. Beyond those, the three towers that made up Texas Health Presbyterian Hospital of Plano stood on the left.

"Did they say which tower?"

"The second, I believe."

He pulled into the parking garage and found a parking spot on the third floor.

"Doesn't seem like we had any company on the way." Thankfully, no blue sport-utility had followed them.

"Nope."

And, yet, Sadie had an uneasy feeling.

"You don't look relieved."

Most likely her alert system was set to high beam again. "It's probably nothing."

"Gut instinct has kept me alive more than once." Nick scanned the parking garage as they walked toward the white building.

An ambulance, sirens blazing, roared toward the emergency entrance.

Sadie's nerves were already stretched to their limits. The blare of the sirens caused her muscles to pull tighter with each step toward the elevator.

She caught herself judging every person who passed by, evaluating their threat. Being outside in daylight had her feeling vulnerable even though she wore a disguise.

Nick squeezed her hand reassuringly as they walked inside the building and to the elevators. He seemed to second-guess himself when he glanced at a metal door with a sign over it that read Stairs. "Let's take those instead."

"What floor are they on?"

"The third." He pulled out his phone and thumbed through his texts as the metal door *cu-clunked* behind them. He stalled on the first step. "She's in room three-fifteen."

They'd climbed one set of stairs when Nick's cell buzzed, indicating a text. He checked the screen. "It's from Riley."

Sadie's pulse increased. "What did he say?"

His eyes stayed on the screen for a long moment as though he needed a second for the words to sink in. He muttered a curse. "Men are in the room asking questions about me and he doesn't like it."

"What? How can that be?"

"Riley's telling us to get out of here." His jaw clenched.

"Wait a minute. Isn't this the break we need? Shouldn't we call the police? Have them arrested? Or at least hauled in for questioning?"

"For what?" He paused. "Asking questions in a hospital? If these guys are flashing badges, then local police aren't going to touch them."

"What about the envelope we found in the warehouse last night?"

"Inadmissible in court. We could go to jail for breaking and entering."

"Oh, right. I forgot."

"I need to check in with Smith. Let him know what's happening. And he damn well better be prepared to send extra resources to make sure nothing happens to my family."

He'd already turned around and started back down the stairwell when the door to the first floor flew open. He froze and ended the call before Smith could answer, biting out another curse word under his breath—the exact one Sadie was thinking.

Sadie followed Nick up the stairs as quietly as she could, fearing the people below would hear her heartbeat for how loud it hammered against her ribs.

She heard the unmistakable click of a bullet being loaded in a chamber. She bit down a gasp, staying as close to Nick as she could manage as he ascended the stairs.

Feet shuffled below, climbing closer. By the sounds of it, someone was in a hurry.

She and Nick had two floors on whoever was chasing them, but they were gaining ground fast.

Nick popped out on the seventh floor and immediately pressed the elevator button.

Hurry.

The elevator dinged and a set of doors opened. Nick rushed inside. "Get against the wall."

She pressed her back against the glass, saying a silent protection prayer.

The stairwell door flung open.

"This where they ditched?" a familiar-sounding voice asked. Did it belong to Burly?

Nick jammed his thumb on the L button a few more times.

Come on.

"I don't think so. I don't see anyone. Maybe one up?" another voice replied. Steroids?

The elevator door closed at the same time as the one leading to the stairs.

"You know who that was, don't you?" she asked.

"I do. They sure have come a long way from the cabin to find us," he said, staring at the screen on his phone intently.

"My thinking exactly. Is it possibly they work for the agency?"

"No. I'd know if they did. Those guys are hired."

She gasped. "You mean professional killers?"

He nodded. "We need to get to my truck and I need to get ahold of Smith. But I want to see who else comes out of the front door before we leave."

The elevator stopped at the second floor. Sadie's heart lurched to her throat.

Nick drew his weapon, and hid it behind his leg. Sadie went shoulder-to-shoulder with him, frighteningly aware of how close the gun was to her own leg, in order to shield the weapon from view. Her body started to shake.

Four or five people pushed in before the elevator doors closed again. A man in scrubs, two nurses and an older couple squeezed inside, making the small space cramped.

The lobby was a welcomed sight.

Nick walked quickly the few steps away from the elevator then broke into a run, not stopping until he was out the front door. He walked across the pathway to an uncovered parking lot and phoned Smith.

"Meg's in the hospital getting ready to have her baby. She had visitors. I need people on her, Smith. My life is one thing, but keep my sister safe."

Sadie only heard one side of the conversation, mostly Nick stressing the need to provide adequate protection for his family.

He asked his boss to hold then checked a text message. "My brother-in-law says the men who stopped by gave names. They also claimed to be coworkers of mine."

By the time he closed the call, he'd relayed the message whoever visited Meg claimed to work with him said their names were Young and Turner.

Based on Nick's reaction, those identities didn't sit well with his boss.

"What did he say?" she asked as soon as Nick looked at her.

"It's impossible for Young and Turner to be here because they're on assignment in Virginia."

"He's sure they're there? I mean couldn't they say they were in one place but actually hop a plane and be here in a few hours?"

"Yeah." His gaze constantly shifted, scanning for possible threats. "But they didn't."

"What makes him so certain? I mean it's not as if

someone follows you guys around checking out your every move."

"He knew because he'd just left them at breakfast. They had a meeting about the case they were working on. No way could they eat with him then make it here in an hour."

"Then clearly someone is getting away with impersonating marshals. How can that happen?"

"Jamison would have access to everyone's personnel records. All he'd have to do is find men who looked similar and then have their credentials faked."

"And his association with Grimes would give him access to a variety of known criminals and channels. Men who would be good at pretending to be someone else when they needed to. Men who could fake government documents skillfully."

"Men who wouldn't be afraid to kill someone to get what they wanted." He finished for her.

Shock wasn't the word for what Sadie experienced. "Isn't it pretty brazen of them to come to the hospital like this? I mean they have to know Meg and Riley are cops."

"Why not? They've already gone to prison and fooled guards. Killed a U.S. Marshal. They're good at this and clearly comfortable with what they're doing."

"What did Riley say to them?"

"He told them I was driving in from Houston, and that I'd be there in two hours. He also asked them to stick around. He said they couldn't get out of there fast enough. He had no reason to detain them, so he had to let them go."

"Not to mention his wife's in labor, and he has no backup." Sadie pointed out.

"Even so, he would've done anything necessary to keep her safe. Even if that meant placing them under arrest."

"What was Smith's reaction to the news?"

"He has extra security coming. I'd like to stick around in case Riley needs me until they arrive." Stress gave way to a long face.

"I hate that you can't be there for Meg while she's in labor."

"Me, too. At least she has Riley with her. He said she probably wouldn't let me come inside, anyway. Something about not wanting to scare me off ever having children." His smile didn't look forced, but faded quickly.

"Who are we looking for?"

"For one, I'd like to know more about the two men who seem to be behind us every step of the way." He checked his messages. "Then there's the pair of men wearing dark suits. Riley said they should stick out."

Sadie studied each person as they came out of the turnstiles.

Five minutes passed before anyone fitting the description came out of the revolving doors of the main building.

"Looks like we have them." Nick switched his phone to camera mode and snapped a couple of pictures. "I'll send these to Smith, and we'll hope for a positive ID."

"You think they might be deputies?"

"Could be. If Jamison sent them and they're following his orders then it's possible they might not even know what he's really after. If they're known criminals, they'll show up in the database, and we'll get a hit." He sent the photos to his boss with a couple of clicks.

"We haven't seen Burly and Steroids. Where could they have possibly gone?"

"It's a big building with multiple exits. They could've gone out somewhere else, and we'd never know. Or they could be in the building. I should warn Riley." He fired off a text to his brother-in-law.

"Can't he detain those guys?"

"He needs to have probable cause." He studied the screen intently.

"Any word from Smith?"

"Not yet. It could take a while to get a match."

"Should we wait here for backup?"

"Let's see where these guys go first. We might want to follow them. At least get a good look at the license plate."

The men walked to a white sedan.

Nick repositioned. "Damn. I can't get a good look at the plate. Too many cars in the way."

He crouched low and moved behind another car, trying to get a better position.

Sadie saw a man in white shirt and black pants heading toward them. "Security's coming."

The radio squawked.

"Keep an eye on him." He moved up another couple of cars.

"He's heading right this way, Nick."

He dropped to his knees and fanned his hands out on the ground, feeling around. "Can you see them, babe?"

"Looking for something, sir?" the guard looked concerned.

"My keys." He felt around underneath a different car. "Dropped them."

The security officer bent down, placing his hands on his knees for support. He had to be close to fifty, and his belly prevented him from bending too far.

Sadie pointed toward the key Nick had dropped moments before. "That it?"

"Where?" He played the part perfectly.

"There. Near the grass by the front tire."

"Look at that. Sure is."

The officer stood to his full height, which looked to be five-foot-ten, as Nick rose to his and offered to shake hands.

"I'd be lost without her."

The officer smiled and nodded, shaking his head and walking toward the building. "I wouldn't be caught dead admitting that to mine. She'd never let me hear the end of it. But it's true."

Sadie turned in time to see the white sedan turn the corner onto Communications Parkway and disappear.

Nick muttered a curse. "You didn't happen to get that number, did you?"

"Nope. I didn't. And we wouldn't be able to catch them at this point, either, would we?"

He grumbled while he shook his head. "Not even if we ran to the truck. Besides, being in a hurry might cause us to make a mistake and be seen. Burly and Steroids might still be in the building."

It was most likely her danger radar overreacting again, but she didn't like the thought of those men being any-where near Nick's pregnant sister.

THIS SITUATION COULDN'T get more frustrating to Nick. If they went inside, where he wanted to be to watch over his sister, they risked Burly and Steroids seeing him. Jamison's camp had been led to believe Nick was no-where around. His henchmen would be expecting him and Sadie to be on Interstate 45 heading north. They would most likely put some resources there.

Riley's knee-jerk reaction to throw them off the trail had been brilliant. Jamison wouldn't be happy waiting around for Nick to show up at the hospital. He'd send resources to cut him off and dispose of him long before he had a chance to make it to Plano. Jamison's life depended on getting rid of Nick and Sadie.

Spreading out Jamison's men improved Nick's odds greatly.

He pulled his cell from his pocket and informed Smith, so he could put resources on I-45. In exchange, he learned support should be arriving at the hospital any second.

Glancing at Sadie, he could see how stressed this situation had been on her. He wanted to reach out to her, to be her comfort, to take all her fear and anxiety away.

He hated that he couldn't.

Another part of him wanted to find Burly and Steroids, if only to force them to talk. He had a few other ideas of things he'd like to do to them, but jail sounded like a good enough option.

Leaving Sadie alone so he could track them was a bad idea.

Bringing her along wasn't an option.

He had no doubt if he was alone he would find them if they were still in the building. Two people would be harder to hide.

Sitting and waiting was a bitter cup of tea for Nick.

Yet, that was what he had to do.

Once he knew Meg, Riley and baby were safe, he could leave. Stashing Sadie at the safe house was his best bet until he heard back from Smith. His men were zeroing in on Jamison, and it wouldn't be long before they had a location.

Until then, Nick would be better off in hiding, too.

The last thing he wanted to do was lead Jamison to Sadie. She was the only one who could identify him as one of her abductors. They needed her statement against Jamison to be able to make an arrest. He had another more personal reason for keeping Sadie safe, but this was not the time to get inside his head about what that meant.

Without proof, Jamison would most likely get off scot-free if Nick and Sadie were killed. She was the only person who could identify him and put him away.

It was bad enough they had to deal with an out-of-control marshal, but Grimes was another story. He had a vested interest in seeing Sadie dead, too. He also seemed hell-bent on making sure she was erased for good. Dead would do it.

Nick's cell buzzed. Smith's name popped up on the screen. He showed it to Sadie before answering. "What's the word, Chief?"

"My men have arrived. It's safe for you and 'the battery' to leave." The boss must've realized Nick wouldn't leave the grounds until he knew his sister was out of danger.

"I appreciate this. You'll keep someone here until she checks out in a couple of days?"

"I'll send someone home with them if it means you won't worry. They'll have twenty-four-hour security. You have enough on your plate right now without wondering if your family's safe."

"What next?"

"I'm in the process of trying to attain a search warrant for Jamison's house. Sadie's word and the bank account might just be enough."

"Jamison lives in Dallas, I presume."

"Right."

Nick would like to be part of the guys serving that warrant, but he suspected the place would be empty.

"He's smart enough to know better than to hide evidence at his house."

"I suspect you're right."

"Doesn't hurt to take a look, anyway," Nick conceded. "Keep me in the loop."

"You know I will."

Nick ended the call. "Back to the safe house."

Waiting made him want to go insane. He also wasn't thrilled by the fact he hadn't heard from Lucy.

He could see fear in Sadie's eyes when she looked at him and nodded. His muscles tensed. She shouldn't have to hide for the rest of her life. Just thinking about how afraid she'd been—how afraid she'd most likely be forever—stirred anger that pierced another hole in his armor.

Grimes needed to be behind bars. Jamison especially needed to be in a cell. And there were a few things he wanted to do to the both of them first that he was sure the agency wouldn't approve. And, yet, if he got his bare hands near them, he'd make sure they knew he'd been there.

He needed to tuck Sadie away until they found Jamison and made sure he couldn't hurt anyone again.

Sadie was quiet on the drive back to the safe house. Nick could feel fear radiating from her. He occasionally reached over to squeeze her hand, to reassure her.

He told her everything would be okay and that they'd find them first.

What he refused to tell her was that this had just become a high stakes game of hide-and-seek…and both of their lives depended on not being found first.

Chapter Seventeen

Nick pulled onto the parking pad with the ever-present feeling of eyes watching him. His instincts didn't normally lead him down the wrong path, so he didn't ignore them.

Yet, scanning the houses, yards and vehicles parked on the street didn't reveal anything out of the ordinary. Kids were still in school, so the streets were quiet.

The winds had kicked up, typical late-November weather. It was noon but the clouds rolling in covered the sun, making it feel more like nightfall. In six hours, the sky would already be dark this time of year.

"Think it's going to rain?"

He shrugged as he exited the cab. "Never can be sure with Texas weather."

"One minute the sun's shining, the next it can be raining. I'd heard about the storms that come this time of year and how the wide skies open up and pour rain. The thunder that cracks right in your ear."

"I never minded a big storm. We can always use the rain." He caught a glimpse of something moving out of the corner of his eyes. He quickly moved next to Sadie, and realized, for the first time, she was trembling. Anger hit him faster than a bolt of lightning.

He put his body between her and whatever had

moved. Might be nothing, but he knew better than to take chances.

Unlocking the front door, he urged Sadie inside. If someone knew where the safe house was, they could be waiting inside. He thought about the blue sport-utility that had been parked a few doors down earlier. He glanced over his shoulder in the general direction where it had been parked. The vehicle was gone.

Was it a coincidence?

Instinct told him not to take anything for granted.

Once inside, he hauled Sadie behind him and drew his gun. He leveled his weapon in front of him.

The lights were off. Without sunlight filtering in through the windows, the place was dark.

He had to take into account the possibility that Paul's relatives had come home early. The scenario was unlikely but had to be considered. "This is Marshal Campbell."

No one responded.

If someone was in the house, they didn't want to be found. Not yet.

Sadie's body shook from fear and probably cold, since the temperature had dropped twenty degrees in the past hour, and they didn't have coats.

With her pressed against his back, he felt every rigid muscle in her body. Everything in him wanted to take away that feeling for her. Make it go away forever.

From his vantage point at the front door, he could see the living room, kitchen and dining room. He swept the area. No surprises there.

The bathroom and pair of bedrooms yielded similar results. The laundry room in the hallway was clear.

Now to assess any threat outside.

He could leave Sadie inside where he was relatively sure she'd be safe. Or risk taking her outside with him.

Leaving her alone could be exactly what Jamison or Grimes would want. Could someone be setting a trap?

On balance, bringing Sadie was a risk he had to take.

Nick moved to the big window in the living room, leaving the lights off.

He peered outside and waited. *Patience.*

A text came through. Everyone had checked in but Lucy.

Movement around the back of Luke's truck caught his attention.

This was no coincidence.

"Stay behind me. Don't move unless I do."

Her eyes were wide, but she nodded.

He moved to the door leading to the small backyard. There was enough of a glow from the lamps across the alley for him to see lines for clothes and winter melon plantings that led from the house to the back fence. The gate was on the opposite side of the house as the parking pad. Nick slid outside with Sadie practically glued to his back.

Gusts of winds blasted, sending leaves thrashing through the air. Tree branches bent and snapped. A big storm was brewing.

Nick dropped down on all fours and crawled toward the front of the house, his shoulder scraping against the building as he moved, urging Sadie to follow along. He stopped at the corner, checking the building next to them, across the street and then behind them.

Rain pelted his face and made it hard to see clearly.

Wind whipped sideways, and a cracking noise split the air. Thunder.

Nick needed to get a visual of the front of the building and see what was going on. With his weapon drawn, he peeked around the building. He was greeted with a spray of bullets.

He planted on his chest, dropping flat on his stomach with Sadie on his heels. He fired a shot toward the figure moving behind the truck as the guy backed away, using the building as cover. His bullet went a little wide and to the right. Between the darkness and the wind, he'd have a difficult time getting off a good shot. *Patience.*

The rustle of someone running toward them came from the yard behind. Stay put and they'd be trapped.

"Listen to me carefully. We're going to have to make a run for it."

Sadie's mouth moved to speak but no words came out. She had been freezing just walking in the house. She had to be in bad shape by now. She'd warm up when she got her blood pumping again. He needed her to move when he gave the signal.

He also knew exactly what she was thinking. "I want you to go first so I can cover you. Once you pop up and get your footing, don't stop running. Got it?"

"Run where?" Panic brought her voice up an octave. To her credit, she fixed her gaze in the direction he pointed.

"Away from the sound of fire."

She nodded.

"On my count. One. Two. Three."

By the time he said the last number, she was to her feet and sprinting across the neighbor's yard.

He covered her, firing a warning shot directly toward the location where bullets had come from.

A figure moved behind the truck, firing one shot after the other. He had to be using a Glock or Beretta or a Sig—there were lots of choices for an automatic—as he dashed toward the tree in the front yard, ducking and rolling to avoid Nick's shot. The guy knew what he was doing. Could it be Jamison?

If so, maybe Nick could end this right there. Arrest him. Put the bastard in jail where he belonged.

Not a chance, a little voice in the back of his head said. Jamison was in too deep. He wouldn't go out willingly. Not after coming this far or going to these lengths to protect his investments. If the supervisor was around, he was there for one purpose. Erase Nick and Sadie.

Nick discharged his weapon again.

The male form used the tree in the front yard as cover. He wasn't running away from anyone, so much as he was running toward Sadie.

Nick heard voices in the backyard. Two, maybe three men were coming from behind. There were too many for Nick to fight off for long, even with his second clip. He was in over his head. He needed to send out a distress call.

Nick fished his phone out of his pocket to call for backup at the same time he heard a shot. Shock overwhelmed him. Was he hit?

He glanced down and saw blood. He made a move to stand, but everything went blurry.

Someone yelled, "Got him!"

Sirens blared.

Could he hide? He belly-crawled toward the vegetable bin he'd spotted earlier. His limbs were weak. His head spun. Where was Sadie? She'd disappeared after she turned the corner around the neighbor's house. Was someone there? Waiting?

No. Couldn't be. She would have screamed. She didn't. And that meant she'd made it to the shops. She could hide there until Nick could find her.

He hauled his heavy frame inside the bin, closing the

lid as he heard footsteps nearing. Another flash of light followed by a crack of thunder sounded overhead.

It was only a matter of time before they would find Nick. He'd left a trail of blood, leading to the bin.

"I saw her turn this way," one of the bastards said. He couldn't be more than five feet from Nick.

His muscles tensed, ready for a fight, then everything went black.

SADIE RAN. HER thighs burned and her lungs clawed for air, but she dragged in another deep breath and pushed forward.

Footsteps were close, closing in, and she had no way to defend herself if the attacker caught up.

Every gunshot blast sent her pulse rocketing into the stratosphere.

"Please, God, let it be Nick behind me." She knew he wasn't there but repeated the prayer, anyway.

There were too many men for Nick to take on by himself.

Thunder cracked, and Sadie let out a yelp before she could squash it.

If someone was behind her, chasing her, wouldn't that mean they'd stopped Nick?

Her mind screamed, *"No!"*

She expected fear to grip her, to paralyze her. Instead, white-hot anger roared through her veins.

If they did anything to Nick, hurt him because they were looking for her…

She wanted to scream.

Maybe she could make it to the strip mall, ditch them and circle back to Nick. The possibility of him lying on the sidewalk, alone, in a pool of his own blood sent anger licking through her veins. If she could get to him—get help—surely paramedics could save him. *Cling to positive thoughts,* she reminded herself. Nick was good at his job. He knew how to handle men like these. He would survive.

She dashed behind one of the houses that backed up to the lot and scrambled up the brick wall separating the neighborhood from retailers.

Nothing bad could happen to Nick. She couldn't allow herself to go there mentally…he would be fine, and they would be together.

If she could get inside one of the stores, she could hide. She still had her cell phone. She could get a message to Smith. He'd send reinforcements. *Stay alive, Nick.*

The reality of him staying back there, alone, to give her a chance to escape pressed down on her chest, making breathing even more difficult. His act of valiance was commendable. Except she couldn't face losing the only man she'd ever loved. Love?

Yeah. Love.

No man had ever made her feel the way he did.

She pushed on.

Rounding the corner to the strip mall, she glanced back in time to see a large man hopping over the brick wall. Not a good sign that he'd gotten past Nick.

Did that mean…?

No.

She refused to think negative thoughts or let fear overtake her. She needed a clear head.

Sadie kept her feet moving forward even though her heart wanted to turn around and find him. He'd said run. He'd told her not to look back. He'd saved her life.

She wouldn't repay him by getting caught if she had anything to say about it.

Turning the last bend to the storefronts, she glanced

across the parking lot. The terra-cotta warriors standing sentinel had men ducking behind them.

She checked behind her. Another minute and the man chasing her would catch up.

Sadie couldn't allow that to happen.

In a sea of black-haired people, she was grateful for the wig. The fact she was a few inches taller than almost everyone else made her easy to spot…not so good.

Luckily, there were lots of shoppers. She pushed through them, keeping as low a profile as she could. When she'd made it past a barbershop and a restaurant, she spotted a supermarket. Perfect.

It was in the middle of the shopping center, but if she could make it there, she could disappear in the aisles. Maybe even slip out the back door, which would lead to the loading dock. She could circle her way back to Nick. He was alive. She refused to think otherwise. He had to be worried about her by now.

Nick was fine. She would find him. They'd get through this.

She'd testify again in a heartbeat if it meant she and Nick could live out the rest of their lives in peace. Maybe even together?

A chest pain so strong it nearly brought her to her knees pierced her.

For a split second, she almost thought she'd been hit by a bullet.

The agony in her chest, she realized, came from knowing deep down that something had happened to Nick.

Otherwise he would be coming for her.

She had to know what happened. What if he lay there, bleeding, and she could help him? Could she get to him in time?

Sirens wailed and her heart stuttered as she made it to the grocery store.

She pulled the cell Nick had given her in Creek Bend from her back pocket. The one she was only supposed to use if he wasn't there—the one she wasn't supposed to need—and hit the only other name in the contacts as she bolted toward the stockroom.

Smith's phone ran into voice mail. "This is Sadie Brooks. We're in trouble…"

A few more steps and she would be able to hide among the boxes of food waiting to be stocked.

A few more steps and she had options.

A few more steps and she could make it to freedom.

Sadie pushed her legs, full force, ignoring the cramp in her calf.

The set of double doors was in reach.

They both flew open at exactly the same time.

There stood Burly.

Chapter Eighteen

Instinct kicked in the moment Burly clamped her in his meaty grip. Sadie wheeled around, trying to break free.

He grinned and tightened his hold on her, forcing her to face him.

She grabbed two fists full of his shirt at chest level, screamed and pivoted her body, sticking her leg out to trip him using his own body weight against him.

He broke into a laugh as he widened his stance. "You think a little thing like you can take me down?"

The leg wheel technique had failed against his two-hundred-plus pounds.

"Help me, somebody," she pleaded.

The small crowd of Asian onlookers dispersed quickly, diverting their gazes away from Sadie.

No one would make eye contact.

Burly hauled her into the stockroom before she could get her mental bearings again. Fists like pit bull jaws locked around her upper arms.

She bent as low as she could, fisted her hands and in one quick motion burst toward the ceiling, breaking free from his hold.

Before he could snatch her again, Sadie wheeled around and exploded toward the metal doors, toward freedom.

Certain she could outrun Burly, hope ballooned in her chest. If she could escape, she could find Nick.

Just shy of reaching the doors, they sprang open.

Steroids.

Sadie screamed a curse as her forward momentum forced her to run smack into his chest. Hopelessness clawed at her. *Not happening. Not again.*

They'd taken away her life before. She'd had to separate from Boomer because of them. They may have killed Nick. She would not go down without a fight.

Rage, not fear, burned hot through her veins.

"In a hurry?" Steroids coughed, closing his arms around her as she kicked and screamed.

This time, she would fight back.

Burly must've drawn his gun. Cold metal pressed to the side of her head, and her arms went limp at the memory of what had happened before.

Give up and they win.

Those bastards wouldn't get the satisfaction. She leaned forward and bit Steroids in the chest as hard as she could.

"Bitch!" He pushed her back a step until she slammed into Burly, whirled her around and tied her hands behind her back.

Sirens grew louder. Thank God, someone had called the police.

Maybe she could stall long enough for the cops to save her?

They dragged her a few steps toward the back door. She made her body go limp.

A blow below her left cheek made her eye feel as if it might pop out of its socket. She spit blood.

Tires squealed out back.

The cops?

No. Couldn't be. There'd be sirens.

Realization crashed down on her, squeezing her lungs. Her heart sank.

The getaway vehicle had just arrived.

Let them take her out of that market, and she may as well be dead.

Sadie kicked and screamed, but they hauled her hands tighter and kept dragging her.

Steroids stuffed a piece of cloth in her mouth, muffling her cries.

Tears burned down her cheeks as fury detonated inside her.

Another ten feet and they could take her anywhere they wanted, do anything they wanted to her. The ICU would be a gift this time. She knew with everything inside her if they got her out the door this time, she'd end up in the morgue.

Her body railed against the bindings on her wrists.

Instead of feeling fear, she felt…resolve.

They could take away her body. They could do anything they wanted to her physically. They could end her life and erase her existence. But while she had breath in her lungs, they would not control her mind.

She felt herself being hauled up and tossed into the back of the sport-utility. Burly got in on one side, Steroids the other. There were two men in the front. The one on the passenger's side was bleeding, losing a fair amount of blood. He held a blood-soaked T-shirt to his left-arm triceps.

She memorized every detail of their faces before the two in the backseat forced her onto the floorboard.

If, no *when,* she escaped, she would testify against the whole lot of them. She would ensure these men were locked away forever. They would not hurt another soul.

Moving her jaw back and forth, she was able to get her tongue behind the cloth to force it out of her mouth.

She remembered sticking her cell phone in her right front pocket. Could she get to it without them noticing?

With her hands tied behind her back, it would be challenging. Could she stretch far enough?

Think. Think. Think.

Lying on her left, facing toward the back, pretty much ensured they'd see her trying to reach into her pocket. Maybe she could distract them somehow? Or bait them into rolling her over to her other side.

"You're a bunch of idiots if you think you'll get away with this. A U.S. Marshal is right behind me. He knows who you are. He knows who your boss is. And he'll find me. When he does, you're all going to jail where you belong."

"I don't think so," Burly said.

A glance passed between them that parked a boulder on Sadie's chest. *Oh. God. No.*

Nothing could happen to Nick.

And, yet, she knew he'd have to be shot or dead not to have come after her already. He hadn't made an attempt to reach her. Her cell hadn't vibrated. No one had called her name or ambushed the men who'd abducted her.

Her heart lurched, threatening to lock up and stop beating.

And let those bastards win? She didn't think so.

She had to reach out to someone.

If she was able to palm her cell—and that was a pretty big if—she'd have access to Smith. For a brief moment, she wondered if Smith had put a tracer on her phone. Maybe he was tracking her right now?

A little voice inside her head reminded her that wouldn't happen. Smith would have given them an untraceable phone. He'd been specific about not wanting to know where they were. It was a safeguard. He'd do it to protect them.

She kicked up at Burly, connecting with his shin.

"Dammit," he grumbled. He tied her ankles together, making it impossible to kick again.

She fought back, not because she thought she'd win, but in order to sell switching positions so she could roll on the other side and access her phone.

By the time they finished, she was facing the opposite direction. On her right side, she could hide the fact she was slipping her phone out of her pocket.

Tears pricked the backs of her eyes.

Despair was an ache in her chest. Sorrow for Nick threatened to suck her under like a riptide and spit her out into the deep.

Before she could say another word, the cloth was being jammed into her mouth again. This time, they tied a strip of material around her head to secure her gag.

Sadie couldn't afford tears.

She had to keep herself calm and force herself to believe that Nick was out there, somewhere, making his way back to her.

Every movement hurt. The bindings around her wrists tightened as she tried to angle her hands toward her right front pocket.

With two fingers, she managed to grasp the corner of her cell well enough to slide it free. She scooted forward, managing to block it with her hip. The phone was already set to vibrate mode. She switched to mute, touched the second name on her contact list, Smith, and covered the speaker with her finger, just in case.

"Where are you taking me?" Her words were muffled

by the gag. She knew full well these guys wouldn't hand over the answer easily.

"Someplace no one will hear you when you scream," Burly said.

NICK BLINKED HIS blurry eyes open. Darkness surrounded him. He couldn't quite put his finger on why he had the urge to run. And what the hell was up with the hammering between his temples?

His body ached. His knees jammed into his face. There were hard walls all around him.

Where was he?

He felt around on his head for bumps, located a couple.

Memories flooded him, coming back all at one time, as if someone had unlocked the gates and sprung open both doors.

"Sadie."

He tried to kick. Only managed to thump his lip with his knee when he moved. He was inside some kind of compartment. No signs of light either meant it was nighttime, or the storm still hadn't passed. The place was airtight.

Rocking back and forth, he tried to free his arms.

Thoughts of the gun battle broke through his mind. He'd told Sadie to run. He'd known they were outnumbered, but he'd tried to get the attention on him and allow her to escape.

He knew they were both in trouble when he saw the shooter immediately give chase.

The vegetable bin. He'd made it. Must've hid him long enough for the police to arrive and scare off Jamison and his men.

Nick felt around. He'd wedged himself inside in a position that was impossible to get out of.

There was no escape.

He heard a familiar voice.

Paul?

Shouting to his friend was a risk. Nick couldn't be sure how long he'd been in that box. Could be minutes or hours. The cops could've come and gone, and so could Grimes or Jamison.

Nick listened intently through the pounding in his temples, straining to hear if there were other voices.

A neighbor must've phoned the police after hearing gunfire.

When he was reasonably certain Paul was alone, he shouted.

"Paul," Nick repeated, louder this time. Shouting made everything hurt, and his head feel as if it might explode. He ignored the pain. Sadie was in trouble. He had to get out of this box and find her.

"Paul!"

Nick heard sounds outside.

"Who is that? Who's here?" Paul's voice trembled.

"It's me. Nick. I need your help to get me out of here."

"Nick?" came the trepid response.

"Open the door, Paul. It's me."

Light split what was left of Nick's head. Yet, it was welcomed.

"What the heck happened to you? How'd you end up in my aunt's vegetable bin?"

"What time is it?" Nick asked, trying to muscle his way out of the container.

"Here. Let me help you."

Where was Sadie? "The woman I was with earlier. Where is she?"

"I don't know. She's not here," Paul said, offering a hand up.

Nick took it and, with a push, broke out of the small container he'd forced himself in. He scanned the area.

"The police are out front. They're asking a lot of questions. I told them I don't know what happened. My neighbor called me when he heard the guns. The old guy kind of freaked out. Called the police, too."

"Did they arrest anyone?" If the police were still there, then Sadie couldn't be too far.

"No one here. My neighbor said he saw everybody run. I didn't expect you to be here, either. I jumped when I heard your voice. That's for sure."

"Which way did they go?" He remembered telling Sadie to run, some of his thoughts were still jumbled, and he'd already lost precious time. He didn't want to risk going off in the wrong direction while his brain was still scrambled.

"The old guy said she went this way." Paul inclined his head toward the left.

"Good. Now do me a favor, and go get the police." Nick needed as many hands on this case as he could get. He checked his pockets for his cell.

His legs cramped.

He tried to walk, but they gave.

Paul grabbed Nick's arm in time to keep him from losing balance and landing on the ground.

"You wait right here, my friend. I'll get the police."

"I lost my cell. It might be on the side of your house." He was grateful to be alive, but what about Sadie?

With him out of the picture, they could do whatever they wanted to her.

Maybe she'd escaped?

Not likely. There were too many men. Jamison must've brought everyone to this fight.

Damn, Nick needed his cell. He needed to make contact with Smith.

The thought of anyone hurting Sadie was like an acid burn on his skin.

A uniformed officer approached. "I need to see some ID, sir."

Nick produced his badge and gave a statement.

"Nick," Paul shouted from the other side of the fence. He burst through. "I found it. These belong to you?"

He held out a cell and a gun.

"Looks like mine." His Glock felt right in his hand. He checked his cell. A dozen missed calls from Smith. "I need to check in with my boss."

The officer nodded.

Smith answered immediately.

"Is she alive?" Nick asked.

"Someone activated her cell phone and used it to call me. I believe it was her."

"Any idea where she is?"

"No. I can tell she's in some type of vehicle. She asked the question of where she was being taken and a man replied they were taking her where no one would hear her scream. It was tough to make out her words. Sounded like something was covering her mouth." He paused. "They could be taking her to a field out in the middle of nowhere for all we know. Without GPS on that phone, I can't track her."

Nick's brain immediately kicked into gear. "There's a place I can think of that no one would hear her scream. The warehouse."

The sounds of fingers flying across a keyboard came through Nick's line. "My closest man is a half hour away."

"I can be there in fifteen minutes."

"Nick," Smith said. Nick didn't like the sound of his

voice when he said it. "They've sent word through one of my informants that they've got Lucy."

Nick ground out a curse. "Can you confirm?"

"I spoke to your brother Luke and she hasn't checked in or answered her phone. Doesn't mean they have her. I just can't confirm one way or the other. They're threatening to drop her body off below the Ferris wheel ride in Fair Park."

Nick's knees buckled. The officer held him steady. "I go to Fair Park, and they'll kill me and Sadie. I go to Sadie and they'll kill Lucy."

"If they have her."

Was it a risk he was willing to take? Jamison clearly knew how much Nick loved and protected his family.

"I can send people to either place, or both. It's your call," Smith said quietly.

Could Sadie already be dead? No. They'd use her to bring Nick out. As soon as they got to him, they'd kill her.

His mind clicked through other possibilities. If he went to Lucy, they'd be ready for him. As soon as they got him, they'd kill Sadie.

He had one advantage. "They don't know that I know about the warehouse. That's where they'd take Sadie. I go to Lucy, and we're all dead."

His stomach lining braided. Make the wrong call and two of the people he loved more than anything in the world would be dead.

"Send your people to Fair Park, but have them wait for my word."

"Got it."

Ending the call, Nick locked gazes with the officer. "I need a ride."

The man in uniform was already bolting toward his squad car.

Running sent a wave of nausea rippling through Nick. He ignored it and pressed on. The thought of anyone hurting Sadie or Lucy sent him to a dark mental place.

He forced all thoughts out of his head that he might be too late.

En route, he bandaged his gunshot wound using supplies from the officer's first-aid kit. They'd split his shoulder with a bullet. He packed gauze on it to stem the bleeding, and secured it with tape.

"No chance you'll let me investigate this lead after I drop you off at the hospital?"

"None whatsoever."

"Then I'll have an ambulance waiting a block away."

"No sirens. I don't want to give these scumbags any warning," Nick said.

The officer nodded before calling it in.

With lights blazing, the cop beat the time by two minutes. He'd cut the lights a block away. "I'll take the front entrance."

"You already know this, but these men are armed, and they're not afraid to shoot an officer. Be careful." Nick hopped out of the car before it came to a complete stop.

He moved to the back of the building, fighting the pain and nausea threatening to buckle his knees. There was a beige sport-utility parked in the back of the building.

Crouching low, he made it to the rear of the vehicle. His gun drawn, he raised high enough to see through the dark window. The vehicle was empty. He moved to the side.

Whoever sat on the passenger's side sure lost a lot of blood. The thought this could be Sadie's blood cut through him. He bit back a curse.

Could belong to anyone. Nick had fired quite a few shots at the jerks, he reminded himself.

A thought nearly leveled him.

Was she even here?

He canceled the thought. This was the most logical place to take her. She had to be inside. He would find her and give her life back to her. A life with him? The thought of opening himself up to that kind of potential pain usually almost flattened Nick.

Not when it came to Sadie. She was different.

Yet, no matter how strong Nick's feelings were, he couldn't ask her to spend the rest of her life waiting up nights and wondering if he'd be coming home. She deserved so much more. Could he give her everything?

A piece of him wished he could.

He loved her. And because he did, he planned to give her something she could only have without him. Peace.

The bay door was half-closed, providing an opportunity to slip into the back of the warehouse.

Breeching the building was easy.

Too easy?

Nick might be walking into a trap.

The main floor of the warehouse was empty.

He glanced up a small flight of stairs into the office.

Several men were there.

His heart raced when he saw her. Sadie. She was there. In the upstairs office.

There were too many men for him to take on, even with the officer who was making his way through the front of the building as backup.

Two against five. Grimes was there. As was Jamison. There were three others in the office.

Nick heard a door open to his left. He pressed his back against the wall and eased toward the sound. A bathroom?

Two against six. He liked those odds even less.

Burly walked out, zipping his pants, his gun holstered.

Nick hit him in the back of the head so hard, he knocked Burly unconscious, catching him on the way down.

The move took almost all of Nick's strength.

He leaned against the wall and took a deep breath.

Glancing up, Nick saw the officer moving toward him. The officer inclined his chin, moving silently.

When he approached them, he pulled out handcuffs. Nick hesitated, almost unsure who those were meant for. But the officer went right to work on Burly.

Five to two increased the odds. Sadie was a fighter. Maybe he should count her as a third.

The officer grabbed the scruff of Burly's neck and hauled him outside.

He returned a moment later. "He's not waking up anytime soon," he whispered. "And if he does, he's not going anywhere."

"Good job. And thanks."

"What do you want to do next?"

The correct answer would be to wait for backup. As long as the men in that room gave him time, Nick would take it. They make a move toward Sadie, and game on. "Keep an eye on them until more men arrive."

He motioned the officer to follow him.

They made it up the stairwell without giving away their position.

The sight of a gun aimed at Sadie's head forced Nick's hand.

He burst into the room, hoping like hell they would believe Burly was returning from the restroom. "I'm Marshal Campbell. You're all under arrest."

Catching them off guard gave him the advantage.

Grimes redirected his weapon toward Nick, but he'd already leveled his and fired.

The officer came in behind Nick, weapon raised.

Steroids put his hands in the air, as did the other pair of men in the room.

"You think you can arrest me?" Jamison aimed his weapon at Sadie.

If Nick fired, Jamison might pull the trigger out of reflex.

Sadie would be dead.

She looked up at Nick, and he expected to see fear in her big green eyes, and he did. But he also saw anger and determination. Good. He could work with that.

If she could distract Jamison, Nick could make a move. Could he signal her somehow?

Her gaze was intent on him. He glanced from her to Jamison's knees.

She gave a slight nod. Bent over on all fours, with Jamison standing over her, she dove into his legs.

He buckled. Nick surged toward Jamison, knocking him a couple of steps backward and away from Sadie.

Gunfire split the air as Nick landed on top of his target and wrestled for control of the weapon. Jamison threw a jackhammer of a punch, connecting with Nick's nose. Blood spurted.

Nick counterpunched, his fist slamming into Jamison's jaw.

Jamison bucked and rolled, causing Nick to lose his grip on Jamison's wrist. Nick adjusted, popping to his knees. He squeezed powerful thighs to hold Jamison, facedown, in place.

Blood poured down Nick's shirt as he cuffed the snake.

Shock overtook Nick as he realized the blood was his.

Once Jamison was secure, Nick folded over to the

sounds of officers rushing downstairs. The one who'd breeched the building with him stood over Jamison, his gun aimed at his temple, as Nick rolled over onto his side, fighting the nausea and fatigue gripping him.

Damn.

He was shot? He immediately thought of Sadie. She was safe now.

The next thing he knew, she was over him, tears streaming down her beautiful cheeks.

"Stay with me, Nick," she begged. The desperation in her voice was palpable. Almost enough to force him to come back to her.

She was safe.

What about Lucy?

As the scene in front of him played out in slow motion, he watched officers handcuff the dirtbags. One of them moved to Nick's side and held his cell phone to his ear. "Someone wants to speak to you."

"Nick? It's Lucy. I'm okay."

Relief flooded him. Sadie was safe. Lucy was okay. Nothing else mattered.

All he wanted to do was close his eyes and go to sleep.

Sadie's voice became distant. Her pleas for him to stay awake faded.

Nick closed his eyes and allowed darkness to claim him.

NICK WOKE WITH a start.

He glanced around the stark white room. His vision was blurry. Where was he?

He tried to push up, unwilling to admit the fear creeping through his system, its icy tendrils closing around his heart.

The case was closed, and he'd most likely never see

Sadie again. The thought caused worse pain than the bullet hole in his shoulder. A few stitches, a little physical therapy, and he'd eventually heal from that. Being without Sadie for the rest of his life put a hollow ache in his chest he'd never recover from.

"Nick?" the voice sounded uncertain and afraid.

Sadie?

He forced his eyes to stay open through the burn and glanced around the room. She was already to the side of the bed before his eyes could focus properly.

"How do you feel?" she asked, reaching out to touch his face.

The sight of her quieted his worst fear—the fear he'd never look into those beautiful eyes again and tell her just how much she meant to him.

"Dizzy. Nauseous." *Relieved.*

"You lost a lot of blood when you were shot," she said. "You must be in pain. Let me call the nurse."

Of course, he just realized, he was in the hospital. But he didn't want the nurse. He had everything he needed right next to him. Sadie.

He covered her hand with his, preventing her from pushing the call button. The whole scenario came back to him in a flood. The warehouse. Grimes. Jamison. "How long have I been out?"

"Two days."

"You've been here the whole time?"

Her cheeks flushed as she nodded. "Luke sneaks Boomer in every chance he gets."

"Tell me what happened."

"Grimes is dead. Jamison shot you. They arrested him, and he's going away for a very long time. So are the others in the warehouse. A few more of his men were arrested at Fair Park."

"And Lucy?"

"She's fine. Calls every hour to check on you, though." Her smile warmed his insides.

"And Meg?"

"She had a little boy."

He couldn't stop himself from reaching out and touching her beautiful face. "You've been keeping track of everyone?"

"I knew you'd want to know as soon as you woke up."

"How's Boomer?"

"He's keeping Gran company at the ranch. She texts me pictures of him every hour." She laughed.

"I remember what you did in the warehouse. I'm proud of you." His chest filled with an emotion that felt a hell of a lot like pride.

She leaned into his palm, and then kissed his hand.

"You been here the whole time?"

She nodded. "There's nowhere else I want to be."

He couldn't believe the love of his life was sitting right there. It would be better if they were somewhere else besides the hospital for what he needed to say. He wished they were somewhere romantic. He needed to ask her something, and he wanted everything to be perfect.

He canceled the thought.

Fact was there would never be a better time than now. "I need you to know that I've fallen hard for you."

He was rewarded with a bright smile. She leaned over and pressed a kiss to his lips. He kept her close when he whispered, "I love you."

She kissed him again, with more enthusiasm this time.

"I love you, Nick Campbell."

This time, he wouldn't be stupid enough to let Sadie walk out that door without knowing exactly what she meant to him. He had no intention of repeating his past mistakes.

He knew what he wanted for the rest of his life, and he wanted Sadie.

"I'd prefer to do this on one knee, but I'm guessing that would cause a whole host of people to come rushing through that door…"

She gasped, tears streaming down her cheeks.

"I don't have a ring to offer you right now. But I sincerely pray my heart and the promise of forever will be enough. Sadie Brooks, will you marry me?"

The minute she took to answer felt like an eternity.

She nodded through her tears. "Yes. I will marry you, Nick Campbell. I want very much to be your wife."

"And I want to be your protector for the rest of our days."

* * * * *